SEIZE
ON THE HIGH SEAS
A Sophie Star Series Book Four

AUTHOR
L. J. WEBB

SEIZE
ON THE HIGH SEAS
A Sophie Star Series Book Four
BY L. J. WEBB

Copyright © 2023 by Linda J Webb
Published by L. J. Webb
Longview, WA

Cover by Adebayo S. Oluwatosin

Some of the Bible Stories in this book are paraphrased by the author to move the story along.
Scriptures that are quoted are from the following versions.
King James Version
Or the
New King James Version®

eBook ISBN 979-8-9855798-8-8

Paperback ISBN 979-8-9855798-9-5

Library of Congress Control Number 2023903218

Table of Contents

It was right that we should make merry and be glad, for your brother was dead and is alive again, and was lost and is found.

Luke 15:32

PROLOUGE

It was dark outside, looking through the little window of the private plane. Marci knew they were flying above a storm because she could see fiery streaks light up the clouds intermittently. And even though she hadn't heard the thunder yet, she knew it was coming. She had no idea what country they were flying over. The plane made one stop for fuel since they left the South Korean compound 12 hours ago. They should be in DC in the next few hours.

One would think Marcella Beauchene would be used to this kind of wealth after being married to Roman for four years. Her parents were upper middle class and lived in a beautiful condominium not far from the Eiffel Tower in Paris. But the type of wealth Roman and Rocky DeCarlo had was overwhelming.

Roman had his eyes closed in the seat next to her on the luxury Super Mid-Size Jet he had on retainer. She looked over at him and smiled. He felt her looking at him, took her hand, and kissed it. Marci loved him more than she thought she could love again.

"You're not sleeping, tesoro. Is something bothering you?" Roman asked.

"No, dear, I like watching the lightning in the clouds below us. I learned to love lightning living in Austin."

"Why have you never asked me to take you back there? You speak so fondly of your friends."

"I do love them, but there is also great tragedy and heartache associated with it."

"You speak of your first husband and Duke?"

Marci turned her head back to the window, "so much heartache. I don't know what it would be like now after all these years."

Roman put the armrest up between them and snuggled her close to him.

"I'm so sorry for all the pain you suffered in your past. But it was that pain that brought you to me. I don't know how to reconcile the two."

"I know, darling. I didn't think I'd ever fall in love again," Marci said. Roman kissed her.

Roman and Rocky DeCarlo were twenty-one, living in Italy on their parent's compound. When they unwittingly fell into the Brokerage business. More precisely, they were approached by a man wanting to sell a ground-to-air missile he came upon. The man offered them a lot of money to find a buyer. After a month of trying, they finally brokered the sale, making their first large commission. They soon became known as the 'Brokers' and could only be contacted anonymously by a dead drop online.

A seller that had illegally come into possession of equipment, military or otherwise. Or, in control of research of any kind, they would contact the 'Brokers' to find a buyer. In some cases, it was the buyers who were looking for a specific item and contacted them.

The brothers had a virtual Rolodex of every unsavory character looking for such items and would match them up. They would provide a mutually acceptable place for the exchange. The seller and the buyer would never meet, and the money would change hands through the brothers on the dark web. They would take their cut and pass on the balance to the seller.

It was the safest and most efficient way to get rid of or buy illegal items. They never dealt with drugs. However, they made counterfeit money exchanges, mainly US or UK currencies.

They were multi-millionaires by twenty-five and became billionaires by their thirty-fifth birthdays. But along with the money came paranoia; Roman seldom left the compound.

As time passed, more dangerous criminal elements wanted to use their services. They declined until they met an American woman who had a proposition for them.

Emma Leppo joined the CIA out of college. She worked in the clandestine unit, where she found and managed assets for the intelligence unit of the CIA.

Emma traveled the world using the cover of a flight attendant when needed. That's how she ran across the brothers.

Word had gotten out that a 'Broker' was making big moves in the black market. One of the intelligence agencies came across a lead. They were confident the 'Brokers', were heading to Spain. Emma used her cover to try to spot them.

By the end of the flight, Emma was sure she had them in her sights. She managed to weasel a dinner invitation, and that's how she approached them to work as a CI for the US.

By that time, several countries were searching for the 'Brokers. But no one knew who they were or where their compound was.

The brothers couldn't see the benefit of working with the US and declined. Emma stayed connected and continued to work on them. They became friends, and she would spend time with them in Italy at their compound.

A few months later, the Agenzia Informazioni, the Italian version of the CIA, finally caught up with the brothers. They raided their compound. Emma was there and escaped with them.

When they got away, the brothers realized they had nowhere to go and no way to get there without being caught. There was a dragnet across the country, and several agencies were hunting them.

Emma made calls to her boss, Director Rylie. They negotiated a deal with the brothers for protection and a new location. In exchange, the brothers would tell the US of any activity that would be dangerous to the US. The brothers agreed to work with terrorists they had previously refused and pass on the information.

For this, the US would turn a blind eye to their other business and find them a new headquarters in South Korea.

The arrangement was mutually beneficial. The information provided prevented bombings and chemical attacks in the US, the UK, Germany, and Spain.

The DeCarlo brothers were still being hunted and were always at risk of being captured, so they changed their tactics. When information came in involving European countries, they asked Emma to negotiate a trade. The info for a clean criminal slate. Emma negotiated the agreements with all but Italy. Italy was not willing to negotiate.

The seat belt sign came on, and soon after, the plane descended into Dulles Airport in DC.

As the driver drove onto their street, Roman got a text from his brother, Rocky.

Contact me when you get home.

"I wonder what this is about. We just left him," Roman showed the text to Marci.

After changing, Marci and Roman went into the small SCIF. The CIA built it for them before they retired four years ago.

"Rocky, why the need for the SCIF? You're on speaker, Marci's in here with me."

"Hi, Marci, we miss you already. Roman, not so much," Rocky always joked with his brother. They were very close, almost like twins.

"What's up, fratello?"

"We received a contact from the son of Mukhtar Hijazi; he is asking us to get him transportation from Switzerland, where they've been hiding for the last year or so. He wants to go to a hospital in Austin, Texas. A heart doctor there created a device that can add ten years to his life."

"He's on NATO's terrorist list. The most wanted man in the world," Marci leaned into the secure line.

"Just tell him we are retired, Rocky. I don't want anything to do with him," Roman said.

Marci interrupted, "No...no. Wait. If we can capture him and his two sons, we need to do it, Roman."

"Marci, the risk is too great. His followers would hunt us down if he found out we work with the CIA. No, I won't put my family at risk. Turn him down."

"Rocky, wait. He's the one that bombed the hospital in Milan that killed the president of Italy and eight hundred people. What if I could negotiate a deal with the Italians? We can negotiate a trade. The Hijazi's for a clean slate for you and Rocky and the return of your properties." Marci turned to Roman and touched his face. "I know how it hurts you and Rocky that you can never go home again. I can do this for you, love."

Roman considered it. "No, you don't have to remind me of what he did to my countrymen. I won't put my family in their headlights."

"Roman, we could go home again. Marci, could you do that?"

"I think so; they have hunted him all over the world. It would be a small price for them to pay."

"But even so, the CIA won't let us give him to the Italians," Rocky said.

"I'm not so sure. I think it could work if I can find something the CIA wants more than the collar."

No one said anything for a while. Finally, Rocky spoke.

"What do you say, fratello?"

Roman looked at his wife, "going home again would be a dream come true, but not if, in the process, I lost you."

"Rocky, tell him we need twenty-four hours to see if we feel we can accommodate their need," Marci said. Roman agreed.

CHAPTER ONE

DC

Director Cosby was speaking to the president's task force. They were assembled in the conference room of the command center in the DC FBI headquarters.

"The President wishes to extend his appreciation for the excellent work completing your last mission in this facility. He would have been here himself, but he had to fly to Florida to survey the damages of the recent hurricane.

"You are all aware we will have a new home in either Prince George County, Maryland, or Quantico the decision is still tied up in bureaucratic red tape.

"Regardless, we are not planning to call you back for the next few weeks. However, if something unexpected comes up, we will borrow the facility at Quantico. That means that everything in here needs to be dismantled. Though it is unlikely it will be moving with us, it could be used elsewhere. So, it is imperative that all the equipment is scrubbed.

"The President will want you all back for the White House Spring Ball, the third week in April.

"Like always, you will be paid for a thirty-day leave before you need to report to your secondary positions.

"If you have any questions or need anything, I will be here until we move. I will maintain my office number and my cell, for those who have it. I will expect all the hard drives in my office before you turn out the lights this evening.

"Special Agents in Charge Townsend and Rodriguez will take it from here."

When Houston stood, Director Cosby moved him aside for a moment. "Where's Miss Star?"

"She went home."

"She still having troubling dreams?" Cosby whispered.

"Yes, sir, the dreams don't allow her to get much rest when she does sleep."

"You need to get her help. The President and First Lady know the issue and want it tended to."

"Yes, sir. And, sir, we are taking a ninety-day leave of absence. We won't be on standby."

"Agent Townsend, the entire team is perpetually on emergency standby. It's what you signed up for when you joined."

"I know, sir, but I'm concerned about my wife. If you can't grant me the leave of absence, I'll be forced to resign."

"That is a threat you don't want to use with me, Agent."

"Sir, I mean no disrespect. But it hasn't been that long since the Chinatowns flesh peddlers put a bounty on Sophie's head and tried to abduct her. She needs a break. We all do, sir."

"I'll talk to the President about it but threatening to resign will not get you what you want," Cosby headed to the door.

"Sir, it's not a threat. Sophie didn't sign up to be in law enforcement. She is a consultant, but it seems she's always the one who gets in harm's way," Houston walked with him to the door. Cosby stopped and looked Houston in the eyes, then left the room.

Special Agent Alfonso Rodriguez, Houston's partner, saw the exchange. "What was that about?"

"I told him Sophie and I want ninety days leave of absence or else."

"He didn't take it well?" Fons stepped back toward the room with Houston.

"He took it as a threat," Houston said.

"The way you meant it," Fons smiled.

Houston didn't answer; he just looked at Fons. They both knew a threat was precisely what it was. The two men went back to the conference room to give instructions on tearing down the command center.

Sophie and Bully walked into the house; they hadn't been there for days. The last operation at the command center ran day and night. She stayed on-site in her office. The office had a private bathroom and a hide-a-bed. She kept a change of clothes and duplicates of everything Bully needed.

Sophie filled Bully's bowl with the homemade dog food she bought from Carol, her private chef.

Carol lived upstairs with her husband and Houston's best friend and partner, Fons. Carol vlogged cooking classes on the internet. She made money through the ads, and companies paid her to advertise the kitchen items she used during her classes. She still did some catering, but her stable income came from being Houston and Sophie's private chef.

After Bully ate, she let him out in the backyard and went to change out of her silk shirt and slacks. Sophie changed into an oversized shirt and leggings, then let Bully in and went to lie down on the couch. Bully laid down on the floor next to her.

Sophie hadn't been honest with Houston. It was true she didn't remember the dreams when she woke up, but she remembered the emotions they brought up. Some good and some traumatic. It was only after the dreams started that she realized she hadn't suppressed her memories like she thought; she just stored them away.

Sophie had spent years at college vanquishing any memory that dared penetrate the wall she erected when she drove away from her home in Austin. She had done such an excellent job of it that if a memory came up, she looked at it like it was a memory of someone else's life. Doing that allowed her to keep a promise she made to herself. *There was no past, only the future.*

Sophie closed her eyes and fell into a dream state.

Two of her friends, a young couple, Lizzy, and CJ, had come to her house and helped her load her things into the older Red Olds Cutlass Supreme her dad passed down to her on her 16th birthday.

Two younger boys, Ricky and Liam, came from across the street. One was Lizzy's brother, the other CJ's. The boys clung to Sophie and begged her not to go. She kissed them on the cheek and got into the car. When she opened the car door, Teddy jumped in. Sophie grabbed him and handed him to Ricky.

'Please hold onto him, so he doesn't chase the car,' Sophie was beginning to feel the brunt of her decision. She started to cry. Sophie gave everyone a last hug and got in the car. She backed out of the driveway and realized she hadn't prayed about her decision. But then again, she hadn't prayed since her father died or gone to church either, for that matter. She had always been taught to run to the Cross when life overwhelmed her. But Sophie wasn't running to the Cross; she was running away from it. And she wasn't sure she wanted to know what the Lord thought about her decision. She knew it wasn't right, but it was how she felt.

Sophie hadn't driven far when Teddy jumped out of Ricky's arms and started chasing the Cutlass. He knew she was leaving for good without him.

Sophie's window was down, and she heard him barking. She stopped and got out of the car. Ricky was trying to catch up with Teddy.

Teddy jumped into Sophie's arms; she caved. She couldn't leave him behind. The boy finally caught up.

'Tell your sister I'm going to take him with me,' Sophie said as she put Teddy in the car.

The boy stood there, 'please don't go, Sophie. I love you, and it will break my sister's heart.'

'I need to go. I'm sorry. I hope you can forgive me someday.'

Sophie got back in the car and drove off. She knew if she looked back, she could never leave. But she needed to go; Sophie was convinced of that. It was true she was leaving behind people who loved her and who she loved with all her heart. She almost stopped; instead, she dropped a curtain on her past.

'I have no past. There is only the future. I will not think of them again.'

Sophie turned off Scott Street, said goodbye to the Purple Cow Candy Store, and turned the corner. Teddy crawled onto her lap, and Sophie drove on. To what, she wasn't sure, but away from her past and all the pain.

Sophie's body twitched, but she didn't wake up.

'Daddy should be home soon, Sophie,' her mom said as she opened the door. Sophie would sit on the concrete step leading into their small home on the Army Base waiting for her daddy. She was three years old then.

When her daddy drove up, she stood up and clapped; he hurried to her, lifted her in the air, and then kissed her cheeks. She loved when Daddy did that. She reached for his briefcase and carried it into the house. Or at least she thought she did. He was lifting it from the back so she could move it.

Her mind was leaping from one memory to another.

Sophie was in first grade, they moved into a bigger house not far from the Army Base in Virginia. Her daddy sent her up to bed after dinner. He never did that. She snuck down the stairs, sitting on the third step from the bottom, and listened to her mommy and daddy arguing. Her mommy was leaving, and she wanted her daddy to sign papers. They argued until finally, they came into the entry and saw her. Sophie wrapped her arms around her mommy's neck and begged her not to go, but her daddy pulled her away and took her upstairs. Mommy was leaving them both.

Sophie woke up crying. She remembered every painful detail. The thing she dreaded the most was having her heart broken again by remembering the pain of the past.

She closed her eyes again.

It was the first day of second grade, and Daddy stood with Sophie while she waited for the bus. He had moved them away from the pain of their home in Virginia. He decided to put in for a tour overseas. The only one available where he could take Sophie was at the Incirlik Air Base in Adana, Turkey.

'I can drive you to school,' Daddy said.

'No, Daddy, Lizzy rides the bus. I want to go to school with her.' Sophie had met Lizzy at the park in the center of the military housing next to the Base. Her daddy took her there the day after they arrived.

That dream ended, and another scene took its place.

Clair called and asked her daddy if Sophie could visit her and her new husband in Paris, where they lived. Her daddy was hesitant, but he knew she needed her mother. So, after that, she would spend time in Paris with her mother every summer.

That dream morphed into another.

The four-year tour in Incirlik was over. Her daddy's friends had asked him to join them in Austin, Texas, instead of re-upping as a Jag officer in the Army. They wanted to open a law firm, and they wanted him to be their criminal defense attorney. He agreed, and when his time was up, he took Sophie to Austin.

As the plane landed in Austin, news Sophie's mother died after being hit by a car while crossing the street was waiting for her. Sophie was heartbroken.

Sophie's crying stirred her, but she didn't become fully awake. Her mind jumped to another memory.

Sophie and Lizzy were at a country estate outside London, England. Her stepfather had invited her to visit like she did when her mother was alive. She was driving a surrey with Lizzy exploring the property when they spotted a young boy taking apples off the ground. When the boy saw them, he dropped the apples and ran.

The girls felt bad they scared him and followed. They lost him, but the next day they searched again and found him. He lived in a dilapidated barn with an older sister, a toddler, and an older brother. They were orphans.

At first, they left them food, but they worried about what would happen to them when they went back home. Finally, Sophie told her stepfather and his fiancé. The couple became their guardians and eventually adopted them and another orphaned boy.

Her dream morphed again.

In her first year of college, Sophie worked the summer at her dad's firm.

Sophie's Dad was just passing the reception area when he collapsed. An ambulance came, and he was taken to the hospital and immediately into surgery. The doctor said he had a massive heart attack resulting in considerable damage. Luke came out of the surgery, but a few days later, a blood clot went through his heart and killed him. He died one month before Sophie was to be married.

Sophie wept and wept, but her body refused to wake up. Several quick flashes passed through her dream. *She saw Duke's face appear. Duke was one of her best friends; she had grown up with him since second grade.*

Sophie saw him on one knee proposing to her at Lizzy's wedding reception.

Sophie remembered postponing the formal wedding ceremony because her dad had just died. But they had decided to have a private ceremony instead and a formal one later in the year.

Sophie asked Duke to stop on the way to the church at a street vendor selling flowers. She wanted to make a bouquet for herself. Duke decided to stop next store and get gas while they were there. After the private wedding ceremony, they planned to spend the weekend in San Antonio at a hotel on the Riverwalk.

Houston and Fons loaded all the boxes Sophie had packed from her office. Houston had already taken all the hard drives into Director Cosby's office.

Matt, Sissy, and Ken stayed behind at the command center. Denny needed help scrubbing the computers and tearing down the media center. Even though the hard drives were taken out, computers often save some information to the C drive. It would take them several hours to finish the job.

Houston carpooled with Fons since Sophie took their SUV home.

"Houston, have you been able to glean anything from Sophie about the dreams?" Fons asked.

"No, she doesn't remember them once she wakes up. Last night she cried out for her father, begging him to come back to her. The only thing she has ever told me about her past was that she loved her father very much. He must have died young."

"Could it be flashbacks from her time with Nikko?" Fons asked.

"No, it's not like that. This seems to be some tragedy or trauma from her childhood," Houston said as Fons slowed down to turn into the driveway. "It must have been bad for her to suppress her entire childhood all these years."

"Why do you suppose it's coming back to her now?"

"Maybe the Lord is saying it's time for her to deal with it. You know how much I love my wife, but I have always known a piece of her was missing."

Fons pulled into the carport next to the double-car detached garage in the DC home in the suburbs. Fons helped Houston pack the boxes to the back porch. Houston didn't want to bring them inside. He figured he would unload them individually instead of taking the mess into the house.

"Thanks for your help, Fons," Houston said as Fons headed up the outside stairs to his apartment. Fons waved back a response as he took the stairs, two at a time.

Sophie took the gas money inside so the attendant could turn on the pump. Out of nowhere, Duke flung himself in front of her and took her to the ground as the glass door shattered behind them. Sophie didn't understand what was going on.

'Duke, why would you do that. It hurt.' But when he didn't respond, she untangled herself from him and saw blood everywhere.

She started screaming for help. Duke tried to speak to her, but it was hard for him to breathe.

'I'm sorry, Sophie, for leaving you. I love you; please forgive me.'

'No, Duke, don't you die on me, you promised. You keep breathing…. You should have let me die.'

Sophie sat up screaming as Houston stepped into the glass door entry of the house. Houston ran inside, thinking Sophie was in danger. He pulled out his gun and ran into the living room.

Houston saw Bully jumping up on the couch, trying to wake Sophie. Houston ran over to the couch and sat beside her. He wasn't sure she was awake and didn't want to startle her.

Fons came running down the stairs, gun in hand. When he got to the bottom step, he saw that Houston was sitting next to Sophie. Houston turned and whispered, "it was a dream."

Fons nodded and went back upstairs, worried about his friends.

Sophie could barely breathe. She was so broken, sobbing.

Houston couldn't be sure, but it sounded like she was saying, 'You should have let me die'.

Sophie was in such distress Houston decided to take the chance and touched her.

"Duke? Duke?" she opened her eyes.

"No, sweetheart, you had a dream; it's me."

Sophie scooted to the corner of the couch and pulled her legs up to her chest. She wrapped her arms around them, put her head on her knees, and sobbed.

"Sophie, did you remember your dream?" Houston didn't try to touch her again, but he stayed next to her. She only nodded. "Do you want to talk about it?"

"No," Sophie said. She wasn't ready to talk about it. "Houston, I want to go home."

Home for Sophie was the penthouse in Manhattan.

"Ok, sweetheart, I'll close the house down tomorrow. Then we can go home the next morning. Will that work?"

16

"Yes," Sophie reached out and touched Houston's face. He was such a good husband. She hated keeping this from him, but she wasn't ready to share.

The words Sophie had spoken, 'You should have let me die,' kept rambling through his brain. Now he was afraid that her remembering her dream was too traumatic for her to manage.

Houston put one of Carol's prepared meals in the oven for dinner. Sophie was doing the dishes after they ate when a knock came at the door.

"I'll get it," Houston said, Bully walked alongside him to see who knocked. Houston opened the door to find a messenger holding an envelope.

"Houston Townsend?"

"Yes." The messenger handed him the envelope. Houston got out his wallet and gave the young man a tip. "Thank you."

Houston opened the envelope and read the note attached to two tickets to a concert in New York in three days.

Agent Townsend,

My wife loves this pianist from the UK. He has only toured in the US for two years. She attended his last performance, and he is now her favorite musician. But the president has asked us to join him at the hurricane site in Florida.

Trish thought Sophie might enjoy the concert since she also plays the piano.

Director Gram Cosby
P.S. The President approved your ninety-day leave.

NEW YORK

They had made it home to Manhattan. Houston hadn't told her much, just that Trish wanted her to have the box seat tickets.

Sophie was excited about going to a live performance; she still had the long black gown she had worn a few years ago to the ballet. There wasn't time to shop for a new dress. It was an off-the-shoulder fitted designer gown with a slit on one side to her knee. The gown was a little loose but not noticeably so. She wasn't surprised since she had recently lost weight. The dreams had her too upset to eat.

Houston kept a fancy black suit at the penthouse, so he was set too. She was putting on her earrings when he called out to her.

"Darling, our driver is here. We don't want to be late." Houston had set up a car service for them when they got married. Because of their undercover work, he had several of the drivers vetted. They were the only ones authorized to pick them up.

Sophie loved watching people and enjoyed seeing the gowns and fancy suits they wore. She eavesdropped on their conversations when she could. Houston didn't understand her fascination with listening to other ladies chatting about nothing of consequence. But he indulged his wife because it made her laugh.

They found the box on the mezzanine. It had a perfect view of the entire stage and the audience.

"Houston, look at that woman; she is beautiful," Sophie whispered.

"Darling, there isn't a woman here that can hold a candle to you."

18

Sophie elbowed him. "No need to butter me up. You won me over years ago."

Houston laughed and kissed her hand. He was sitting on the outside seat like always. That way, no one could get to her without going through him. It wasn't something other couples in this Hall had to consider.

Sophie was feeling guilty that she hadn't told Houston about the dreams. She wasn't sure why she thought she needed to keep them to herself. Maybe the painful ones had formed a keloid scar and were too raw. She needed time to reconcile them herself.

CHAPTER TWO

Cade Leggett Cornish was a musical prodigy, although it wasn't discovered until he was twelve. His adoptive parents had tutors come in and give him and his siblings music lessons. His siblings were fluent in at least one instrument, but Cade had mastered several. He was a virtuoso at the piano, the violin, and adept at the trumpet.

Cade was accepted into the Royal Academy of Music in London at 16, but Wes and Lady Be did not want him away from home at that young age. They found a retired professor from the Royal Academy who lived in Chertsey to come work with him twice a week. When he turned eighteen, they registered him and set him up with a car service. Lady Be's flat was closest to the school, so he stayed there. On the weekend, Cade drove home. Sometimes the family would come and stay in London for the week.

The day Cade graduated; he was immediately approached by the London Symphony Orchestra. He wasn't sure if that was what he wanted for his life, but he knew it was a great honor and decided it would be good for his resume.

Cade was doing solo pieces in the first year. More importantly, he found the love of his life, Chantel Petit. She was a violinist, a beautiful woman. She was always kind to everyone and generally happy. She reminded him of his sisters.

They married less than a year after they met at Lennox Estate. Her parents lived in a small suburb outside of Paris and stayed at the estate for a week prior to the wedding. It was a beautiful affair.

Cade told Chantel about Sophie and how she disappeared after the tragedy of Duke's death. He told her he wanted to hunt for her but didn't even know where to start. They discussed it and decided to quit the London Symphony and go on tour. They only toured three months a year. They spent two weeks of the tour in New York searching for his sister.

Cade confided in Dex about what his plans were. Dex agreed to come to New York with him during that two weeks and help him search.

Dex was married now too. He met his wife, Rayne, her father, Senator Hawk Newhouse, and her mother, Pricilla, at a fundraiser.

Wes and Lady Phoebe spent a lot of their time raising funds around the UK for orphaned girls' schools and homeless underage boys.

Senator Newhouse was a friend of Earl Ellingham and was in London on state business when they were invited to attend.

Dex fell for Rayne at first sight and flew to DC six times the first year they met. They married in DC; Dex's family flew from the UK and Austin to attend.

On tour, Cade and Chantel performed duets on the piano and on the electric violin. Cade also played the banjo and the trumpet. Dex and Rayne were backstage, visiting with them before the performance. The Senator and his wife were in their box on the second level.

"Cade, tomorrow we can spend the day looking for Sophie," Dex said.

"Good..." Cade started to answer.

"Cade, the chances that you will ever find someone who doesn't want to be found in a city like New York is next to nil."

"Chantel, it's worth the effort. You don't understand how close we all were. It's been nine years, and I never go anywhere without looking into faces I pass by, hoping I'll see hers." Cade took Chantel's hand. "I know you are trying to keep us from being disappointed again. But we have to try."

"What will you do if you find her, Cade?" Rayne asked.

"I don't know."

The giant velvet curtain opened, revealing two grand pianos set up back-to-back so the musicians could see each other. On stands nearby were two electric violins, a banjo, and a trumpet. A young man stepped out, and the audience started applauding. He bowed and sat at the piano. He needed no introduction since his was the name on the marquee.

Sophie gasped when she saw him, "Joe," she put her hand to her mouth.

"No, his name is Cade Leggitt Cornish, see." Houston handed her the small magazine they were given as they walked in. It displayed pictures of him and his wife performing at other concerts and a list of their accomplishments. But Sophie's eyes were glued to the stage.

The virtuoso played Beethoven's Hammerklavier, widely accepted as the most challenging piece. He did so because he knew the audience wanted to rate his skill level for themselves. Then he played contemporary pieces and pop music, including Elvis' version of 'A Bridge Over Troubled Water.'

After playing Elvis's song to thunderous applause, Cade stood to introduce and bring out his wife. He looked at Chantel off staged and started to reach out to her when he paused and turned back to the audience. He asked the lighting director to take down the stage lights a little and bring up the audience lights so he could see them.

"I don't normally do this, but I'd like to take a minute to tell you about my family. I have been so blessed to have a large family and an even larger extended family. Tonight, my older brother, Dex, and his wife, Rayne, are with me." Cade looked up to the box where they were seated.

"I'm also honored to have Rayne's parents in attendance, Senator Newhouse and his lovely wife, Pricilla." Cade found himself scanning the crowd as he spoke. "My wife and I only tour three months of the year because we miss our families when we're gone. I have a little sister, China, who gets very anxious when any family member is gone for long.

"China has already called me twice today to make sure we will be coming home soon," he chuckled, and the audience did too. "You might think I am the star of my family, but I assure you I'm not. Every member of my family has extraordinary abilities in their own field. None of us were born into this family; we were adopted. But I can assure you we couldn't be any closer if we were blood.

"Each of our stories is tragic, but what we have now is pure...." As Cade was scanning the private boxes, he stopped when he saw her. *Sophie.*

Dex noticed the change in Cade's speech; it became shaky. "Something's wrong," he whispered to Rayne. Dex stood to see where Cade was looking, but the angle wasn't right.

"I remember one of the last times I was with my oldest sister before she left, nine years ago, we played a duet together. I wonder if she would play with me again."

Cade was staring at her. Sophie knew it was time to start facing the devastation she had left behind nine years ago. She didn't know where she got the strength, but she stood up.

Houston stopped her, "Sophie, what's going on?"

"That's my brother," she gave no more explanation.

Houston stood up and followed her as she made her way backstage.

Dex still couldn't see her. He got up and ran from the box to backstage, hoping it was Sophie.

Cade needed to do something; he couldn't have dead air in the middle of a concert. He turned and introduced his wife and asked her to play the violin. She was part of the program anyway; he was just taking her out of order.

Cade moved off stage, hoping Sophie wasn't running away again. Dex made it there first.

"You saw Sophie?"

"Yes. Dex, she was sitting in the box just below you on the mezzanine."

"Is she coming down?"

"She got up, so either she's running again, or she's coming backstage." Cade was standing by the stage door, knowing Sophie couldn't get in without approval.

"I'm not running again."

Cade and Dex were startled by a voice behind them. They turned to see Sophie standing with a tall man that looked like he had stepped off an FBI recruitment poster.

"I'm here," Sophie repeated. Cade and Dex went to hug her. The three of them cried. Cade heard the final stanza of the piece his wife was playing.

"I have to get back on stage. Come play our duet," Cade prodded.

"Cade, I'm not your caliber; your audience would be disappointed."

"No, they won't, but I wouldn't care if they were. My sister was lost, and now she is found."

Houston handed her his handkerchief so she could wipe the mascara from her face. There was a mirror close to the door.

As Houston stood by Dex, astounded at what was happening, Sophie and Cade took the stage, hand in hand.

Cade kissed his wife's cheek and thanked her, then turned to the audience.

"My sister Sophie thinks you will be disappointed if she tries to play a duet with me, but I assure you, you won't."

Cade walked Sophie to the second piano and waited for her to be seated before he took his place at the other piano.

They looked at each other, and Cade nodded. They started playing 'Let It Be,' a song by the Beatles they had played together when her father had passed away.

As they got further into it, Cade started adding embellishments and trills. They sped the song up and kept playing faster and louder until they finally reached the end. They threw up their hands and laughed. They had blocked out the audience and played like they were at home messing around. Sophie was surprised when the audience applauded and gave them a standing ovation.

Cade went to her, took her hand, and moved her in front of the pianos to take their bows.

Cade whispered, "please don't go anywhere, Sophie. I need to finish the concert. Stay backstage. Please."

Sophie kissed his cheek, "I will wait for you," and walked off. Chantel came back on stage, and they played together on several instruments.

Houston was standing off-stage. Sophie introduced him to Dex.

"That was amazing, sweetheart," Houston kissed her cheek.

Dex rushed up to the box where his wife and in-laws were before the final performance and asked if they would like to meet his sister backstage.

They made it backstage as Cade and Chantel took their final bows.

"Houston, Sophie, this is my wife, Rayne, her father, Senator Newhouse, and her mother, Priscilla." The group said their hellos.

Houston recognized Senator Newhouse; he was on the Senate Intel Committee. After each task force operation, a summary was sent to them to review.

Houston didn't indicate he knew who he was; most of the task force were cloaked in top secret covers. The Intel Committee knew of the task force but not the individuals that made up the team.

Cade and Chantel came off stage. The crowd was still applauding, but he was worried Sophie would leave before he could talk to her.

"Cade, go take your bows. I'll wait for you," Sophie insisted.

After the final bow, Cade returned and insisted everyone come to his and Dex's suite at Trump International.

Senator Newhouse and his wife thanked him but declined. Dex and Rayne were in the same two-bedroom suite at the hotel with Cade and Chantel.

"Sis, we need to talk; please come," Dex took her hand.

Sophie looked over at Houston, "It's up to you."

"Ride with us, Soph. I have a limo waiting," Cade led them to his dressing room so he and Chantel could gather their things. They still had two more nights of performances, but they took their personal items home every night. Their instruments remain; the pianos were rented from a local music store and were insured. The other instruments belonged to Cade and Chantel but were heavily insured.

Sophie agreed to go with them. Houston texted his driver and said they were going with friends to Trump International. He would text him from there when they were ready to go home.

The first thing the group did when they got there was order food from the hotel's restaurant and get changed. Rayne was closest to Sophie's size and offered her a pair of jeans and a top to change into. Houston just took off his jacket and tie.

They kept the conversation light during dinner, but after, Cade asked.

"Sophie, I understand why you felt you had to go after Duke was killed, but why didn't you come back to us?"

They were sitting in the conversation area in the living room. It consisted of two couches, a love seat, and two overstuffed chairs, upholstered in the same cotton material with a subtle floral pattern.

Sophie looked out the large picture windows on one wall of the living area before she answered. It was dark out, but the city's lights reflected off the glass.

"When I drove away that day. I hadn't prayed or talked to God since my dad died. I was so broken. It was my fault Duke was killed."

Dex started to correct her.

"No, Dex, it was my fault. I wanted to take flowers to our private wedding. If I hadn't asked Duke to stop, we would have never been caught up in that robbery, and his family would still have him. What did it matter if I died? My father was gone. I had no family left."

"Sophie. Stop that. It's a lie. You had us. We loved you, and you know it," Dex admonished her.

"I know that's true now and even then. But I couldn't take another loss. If something had happened to another one of the people I loved, I would have died."

"But you never came back, Sophie. Do you know how that affected the rest of us? We love you so much."

Sophie began to cry. Houston wondered if he should shut this down. But it was her family, and he didn't want to interfere. It was the first time he had heard anything about her past.

"I know you loved me...."

"*Love* you, present tense," Dex interrupted.

"When I left that day, I did my best to shut out my past. It took a long time, but I managed to gain distance from it and put it away. My dreams have only recently forced them to the forefront again."

"You forgot us?" Cade was hurt.

"No, Cade. You were always with me in my spirit. But you were in a holding place in my mind. I can't explain it."

"Sis, you have to come back and make things right," Dex said. He leaned across the arm of the couch to reach out to touch her hand.

"I can't. China will never forgive me, and I can't take that rejection. I'm sorry."

"It doesn't matter that it will be difficult; it's the right thing to do, Sophie," Cade added.

None of the spouses injected anything into the conversation. This was obviously a family issue that had been painful for a long time. They needed to address it without interference.

Houston was surprised at how different she was with her family. She was vulnerable and took all the admonishments they dished out about her leaving.

Houston had to admit he was upset with her for not sharing her dreams when she remembered them. But this wasn't the place to tell her that.

"Soph, I'm not going home and lying to the family," Dex said.

"You don't need to lie, just don't say you found me," Sophie said.

"No, that's not going to work, sis. You need to face your family. Not just at Lennox Estate, what about your family in Austin. They were heartbroken when you left...you left Lizzy. The best friend you ever had."

"You think I don't know the hurt I caused, Dex. But I can't go back. They are better off now that they don't think about me anymore."

"But they do. I know Grandpa Emmett and Manny found where you were a couple of times, but when they got there, you were gone," Dex said.

"They came to look for me?"

"Of course, Sophie. You disappeared. They never stopped looking for you. What happened to you?"

Sophie felt she owed them an answer to that question. She told them everything. How she got involved with a criminal empire and ended up being beaten by a man obsessed with her.

She told them how she hid in a small town in Washington to escape him and gave her life back to Christ. She spoke of how she went back to try to make things right by taking down the criminal empire and how all of that came to pass.

"It's how I met Houston. He was assigned to protect me during the takedown."

"Sophie, I can't believe you went through all that by yourself," Dex said.

"When I left all of you. I was so lost. I had left my family, my God and saw a side of life I had always been sheltered from. God had to go to great lengths to get me back to a place where I saw my need for Him.

"I wish I hadn't taken that road. But it brought me back to Jesus, so it was worth it."

"What do you do now?" Cade asked.

Sophie looked at Houston. "I don't care about the consequences. I'm not going to lie to them, Houston."

"Do what you have to, Sophie."

Sophie told them they could never tell anyone what she was about to say.

"Houston and I work on the President's Task Force, which takes down national and international threats to our country. It's under the FBI supervision and is top secret; we work undercover and behind the scenes."

"Sophie, that's incredible. I guess you became a spy after all," Dex laughed.

"I guess I did."

The rest of the night, Sophie asked to hear everything that had happened in the last nine years at Lennox Estate and in Austin. Cade told her Lizzy and CJ had a boy.

"He is two now, Jerimiah Emmett Young, but China decided that was too long, so she combined the names and called him Jett. It stuck."

"Lizzy has a child. How wonderful," Sophie whispered to herself.

It was one in the morning when they decided to call it an evening.

"Sophie, you have to promise you won't disappear on us again. We can talk about you coming home later. But you can't disappear again."

"We live here...part of the time. Why don't we meet up tomorrow and go ice skating at Rockefeller Center," Sophie said. "We'll talk more."

Houston sent a text to his driver to pick them up in twenty minutes at Trump International. After he gave Dex their address and everyone said their goodbyes, they headed downstairs, her formal gown over her arm.

Houston was quiet on the drive home. "Houston, what's bothering you?"

"You are so different around your family."

"Different, how?"

"You're so open and vulnerable like I imagine you were as a girl."

"Is that a bad thing?"

"No, it's just a side of you I don't know."

"And?"

"I'm hurt you didn't share your dreams with me. I feel like you have held back a part of yourself. I thought we were closer than that."

Sophie turned to Houston in the seat. "Houston, you don't have the right to be hurt. It's my past, and I need to deal with it in a way that works for me."

Houston didn't respond but turned his face away from her and looked out the window.

It wasn't Sophie's intention to shut him out; she needed time to process it. If Cade hadn't called her out tonight, she had no idea when she would have told him. She knew she hurt him.

Sophie took Houston's hand in both hers; he turned to her. "I'm sorry, I planned to tell you everything. I wasn't expecting tonight to unfold the way it did."

"You were almost married to someone else?"

"Yes, when we get home, I'll tell you everything about my childhood from my first memory. You're everything to me. But the pain it brings up remembering it…it's hard to talk about.

When they got home, Sophie put on a pot of coffee while Houston changed and hung up his suit and Sophie's dress. She took two large cups from the cupboard and filled them up, placing them on the coffee table in front of the couch, Bully crawled up beside her.

When Houston sat down, she told him the story of her life. When she told of her father's death, she broke down. He held her and stroked her hair. After she composed herself, she told him about the day she was supposed to marry her best friend and how it was her fault he had died.

Sophie thought she would break down again, but she didn't. She had cried herself out about Duke that day she dreamed of him on the couch.

Houston hadn't said anything the entire time she talked of her past. The first thing he said was, "are you telling me Blaze Walsh Cornish, the best soccer player in the world, is related to you?"

Sophie couldn't help but laugh. "After everything I told you, that's what you want to know?"

"Yeah," he kissed her and held her close. "You must have truly loved Duke if you were going to marry him."

Sophie knew what he was asking. He was worried he was a second choice. "Houston, if life had turned out differently, I would have never met you. And I'm sure Duke and I would have had a good life.

"But that never happened. Did I love Duke? Yes. But if you are asking if I loved him more than you. No. You are my love, my life; God sent you to me. I don't want to imagine my life without you."

They were both exhausted; it was 3 am. Houston stood, scooped up his wife in his arms, and headed to the bedroom.

CHAPTER THREE

DC

Roman was still not convinced that taking on this job was a good idea. "How do you think Hijazi found our contact?"

"I don't know, Roman. But I think we should talk to Director Perry right away."

"I'm not sure about this, amore mio, it's too dangerous. This is not a man who has a soul. He is evil. He bombed the hospital in Milan and killed eight hundred people just to kill our president. If he is sick, he needs to die."

"I don't disagree with you, darling, but he should have to face the Italian people and go on trial publicly for his crime. They need that closure. And if we can do that for them and get you back your citizenship and property, I want to do that for you."

Roman embraced her. "I know you do. But I would have no life left if I lost you in the process."

"Let's just talk to the director about it."

"All right, but not tonight. Tomorrow."

After breakfast, Marci went into the SCIF and used the secure line to call Director Perry.

"Director Perry's office."

"I need to speak with Director Perry, please."

"Your name."

She gave her name, and the director's Secretary put her on hold. A moment later, he came on the line.

"I thought you were retired?" he laughed. "Are you bored already?"

"No sir, but I need to see you right away; this can't wait."

"Do you feel comfortable coming here, or do you want to meet somewhere else?" Director Perry asked.

"Can you come here, sir?"

"I'll be there."

At 2:30 that afternoon, a cable truck pulled up, and a man in full 'cable guy gear' stepped out and knocked on the door.

Marci opened the door and chuckled. "I like this look on you, sir."

"Yeah, yeah. Have your laugh." The director stepped in and took off the gear belt around his waist. He pulled out a black box voice scrambler, turned it on, and set it on the kitchen table.

"This must be urgent, or you wouldn't have called me, Miss Beauchene."

Roman didn't like that the agency still called Marci by her maiden name. He knew it was a security precaution, but he was old-fashioned and preferred her to use his last name.

"Mr. DeCarlo, you look well," the director said in the way of a pleasantry.

"Thank you, Director Perry, as do you." Roman stood and pulled out a cheese and fruit tray from the refrigerator for their guest. "You care for coffee or tea?"

"Coffee, thank you." The director was not one for social protocol. But he knew enough about Roman to know things would get off to a lousy start unless he let him do his thing. In some ways, the director wished he were more of a people person. But then he wouldn't be fit for this job.

Roman and Director Perry never directly spoke about the intel he gave to the US. Marci was the handler and managed every contact with the agency.

"Sir, we have been contacted by Mukhtar Hijazi," Marci paused to let that set in. Marci could see the look of surprise on the director's face. He was rarely taken back.

"How?"

"The message came through Roman's contact. How Hijazi found him, I have no idea. I know it's no surprise to you that Hijazi is ill. He wants Roman to find a way to get him into the US. A heart doctor in Austin has invented a device that can add ten years to his life."

"Why would we want to help him live longer?" the director asked.

"My sentiment, exactly." Roman set a plate and a fork in front of the director so he could take what he wanted from the tray.

"Sir, Mukhtar Hijazi should stand trial in Italy. He bombed a hospital and killed over eight hundred people just to assassinate the Italian president."

"So, you want me to get the information to the Italians, Marci?"

"No, we should bring Hijazi to the US and let him get the operation. Then we get him in international waters and hand him over to the Italians," Marci corrected.

"Why would we do that? I don't mean, why not capture the Hijazi's. Why would we turn him over to the Italians if this is our op?"

"Because the US has damaged their political relationship with Italy, a close ally at one time. President Stevens didn't respond to the tragedy timely. This would be a way to get back in good graces with them. And the Italian courts will make sure Makhtar pays for his crimes."

Director Perry was working as assistant to the previous director, Director Rylie, at the time of the bombing. Perry was in the room when Director Rylie advised President Stevens to immediately send aid and condolences. But the president didn't care for the Italians and waited until he got slammed in the press before he responded.

"Ok, Marci, there is more to this. What is it?" Perry asked.

"For Roman's part in facilitating this, I want the Italian government to expunge his criminal record and take him off the most wanted list. We want them to grant Roman and Rocky immunity for past crimes and their citizenship and properties back."

"I don't know that President Madden will agree to turn the most wanted man in the world over to the Italians. Especially on our dime."

"Director, it wouldn't be on the government's dime. Hijazi will pay for all of it. The US wouldn't be involved at all, the governments' fingerprints can't be anywhere on this. Hijazi would find out. This has to come entirely through Roman's sources," Marci said.

"Marci, we can't have an operation running on our soil that is not controlled by one of our agencies."

"I understand, sir; he could have his task force shadow it. They just can't intervene under any circumstances until it's time."

"Even if the president wanted to improve our relations with Italy. And I can see the benefit of that. He would want someone connected to us imbedded with the Hijazi's while on US soil. How do we know that while here, they don't plan to do some terrorist act?

"These people are zealots. They give no thought to human life," Perry lifted his coffee cup to take a drink.

Roman finally stepped in. "I have occasionally hired a freelance operator to travel with items being transported if it was of great value. It would not be out of character.

"But in this case, it would have to be a woman. These men put no value on women and would not be threatened by having one travel with them. A man would be too threatening. I'm sure his two sons and daughter will travel with him."

Director Perry sat for a while, staring at his empty plate. Marci could see the wheels turning. The Italians would make sure he was punished for his crimes. Makhtar's lawyers would appeal the verdict for years to higher and higher courts. The US would be assuaged from the cost of those trials and housing Makhtar and his sons in a maximum-security prison. It would also give the US back the good standing they once had with the Italian government. *It could be a win, win*, Perry thought.

"Alright, I'll take it to the president when he returns from Florida. He would likely want to use his task force to shadow Hijazi across the US.

"Director Cosby shut down the unit because their headquarters are being moved. But they can use the facilities at Quantico." Perry was basically talking to himself. He looked up at Roman.

"When is Hijazi supposed to have this surgery?"

"We have no information yet. We told Makhtar we would need twenty-four hours," Marci was the one who answered. "But before we do anything, I need to negotiate terms with Italy."

"I'll contact the Italian Ambassador at their Embassy, and you can meet up with him. He can get you in contact with the right people."

"Thank you, sir."

Director Perry stood up. Marci and Roman followed him to the door. He put on his 'cable guy gear' before he left, and they watched him get into his truck.

NEW YORK

After ice skating at the Rockefeller Center, the small group walked to the nearest Chinese Restaurant.

"You did not win, Cade. I got there first," Dex said.

"Neither of you won; I was first. Wasn't I Houston?" Sophie turned to him for support.

"Houston, I don't think this family ever does anything without competing. You should hear the stories about the pedal boats in London on the lake," Rayne laughed.

"Really? Well, I have a story about Sophie and go-karts," Houston added.

"I won that fair and square; even Fons said so," Sophie laughed and slapped Houston's arm.

"Ow," Houston chuckled.

"You think we're competitive? We are nothing compared to Blaze," Cade said. Everyone agreed, laughing.

"No kidding, even as kids playing football. If we were on his team and didn't play like a professional, he would get upset," Dex said. "That's why our pa and uncles would step in and cheat for the opposite side," Cade added.

"You mean soccer, right?" Houston chuckled.

Sophie got quiet; Dex noticed. "Sophie, you don't want to quash all the great memories because you miss your dad. Uncle Luke was such a great one for trying to even the score for you girls in our games, not just football."

Sophie smiled, "yeah," she whispered. Their lunch came, and the group was quiet for a time while they ate.

"Sophie, you'll come to our concert tonight, right? You can watch from backstage. But I want you to do our duet again," Cade grabbed another egg roll from the family plates in the center of the table.

"Oh, no one wants to hear me play. The audience comes for you and Chantel. They only applauded last night because you introduced me as your sister."

"Not true, Sophie; you played beautifully," Chantel said.

"Yeah, and Dex and Rayne will come too. Won't you?" Cade looked over at them. Dex started to answer, but Rayne spoke.

"Cade, we'd love to, but we promised my father we'd attend a political fundraiser with him."

Dex lowered his head, "oh, yeah, I forgot." Then looked up at her with pleading eyes.

"Oh, all right. Don't give me those puppy dog eyes. I'll make excuses for you, but I can't back out."

Dex kissed her cheek several times, "thank you, my love; you are the best."

"And don't think you don't owe me one for this."

"Anything, Rayne.

"You say that now," Rayne snickered.

The concert was another huge success; the duet Sophie and Cade played was one of the highlights.

Afterward, they headed back to Cade's suite at Trump International. This time Sophie and Houston brought clothes to change into. Sophie washed the clothes Rayne lent her and brought them back. They ordered food from the hotel's four-star restaurant again.

"Rayne texted me; she should be here soon," Dex said.

"Dex, your wife is a treasure. I'm so glad you found someone perfect for you. But doesn't she work for her father? And don't you still help Mr. Gray at the estate?" Sophie poured Houston another glass of tea.

"Help?" Cade said. "Dex manages everything; he runs the entire estate and supervises a full bunkhouse of unpapered minors who fell through the cracks. And now he wants to build on the property pa bought that had the barn they once lived in."

"Wes bought that property?" Sophie looked at Dex, surprised.

"Yeah, you know how sentimental pa and ma are. He didn't want it to go to strangers. He's never torn down the barn. He goes there sometimes to remind himself how much God has given him and how desperate other people are," Dex said.

"I think God dropped an extra-large capacity in him to love people when he got saved," Sophie said. "What would you build, Dex?"

We have so many minors coming to us now for work. But we can't employ them all. I thought of building a dorm and bringing in tutors. They could get an education, then learn a trade or go to college. You know ma and pa have a charity now for fundraising to keep the girl's school going. It also supports underage boys, who are homeless. We would add the dorm to the charity list. They would have to work on the property part-time."

"Would you plant more orchards?" Sophie asked.

"I'm thinking something more practical, like vegetables, corn, herbs, that sort of thing. They could sell what they don't use at the street market on Saturdays and learn a little about business."

"Wow, that's awesome, Dex. Houston and I would financially back that, too. Wouldn't we, darling?"

"Yes, helping a child get a chance at a good life is a perfect charity for us to back," Houston added.

The group turned as the door opened, and Rayne came in. Dex got up to greet her.

"Sweetheart, I had some of your favorite foods sent up for you."

"Thank you, Dex. You know I can't eat at those fundraisers; they make me too nervous." Rayne went to change and came back to join the group at the table. "How was the concert?"

"It was amazing. Cade and Chantel are incredible performers. The audience loved them," Sophie gushed. She was so proud of her brother. She looked at Rayne, "I was asking your husband how you two manage, when you work in DC, and Dex lives and works in Lennox County."

"The first year, I stayed in DC while the Senate was in session. I flew to the UK when they were out. Dex would fly to DC in the winter after he and Mr. Gray made sure they prepared for the frost. Finn would take over supervising the bunkhouse with Wes' help.

"But it was hard, so I quit. I spend most of my time in Lennox now, but I still come to DC for two months to help my father when the Senate is in session. And then we come off and on to visit them through the year."

"Your life sounds very complicated," Sophie said.

"Look who's talking," Dex laughed. "My sister, the spy."

"You'll come to our final concert tomorrow, won't you?" Cade asked.

Sophie looked at Houston, "It's up to you, sweetheart," he said.

"Yes, but I'm not sure I'm up to a duet with you again."

"We'll see about that," Cade winked at her.

"Would you all like to come to the penthouse for lunch tomorrow? I'll BBQ," Houston said.

At 11 am, a call came in from the building's security guard, saying they had guests coming up. Houston had let him know earlier who they were expecting.

Sophie and Bully waited at the door to greet them. After introducing Bully to everyone, they headed to the balcony. Houston was setting up the grill. Dex and Cade headed straight for it.

"It seems a grill is like a magnet for all men. I remember the BBQs in Austin; it seems it took every man there to grill steaks and chicken." Sophie remembered the scene fondly.

Rayne chuckled, "It's true; I've seen it with my family too."

"Bully is a beautiful animal, Sophie. What breed is he?" Chantel asked.

"He's a Belgian Malinois. He is a brilliant dog and special in so many ways."

"China has a miniature poodle called Teddy Jr. I understand he was named after your dog. He came with you to New York, right?"

"Yes, but shortly after I graduated, he died of cancer. It was hard to lose him. He was my only friend when I came to the city," Sophie said. Chantel could tell she wanted to change the subject.

"Your place is beautiful, Sophie. Can we have a tour," Chantel asked.

After they toured the penthouse, Sophie said, "I want to know more about my new sisters."

As the women chatted, sitting on the patio furniture, the men grabbed the food prepared from the fridge and put the steaks and chicken on a platter. After saying grace, they all dug in.

"Sophie, this potato salad is wonderful. Will you give me the recipe?" Chantel asked, putting another forkful in her mouth. The men chuckled. Sophie gave the guys a dirty look.

"What's so funny," Rayne asked.

"My sister cannot cook," Dex snickered.

"Shut up, Dex. Yes, I can. Just ask Houston."

"Yes indeed, my wife makes the best waffles and pancakes in town," Houston couldn't keep himself from smiling.

"Sophie, don't listen to them; I'm sure you are a great cook," Chantel said.

Cade finally couldn't stop himself and laughed. Sophie elbowed him.

"I don't get it," Rayne said.

"Whenever Sophie tried to cook when we were in Austin, it always ended up with a smoke detector going off. Duke told us the one time she got something as far as the table, he and Uncle

Luke didn't want to hurt her feelings and tried to eat it. It was stew, but it tasted so bad that when she wasn't looking, they fed it to Teddy," Cade said.

"Yeah, from what I heard, even Teddy had a hard time getting it down," Dex burst out laughing, and the others couldn't help but join in.

Sophie put her hands on her hips like she did when she was a kid and blurted out, "That's not true. They said they liked it." The guys only laughed harder.

"Well, this potato salad is delicious, Sophie. Don't listen to them," Rayne defended her.

"To be honest, Rayne, I didn't make it. I have a private chef who makes us meals three times a week. Houston grills the other nights if we don't decide to eat out. I don't know why but I can't seem to follow a recipe without ruining it."

"Well, I'm not the best cook either. I occasionally cook for Dex in our apartment upstairs in the manor, but we eat with the family most nights we're there," Rayne said. "When in DC, my mother has a cook and housekeeper. She has too many events to attend with my dad, to do it all herself."

"Sophie, you and Houston *are* coming tonight?" Cade asked.

"Yes, we planned on it."

"Our final stop on our tour is in Austin. We have to be there next Wednesday. We have performances on Thursday, Friday, and Saturday.

"Will you consider traveling with us?" Cade asked.

Sophie looked down at her plate and moved her food around. "I don't think so, Cade. I'm not ready."

It was hard for Cade not to push it, but he felt it was best to give her time.

"So, will you stay in New York until then?" Sophie asked.

"We will," Chantel answered for Cade. Last year they stayed to look for Sophie.

"I'd love to take you to Trenton, New Jersey, to meet Houston's family and some of our extended family," Sophie said, looking at Houston to help encourage them to say yes.

"My parents would be hurt if they found out Sophie's family was in town, and they didn't get to meet you."

Dex looked at his wife; she nodded, "We'd love to."

CHAPTER FOUR

DC

Director Stew Perry walked to Director Cosby's office when he heard he was back from Florida. His long-time administrative assistant, Cassi, retired. The director didn't like change; Stew wondered how his new assistant was working out. She was away from her desk, and Cosby's door was open, so he knocked and waited for him to look up.

"Stew, what are you doing here? Come on in."

"Sorry, Ms. Deasun wasn't at her desk. How is she working out?"

"Close the door behind you and have a seat."

"Patsy is efficient, but I won't hold my breath that she plans on moving with us once we move to Prince George County."

"Is that where they finally decided to move you to?"

"Who knows. You know how government bureaucracy works. What brings you to my office, Stew?"

"I'm aware you don't know my people. But I inherited Director Rylie's handlers and assets when he retired."

"I'm aware."

"We have one asset that Emma Leppo brought in before she got involved with politics and resigned. He has been a goldmine for us. Saved thousands of lives. Not only in the US, but in Europe also."

"I was read in that he exists but not given a name or the name of his handler."

"He married his new handler and retired a few years back. From time to time someone still tries to contact him for his

47

services. If it's valuable, he will pass on the information. While you were gone, I received a call from his handler to meet." Perry paused when Cosby got up, moved to his small wet bar, and lifted a cup in way of asking if he wanted coffee. Perry nodded, then continued. "Makhtar Hijazi had contacted him."

Cosby almost stopped in his tracks. "You're kidding? Are we talking about the same man?"

"Yes. After the bombing in Italy, he had to go into hiding because of the worldwide hunt for him. We found out recently he has been ill for some time."

"Yes, but he still runs his terrorist group."

"Not so much in the last year. His sons are stepping in for him in the videos. We haven't been able to track where he is, but we believe he doesn't have long to live."

"Too bad. I wish we could put Makhtar and his two sons on trial for crimes against humanity."

"That's what I said, but Ms. Beauchene wants us to let him get treated here in the US and then turn him over to the Italians."

"I can see luring him over here to capture him and maybe even letting him get treatment so he can stand trial. But why on earth would we turn him over to the Italians?"

"During our CI's time with us, he negotiated with most European countries. Exchanging lifesaving information for immunity for past crimes and records of them expunged. He's Italian, and they are the only ones who refused. The Agenzia Informazioni almost captured him once. He escaped. It made them look bad; they haven't gotten over it yet."

"I can see why your asset wants to give him to Italy, but why would we?"

"You were around when Hijazi bombed the hospital in Milan. His target was Italy's president, who was visiting his mother. They lost their president and over eight hundred citizens in that bombing."

"I'm aware."

"And I know you remember President Stevens didn't like the Italians. He waited until the press crucified him before he finally sent aid and condolences."

"Yes, that was a huge political faux pas, and likely is what unseated him and made him a one-term president."

"Rightly so," Cosby answered.

"Ms. Beauchene thinks giving Hijazi to Italy will heal the political animosity. The Italians still hold it against us."

"And?"

"And she wants to negotiate a way for her husband and his brother to get immunity. She also wants the brothers to get their citizenship, and their property returned."

Director Cosby didn't say anything. Instead, he looked out the window and rocked in his office chair. Perry sat quietly, drinking his coffee.

"President Madden has tried several times to make things right, politically, with Italy. Nothing seems to work. He might be interested.

"But there is no way we can have a terrorist roaming our country without us managing it. They could wreak havoc on their way out," Cosby said.

"I agree. I expect the President would want to have his task force shadow the Hijazis."

"They'll do more than that. They will have to organize and run it."

"No, Gram, the asset was right about that. Roman needs to use his own sources. If Hijazi gets wind, the 'Broker' isn't in charge; he'll bolt. And the DeCarlo's have resources and means we don't have."

"Ok, but we need to have someone imbedded with them. We can't give them free rein in our country," Cosby said.

"Our asset agreed to that. But DeCarlo said it would have to be a woman. A man would be too threatening," Perry said. Cosby stood; Perry followed suit.

"I'll take it to the President. Thanks, Stew. I'll get back to you as soon as I have an answer."

Ms. Deasun was startled when she saw Director Perry coming out of Director Cosby's office. She stood.

"Sorry, sir, I didn't know you had someone in your office."

"Ms. Deasun, will you please call the president's administrative assistant and find out when he can see me."

"Yes, sir."

"Ok, Gram, I'll wait to hear from you."

TRENTON, NJ

Houston and Sophie headed to Trump International to pick up her family. Bully was in the third row. Sophie planned to sit there with him on the drive. She couldn't bear to leave him home alone. Bully loved going to Trenton. His best friend, Tora, Bully's brother, lived there. Sophie gave him to Katsumi when he was still the Kumicho of the Akuza.

Dex took the front seat with Houston. Chantel, Rayne, and Cade sat in the second row. They were leaving early so they could make the church service in Trenton. Houston and Sophie's home church. The women chatted; Cade was stuck in the middle. He scooted up, leaning forward to converse with the guys in the front seats.

During the trip to Trenton, Sophie felt she needed to explain her relationship with Izumi and Katsumi.

Sophie told them how she was hunting for a tender-age girl, feared to have been trafficked by the Chinese gangs to be used in their brothels. Sophie and the police started taking down brothels one by one, hunting for her. Eventually, the task force got involved and they found the girl and, in the process, released over 1400 women from the grasp of the flesh peddlers.

"Katsumi didn't know I was with a task force. He only knew I was looking for a girl who had been taken. He protected Houston, me, and Houston's partner when we were led into a trap. And when a bounty was put on my head by the Chinese gangs: Katsumi hid us at his compound and protected us.

"Through all this, he and his son Izumi became Christians and left the Akuza. They live in Trenton now; they still don't know we are with the President's Task Force. But we are very close, like our uncles in Austin. I refer to Katsumi as Ojisan, which means uncle, but he refers to me as musume, which means daughter. And Izumi refers to me as his sister."

"That's amazing, sis. I'd like to hear the whole story sometime," Cade said.

The trip took an hour and a half. When they turned into the church's parking lot. Houston saw his parents, his siblings, Izumi and Lee, Katsumi, and Mr. Jo, waiting outside for them.

They exited the SUV and headed to the church. The family spotted them giving hugs and greetings all around.

Bully sat on the porch during church; he wasn't allowed inside.

After church, Izumi moved Sophie away from the crowd to speak with her. "Imoto, please bring your family to our home for lunch. When Lee heard you were bringing your family, she insisted we cook an elaborate lunch for you. She spent all day yesterday cooking."

"Of course, we'll come, Izumi. Have you already told Houston's family?"

"Yes. Miss Lily said she would bring some of your favorite dishes too."

"All right, we'll head over there as soon as I can corral everyone back in the SUV," Sophie chuckled.

Chantel and Rayne were taken by the beauty of Izumi's home and asked for a tour. When they found out Katsumi lived on the grounds, they asked if they could see his and Mr. Jo's home after lunch.

Tora and Bully played outside. The conversations were lively, and a bout of laughter often broke out at one end of the table or the other.

Sophie always sat by Katsumi; they enjoyed each other's company.

"Watashi no musume, you have never spoken of your family. How is it we now have the honor of meeting them?"

Sophie told him how she forced down memories of her childhood because of the great tragedies.

"I understand great tragedy. When my wife died, I didn't care to live anymore. I shut myself off from loving anyone and lived to be the Kumicho of the Akuza.

"If it weren't for you.... I would still be living that life. Such a waste. All those years without knowing Jesus as my savior," he took Sophie's hand. "Without my daughter and my son. I wasted so many years." Katsumi's eyes watered. Sophie reached up and touched his face.

"But look at your life now. You love and are loved by so many. You do great acts of charity and work for the Lord in many ways."

"Yes, musume. I need to remember how blessed I am. But you haven't explained how you came upon your brother."

Sophie told them about the tickets they received as a gift for Cade and Chantel's concert. She said Cade spotted her in the audience and asked her to play a duet with him.

"They had been looking for me for years. Cade was as shocked as I was that he found my face in a full concert hall."

Izumi ushered everyone to the backyard after the meal to enjoy the weather. Bully and Tora came to get attention from the crowd. Tora never ventured far from Katsumi.

After the group walked through the beautifully sculpted garden and admired the flowers, they sat on the patio. Lee brought out beverages. Sophie got up to help her serve them, as did Lily and Spring, Houston's sister.

The sun was going down, and the lights in the yard turned on. Katsumi stood and made a request.

"I understand we have celebrities among us; it would be rude of us not to acknowledge them. Sophie's brother, Cade, and his wife, Chantel, are virtuosi on the piano. Would you honor us with a duet?" Everyone clapped and encouraged them to play.

"We will be honored to play for you, but I must insist that my sister also play a duet with me," Cade turned to Sophie. She smiled and nodded.

The group moved into the large piano room. Chantel and Cade sat on the bench together and played Leonard Bernstein's, 'West Side Story'.

It was an excellent choice, and everyone enjoyed it. When they finished, Cade looked at Sophie. She sat down with him like they did at her home many years ago and played 'Let It Be' by the Beatles.

Sophie and Cade had a blast playing together again, and the group loved it.

"We need to practice another duet, Cade," Sophie said. "We do need to come up with something new," Cade agreed.

It had been a wonderful day, but it was getting late. The group had already eaten leftovers for dinner and cleaned up the kitchen.

"How long are you and your family staying, Sophie?" Izumi asked.

"I'm not sure, but we will be at Lily and Jack's tonight."

"Will you bring your brothers to my store tomorrow; I will fit them for suits as my gift."

"Izumi, you don't have to do that. People pay a boatload of money for one of your suits."

"Imoto, they are part of our family now. It is tradition to give a gift. I wish to honor them."

"All right, Izumi, I'll bring them over."

Before everyone left, Izumi and Lee asked for everyone's attention.

"Lee and I have an announcement to make...." he paused and looked at his wife. "We are going to have our first baby."

There was a moment of surprised silence; then applause broke out, and everyone went to hug and congratulate them.

"If we are telling secrets," Josh Bennet, Spring's husband, said. "Spring and I are expecting too." Again, the group applauded, whooped, and hollered.

When they thought the excitement was over. Cade spoke. "Chantel and I would like to say something," he looked around for his brother and sister. "Chantel and I are having a baby too."

Sophie's hand flew up to her mouth. She was shocked but excited. Again, congratulations rang out from everyone.

Dex moved over to Sophie and whispered, "I think we are going to have to create our own cul-de-sac," he laughed.

Of course, babies were the subject on the drive over to Houston's parents' home, where they were staying. Houston and

Sophie's apartment was too small for all of them, and they didn't want to stay in a different location.

Lily settled her guests in their rooms and said she would have breakfast ready for them around 9 am. But they were welcome to sleep in if they wished.

After saying their goodnights, Sophie was in the bathroom brushing her teeth. Houston was already under the covers. Sophie was at the bathroom door looking at him, talking. Houston couldn't understand her.

"Sophie, I can't understand a word you're saying. Wait until you are done brushing your teeth."

Sophie gave him that look she gave when she was annoyed and finished brushing and got in bed.

"I was saying Izumi wants us to take Cade and Dex to his shop tomorrow so he can fit them for suits."

"Wow, that's generous of him. Those suits are top of the line."

"I know, I told him he didn't have to do that, but he said they are part of the family."

When Sophie slipped into bed, Houston took her hand and looked at her. "Sophie, you are so happy and at ease with your brothers. Why won't you go to see the rest of your family?"

Sophie didn't speak. She looked at the bathroom light she forgot to turn off. Tears started to make a path down her cheeks. Houston reached up and wiped them away.

"Please tell me why, sweetheart."

"If Cade hadn't called me out and welcomed me with open arms, I would have never approached him at the concert. If I show up in Austin or Lennox County and they reject me.... I couldn't stand it, Houston. I couldn't take it."

"But there was no hesitation with Dex and Cade; they welcomed you without reservation."

"But what if the others don't. I know China will never forgive me. And Lizzy, I walked out on my best friend. Drew may not remember me, but he and China were inseparable; she probably told him how I walked out on them.... No, Houston, I can't take the chance." Sophie laid her head on his chest and cried. He held her, kissed the top of her head, and stroked her hair.

DC

Ms. Deasun knocked on the director's door.

"Come," he said.

"Director Cosby, the president said for you to come at your convenience; he would make time for you.

"Thank you," Cosby stood, grabbed his leather-bound notebook, and headed out the door.

DC traffic was brutal during the day. It took his driver almost an hour to get him to the White House. President Madden's administrative assistant stood to greet him and walked him to the door. She knocked and stepped in without waiting for an answer.

Director Cosby smiled when he saw Emma sitting with Michael. They had all been friends for years. Their sons grew up together. Emma was one of the president's closest advisors.

"Good morning Mr. President, Madam First Lady."

"Have a seat, Gram," The president and his wife moved to the seating area to sit with him.

"Alright, Gram, what is so important."

"Director Perry came to my office today with some compelling information," he went on to tell him everything he was told.

Emma looked at Gram. "When you say asset and handler, you mean Roman and Marci, right?"

"Yes, that's right," Gram acknowledged.

"I'm not convinced of Marci's reasoning to hand Hijazi over to the Italians," Michael argued.

"Michael, you can barely get the Italian President to answer your phone calls. And isn't the important thing that Hijazi is captured. I believe Mukhtar himself planted that bomb and detonated it. The loss was massive, and you know how we feel when one of our presidents gets assassinated. They should have first rights to him."

"But they don't have the death penalty."

"They have made exceptions, but even so, life in an Italian prison is more of a punishment than death."

"But why let him traipse all over the US and get the surgery. Why not just turn him over and let the Italians care for him?"

"For one thing, sir, to get credit for handing him over, we have to have him. And the surgery that he needs is so new the only doctor that can perform it at this time is the one who invented the device.

"Besides, Michael, his sons would want to accompany him to the surgery. Capturing Mukhtar won't mean as much unless we get his two heirs."

The president sat for a while. Emma got up, poured him and Gram a cup of coffee, and handed it to them.

"My task force would have to be in charge. We can't take the chance of them harming our citizens," the President finally said.

"Sir, Stew, kiboshed that idea. And he's right. We can't have our fingerprints on this in any way. DeCarlo has the resources to do this. But he agreed to have someone imbedded with them as they travel, as part of the agreement."

"Then Agent Townsend and Agent Rodriguez come to mine," Michael said.

"I would have agreed with you, sir, but I was told it would have to be a woman. Men would be too threatening."

"Marci could do it, Stew," Emma said.

"From what I understand, she is a private contractor. Ms. Beauchene doesn't have the training," Gram said.

"No, but she knows Roman's sources inside and out, and she could manage any complication that may arise."

"I was thinking more along the lines of Miss Star," Michael said. "She certainly has the ability. I have never seen anyone so capable of reading a conflict and knowing how a target will respond. And my task force can shadow them. They can predict her moves."

"True, and it wouldn't be prudent to send a woman alone on this mission. The two of them could go," Emma said.

"Sir, you approved Houston's request for a 90-day leave of absence. I don't think they will come back for this. Houston was adamant about it."

"I need to trust the people I send on this mission, and I don't know anyone I trust more. Call them and get them to agree," Michael said.

"Emma, you and Marci are close. Why don't you talk to her and Roman about it? I'm sure she would do it for you," Michael said.

SEIZE ON THE HIGH SEAS

CHAPTER FIVE

Emma wore a pair of blue jeans, a ball cap, and a hoody as a disguise when she drove herself over to see Roman and Marci. She hadn't called ahead but sent her security to drive by to see if their vehicle was there.

Emma pulled into the driveway and went to the door. She knocked, and Marci answered moments later.

"Emma?"

"Can I come in?"

Marci stepped aside and led her to the kitchen nook. Roman and Marci were having a mid-afternoon snack and reading.

Roman stood up, went to her, and kissed her cheek. He had been in love with Emma once, years ago. He didn't handle it well when she turned down his proposal, but that was water under the bridge. Roman knew now that God had someone else in mind for him.

"Marci, please sit; Roman will bring you a plate. I know you love cheese and fruit trays," Roman went to get her something to drink. "Coffee or tea, Emma?"

"Iced tea if you have it."

Emma and Marci sat while he brought the women iced tea and a plate and fork for Emma, then sat down with them.

"Yes, Roman introduced me to the mid-afternoon snack, and I try to have it as often as possible," Emma said as a compliment to Roman.

"I take it our proposal has reached Michael," Marci said.

"Yes. We can see the benefit of improving our relations with the Italians. And you're right; they should have the first right to put him on trial for what he did."

"But you have concerns?" Marci asked.

She addressed Roman, "Do you still have the contacts to run a complex operation like this? How will you get him traveling papers? Those are my main concerns," Emma said.

"Yes, all my contacts are still in play. I would get them forged Italian passports and medical visas from the US."

"Why forgeries? If the Italians know what we're doing, they will give you the real thing. The same with the US medical visa."

"Because it would be suspicious if we have the real thing. These men are smart. They will be expecting to spot the imperfection of a forgery, but they will also know a good forgery will pass inspection at any security check."

"That makes sense," Emma agreed. "Now, about who to imbed with them. Michael only trusts his task force to do such a sensitive job. He wants them to shadow your operation and imbed one of his team. Her name is Sophie Star, and she leads the task force with her husband."

Roman looked over at Marci. The look on her face confirmed what he was thinking.

"Did you say Sophie Star?" Marci asked.

"Yes, why?" Emma thought for a moment. "You don't think this could be your stepdaughter, do you? Didn't she disappear nine years ago?"

"Yes. Do you have a picture of her?"

"No, she works undercover. Her file is sealed."

"Describe her to me."

"She is beautiful, with auburn hair, hazel eyes, about five-six."

"It's her, Roman; it has to be," Marci said. Roman took her hand.

"Where is she?" Marci asked.

"I don't know. Mis Star and her husband are on a 90-day leave. But we are trying to get them to come back for this operation. Michael thinks she is the best one for this job; I suggested you accompany her. I don't like the idea of a woman going solo on this."

"Marci? No, Emma. I'm not putting my wife in danger for this," Roman said. Marci squeezed his hand.

"Roman, more than anything, I want to give you your heart's desire to be able to go home again."

"Not at the cost of losing you, Marci."

"If Sophie is going, I won't let her go without me. I would never forgive myself if something happened to her."

"We do have a snag with that. Sophie's husband insists she needs this time off. He might turn in his papers before he lets her do it."

"We are getting ahead of ourselves anyway. We haven't taken the contract, and we don't know the timeline for the surgery. There may be a waiting list, or maybe the doctor will say he doesn't qualify," Marci said.

"All true. You get things going on your end. Know that we will give you whatever help you need."

"I'm waiting to get in touch with the right person in Italy. Director Perry is contacting the Italian embassy for me," Marci said.

The group snacked and visited as old friends for an hour, then Emma left as she came.

TRENTON, NJ

Dex woke up from a fretful night's sleep. He looked at the time on his cell: it was 6:30. He got up and slipped on a pair of jeans and a T-shirt, then sent a text to Cade, hoping he was having as much trouble sleeping.

If you are awake, meet me out on the kitchen porch.

Dex brushed his teeth and headed downstairs. He was surprised to see Jack sitting in the kitchen having a cup of coffee.

"Coffee is fresh. Help yourself," Jack said.

"Thank you, Jack. You're up early."

"After years of getting up at dark, it's hard to sleep in. But I don't like disturbing Lily, so I just enjoy the quiet time."

"I don't mean to invade your space," Dex poured himself a cup.

"I'm happy for the company. Sit with me for a while."

"Thank you."

"Your sister is a remarkable woman. My son loves her more than life, but she never told us anything about her family. You seem very close; why would she leave home?"

"It's a long story, but it boils down to her losing her father and her fiancé within a few weeks of each other." Dex took a sip of his coffee and reached for the sugar on the table. "She blamed herself for Duke's death. It isn't true; he was killed in a robbery. Duke took a bullet meant for her. She couldn't get over it, so she left us behind and disappeared."

"Sophie did the same thing when the man who kidnapped her was shot in a standoff with the police. Sophie blamed herself. She ran, leaving Houston behind devastated.

"Fortunately for Houston, she had a change of heart. Whenever anything bad happens, she tends to blame herself. As if she could have prevented it somehow. I don't know where that comes from," Jack said.

"It's in her nature to want to fix things for people. It's how my siblings and I ended up at Lennox estate. She found us living in a dilapidated barn, starving. She couldn't just walk away. It's who she is.

"The family was heartbroken when she took off. And now she doesn't want us to tell them we've found her. I'm not sure I can do that."

"Dex, she is your sister, and it's not my place to tell you how to handle it. But spending time with you and Cade may help persuade her. I understand she fears rejection if she appears on their doorstep. Sophie is sensitive; it would break her."

"Yes, that is exactly what she is afraid of...." Dex was distracted when a text vibrated on his cell. "Excuse me." Dex looked at his cell. It was Cade saying he was on his way down.

"It's Cade. I asked him to come and talk with me. We need to figure out what to do."

"Know this, Houston will honor your place as her brother, but he will not let you push Sophie into doing something she doesn't feel comfortable doing. He is very protective of her," Jack said. "You can have some privacy on the porch."

"Thanks, Jack."

Dex refilled his coffee, added more sugar, and poured a cup for Cade. He handed it to him as they walked out to the porch after Cade said hello to Jack.

"Cade, I don't think I can go to Austin with you," Dex took the closest wooden chair by the door. Cade sat next to him in an identical chair.

"You want to stay with Sophie?"

"Yes. If she gets used to being with us, she may reconsider returning home."

"Chantel and I can't stay. We have to finish the tour."

"I know, but after you are done, will you come back?"

"Yes, of course. But the family will question why you are not with me and why I'm not staying. And you know I'm a terrible liar."

"Yes, you are. That is why pa always asked you when he wanted to know what was going on with the rest of us."

"You can't still be mad I told him you snuck out on your motorcycle to meet that cute blond from the village at midnight."

"I lost the bike for a month, Cade."

"Get over it," Cade laughed.

"I noticed you never told on China."

"Yeah, but that's China. No one tells on her."

"Ok, true enough. Let's get back to Sophie...." Dex's cell rang. "It's China; she must have ESP," he accepted the call.

"Hello, China. I'm here with Cade. I'll put you on speaker."

"Hi, Dex, Joe. I want to know when you are coming home. You have been gone a long time." China was very young when Cade came to live with them. His mother had told him to run to Lennox Estate if he was ever in trouble. He showed up with a broken arm and bruises, the night his mother was murdered. They found him sleeping against their equipment barn. He lied and said his name was Joe. China never called him anything else.

"China, you know my tour isn't over yet. I still have to go to Austin."

"Will you promise to come home right after you're done?"

"We might stay and visit with family. And Rayne might want to work with her father for a while," Dex said.

China was quiet. After Sophie disappeared, she never liked her family being away. She developed an irrational fear they would never come back.

"China, we are not going to disappear. You need to stop having anxiety over it," Cade said.

"But you haven't called in three days. You always call me."

"I'm sorry, China, we should have been more thoughtful," Dex said.

"Yeah, sorry, sis," Cade added. "Is everything alright at home?"

China went on for ten minutes, telling all the news. "And I'm going to spend most of the summer in Austin with Drew."

"How come you give us a bad time about being away when you spend months away in Austin?" Dex laughed.

"Because it's different. If you were with the family in Austin, I would know exactly where you were. But you are traveling all over, and I don't know where you are or when you'll be home if you don't call me."

"True. Alright, China. Tell the family we love them. And don't get caught riding my motorcycle on the property. I'm sorry now I taught you."

"I won't get caught. Ma and Pa are in London at another fundraiser. I didn't want to go."

"You're home alone?" Dex asked, concerned. She was almost fourteen but still too young to be on her own, as far as he was concerned.

"No, Emmi and Bridgett didn't want to go either. Scarlett went with them. I think there is a guy she likes in London."

"Really, what do you know about him?" Cade asked.

"Only that he is tall and handsome."

"Alright, take care, and we'll call you tomorrow," Dex said.

"Love you, China," Cade and Dex echoed.

"Love you more," China said and ended the call.

"We are not going to be able to keep this a secret from her," Cade said.

"I know. Just get back here as soon as you can. Given a little time, I think we can change Sophie's mind."

Dex heard Lily's voice in the kitchen, and the two decided to go back inside. "Good morning, Miss Lily," Cade said.

"Hello, you two. Jack said you were up early. What do you say I make breakfast for you."

"Do I get a vote?" Jack asked.

"No, dear, you're not a guest," Lily chuckled.

"We'd love to eat, thank you," Cade took a seat at the kitchen table after refilling his cup with coffee.

The smell of bacon filled the kitchen, and a few minutes later, Houston walked in, following the smell. Bully walked next to him.

"I think you have a bacon radar, son," Lily said as her son kissed her cheek.

"Good morning, Mom, Dad, Cade, Dex." Houston let Bully out and filled his water and food bowls on the porch.

"Good morning," everyone echoed back. Houston went to the cupboard, grabbed a cup, filled it with coffee, and then found a seat at the table.

"After breakfast, what do you think about taking the horses out?" Houston directed his question to Dex and Cade. "I don't know about your wives, but Sophie won't be downstairs before we get back.

Cade looked at Dex, "Sounds good to us."

Houston, Cade, and Dex headed to the trails, giving the horses a chance to warm up before they ran them. At one point on the path where the three could ride side by side, Houston spoke.

"Last night, I tried to talk to Sophie about going back to Austin or Lennox. She's not ready, guys; she's afraid some of the family will reject her. She cried in my arms until she fell asleep.

"I'm telling you because even though I agree with you. I won't let you push her to go home unless she's ready." Houston stopped walking his horse. Dex and Cade went a few more steps before they realized he had stopped.

"You can't tell your family you found her," Houston said.

"Houston, I respect that you are her husband and want to do what's best for Sophie. But getting her back with a family who loves her is the right thing." Dex saw that Houston was going to interrupt him and raised his hand to stop him. "But we agree. That's why, if you don't mind company for a while, I plan to stay while Cade goes to Austin to finish his tour."

"You think Sophie may feel she could face the family if she gets more comfortable with you?"

"I think so. And she is right about possible repercussions. China and Emmi were heartbroken when she didn't return. They still are after all these years. I don't know what their first reaction will be. But their anger is bred from their deep love for her. They'll get over it."

"The rest of the families will see it like we did," Dex nodded to Cade.

"Houston, I don't plan on telling her secret when I'm in Austin, but you have to know I'm a horrible liar," Cade said.

Houston gave his horse a jab, and he started forward again. "Just so you know where I stand. I'll do everything I can to encourage her, but my support ends if Sophie gets hurt."

When the guys were done rubbing down the horses and letting them out in the field, they headed to the kitchen door. They could hear the ladies laughing before they opened it.

"Lily said you guys went riding," Sophie addressed her brothers. "Isn't the ranch beautiful?"

"Yes, it is," Dex said, Cade nodding agreement as he went to kiss his wife on the cheek.

"We'll go take a shower and come back down. We smell like horses and sweat," Cade said.

As the guys left, Sophie hollered after them, "Don't forget, Izumi is expecting us at his shop by 10:30."

"Sophie, while you take your brothers to the shop, Spring asked if Chantel and Rayne would like to go with me to her house. She was hoping they might have ideas for the nursery. Then she wants you all to meet us there for lunch."

Sophie turned to her sisters-in-law, "It's up to you."

"I'd love to. What do you think, Chantel?" Rayne asked.

"I think it's a great idea; maybe I can get some ideas for the nursery at Lennox, too," Chantel smiled.

Izumi's Fine Men's Clothier Store was like walking into a fine jewelry store. The floor was marble, and the walls were covered with subtle gold and tan wallpaper. A large Persian rug covered the center of the room. A table set on top of it with beautiful silk ties Izumi designed and made in back where all the seamstresses worked.

The wasn't a counter with a cash register. The twelve different designer suits were displayed on mannequins. Four suits in assorted sizes hung behind the display. Izumi made suits to order but kept a few for those men who needed one immediately. His tailor was always on site and could make adjustments in less than a day when necessary.

"Izumi has clients come here from around the world to get his silk suits and ties. Izumi gives the silk producers the subtle patterns he wants in the material, then brings it home and has the suits and ties made by hand here.

He started by training some women freed from the Chinese gangs to give them good jobs. He taught them English and brought tutors to help them get a high school equivalency certificate. Then he helped them find other jobs if they wanted. Most chose to stay. He and Lee are excellent employers."

Cade stepped up to one of the displays, touching the material. "It feels like a million bucks."

Sophie laughed, "If he put price tags on them, you'd see you're not far off."

"It's the old saying, if you need to ask, you shouldn't be here," Dex said.

"Exactly," Sophie responded. "He private labels for high-end department stores. But he won't use the same silk he uses in his shop, and they don't get the current season's designs."

Izumi interrupted, "I hear my sister is filling your head with accolades of me. I'm afraid she exaggerates."

"Not true, Izumi," Sophie said as Izumi stepped to her and kissed her cheek.

"Thank you for coming to my humble shop. It is an honor to have the brothers of my sister bless me in such a way. It would give me immense pleasure if you allowed me to fit you in a suit. A gift to my new brothers."

"Izumi, thank you for the offer, but that would be too much," Dex said. Sophie stepped up to him and whispered.

"Dex, if you refuse, it will be an insult."

"However, if, you are sure. We would be honored," Dex said.

After Dex and Cade picked a suit design, they liked and were fitted by the tailor. Sophie reminded Izumi and Lee, who came down from her upstairs office to greet them, that dinner at Lily's was at seven.

Houston texted Spring to tell her they were on the way for lunch. When they walked in, lunch was being put on the table. Spring had grilled salmon, asparagus, and potato salad. The potato salad was to keep her brother, Houston, happy.

"This is an amazing spread, Spring. Are you a chef?" Cade asked.

"No, I just love cooking. When Josh and I decided to remodel instead of sell. I had free range to put in a chef's kitchen. Then he suggested I take classes to learn how to use all the new equipment," she laughed.

"She is a marvelous cook," Lily bragged on her daughter.

"I plan to invite the families over for dinner, if you plan on staying a while."

As the platters of food were being passed around, Cade answered. "Chantel and I have to finish up our tour in Austin, but if we are welcome, we would like to come back when we're done." Chantel looked at him quizzically. He mouthed, *'we'll talk later'* to her.

"Of course, you are welcome to come back. You can stay with us as long as you like. Does that mean you and Rayne are staying here while they are gone, Dex?" Lily asked.

"I thought it would be nice to spend more time with Sophie."

"Of course, you want to stay with your sister. And I insist you stay with us," Lily responded.

"I'm glad you're staying, Dex. How long will you be gone, Cade?" Sophie asked.

"We have our final performance on Saturday night. So, we'll be back Sunday or Monday."

"Mercer Airport will have direct flights to Austin. That way, you don't have to fly out of LaGuardia or JFK."

"We'll come back that way, but we need to pick up our things at Trump International. We can hire a car to take us back on Wednesday."

"Don't be silly. Jack and I will take you back. I wanted to do some early Christmas shopping anyway. And we can bring back Dex's things too."

"Thank you," Dex said. "Rayne packed our suitcases, expecting to stay here until we left on Wednesday."

CHAPTER SIX

DC

R oman sent a message to Rocky to accept the job. Roman had seen pictures of the Hijazis on television when they took credit for the bombing. They had the coloring of an Italian and wouldn't have been surprised if they had Italian in their DNA. Rocky sent a message to Makhtar to send his medical records in his new name, Enzo Ricci.

Rocky sent back a message confirming the instructions were passed on. The cost of the job was a million dollars. He knew Hijazi would have no trouble coming up with the money. A fourth of the money would go to the hospital for surgery, and another fourth would go to the intermediaries that would help with the job.

Marci was not pleased that he had agreed to do the job before she had negotiated with the Italians.

"Darling, I know you are looking out for me. But I am an Italian, whether they restore my citizenship or not. What the Hijazis did to my President and my countrymen is unforgivable. My country has the right to exact justice for it."

Marci kissed him, "I won't mention you've already agreed when I negotiate. Director Perry connected with the Italian Ambassador. The Director only told him I had information for the President of the Council of Ministers of the Parliament's ears only. Director Perry had developed a relationship with the Council's President, Lorenzo Vittore in the military. Lorenzo Vittore was asked to call me from a secure line."

The next morning Roman was awakened by a buzz on his cell. He sat up, grabbed his cell, and moved out of the bedroom, not to disturb Marci.

It was a text: **Medical info sent.**

Roman went to the SCIF and opened the secure connection. He clicked on the medical records file with a note with the name of the Doctor in Austin. Roman also found a receipt for one million dollars deposited in the numbered account set up for this purpose.

Roman wasn't a doctor, so he couldn't tell how severe Makhtar's medical condition was. But he had done some research on the device Makhtar needed. It had yet to get the final approval by the FDA, but in the US, there was legislation called 'The Right to Try'. It gave doctors permission to use experimental procedures on terminal patients. Roman had no idea if Makhtar fit that criterion.

Roman would have to lure the Hijazis here some other way if he didn't. But he wasn't going to let this opportunity pass by.

Roman told Rocky to order the Italian passports and US medical visas from their forger as soon as the Hijazis sent their passport photos. Rocky told him the Hijazis were sending pictures today.

AUSTIN, TEXAS

Saturday night, Cade and Chantel took their final curtain call and found his Austin family waiting for them backstage.

"That was amazing," Lizzy said, hugging Cade and then Chantel. The rest of the families congratulated them on their performance.

Blaze and Xander had convinced Emmett to build them a small, gated community on the part of the undeveloped land around his house. There were fifteen triple-size lots on a cul-de-sac behind the gates. All of Blaze's family had access to it. Blaze only spent three months a year there besides the holidays. But Lizzy insisted Cade and Chantel stay with them since Dex and Rayne hadn't come.

"Lizzy, I must ensure our equipment gets properly packed for shipping back to the UK. I'll meet you at your house. Chantel can ride with you."

Emmett heard what he said and offered to stay with him and drive him to Lizzy and CJ's when he was done.

Cade knew he couldn't refuse without people asking questions. He wanted to talk to Dex and tell him they would take a flight back to Trenton on Monday. He'd have to wait.

Cade managed his own concerts, so he was the one who made sure everything went back where it came from. Emmett helped Cade pack his instruments and signed them over to the transportation company. The pianos were rented, and he waited for the music company's truck to get there and haul them away.

"Thanks for staying with me, Grandpa," Cade signed the papers the movers set in front of him. Chantel asked him to recheck the dressing room in a text.

"Chantel wants me to check the dressing room one more time. She left a set of earrings I bought her for her birthday in a dressing room while performing in Germany. She still feels bad about it."

"I would do things like that for Carol all the time. It's one of our jobs," Emmett smiled.

They finally went to the parking garage and got in Emmett's SUV.

"You still plan on staying for a week?" Emmett asked.

"No, Grandpa, Chantel, and I are leaving on Monday."

"Cade, what's going on. It's not like Dex not to come with you. And now you have to rush off."

"Dex ran into a friend, and he wanted to stay in New York and visit with him and his wife. That's all. I promised I would come back and spend time with them too."

"What friend?" Emmett knew something was going on.

"Oh, you don't know him, Grandpa. His name is Houston Townsend."

Emmett took his eyes off the road for a moment and looked over at Cade, "You found Sophie?"

When Sophie didn't return after college, Emmett and Manny started searching for her. They had left her alone for those college years, thinking she needed the time to recover from her losses. But when she didn't return, Manny started a search. Sophie had left no forwarding address with the college.

Every year Manny would do parcel searches in New York County. Finally, he found a penthouse in her name in Manhattan. Emmett and Manny flew there to check it out. They went to the building and spoke with the security guard.

Manny told the guard he was Sophie's uncle and the family had been looking for her. The security guard apologized for being the bearer of bad news and told him Sophie had disappeared from the hospital. The police were trying to find her.

Emmett and Manny went to the police, but Detective Cartwright, who was in charge, told him they had no leads, and it was a cold case.

Manny expanded his parcel search yearly and eventually got as far as the District of Columbia County. He found a property owned by Houston Townsend and Sophie Star Townsend.

This time Emmett went alone. He found the property and knocked on the door. When there was no answer, Emmett wandered around the house looking in windows. When he returned to the front yard, two black SUVs were parked at an angle on the street. Six men in FBI jackets and bulletproof vests pointed their guns at him.

Emmett raised his hands. The lead Agent told his men to lower their weapons after he searched Emmett and found he wasn't carrying.

'Sir, what are you doing here?"

'I'm looking for my granddaughter.'

'What's her name?'

'Sophie Star.'

Emmett knew the Agent recognized her name. 'Sir, you need to leave the premises.'

'Do you know my granddaughter? Is she in trouble?'

'No, sir, you have the wrong address. You must move off the property now, sir, or I will have to detain you.' He escorted Emmett to his car. Then he whispered.

'Sir, don't come back here again.'

Emmett wasn't afraid of being detained, but he knew agency protocols, and this house was being protected. From what, he did not know, but he wasn't going to mess up an operation. And he had no idea if it would put his granddaughter in danger.

Emmett had no way of knowing that a bounty was placed on Sophie's head, and she was being protected at Katsumi's compound.

"What? No. Why did you say that?" Cade stammered.

Emmett pulled into a gas station and parked the SUV.

"Cade, you are a terrible liar. I know Houston Townsend is Sophie's husband."

"How do you know that?"

"Manny and I have kept searching for her over the years. That's why Dex didn't come and why you are leaving early. You want to spend time with her."

"Grandpa, we are trying to convince her to come home, but she is afraid. Sophie said she couldn't take being rejected by people she loves so much."

"Where is she, Cade?"

"In Trenton, New Jersey. Houston's family lives there."

"Do they live there too?"

"No, they have a penthouse in Manhattan and a home in DC."

"I'm going back there with you, Cade."

"Grandpa, you can't. Sophie made me promise not to tell. If she doesn't trust us, she will never come home."

"I'm coming with you."

"How will you explain it to the family."

"I'll figure something out."

TRENTON, NJ

Jack had scored tickets Friday to a baseball game at Arm and Hammer Park Saturday night. Trenton's favorite team won in a close game that everyone enjoyed.

Saturday morning, Katsumi took Houston, Sophie, Dex, and Rayne to the Farmers Market. He bought fresh ingredients for dinner he planned at his house.

Cade had called and said he would be coming in on Monday. Sophie and Dex fell back into their friendship naturally and spent a lot of time together. Rayne made an effort to leave them alone so they could talk.

After lunch, Houston's brothers, Sam, and Teddy, took on Dex and Houston outside for a 'pick-up game'. Lily told them it was time to get dressed for dinner at Katsumi's.

Mr. Jo, Katsumi's one-time groundskeeper at the Akuza compound, became a Christian after Izumi testified about his miraculous conversion. He and Katsumi shared the large home Katsumi built on part of Izumi's property. Mr. Jo attended a Korean Bible study with Yon Moon. Yon Moon moved there to be close to her son, who was in prison nearby. Yon Min-ji was in jail in Trenton for counterfeiting millions in American currencies. He was given a light sentence because he helped the task force take down several terrorist cells. He would be out soon.

Mr. Jo and Yon Moon had been keeping company for the last few months. They were both Korean and were learning English at the Korean community center. Though most thought there was more to it than that.

The Korean, Japanese combination dinner was so successful that the hosts had to refill empty platters more than once. When everyone had eaten twice what they had intended, the guest cleared the table.

Sophie washed Katsumi's hand-painted China dishes by hand. She knew Katsumi would never put them in the dishwasher. Dex dried, and Houston put them away. The others put the leftovers, what little there was, in the refrigerator and cleaned the table.

The party moved to the glass-enclosed patio. It was dark, so the small globe lights lining the patio perimeter and the ground lights in the gardens out back gave off a feeling of paradise.

Sophie caught Katsumi sitting, watching the group laughing, and chatting. She saw the contentment on his face and went to sit with him.

"This is what your heart searched for all those years. Isn't it, Ojisan?"

Katsumi looked at her and took her hand. "I didn't understand what the scripture meant that said, 'joy unspeakable and full of glory'. Jesus has given me so much, yet I offer Him nothing in return," a tear slipped from his eye. "I am nothing, and He is everything, yet look at what He has given me."

Sophie patted his hand with her free one. "Katsumi, God sees us through the righteousness of His son. It is a gift none of us deserve. All we can do is be grateful and live in His service."

"Of course, you are right, musume. It's hard for me to forget who I was. I was so blind...." Katsumi changed the subject and looked up at her. "Musume, I am happy to see you have found your brothers, but why would you not go to see the others in your family?"

"Ojisan, you don't understand. I hurt them. My father died a few weeks before he was to walk me down the aisle to marry a man who I loved very much. I couldn't bear having the ceremony without him, so we agreed to postpone the formal ceremony. We decided to have a private ceremony with just the family.

"On the way to the church, I saw a street vendor selling flowers, and I asked Duke to stop so I could make myself a bouquet. There was a gas station right there, so Duke decided to get gas. I headed inside to give the cashier the money for the gas, but Duke saw something through the glass doors that I didn't. The place was being robbed. He knew my opening the door would startle the thief. He ran to me and threw his body in front of mine, taking me to the ground as the glass door shattered behind us.

"Duke took a bullet meant for me. I took Duke from his family. I caused the pain they suffered from his loss. I was the one who wanted to stop for flowers...." Sophie started to cry. "I couldn't stay and watch all the suffering I caused, so I left. I knew it would cause them more pain, but I couldn't stand it. I left and never went back."

"Watashi no musume, you are afraid of their reaction. But I have seen you stand toe to toe with some of the most dangerous heads of Chinatown's gangs. You are fearless, my daughter."

"Ojisan, those men could only hurt my body. I could survive that. My family could break my heart. That, I can't survive."

"Your brothers have not rejected you."

"That's true; they have shown me grace. But my little sister... my best friend. I don't know that they can forgive me."

"In God's Word, he told of a man whose son took his inheritance and left him...."

"Yes, The Prodigal Son. But his brother did not forgive him."

"True, musume, but sometimes it has to rain so the clouds will pass, and the sun can come out."

"You think I should go make things right," Sophie looked up at Katsumi.

"I miss you when you are gone. But I want you to do what will give you the greatest joy in the end. Not what is most comfortable for you now."

Houston had noticed Sophie talking with Katsumi. He knew she would listen to his advice; Katsumi was a wise man. Dex had been talking to Ted but looked around for Sophie and saw she was with Katsumi, crying. He wanted to see what was wrong, but Houston touched his arm.

"Let them talk. Katsumi will give her good advice."

Dex nodded and felt his cell vibrate. He looked at it; Cade was calling.

"I need to take this," Dex stepped away from the group.

"Hello, Cade."

"We have a problem."

"What?"

"Grandpa Emmett is coming."

"Cade, we promised we wouldn't tell."

"I didn't. We knew someone would ask why you and Rayne didn't come, so I told him you ran into a friend and wanted to visit."

"Emmett asked who it was. The only name I could think of was Houston Townsend."

"That should have worked," Dex said.

"Well, it didn't. Grandpa knows Houston is Sophie's husband."

"How did he know that?"

"You know, Grandpa and Uncle Manny have been searching for her for years. Apparently, a year or so ago, Uncle Manny did a property search in DC. Houston's name came up with Sophie's on their property. Grandpa went to DC, but when he got there, they were gone."

"I need to tell Houston; he will not be happy with us. Text me your flight information. See you soon, Cade."

When Dex got off the phone, he took a deep breath and went to Houston. "Can I speak with you for a moment?"

Houston followed him to the kitchen.

"Cade called. He's coming in on Monday."

"That's great. I can pick him up if that's what you're worried about."

"No, Houston. Grandpa Emmett is coming with them."

"DEX! I told you I would back you up if you didn't push her too far. Cade broke his promise," Houston started to pace the kitchen. He considered taking Sophie back to New York before they got here.

"Houston, listen. Cade didn't break his promise. He had come up with a cover for why Rayne and I didn't travel with him. He said I ran into a friend and wanted to visit with him.

"Grandpa asked what friend and Cade used you. But grandpa knew who you were; he knew you were married to Sophie."

"How would he know that, Dex?" Houston was in Dex's space. Dex told him what Cade said.

Houston calmed down. "Maybe I should take her home before he gets here."

"No, Houston, don't. Emmett and Sophie were very close. Besides her father, Emmett was always the one she ran to when she was sad. I know him; he would never say anything to hurt her.... Please don't tell her. Once she sees him, she will run to him, not away. Trust me, Houston."

Houston looked at him. "Alright, I'll keep quiet for now." The two men went back to the group.

DC

Marci heard a faint ring of the secure landline in the SCIF. She ran to get it. "Hello?" Roman slipped in when he woke and saw she wasn't beside him.

"Ms. Beauchene?"

"Yes."

"Minister Lorenzo Vittore here," Vittore spoke English well but had a heavy accent.

"Yes, sir, I was expecting your call."

"Director Perry tells me you have information I will want to hear."

"That is correct, sir. Before we begin, I need you to pledge that everything I tell you will go no further."

"Va bene."

"I know you are still hunting the terrorist Makhtar Hijazi and his sons for the assassination of your former President and murder of hundreds of your citizens in the hospital bombing. The

Agenzia Informazioni has them at the top of their most wanted list."

"True, but that is not news, Ms. Beauchene."

"No, sir, but the fact that we can turn that man over to you is." Marci could hear Vittore's chair scrape the floor as he stood up.

"Are you telling me the United States has Makhtar Hijazi and his sons and is not telling us?"

"No, sir, no one has him yet, but Roman and Rocky DeCarlo have a way to entrap him and are willing to turn him over to the US. Who, in turn, is willing to turn him over to you to improve your political relations."

"Ms. Beauchene, you need to tell me what you are talking about," Vittore sat back down.

"First, I need to negotiate with you."

"Negotiate?"

"The DeCarlo brothers have given vital information to you over the years that protected your citizens. In return, they asked that you remove them from your criminal database and your most wanted list. Other countries in Europe have agreed. But your government continues to refuse."

"The DeCarlo brothers are criminals. They need to pay for their crimes."

"Sir, you know very well that your justice system has exchanged information for leniency as a routine. As does everyone else in the world."

"True, but someone high up has a grudge against them and promised never to negotiate."

"Well then, sir, there is no need for us to continue this conversation." Marci waited a few seconds before hanging up, hoping he would stop her.

"Wait. Can you guarantee that DeCarlo's can hand over the Hijazis?"

"No one can guarantee 100%, but yes. However, now they want more than immunity for their past criminal actions in Italy. They also want their citizenship reinstated, and their confiscated property returned."

"Ms. Beauchene, you are asking a lot."

"And they are giving a lot."

"These are things I cannot do on my own. I would need President Giordano to sign off."

"None of this can get out. If it leaks that the brothers are in league with you, the Hijazis will go back underground. This is our only hope to capture them."

"I assure you, Ms. Beauchene, I understand what is at stake here. But other agencies need to be involved to remove them from the database and return their property. And people will begin to ask questions. The reinstatement of his citizenship, the President, can do on his own."

"I understand. We want a letter of intent with your seal, and if you must get the President involved, his seal also. We will trust that you will keep your promises once we have turned the Hijazi's over to you."

"How much time do we have to think about this?" Vittore asked.

"Twenty-four hours. I'll be waiting for your call."

"I'll get back to you," Vittore didn't say goodbye; he disconnected.

Marci took a deep breath. She couldn't remember if she breathed during the negotiations.

"You have done everything you can for me, love. Now you must understand that I must do this whether or not they agree."

"I do, sweetheart."

CHAPTER SEVEN

TRENTON, NJ, MONDAY

Houston and Dex headed to the Trenton-Mercer Airport to pick up Cade, Chantel, and Emmett. Houston was still upset that an uninvited third member of Sophie's family was showing up.

Houston and Dex were in the waiting area next to the security checkpoint. Dex spotted Cade first and waved at him. As they got closer, Houston stood to meet them. Emmett introduced himself to Houston and reached out his hand. Houston didn't reciprocate.

"Mr. Scott, I don't want to be rude to anyone in Sophie's family, but I told her brothers I won't allow anyone to hurt my wife. If you came here to give her a piece of your mind for disappearing, I prefer you turn around and return to Austin."

Emmett smiled, "Houston, I have loved Sophie from the first day I met her, and she asked me to be her grandpa. I have been there for her through all the tragedies in her life. There is no way I would ever hurt her."

Houston looked at him for a moment longer. "That's good to hear," Houston reached his hand out to Emmett. Emmett didn't hesitate; he shook hands with him, and they headed to the luggage carousel.

Sophie and Rayne were drinking iced tea on the porch, waiting for the men to return. Bully was chasing something in the yard.

"Sophie, I understand why you left Austin. The trauma of your losses was great. But why not come home."

"It isn't that simple, Rayne. When I left, I worked hard to keep all memory of my past at bay. By the time I left the University in New York, I had successfully cocooned them in a hidden place in my mind.

"I'm sure I would have been able to bring them back up if I had made an attempt to do so. A few weeks before I went to Cade's concert, I began having dreams. I couldn't remember them, but I would wake up crying. Although the dreams were a mystery, the feeling of loss was familiar. About a week ago, I dreamed again, but this time I remembered everything. I never told Houston because the pain that came with the memories was still too raw.

"When Cade called me out at the concert, Houston had no idea what was going on."

"Dex told me how much you loved your father and Duke. I'm sorry for the pain that caused you."

"It wasn't just that Duke died. I felt it was my fault. I still do."

"Sophie..."

"I know everyone says it wasn't, but they aren't in my head. In my mind, it is my fault, and his parents suffered so much at his loss. Not just them but all the families. You must see how close everyone is."

"Yes, I know. When Dex introduced me to them, I feared they wouldn't accept me. But they treated me like I was already a family member."

"I believe that. They are the most loving people," Sophie said.

"If you know that, why won't you believe they will accept you back as if you never left. I know there are members of my family, cousins, and uncles, that I hardly ever see. But when we get together, it is as if we were never apart."

"I don't..." Sophie was interrupted by the SUV pulling up. Both ladies stood to greet Cade and Chantel.

Houston saw Sophie and Rayne waiting on the porch for them. He stepped out of the SUV and leaned inside to speak to Emmett. Bully came running to him to get some attention. Houston rubbed Bully's face and ears for a moment, then Bully went to stand by Sophie.

"I'll grab your duffle," Houston said. Directing it at Emmett.

Cade and Chantel had already opened their doors and were stepping out. Sophie and Rayne were coming down the stairs to greet them when Emmett opened his door and stepped out.

Sophie froze. Bully sensed her anxiety and started growling at the stranger. Emmett took a few steps forward and opened his arms. Sophie ran to him, and they wrapped their arms around each other. Bully stopped growling but stayed by her.

"I've missed you so much, angel."

"Grandpa, I'm sorry," Sophie was weeping.

"You never have to be sorry with me, angel; you know that."

Houston opened the back of the SUV to get Emmett's duffle and one of Cade's suitcases. Then he stepped close enough to hear what was being said. Once he knew Emmett was just loving her, he took the luggage inside.

Jack and Lily had come out on the porch to welcome their guest when they saw Emmett and Sophie hugging. They looked at Houston for an explanation.

"That's her grandfather."

"Oh," Lily said. "Put his things in Spring's old room. It's the only empty room left."

"Mom, dad, are we putting too much on you with all this?"

"How could you even ask that, Houston," Jack said. "Family is never a burden."

"Thanks, Dad."

When news got around that another member of Sophie's family had arrived, the Townsend house was packed. Lily asked Ted to run to the butchers to get steaks and chicken before they closed.

"I'll have your dad grill tonight. I have leftover tossed green salad and some fresh corn on the cob in the refrigerator. That should feed this crowd." Lily went to get money out of her purse.

"Mom, I'll get this. My place is too small to hold a dinner party. The least I can do is help to pay for one."

When Katsumi, Izumi, and Lee showed up, Sophie introduced them to her grandpa. "Ojisan and Izumi protected me from some evil men once. I owe them a lot," Sophie said.

"I'm afraid your granddaughter embellishes, Mr. Scott. It was her and Houston that saved us from the wasted life we were living." Mr. Katsumi bowed to him. Emmett returned the bow.

When Sophie was alone with Emmett, she told him the truth about the task force. She also told the truth about who Katsumi and Izumi were before Jesus turned their lives around. Sophie was careful not to give away top-secret information, but Houston was not happy at how much she told about the mission.

DC. TUESDAY

The call came from Vittore the next morning. But it wasn't Vittore on the line. It was President Giordano who spoke.

"Hello?"

"Ms. Beauchene?"

"Yes."

"President Giordano, here. Minister Vittore is here with me. We are in a secure room. I will put you on speaker."

Roman had come in the SCIF with her. "Alright, Mr. President."

"Is the information you provided Minister Vittore verifiable?"

"Yes, everything I said is accurate; we can deliver the Hijazis to you."

"What is your time frame?"

"That is to be determined. No more than three months would be our best estimate." Marci read off a note Roman quickly wrote to answer his question.

"We are willing to send you the letter you requested agreeing to your demands and sealed by both of our hands. When the DeCarlo brothers complete their mission. And the United States hands the Hijazis to us; we will make good on our promises and give Mr. DeCarlo and his brother back their property and citizenship papers."

"I was told there is someone high up in your government that will oppose you doing this once it gets out."

"That's true, but by the time he finds out, it will already be done, and he will not have the power to reverse it."

Roman scribbled something on the notepad. Marci nodded. "I would like to know who would oppose these terms?"

"One of the Parliament members, Elio Greco." President Giordano said. Roman recognized the name and nodded.

"Thank you, Mr. President; we will get back to you with more information as we make the arrangements," Marci said.

"You said the United States is supporting you in this."

"They are allowing us to run this operation on their soil and will not interfere with our plans," Marci paused. "Sir, I cannot stress enough the need for arrant secrecy. If the Hijazis get wind of any of it, they will bolt."

"We know how delicate this operation is, Ms. Beauchene."

Marci requested they send the sealed letters of commitment to the P.O. Box in South Korea and a copy to them using their secure email address. She asked they hand the brothers their citizenship papers when the Hijazis are transferred to the Italian escorts, and they ended the call.

"Roman, how do you know they won't send someone to watch the post office box and try to capture Rocky. Then they could force you into doing what they want without having to do anything for you."

Roman laughed, "My dear wife, you have watched too many spy movies. I trust my government to do what they say. But Rocky has a contact that works in the post office where our box is. He takes the mail from the back side of the box and then drops it off in a drop box for us on his way home at night."

"Now, who watches too many spy movies?" Marci smiled.

"It's like you Americans like to say. Trust but verify."

"Who is this Elio Greco?" Marci asked.

Roman explained that Elio was Rocky's best friend when they were at the University Milano-Bicocca. Elio made extra money by stealing tests from the office and selling them to students. His parents were wealthy, but they kept him on a tight leash. He got caught and believed it was Rocky who turned him in. Rocky swore he would never do that, but Elio refused to believe him."

"Well, if he works in a high station in the government, it couldn't have caused him too much damage."

"The University did not want the scandal, and his father made a huge donation to the University. It was swept under the rug, as you like to say."

"So why is he holding a grudge."

"For whatever reason, Elio could never get over the betrayal."

"But Rocky didn't do it," Marci was saddened by the story. Roman just shrugged his shoulders. He had no answer.

Marci contacted Director Perry to let him know the plan was in motion. Roman read through Makhtar's medical records again.

"Marci, I need to get ahold of Dr. Cornett's scheduler. We need to know how far out a surgery could take place. Can you look that number up for me?"

"What hospital?"

Roman looked through the notes. "I don't see any notes on what hospital Dr. Cornett works out of."

"Some surgeons have privileges at more than one hospital. I'll try to find where his office is." Marci looked up the hospitals in Austin. "I should have remembered this; it's the hospital where they took Luke. The Heart Hospital of Austin, on N. Lamar Blvd." Marci wrote down the number for him.

After lunch, Roman sat at the kitchen nook and made the call.

"Heart Hospital, how can I help you?"

"I'm looking for Dr. Cornett; he's a heart surgeon."

"I'll connect you."

"Hello?"

"Yes, are you Dr. Cornett's scheduler?"

"This is Dr. Cornett."

"Oh, I'm sorry; I had no idea you would answer the phone."

"My scheduler is on lunch. Can I help you?"

"Sir, my name is Roman DeCarlo. I'm calling for a man who is out of the country. He is extremely ill and has read about the device you invented. He has the condition that your device was invented to correct. He is hoping he can schedule surgery."

"I'm sorry it's not quite that simple. I need his medical records to see if the heart condition fits the criterion. Not all conditions are helped with this device. Then there is the issue that my device has not received the final approval by the FDA."

"I understand, sir. But 'The Right to Try' legislation is in play for issues like this, correct?"

"Yes, but we have to determine that the gentleman could not live the two years left it would take for the FDA's final approval."

"I believe he would qualify under that criterion."

"Well, if he qualifies, his medical records will determine how quickly surgery is needed."

"The man sent me his medical records. I can have them emailed to you right away. If you give me your email address, I will send it and my contact numbers. He is not a US citizen, so he does not have insurance."

"I don't handle anything to do with payments. I can give you the number to accounting."

"Thank you, Doctor. Please get back to me as soon as possible."

They said goodbye and ended the call after Dr. Cornett gave him the email address.

"What do you think," Marci asked.

Roman emailed Makhtar's medical records and sent his contact numbers. Then answered her.

"I have no clue. But even if he is not eligible for the surgery, I will find some way to lure the Hijazis here.

After hearing from Marci, Director Perry called Director Cosby, who in turn called the President. With a green light from the President, Director Cosby decided he needed to put the task force on standby.

"Hello?"

"Agent Rodriguez, something big is coming down. I need to put your team on standby."

"Do you have a time frame, sir?"

"No, but my guess is within the next week or so."

"I'll call the team, sir, but you know Houston is on leave."

"I know, but this operation will require Agent Townsend and Ms. Star."

"Sir, I can tell you, Houston will not respond to this standby."

"I'll call him myself, Agent Rodriguez."

TRENTON, NJ

Houston's family had to go to work, and Lily and Jack had business they needed to tend out of town. Katsumi invited Sophie and her family to go with him to the Trenton City Museum, where they featured an exhibit of Japanese artwork.

There were sculptures from the first century. Prints by Ōmura Kōyō, scrolls from the 12th century, and ancient garments woven and embroidered in silk; all extraordinary.

The younger crowd broke off and meandered around the large museum. Katsumi and Emmett sat on a bench in front of a particularly complex scroll.

Katsumi explained the writing script by Jōdai Nihon-go. Translating the message. Emmett asked a few questions, then thanked Katsumi for being there for his granddaughter when he wasn't.

SEIZE ON THE HIGH SEAS

"Mr. Scott, I must tell you of the greatness of your granddaughter."

Kasumi told of how he sought her to recover something that belonged to the Akuza. He told him of the missing girl and how Sophie ravaged the Chinese gangs until she finally found the tender-age girl.

"I have never met such a fearless woman." Katsumi finished.

"Thank you for telling me that. But I am not surprised. Sophie has always been a champion against injustice, even as a child," Emmett paused. "Mr. Katsumi, Sophie needs to return and reconnect with her family. We need her, and she needs us. I know she respects you. Has she spoken about it with you?"

"Mr. Scott..."

"Please, Mr. Katsumi, we are family; call me Emmett."

"If you will drop the Mister from my name."

"Done."

"Emmett, I will not dishonor confidence. But I feel comfortable saying I have encouraged her to let go of her fear of rejection and see what can become of going home."

"I can't ask for more than that. Thank you."

Their private conversation ended when the group found them.

"There you are, Grandpa, Ojisan. I thought we'd have to send the troops to find you," Sophie smiled.

"No, musume, it was not us who was missing, but you. We were right here all along."

Sophie laughed. "So, that's your story, and you're sticking to it, huh," she turned to Katsumi. "Did you want to go back to the Farmer's Market today? I think they close in an hour."

"Oh, yes, I need fresh herbs and vegetables. Mr. Jo promised to enlarge his garden next year. Our family keeps expanding, and he enjoys sharing the harvest."

"Mom hates buying herbs from the store now. Mr. Jo has spoiled her with the herbs from his garden," Houston said.

As the group wandered around the Farmers Market, picking up a few things, Houston's phone rang. He looked at the caller ID and told Sophie he needed to take it. She nodded and walked on with Emmett.

"Hello, Director Cosby."

"Good day, Houston. I know you are on a leave of absence, but word has gotten to us about a major operation. I can't tell you over the phone, but I've called your team to stand by."

"I was very clear, sir; Sophie and I will not be on standby during our leave."

"Houston, this operation requires Ms. Star. Come back, and I will fill you in."

"No, sir. Government agencies, by their nature, will use people up, to the detriment of their families and their own health. I don't blame you, sir; it is how government works. But I will not allow my marriage or my wife's health to become one of those statistics. If you need me to formally resign from my position, I will happily do so. My wife, as a private contractor, can refuse any operations she wants."

"Agent Townsend, let me fill you in before you make up your mind. I'll send someone to you. You're in Trenton, right? Staying at your parent's home?"

"Director Cosby, I would rather you didn't. There is always one more operation to save the world, one more mission to save democracy. It never ends. There has to be a point where we just say no."

"Hear us out," Cosby said. Houston paused for a long time. Cosby wondered if he had hung up.

"When would I expect them?"

"Tomorrow by 2 pm. I'll send them by helicopter."

"I'll be here."

"Thank you, Agent Townsend."

After everyone turned in, Houston told Sophie about the call from Cosby. "I told him I would resign before I would cut short our nighty-day leave."

Sophie kissed him, "thank you, sweetheart. I am having a wonderful time with my family, and I don't know how long Dex and Cade can stay."

"Don't thank me yet. Cosby insisted on sending someone out tomorrow to fill us in on the operation."

Director Cosby expected some pushback from Houston, but he didn't expect the diatribe about the agencies. Houston wasn't wrong. The percentage of divorces and suicides in law enforcement in all arenas is unacceptable.

Gram called the president on his private cell and asked if he had time to talk. Michael asked him to come to the residence at the White house for dinner.

AUSTIN, TX

"Lawson, I don't understand why you won't go on, Good Morning Austin. It will be fun, and the host is a beautiful woman, a former Miss Texas. Besides, you do other shows to promote the Heart Hospital and your new devices all the time."

"Mom, it's a puff piece. My friends will never let me live it down. Can you see CJ ever doing it?"

"Your friends will love it. This is the third year in a row you made Austin's most eligible list. It's an honor."

"No, mom, it's an indictment of the fact I can't keep a girlfriend."

"Lawson, just do it for me. Please."

Lawson had never been able to say no to his mother. For years when his father was stationed overseas with the Air force, it was just the two of them. He resented his father for that when he was younger. But after his Freshman year in high school, his father took a station where he could bring his family. They stayed in Germany for two years. His dad, a pilot for the Air Force, retired after that tour. But during that time, Lawson and his father managed to become close.

"Alright, Mom, for you."

"Ok, I'll call the station back and find out when they want you."

DC

Gram Cosby called his wife to tell her he was heading to the White House residence, and they invited him to stay for dinner.

"No problem, sweetheart, I'll work on my new painting."

"I'll be excited to see it, Trish," Gram said. Trish's paintings sell for more than what he makes in six months. Trish didn't want her association with the president and first lady to be why people purchased her work, so she used a pseudonym.

Trish's paintings were whimsical. Beautiful garden scenes in twilight with fireflies and fairies. She gave one of her first paintings to Emma, her good friend. Emma displayed it in a prominent place in the residence. Trish often wondered if that pushed up the price of her paintings.

CHAPTER EIGHT

Cosby used the stairs to get to the residence and was announced by a secret service agent.

"Good evening, Mr. President, Madam First Lady."

"Good evening, Gram, and drop the formality; we're at the residence," Michael moved to meet him and shake his hand.

"Thanks, Michael," then Gram turned to Emma. "Hope you haven't been working your fingers to the bone making dinner," he laughed.

"Yeah, haha. I figured you wanted to talk about something privately, so I had the kitchen send up lasagna and a salad. I put it in the oven an hour ago. It should be ready by the time we finish our salads. Have a seat. What would you like to drink?"

"Pepsi, if you have any," Gram said.

"Do you want a glass with ice?"

"No, thanks. The can is fine."

"What do you want, dear?"

"Coffee for me."

Emma took the salad from the refrigerator and three small glass carafes of the chef's famous salad dressings and placed them on a rolling cart. Then she put the drinks along with a glass of ice for her iced tea and rolled it out to the dining table.

After setting the food on the table, Emma sat down, and Michael asked Gram to say the blessing.

They were partway through the salad when the stove beeped. Emma started to stand to pull out the lasagna, but Michael said he would get it.

Michael set the hot lasagna pan on a trivet that was on the table. After Emma served each of them a generous portion of the cheesy lasagna, Michael asked Gram what was on his mind.

"Now that the mission is a go and we agreed we should shadow it, I put your task force on standby.

"When I called Houston, he refused. He had made it clear; he would not come back during his 90-day leave." Gram took a bite of his lasagna and quickly tried to cool his mouth down with a drink from his Pepsi, but it was empty. He grabbed the water instead.

"Are you alright, Gram?" Emma chuckled. "You have always been too impatient to let your food cool down."

After Gram stopped gulping down water, he said, "Yeah. You could have told me it was hot, Emma."

Michael laughed. "What, you need someone to tell you that cheesy lasagna straight out of the oven is hot?"

"Trish always does." They all laughed, then got back to business while Gram let his food cool down.

"Houston didn't just refuse but gave me a thinly veiled diatribe about the wheels of government. He said there will always be another emergency, another mission. He added by their nature, government agencies don't care how the constant grind damages marriages and even the health of their agents. The bureaucracy casts them aside when they are no longer useful and replaces them."

"You know, Michael, he is not wrong. When I worked for the CIA, the company never cared if they called me back from the side of a sick parent. Once, they called me off a vacation I had planned a year in advance and paid for up front.

"It isn't right. But I know that the work our agencies do is critical to the survival of our country. It's hard to balance the two," Emma was sympathetic to Houston's point of view.

"So, he flat-out refused?" Michael asked.

"Yes, he said he would send in his resignation letter if I wanted."

"Wow. There must be more going on in his life than we know."

"There is. Sophie's bad dreams have him worried. Houston has always looked out for his wife. But since the dreams, he has ratcheted up his protection a few notches. I don't know if the dreams have stopped but he is still protecting her. He complained the only big break she's had was after shutting down the brothels belonging to the Chinese gangs."

No one said anything for a while. The only noise was the click of forks and knives on the good China.

"Michael, we need Sophie on this. We can't send Marci alone, and we can't bring anyone else into the loop. The lid on this must be airtight," Emma said.

"Emma's right, Gram. You must have a suggestion on how to change his mind."

"I do." Gram looked over at Emma. "I think you and Marci can change her mind if you go in person to talk to her. Once they know it is Makhtar Hijazi and his two sons we are trying to capture, I believe they will change their minds."

"You think he will respond better to me than you, Gram?"

"I think Ms. Star will, and wherever she goes, he goes. I told them someone would be there to fill them in at 2 pm tomorrow. They are at his parent's home in Trenton," Gram said.

Emma looked at Michael, "It's worth a try."

"Alright, I'll have Marine One Foxtrot called out for you. The helicopter should get you there in less than an hour."

"That works. After dinner, I'll call Marci and let her know the plan," Emma looked over at her husband. "You know that Sophie is Marci's stepdaughter. Her first husband Luke, his daughter."

"I had no idea. How does Marci feel about her being imbedded with the Hijazis?" Michael asked.

"Marci is aware that Sophie is part of your task force. She wouldn't be on it if she couldn't handle herself."

"Alright, I'll pray Sophie will hear you out," Gram drank the last of his second Pepsi. "Emma, can I take some of this lasagna home to Trish? It's delicious."

"I'll pack some up for you."

"Thanks."

AUSTIN, TX. WEDNESDAY

Lawson was nervous stepping into the local TV station. The segment's producer greeted him and took him to the green room. A sound tech came in and fixed him with a lapel mic. Lawson thanked him, and the man left.

Lawson paced until the producer of his segment came to get him. She directed him to the set where his interview would happen. The host was reading material from a notebook. He guessed it was about him.

Cherysh Chandler, or Cher, as she was known. Was as pretty as Lawson's mother had told him. Her light blond hair, almost white, fell down her back past her shoulders, and she was in great shape. He couldn't help but smile. He knew his mom was trying to set him up again.

Cher Chandler noticed Lawson in her peripheral vision and stood to greet him.

"Dr. Lawson Cornett, it's a pleasure to meet you. You are a hard man to corral."

"Please call me Lawson."

"I will; after our first introduction," Cher moved him up on the set and directed him where to sit. "We have a few minutes before our segment starts. I'll give you a rundown of the questions," she took a note card out of the binder and set the binder down out of sight. "We'll talk about the devices you invented, your family, your background, and childhood memories. Then, of course, you are on Austin's most eligible bachelor list for the third year in a row."

Lawson started to object, but the floor director put up her hand, and Cher directed herself to the camera that was coming live in 3...2...1.

"Good morning Austin. I'm your host Cher Chandler, and today our guest is the illusive Dr. Lawson Cornett. Dr. Cornett made Austin's most eligible bachelor list for the third year." Cher directed her attention to Lawson, and a camera turned to him.

"Good morning, Dr. Cornett. This is your first TV interview with us."

"Yes, my mother insisted I do it," Lawson replied. The crew laughed. "Please call me Lawson."

"Thank you, Lawson." The camera moved back to Cher. "You are a pediatric heart surgeon at the Heart Hospital here in Austin, and you invented a device that gives.... Well, why don't you tell us what it does."

"A small percentage of infants are born with a heart that is not fully formed. Over time the heart defect heals itself. But some infants don't survive long enough for that to happen. My device works as a substitute for the undeveloped portion, temporarily."

"From what I understand, you have also transformed that device into something that can help adult patients."

"Yes, with modifications, the device can add ten years to the life of an adult. This heart defect generally doesn't manifest until late in life. I realized that my device, once modified, could extend life expectancy."

"What gave you the idea that you could modify your device to do it."

"I was at a medical convention, and one doctor spoke about a case he was dealing with. When he explained the issue, I realized my device could be adjusted to alleviate the problem."

"That's very impressive, Doctor. Now I'd like to move on to the subject that brings you here. Your love life."

"I'm afraid my love life is a little boring, Cher," he chuckled.

"Maybe not after this segment, but first, we need to take a break, and we'll be right back.

The camera was turned off, and Cher said, "Lawson, you are doing a fantastic job. We'll go into your personal life in this next piece. Before Lawson could respond, the floor director was putting Cher on notice.

"We are back with Doctor Lawson Cornett, one of Austin's most eligible bachelors. You grew up in Austin, didn't you?"

"Mostly, my mom said we lived in Colorado on an Air Force Base there when I was young, but I don't remember that. My mom and I lived here while my father was deployed overseas. He is a retired Air Force pilot."

"Didn't you travel with him on his deployments?"

"No, the countries he was deployed were too volatile to allow family members to come. But in my sophomore and junior years in high school, we went to Germany with him."

"Did you like Germany?"

"Yes, after I got there. But I hated leaving my friends here in Austin."

"Are you a workaholic, like most doctors?"

Lawson laughed, "I would be, but my friends won't allow it. They insist I spend time away from work. We have regular outings."

"Are your friends' also doctors?"

"Some are. The friends I spend most of my time with are accomplished in their fields, but they are not doctors. They are the friends I went to school with. And I guarantee you, I will hear about doing this puff piece from them." Lawson smiled thinking of the teasing waiting for him.

Cher laughed. "You still have friends from school?"

SEIZE ON THE HIGH SEAS

"Yes, high school. I went to Parkcrest Academy. A group of us ate lunch together and spent most of our time outside school together. We were and are still very close."

"My research says you were in love with one of your friends from school." Cher noticed a strange expression on Lawson's face for a second. She didn't know if the camera had caught it.

"Yes, there was a girl I spent a lot of time with."

"I take it the romance didn't last long. Most school romances don't stand the test of time."

"This one would have."

"What happened?"

"As much as I loved her, she loved someone else."

"So, she is the one that got away?" Cher smiled. But the look flicked across Lawson's face again. She thought there might be something juicy there. "Do you still see her; did she marry the other man?"

"No, they stopped for gas on the way to their wedding and walked into a robbery. He was murdered by the gunman robbing the place."

Cher wasn't expecting his response, "do you see your old flame anymore?"

"No, after her fiancé died, she left town and disappeared."

"Oh! We need to go to a commercial break, and we'll be right back with our guest Dr. Cornett." Cher waited until the camera light was off, then said. "Lawson, I'm sorry; I had no idea that happened."

Lawson looked up at her, "are we almost done?"

"You're still in love with her, aren't you? That's why none of the women you date last more than six months."

Lawson looked up at her. "Don't ask me that on camera, but I do still love her. I have never met anyone as interesting and challenging as Sophie. She's the one who taught me how to be a good friend and look out for others. I will never forget her."

"I'm sorry for that, Lawson, but if you don't get past it, you will never find a wife. No one wants a ghost in their relationship they can't compete with. You made her the perfect woman in your mind when she was probably just like the rest of us."

"That's where you're mistaken. I have not exaggerated Sophie in my mind. Sophie was unique, and all her friends will say the same thing."

Cher's floor director cued her, and she put a smile back on her face.

"So, Lawson, what do you and your friends do for fun."

The segment lasted for five more minutes, then Cher stood and thanked him for coming. "Lawson, if you want to move on with your life, you must find a way to close that chapter."

"Thanks, Cher. I know that, but I can't seem to do it."

After the sound tech retrieved his lapel mic, Lawson stepped out the door. He stopped and took in a deep breath. Bringing up Sophie always brought him pain, but he was better now at controlling his thoughts. His cell vibrated in his pocket.

"Hello, Mom."

TRENTON, NJ

Houston, Dex, and Cade were playing basketball outside after breakfast. Jack and Emmett sat on the porch watching with a cup of coffee.

Sophie, Chantel, and Rayne took the horses out for a ride. Bully was lying on the porch whining as the horses rode away. He wasn't allowed to go with them.

An hour later, Lily brought out sweet tea for the guys. They took a break from basketball and sat on the stairs drinking the sweet drink.

Houston could see the women coming from their ride. Houston, and Sophie's brothers, headed to the barn to take the saddles off and rub down the horses.

The women got off the horses before walking them into the barn. Houston took Sophie's horse.

"Thanks, sweetheart."

"Why don't you ladies change and relax. This won't take us long."

Sophie kissed Houston, and the women headed to the house. Bully was following them when he heard a loud whooshing sound. Bully started barking and the horses got spooked.

The men put the horses in the stall instead of letting them out in the field.

Houston stepped up behind Sophie. "That must be whoever Cosby sent." The helicopter got closer. "That looks like Marine One."

Lily stepped out of the kitchen and stood next to Jack. This wasn't the first time a helicopter landed on their property. Lily remembered when her home was used to trap an Italian assassin hired to kill Sophie.

As everyone watched, the co-pilot stepped out and opened the sliding door exposing the passengers. Two secret service men got out first and scanned the area. After nodding to the co-pilot, he helped the other two passengers out.

Everyone was surprised to see two women step down. One being the First Lady of the United States.

Houston and Sophie immediately went to greet the First Lady. When Sophie took a moment to address the other passenger, she stuttered, "Marci?"

Houston looked at her quizzically. "Houston, this is my stepmother Marci Star." Marci didn't correct her usage of her former last name.

"Please, Madam First Lady and Mrs. Star, let me introduce my family," Houston said.

"Dex recognized Marci, "Aunt Marci?"

"Dex," she hugged him, and he introduced his wife, then she turned. "Cade, you look wonderful," she hugged him and Chantel when he introduced her.

As Houston continued introducing the family, Marci recognized Emmett.

"Emmett Scott," she gave him a hug. "I've missed you."

After introducing Lily and Jack to the First Lady and Marci, Lily invited them into the house and directed them to the living room.

"Mrs. Townsend, this is a lovely home. Thank you for letting us in without an invitation."

"Madam First Lady, it is an honor to have you here. May I get you and Mrs. Star tea?"

"Would you have some iced tea?"

"I have sweet tea made up."

"Oh, that would be lovely. Thank you, Mrs. Townsend."

"Please call me Lily."

After visiting over tea, the First Lady said, "Mr. and Mrs. Townsend, would you mind if I borrowed your son and Sophie."

"Not at all. We have a private study in the back of the house," Jack offered.

"Thank you."

CHAPTER NINE

Once everyone settled in chairs, Emma spoke first. "Houston, I know you refused to be on standby and abandon your 90-day leave. However, the President asked if Marci and I would come and explain why this is so important."

"Madam First Lady, I want to be upfront. I have no intention of returning to DC until my leave is up. I explained to Director Cosby, I am happy to put in my papers if necessary."

"I am aware of that, Houston," the First Lady turned to Sophie.

"Sophie, Marci told me about what happened to Luke and your fiancé. You left your home and friends after that. But I see today that you have reconnected with at least some of your family," Emma said.

"Yes, two of my brothers and my grandfather," Sophie said.

"That is one reason I don't want to come back. It has been nine years since Sophie has seen any of them. I won't cut short their visit," Houston shifted in his seat, interrupting again.

"I understand, but since we came this far, will you hear us out?" Emma asked.

"Of course, Madam First Lady," Sophie said.

"Call me Emma, please. We have all been through too much together to be formal in private. But Marci should be the one to tell you about it."

Marci leaned forward and directed her attention to Sophie. "Sophie, I need to correct something. I'm remarried now; I'm Marci DeCarlo. I worked as a private contractor for the clandestine unit of the CIA...."

Sophie interrupted, "when you were married to my dad?"

"Yes, and he knew about it. When you found me in the bushes by your house, I was just coming off an assignment."

"I took over as handler for an asset when the previous handler quit 'the company'. Roman and Rocky DeCarlo 'brokered' merchandise exchange between criminals."

"DeCarlo, are you married to a criminal, Marci?" Sophie couldn't believe it.

"No. Roman and his brother became Christian's years ago. They wanted to dismantle their business, but the CIA asked them not to. They wanted to keep information filtering through. The brother's intel was and is critical to the security of our country.

"Let me explain. Roman and Rocky have a gold mind of criminal contacts worldwide. Mainly on the dark web and in the underground. Everyone knows where to go if they have something to sell or buy, that is illegal. It could be guns, heavy equipment, stolen artifacts, or corporate espionage. The brothers would manage the transfer and the exchange of money, take their commission, and pass on the rest.

"They never got their hands dirty with any stolen property. One of the CIA's handlers managed to get them to agree to pass on intel that would benefit the US.

"Even though they didn't work with terrorists. Terrorists would contact them, looking for the same kind of deals.

"Roman would turn down the contract and then pass on the information to the US. The US, in turn, would pass the information on to our allies if it involved their countries.

"In return, these countries gave the brothers immunity for their past crimes.

"I give you this background, so you understand when I tell you that we are confident this information is solid."

"Alright, Marci, what information?" Houston asked.

Marci addressed Houston, "Houston, I know you are aware of the Hijazis."

"Yes. They are terrorists who moved from Iran to Afghanistan and then disappeared. But not until they murdered hundreds of civilians in bombings. The most notable in Italy; a hospital. The president of Italy and over eight hundred people died in that bombing.

"After that, the world hunted him, and he dropped off the face of the earth. But intel says he still operates and has a wide following connected to him through video on the web."

"Exactly. Makhtar Hijazi contacted the DeCarlo brothers. He is dying. He wants the brothers to smuggle him, his two sons, and his daughter into the country, so he can get surgery. Apparently, a device can be implanted into his heart that could add ten years to his life."

"Why would we want to help him live longer?" Houston asked.

"The plan is to get them here, and let him have the surgery, then capture him and his sons. The US would then turn them over to the Italians to be tried for crimes against humanity," Emma stated.

"Ok, I understand you wanting to lure them here, but why let him have the surgery," Sophie asked.

"He needs to live long enough to stand trial. The world needs to see these men face justice. Italy may take their lives anyway, but their citizens will have justice."

"I didn't think Italy had a death penalty," Houston said.

"They have made exceptions. I don't know if they will in this case, but my guess is they will."

"And the CIA is alright with these men running free in the US?" Houston asked.

"No. But the brothers have to be the ones that facilitate this. If the US gets involved, there is too big a chance the Hijazis will get wind of it.

"The president wants his task force to shadow them," Marci said.

"If that's all you need the task force for, you don't need Sophie or me. The team is more than capable of doing that," Houston said.

"Houston, there is a little more to it than that. We need to imbed two of ours in with them," Emma said.

"They will never allow it," Houston ran his hand through his hair, tousling it.

"The brothers often send people in their network with the merchandise when it travels. If the Hijazis want their help, they will agree. But we can't send men; it will have to be two women," Marci said, leaning back in the chair.

"Houston, only five people, other than the brothers, and the Italians, have this intel. The president, Director Cosby, Director Perry, Marci, and myself. Now you and Sophie. Your team is on standby but has not been read in. We cannot bring anyone else into the loop."

"So, who are you imbedding with the Hijazis?" Sophie asked.

"Me, Sophie, and I'm hoping you'll go with me," Marci got out of her chair and sat closer to her. Houston started to speak, but Emma held up her hand.

"Sophie, we don't want to send Marci in by herself, but beyond that, we all know you can read a situation. You are our best choice.

"This is a sensitive situation. Makhtar's sons need to be watched. We can't let them go off and blow something up on their way out of the country. We need you, Sophie." Emma said.

"You can't possibly be asking my wife to travel with the evilest men in the world without backup!" Houston scooted to the end of his seat.

Sophie reached over and put her hand on Houston's arm. "Madam First Lady, I appreciate that you think I'm the one you need for this operation, but I'm not sure. I need to talk to Houston about this, and I have family here that I haven't seen in nine years.

I'm not inclined to leave them right now. When does this plan go into motion?"

"We are not sure; maybe a week," Marci said.

"Sophie stood; I won't give you an answer today because if I did, it would be no. We'll pray about it, and Houston will get back to you." The others stood. "I am grateful that you came all this way to speak with us personally. Our families would be honored if you would stay and have dinner with us." Sophie knew Lily would be whipping up something in case they were staying.

"It would be our pleasure," Emma said.

Katsumi came by Lily's to bring hotteok, a popular Korean dessert. Lee made it for them. He had no idea they had company. Sophie introduced him to the First Lady and Marci, explaining she was her stepmother. The First Lady knew the back story but had no idea where he had moved when he left the Akuza. Lily insisted he stay and eat with them.

As the food and plates were being taken away to the kitchen, a secret service agent came and spoke softly in Emma's ear. Marine One Foxtrot would be here in five minutes.

Emma stood and spoke to the family, "I can't thank you enough for your hospitality; the meal was excellent, Lily. And Mr. Katsumi, please let Lee know those sweet stuffed pancakes were delicious. I must have our chef cook this up for Michael."

Everyone said goodbye. Houston walked the First Lady to her ride home.

The First Lady turned to speak to him, "Houston, I know you are against this. But think about what it would mean to capture Makhtar Hijazi."

"Madam First Lady, if Sophie and I had never been part of The President's Task Force, you would have been asking this of someone else. But I know my wife, and it will be difficult for her to let her stepmother go on this mission without her."

"You won't object if she decides to do this?"

"No, I won't," Houston extended his hand to help her into the helicopter. Then helped Marci in. "Thank you for staying for dinner; it will be a memory my family will talk about for years."

"It was our pleasure, Houston."

Sophie was quiet after they left. The family was chatting about the visit, and Lily called Spring and the boys to tell them about it. Katsumi knew something was going on and asked Sophie about it.

"Musume, what would bring The First Lady here. She wanted you to do something for her husband, yes? Like I did when I asked you to recover my property."

"Yes, Ojisan. They want Houston and me to do something to help them."

"Is it dangerous?"

"They don't think so."

"But Houston does?"

"Houston worries, yes."

"Whatever you decide, I will pray for you, watashi no musume."

Sophie took Katsumi's hand. "Thank you, Ojisan."

When Houston and Sophie were in bed, they finally had a minute to talk about it.

"Sophie, I promised you 90 days. I don't want you to do this. There will always be another crisis, another priority mission. They can't lay this on us."

"I agree, but if I don't go, Marci will go on her own. She' is my stepmother; I would regret not being there if something happened to her."

"The same thing that would happen to her would happen to you if you were with her."

"Not necessarily, Ecc. 4:12 says, 'Though one may be overpowered by another, two can withstand him. And a threefold cord is not quickly broken.'"

"Whose your third man?"

"Jesus, and you. The idea that no one would be close by is unacceptable. I would never trust anyone but you and Fons. You two will have to figure out how to do it without being seen, but no one is better than you."

"You decided to do this before they left, didn't you?"

"Only if they let you decide how best to protect us. But yes, if it weren't Marci…. My father loved her so much. He would want me to protect her."

Houston held her. "What about your family?" Sophie laid her head on his chest.

"I'll ask them how long they can stay. I know China has been calling them, wondering when they were coming home.

"My leaving has caused her to worry whenever one of the family is away for very long."

"What have you decided about going home to see the rest of the family?"

"I'm not sure yet. Grandpa Emmett wants me to. Maybe after this mission, I'm not sure."

"What did he say about our visitor?"

"Grandpa and Katsumi both knew she didn't stop by for a visit. They know somethings going on."

Dex and Rayne were sound asleep when Dex's cell phone rang. He was startled awake and quickly picked up the phone, not wanting to wake up Rayne.

"Hello," Dex whispered, then got up and went into the hallway.

"I'm sorry, I dialed the phone before I did the math on the time difference."

"It's ok, Em; what's the matter?"

"I'm putting you on speaker…China is with me. China snuck out of the manor tonight. Ma and Pa stayed in London. I heard a noise in the hallway at 11:30 after all the alarms were set. I peeked out my bedroom door and saw China sneaking down the stairs.

"I slipped on some shoes and followed her. She met one of the boys from the bunkhouse; I watched for a while and saw them kissing."

"Who was it?"

Dex heard China choke out, "Lorin," between tears.

"Aldwin?"

"Yeah, I think that's his last name," Emmi said.

"I saw him watching China a few times. He is a good guy, but I should have warned him off," Dex directed his following statement to China. "He's almost eighteen, China. Way too old for you; you are not even fourteen yet."

"He is really nice… Dex. We just wanted to talk. Then he asked… if he could kiss me. I didn't see the harm," China said, choking back more tears.

"That is exactly why you are too young to date or have a boyfriend. You are naive, China, and Pa said you can't date until you are sixteen, which means kissing boys too."

"I'm not naive."

"Yes, you are, and selfish too. Do you know what is going to happen to Lorin now? He is only months away from completing his grade 12 diploma, so he can attend trade school. Do you think Pa will let him stay now that he broke the rules?"

"But we didn't do anything wrong. He just kissed me," China blurted out.

"Then why did you need to sneak around. You know what Pa thinks about that. He says, 'if you have to sneak to do it, what you are saying is I know it's wrong, but I want to do it anyway'. It's your sneaking that is going to upset him."

"Yeah...," China whispered.

"How long has this been going on?"

"I've only met him a few times."

"Was this the first time he kissed you?" Dex asked.

"Yes. Please don't tell Pa. Please, Dex, I won't do it again. I don't want him to leave because of me."

"Pa trusts me. I can't keep it from him. But I will see if Finn's old apartment above the garage is available. After he and Carla got married, they saved for a house. I think they just bought it. If the apartment is still open, I'll see if Lorin can move in. We'll pay his rent until he's done with trade school. And he can keep working here until then."

"Dex, please don't tell Pa. He will think differently of me. I couldn't stand that."

"That's not true. Do you remember when Blaze got caught smoking, and he said hurtful things to Pa? Pa never once loved him less or thought any differently about him. Parents aren't like other people. They love like Jesus unconditionally."

"But it will hurt him," China sobbed.

"You should have thought of that before you did it. I can't lie to him, sis. I love you. This is a little mistake, but it may keep you from making a bigger one."

Dex must have raised his voice because Cade came out of his room to see what was happening. Dex made a motion that he would be off in a minute.

"I'm sorry, Dex. Please don't be mad at me."

"I'm not mad; I'm worried. You are my little sister. I don't ever want anything to happen to you. You are lucky, me, Blaze, or Cade, weren't there. We would probably have given Lorin a beating for messing with our little sister."

"Do they have to know?" China asked, pleading.

"They will find out one way or another. But nothing you could ever do would make us think less of you. Remember, family only loves more, not less. I love you, sis. Now go to bed and get some sleep. Let me talk to Emmi."

"Dex, she is so embarrassed. You know how much she cares about what you guys think of her. Maybe I should have her sleep in my room tonight."

"That is a good idea. I really reamed her out. You need to reaffirm how much we all love her."

"Ok, Dex. Goodnight."

"Goodnight, sis."

"Dex, what on earth is going on?" Cade asked.

"China snuck out of the house, and Emmi caught her outside the bunkhouse. Lorin Aldwin was kissing her."

"That kid is almost 18; what's the matter with him?" Cade was angry.

"Keep it down; I've already woken you. I don't want to wake the rest of the house."

"I want that guy off Lennox Estate, Dex."

"Yeah, once Pa finds out, Lorin will have to go; his actions don't just break the rules; they annihilate them. I'm going to see if Finn's old apartment is available. The estate will pay the rent until he is through trade school."

"As long as he is away from my sister. I don't care where he goes."

"China thinks we won't like her anymore. We need to soothe hurt feelings in the morning."

"Yeah."

"Goodnight, Dex."

"Goodnight, Cade.

TRENTON, NJ. THURSDAY

At breakfast, Emmett's cell rang, and he took the call outside.

"Hello, son."

"Dad, how is your visit going with Dex and Cade?"

"We are having a good time."

"When are you coming home?"

"Is something going on?"

"Not exactly. Anna and I think it's time to tell Drew he's adopted. I wanted you to be here when we do in case he wants to talk to you about it."

"When did you plan on doing that?"

"This weekend. I'm afraid Drew is going to hear about it somewhere else. I'm worried we already waited too long."

"I'll come home Saturday night."

"Will Cade and Dex be with you?"

"I don't think so; they have other plans."

"Alright, Dad, I'll pick you up at the airport."

"Thanks, David."

Emmett walked back into the kitchen to finish breakfast with the family.

"Grandpa, we are talking about going into Manhattan tomorrow. What do you think?"

"Sounds good. I'm heading home on Saturday."

"You are?"

"Yes, I'm sorry, angel, but David and Anna think it's time to tell Drew he's adopted. They want me there."

"Grandpa, he has no memory of his birth mother. Is there some reason they want to tell him he's adopted?" Dex asked.

"If it were up to them, they would wait until he was older. But you know who his mother was and the way she was killed. He's worried a random reporter will want to do a follow-up story and hunt down Drew."

"Isn't the adoption sealed?" Cade asked.

"Yes, but there are people who were there the night she was killed. They know who took Drew."

"Your right. It would not be good if Drew heard it from someone else. I think we should be heading home soon, too, Sophie," Dex said.

"I will hate to see you all go, but I understand."

Houston contacted Director Cosby and told him they would work on the Hijazi operation. But he had stipulations.

Director Cosby didn't seem surprised and asked when they would be in DC.

"Not before this weekend," Houston responded.

"Alright, call me when you're in town."

DC

"Rocky, I spoke with the doctor a few days ago. He looked over the medical records. Dr. Cornett said the man may not survive the trip to get the surgery. He said to call him as soon as we have an expected date for his arrival. The doctor needs to know to reserve the surgery room and put his team on the schedule."

"Alright, Roman. I contacted Captain Mandrapilias. He is available and accepted the job. But he said they would have to get to the Port of Sanremo at the western port of the Italian mainland."

"Then let's inform Makhtar Hijazi it's on him to get there. Send a picture of the yacht and the port information. It should only be a five or six hour drive from Geneva unless they run into trouble. Did our courier get there with their passports and visas?"

"Yes, they're signed for."

"We'll work on the rest of the travel itinerary while they are on the Atlantic. Have they followed all our instructions?

"Yes, but not without an argument. Makhtar did not want to shave his head and his beard. The boys weren't quite so adamant about shaving their beards. His daughter was no problem. Wearing western clothes was more than acceptable to her."

"Rocky, we need to know when they are leaving Geneva so the captain can be waiting for them."

"I'll get back to you as soon as I have an answer."

Marci was in the SCIF with Roman. She pulled up a map on her computer to see Geneva's distance from Sanremo.

"Can the Captain get to Sanremo if the Hijazis leave right away? Yes, his yacht is generally moored in Greece. Captain Mandrapilias has a large Category 'A' 75-foot motor yacht with fuel tanks that can hold three thousand gallons. That will allow him to travel 25 knots an hour for most of the trip. He flies a white flag from Italy that designates his yacht as a member of the Paris Memorandum of Understanding on Port. It gives him the most protection while in international waters. We don't want them to be boarded by Maritime Law Enforcement. Depending on the weather, it should take him 7 or 8 days to reach the US."

"He can't come in at a main Port. There will be customs and security agents. The facial recognition cameras will pick him out in a second. It won't matter if he's bald or has shaved his beard."

"You're right; we had him shave so that he wouldn't be easily recognizable to the general population or other authorities on the road or at the hospital.

"I have a contact that has a boat slip on his private property in Corpus Christi," Roman decided to contact him.

"Alright, we need to let Director Perry know as soon as we hear back from Rocky."

CHAPTER TEN

NEW YORK. FRIDAY.

Sophie loved hosting her family at the penthouse. They kiboshed the shopping and decided to go go-karting and to a movie instead.

Dex, Cade, Houston, and Sophie ran their go-karts like they were in the Daytona 500. Chantel and Rayne knew better than to get into the competition. It was a no-win situation, so they drove around the track, watching it all play out.

Dex finally got in the lead and swerved back and forth so his siblings couldn't pass him. On the backstretch, Houston and Cade managed to get on either side of Dex, and Sophie squeezed in beside them. They crossed the line simultaneously.

The four competitors argued about who got across first for the next hour at dinner.

"Grandpa, you saw it. Who won?" Sophie asked. Emmett had sat on the sidelines with a cup of coffee and enjoyed watching the family together again.

"It looked too close to call."

"Grandpa, you are no help," Sophie gave him the look Duke used to love and laughed at when she aimed it in his direction. Emmett couldn't help but laugh.

By the time they got home after the movie, they were tired and went to bed. The family was leaving tomorrow.

MANHATTAN-SATURDAY

Sophie came out of the shower and smelled bacon; she dried her hair and got dressed. When she stepped into the kitchen, Houston was making waffles. She got on her tiptoes in her bare feet and kissed him on the cheek.

"Good morning, sweetheart; thank you for making waffles. My favorite."

"Everything is your favorite, as long as you don't have to cook."

Sophie slapped his arm, and Houston smiled at her.

Dex, and Cade sat at the kitchen bar, talking with Houston while he cooked. The men had formed a familial bond.

"Hi, sis; Chantel and Rayne will be out soon. They are getting dressed," Dex got up and hugged her.

"What does everyone want to do today?"

"Chantel said she would like to see the zoo in Central Park. Would that work for everyone? Can we do that and still be at LaGuardia by 2 pm for our flight?"

"What do you think, Houston, will there be enough time?"

"Yeah, we'll keep an eye on the clock."

"Oh good, I'd love that. How about you, Grandpa?" Sophie asked as he walked into the room.

"Sure, but I need to be at the airport by 4 pm. You can drop me off at the same time, so you don't have to make two trips."

"We'll wait and have coffee and goodies with you at the bakery in the airport. I love their scones. I hate to see you go, Grandpa," Sophie put her arms around him.

"Sophie, I will keep your secret, even though I disapprove. But you know where I live and if you want to see me, I'll be there," Emmett kissed her forehead.

The men's favorite animals were the snow leopards. But the women loved the red pandas and watched them for almost an hour.

Before they drove to LaGuardia Airport, they stopped to eat.

Houston parked the car at the airport and helped the guys wrangle the luggage to the drop-off. They walked Dex, Cade, and their wives to security and gave hugs all around. Sophie, Houston, and Emmett watched them get through security and waved goodbye as they headed to their gate.

Sophie found a cool LaGuardia Airport hat. She asked Emmett to give it to Drew without telling him it came from her.

"I will come home, Grandpa. I'm just not ready yet. Lizzy probably hates me, and I can't look Uncle David and Aunt Anna in the eyes. I feel so guilty...." She lifted her hand to stop him from saying what she knew he would say. "I'll get there, Grandpa; I'm not there yet."

"It's not like that with our family. No matter what happens, we always love. But Duke was not your fault. Do you think Duke could have lived with himself if he hadn't tried to save you?"

"I know what you are saying, Grandpa, but it has never made it from my heart to my brain."

When Sophie walked into the penthouse after dropping off her family at the airport. She felt the emptiness. Usually, Bully filled that empty space, but they left him with Katsumi and Tora. Bully couldn't come on this mission.

Sophie stood by the glass patio doors, looking out onto the city as the sun rose slowly up the horizon. She had a cup of the fresh coffee Houston had made. Houston knew she was missing her family. He took her over to the couch and sat with her, putting his arm around her, and pulling her close. She rested her head on his shoulder.

"Soph, I've been thinking. Maybe after this job, we should resign from the task force."

Sophie sat up, "What? You love working with the task force. Why would you quit? What would you do?"

"I don't know. Maybe we want to open our own PI firm."

"Would you still work for the US Marshals?"

"I don't know," Houston whispered, leaning his head back on the couch.

"Would Fons leave with you? He has a wife now. He needs a steady income."

"I have plenty of money to support a business and pay his salary until we get clients."

"I like that idea. We could pick our jobs and take off whenever we want."

"Yeah. And Sophie.... When we get back from this job, you need to see your family and make things right."

"I know."

"You are different around your family."

"No, I'm not," Sophie sat up and scowled at him.

"It's a good thing. You are so relaxed, happy, and open. You are not generally like that. You had a piece missing," Houston adjusted his position to look straight at her. "I have to be honest. I'm a little afraid that if you go home, you will want to stay there. You are whole when you are around them."

Sophie cupped his cheek with her hand. "Oh, Houston, wherever we are together. That is home to me. I may want to visit them often. But I wouldn't take you from your family."

"I want you to know. I would move, so you could be with them if you want."

Sophie laid her head on his shoulder again. "I know that, Houston. You always put me before your own wants and needs. I love you."

"When do you want to head to DC?"

"We might as well head up there now. There is no reason to stay here," Sophie stood to pack a few things. Houston did the same.

DC

It took about six hours to get to DC because they stopped to eat dinner at one of their favorite spots. When they walked into the house, Fons called and asked if he and Carol could come down.

"Since when do you ask, Fons," Houston teased.

"It's my wife; she's a bad influence."

"I heard that," Carol said in the background. Houston smiled. Carol was so good for him.

"Come on down."

"Do I get a prize," Fons always made the same reply.

"Yeah, you get to see me."

"Sophie, Fons and Carol are coming down."

"Great. I've missed them."

They moved to the staircase and waited for them. After they all hugged. They headed for the kitchen for coffee.

"Where's Bully?" Carol placed the brownies she had brought down on the kitchen table.

"We left him with Katsumi and Tora. He isn't able to come with us on this job." That was as much as she could say in front of Carol. Fons had told Carol he worked undercover on a task force before they married. He felt she had a right to decide if she wanted to live with a man who worked dangerous missions. But he never went into detail about the assignments.

"Well, I'm glad to have you guys back," Carol said.

They stayed and ate brownies and talked about Sophie's family until late into the evening. Then Carol went upstairs, and Fons stayed to talk about the new mission. Sophie decided to go to bed.

"What do you know, Houston?" Fons asked.

"The First Lady came to Trenton and filled us in. It appears Makhtar Hijazi needs surgery in the US. Makhtar got ahold of a broker to facilitate getting him into the country. Fortunately for us, the broker, who actually are two brothers, happens to be a CIA asset. Their handler contacted Director Perry of the clandestine unit."

"Wow. So, we're going to lure him here to arrest him?"

"Not quite. The asset has to handle it. If Hijazi gets wind the US is involved, he won't come."

"So, what is the task force doing?"

"They want Sophie and the handler, who happens to be Sophie's stepmother, to imbed with the Hijazis."

"Sophie's stepmother?"

"It's a long story. I'll tell you another time. Anyway, it's common for the broker to send someone to ensure the merchandise reaches its destination. But there is no way I'm letting my wife travel with terrorists without being an arm's distance away if there is trouble."

"I agree. So, what's the plan?"

"I don't have one yet. I'm hoping you can help me come up with one."

"I got a call; Director Cosby wants us all at Quantico at 8 am, Monday. He says they have a state-of-the-art command center. It's used to train techs, and analysts, from the CIA, FBI, DEA, Homeland Security, and the Capital Police. It's been upgraded to a SCIF." Frons grabbed another one of his wife's brownies.

"Hey, leave some for Sophie; you live with a chef."

Fons laughed as he shoved the last bite in his mouth. "I don't think they expected you and Sophie to be here."

AUSTIN, TX. SUNDAY

David and Anna spent time with Emmett late Saturday night. They wanted his opinion on how they planned to approach Drew with the news he was adopted.

After hearing them out, Emmett agreed it was a sound approach. He said he would stick around the house if they needed him.

Anna grabbed the baby picture album that Florence had made for Andrew. She had stored it in the hope chest at the foot of their bed all these years. There was another album of Florence and Bradley Morgan's wedding and honeymoon. There were no pictures of Bradley with Andrew. He didn't want anything to do with his son and told anyone who would listen he felt the baby wasn't his. There was no need for Drew to ever know that.

It was Sunday after the BBQ and Drew was still talking about his time with the guys on Saturday. Every Saturday, there was a standing outing with CJ, Ricky, Liam, Lawson, Xander, Drew, and Cash. Sometimes their dads and some of the other men would come along. But they would rather golf or play handball these days.

They made a pact with their wives or girlfriends to be home by 1 pm and spend the rest of the day and Sunday with their families. To keep that promise, they tended to leave early in the morning. Yesterday they went skeet shooting.

Drew came in from playing soccer with the guys after the BBQ and saw his folks at the kitchen table talking. Drew was still pumped about getting to shoot a shotgun.

SEIZE ON THE HIGH SEAS

"Dad, I want to go skeet shooting again. I like shooting at the clay pigeons. It was so cool. I even hit some. CJ said I have a good eye."

"Yes, you told us. I'll go with you next time. I like skeet shooting too."

"That would be awesome, Dad."

"Can Kato spend the night. We can go to school together.

"Sure, but we need to talk to you first."

"What about?"

"Sit down, Drew. Would you like some juice? It was pretty warm out today; you probably need to hydrate."

"Sure, Mom, orange juice."

Anna placed a glass of orange juice in front of him and sat down.

"Drew, you know China is adopted, right?"

"Yeah, she tells me she adopted me as a brother the same day she was adopted."

"In a way, she did. The judge declared you brother and sister and banged his gavel. She was upset when she found out you couldn't live with them at Lennox Estate." Anna watched Drew drink down his orange juice in one long gulp. Then he answered.

"Yeah, she likes having me around."

"Do you think China loves her mom and dad any less because she's adopted?"

"China? No, she's a daddy's girl, all the way. She loves Uncle Wes and Lady Be."

"Yeah, I think so too. Do you think Wes and Lady Phoebe love her less because she had another mother before them?"

"No way. They love all the kids. The kids tell me that all the time."

"Drew, we want to tell you about a very special woman who loved you very much. She died when you were a baby, so I doubt you remember her.

"Her name was Florence Winsor Morgan. I met Flo when she came into my office to redo her Will and set up a trust. We became friends. Flo wanted to make arrangements for her son to go to a family who would love him as much as she did.

"She picked your mother and me."

Drew got a strange look on his face. "I don't understand."

"Your Dad and I are your parents. But before us, you were Flo's son. She died, and you became our son," Anna said.

"I'm adopted?"

"The day Flo died; your dad was there. He brought you home that night, and we became a family. We never considered you adopted. You were our son from the moment you came into our home," Anna said.

Drew was quiet. "How did she die?"

"It was very tragic. Flo was killed," David put his hand on Drew's arm.

"Like murdered?"

"Yes."

"Did they find who did it?"

"Yes."

"Wow."

"We are telling you this because we promised her, we would. She loved you very much and knew we would be the right Mom and Dad for you," David moved the baby album closer.

"These are pictures of Flo and you when you were a baby," Anna opened the album.

Anna pointed to a picture. "This is a picture of Florence."

"She was pretty," Drew said, mainly to himself.

"She was beautiful and a good person," Anna said.

Drew went through the album, occasionally pointing out a picture.

"I was so little."

"Yes, you were, and such a sweet boy," Anna pointed at one of the last pictures in the album. "That's how old you were when you became our son."

"If you ever want to ask us anything about her, we will tell you everything we know," David said. "And if you don't want to ask us, you can always ask Grandpa."

"Ok, Dad," he turned to his mom. "What's for lunch?"

David and Anna were surprised at his response to the news. "I've got leftover spaghetti. Want some?"

"Yeah. I love your spaghetti."

"You have to go wash up."

David stood with Drew and gave him a bear hug. "I love you, son."

"I know, Dad. I love you too."

Anna stepped over and hugged him, too. "You can talk to us about anything, son."

Drew nodded and bounced off to wash up.

"That wasn't what I expected," Anna said.

"Me either, but it might take time. After it settles in, we might see a response. And I know when Drew becomes a teenager and is mad at us, he'll get a jab in about it."

"Maybe, or maybe the fact that so many of our extended family is adopted, it simply doesn't matter," Anna said.

"God can work it out. We'll keep praying about it."

QUANTICO-MONDAY,

Houston, Sophie, and Fons rode to Quantico together. Carol made a triple batch of peanut butter cookies for the team. But the way the men were eating them on the road, Sophie wondered if there would be any left for the others.

They were pleasantly surprised by the layout when they walked into Quantico's Command Center.

"It looks a lot like ours in DC," Denny said to Fons as he walked in behind them.

Director Cosby wasn't there yet, but their team had assembled. Sophie put the large Tupperware container of cookies on the conference table.

"There were twice this many when we left DC. But the cookie monsters attacked," Sophie opened the lid.

The others bad-mouthed Houston and Fons teasingly.

"Anyone know what this is about?" Denny took several cookies and sat down at the table.

"I'm sure Director Cosby will be here soon to tell us," Fons said, reaching for another cookie, but Matt slapped his hand.

"You had your share."

Before they could ask any more questions, Director Cosby and Director Perry walked in. Two others walked in with them. Sophie recognized her stepmother but not the man with her.

"Please be seated. Thank you for coming back before your leave was up." After everyone found a place to sit, Director Cosby continued. "I'm sure you recognize Director Perry of the CIA clandestine unit. With him is one of his recruiters, Marci Beauchene, and her asset, Roman DeCarlo."

Some of the team recognized the name and looked at each other. Director Perry noticed and stepped in.

"Mr. DeCarlo and his brother have been our assets for fifteen years. The intel they have given us has saved this country and others from serious attacks of terrorism.

"Recently, he was contacted by Makhtar Hijazi," he could hear murmurs around the room. "Yes, that Hijazi. We knew he was sick when he dropped off our radar but couldn't verify it. He needs surgery to stay alive. He wants Mr. DeCarlo to facilitate that for him.

"Mr. DeCarlo is retired but is willing to do this at our request. The Hijazi's bombed a hospital in his homeland, Italy. He has skin in the game." Director Perry gave the floor back to Director Cosby.

"Normally, this team would develop a plan to get him on US soil. But because the Hijazis are well connected and could hear about a US operation. Mr. DeCarlo and his brother will make all the connections. We will shadow the movement while they are on our soil. They will come from a port in Italy to Texas on a yacht.

"The plan is to allow him to get the surgery, recuperate, then get him back on the yacht they came on. We will turn him over to the Italians to arrest them after our Seal Team secures them on the yacht," Director Cosby explained.

Several of the team interrupted.

"Why on earth would we allow him to get that surgery?" Sissy asked.

"And why would we let him travel freely across our country? He could be planning all sorts of mayhem," Agent Ken Smith asked.

"Why are we turning them over to Italy? It should be the US collar," Lt. Flynn Murphy chimed in.

"I understand your frustrations. I'll answer the second question first. The President feels he should be alive long enough to stand trial for his treacherous acts in Italy. That country needs to have a chance to exact justice for the assassination of its President. Not to mention hundreds of their citizens who were in the hospital. And if you remember. President Stevens, at the time, held back aid and condolences for their loss. That caused real cracks in our political relations. President Madden wants to mend those wounds.

"To answer your other question, you are right. We cannot let the Hijazis travel in our country without supervision. So, Mr.

DeCarlo will have two of ours imbedded with them as they travel in the US," Director Cosby said.

"So, some of us will travel with them?" Agent Mathew asked.

"Yes, Marci Beauchene and Sophie Star," Cosby answered.

"You want two women to travel with terrorists? Why not me and Fons," Denny asked.

"The Hijazis would object. Men would be too great a threat and they might back out. We want to be the ones to broker this," Cosby answered.

"You want us to sit here while one of our team is out there on her own? I don't like it, Director," Sissy Corban said.

Director Cosby raised his hand to stop the conversation. "I know this is not ideal, but if the Hijazis get wind of a tail, a drone, or a tracker, this could turn into a blood bath. We need to let Mr. DeCarlo run this his way. But, like I said, we will be shadowing the operation from here."

"Sir, we need to hear the plan; maybe we can give some input, still letting Mr. DeCarlo facilitate it," Houston said.

Director Cosby turned to Roman DeCarlo. "Mr. DeCarlo, will you please brief our team."

Roman stood, "My brother and I have a yacht picking up Makhtar Hijazi, his two sons, Anwar and Khaan, and his daughter Ojala. Captain Mandrapilias is meeting the Hijazis at the Sanremo Port to take them across the Atlantic to Corpus Christi, Texas, in the Gulf of Mexico. They will be traveling under alias'.

"From there, he will travel to Austin, Texas, where Dr. Lawson Cornett will do the surgery...."

Roman stopped when he heard a gasp. He looked around and saw Sophie's face and realized something he said was a surprise to her. He looked over at his wife, she nodded, and he continued. "From there, he will travel back to Corpus Christi and board the yacht. As the yacht gets into international waters, your

Seal Team will secure the men on the yacht. Then the Italians, with your government's permission, will board the yacht and arrest Makhtar and his sons," Roman concluded.

Sophie whispered to Houston, "Ask if it's alright if we take a break for a minute."

"Sir, can we take a break. We want to confer with our team."

Roman turned to Director Perry, who stood and answered. "Yes, let's take a fifteen-minute break."

SEIZE ON THE HIGH SEAS

CHAPTER ELEVEN

The team headed to the breakroom in the back to discuss this operation. Marci walked over to Sophie. Sophie turned to her, "You knew we were going to Austin and that Lawson was the doctor?"

"Yes, but we didn't have an opportunity to discuss it."

"Marci, there are tons of people in Austin that could break our cover. And Lawson...you know he will react when he sees me. There is no way we can be the ones to imbed with the Hijazis."

"As far as Lawson is concerned, we can get someone he trusts to let him know you are working undercover. He's a grown man; he can control his reaction to seeing you."

"Who? Who can do that? No one knows what's going on." Sophie wrung her hands.

Marci thought for a second, "Emmett. I'm sure you gave him an idea of what you do. He won't ask too many questions, and I know he'd do it."

"Ok, but what about everyone we know in the city?"

We will only be in the hospital. Maybe Emmett could stick around the hospital and run interference for us."

"That may work," Sophie agreed.

"Sophie, what's going on? What's the deal with Austin, Texas, and this Dr. Cornett?" Fons asked.

"Fons, the short version is, I grew up in Austin, Marci is my stepmother, and Lawson Cornett was one of my best friends."

"Oh."

"Sissy, I agree with your earlier comment. We can't have Marci and Sophie out there without backup. Instead of an SUV. What if DeCarlo arranges for an RV. Supposedly to keep Makhtar comfortable for the trip to Austin. He can have a driver and a backup on board to get them to Austin," Houston said. "Fons and I could drive."

"Houston, you two exude law enforcement. You can't," Marci objected.

"We can stop shaving, and with the right clothes, we could pass. DeCarlo could say we are also there to protect them."

"That may work, Houston," Matt said.

The team returned to the briefing, and Houston suggested the RV, with him and Fons driving.

"That is an excellent idea, Agent Townsend," Roman said. "But there is no way you can do it. You are too intimidating. My brother and I will drive. No one knows we are the 'Brokers'. We have always kept our identities a secret. And we don't look like Navy Seals."

"That works for us, Mr. DeCarlo, but we are not letting part of our team travel without backup. If you are driving, we can follow from ahead of you since we will know your route. You can drive it in about four hours. Then at the hospital, we can stay out of sight."

"Houston, it's imperative they do not feel like they are being followed. You can stay in Austin, but I'm not sure about you being in the hospital," Roman said.

"It's the only way we can be sure none of them goes off on their own. We have to be able to surveil them," Houston said. Director Cosby agreed with him.

"And I also think we need to bring a drone and our drone pilot with us," Houston turned to look at Navy Lt. Murphy. He was added to the task force during the Chinatown operation.

"I agree," Lt. Murphy said.

Director Perry considered it. "Alright, but don't forget, we need to be invisible."

Sophie spoke up, "Director Cosby. I would like you to call out our SRT team. I have a gut feeling we are going to need them. Knowing who these men are, I have little doubt they have plans."

"Alright, I'll have them set up close to the hospital but not inside," Cosby agreed. Right now, we need to set up house in this command center. We will start tracking them as soon as they hit Corpus Christi. Director Perry has a satellite monitoring the captain's progress across the Atlantic." Cosby was still speaking when Roman felt his cell vibrate. He looked at the caller ID and saw it was his brother.

Roman stepped away from the conference table and answered.

"Ciao, fratello."

"We might have a problem, Roman."

"What?"

"The Captain called to let me know they hit severe weather. It has slowed them down. The captain will try to make it up once the storm passes. But our passenger, the old one, is very ill. He has gotten worse since the bad weather has tossed him about."

"Thank you for letting me know, Rocky. Make sure he calls us when he's within 24 hours of Corpus Christi."

"I'll let him know."

"And Rocky, you need to fly to meet me in Corpus Christi before the yacht gets there. We are concerned about sending Marci and Sophie in without backup. Instead of an SUV, I'm supplying an RV. You and I will be the drivers. The fact Makhtar has gotten worse will be our excuse. Call the Captain and ask him to pass on the vehicle change."

"I never did like them being imbedded alone," Rocky said. Roman hung up and went back to the table. He waited until Director Cosby finished what he was saying, then spoke up.

"Director, I received a call from my brother. Makhtar has gotten worse. If Makhtar dies at sea, the sons may force the captain to turn around and take them to Syria. They'll want to travel to Iran to bury their father."

"How long before they dock in Corpus Christi?" Fons asked.

"They left Italy four days ago," Roman answered. "It would normally be a seven or eight day trip."

"If Makhtar dies, we will have to push up our seize on the yacht. The brothers are on the most wanted list too." Director Cosby turned to Houston. "We need to prepare for that scenario with the Seal Team."

"Yes, sir," Director Cosby stood, "We'll end this briefing here. Make preparations and let Director Perry and me know when they reach Corpus Christi."

"Yes, sir."

Houston and Fons motioned his team to meet in the break room. After everyone grabbed a coffee or another beverage, they sat at the smaller tables.

"Denny, you and Ken will run the operation from here. Matt, you, and Sissy, too. Fons, Flynn, and I will be in the field with Sophie and Ms. Beauchene. Any questions?" No one responded. "Alright, Denny, who do you need here to help you get this command center in shape?"

"If Ken, Matt, and Sissy would stay, we could run some checks and make sure we have a handle on this new equipment.

I want to be linked into the satellite feed Director Perry has monitoring the yacht."

"Alright, then. We will leave you to it and be back when it's time for another briefing. Call us if you find out you need more help." Houston said.

Before Houston, Fons, and Sophie headed home, Marci wanted to introduce her husband to them.

"Roman, this is my stepdaughter, Sophie, her husband, SAC Houston Townsend, and their best friend, SAC Alfonso Rodriguez."

Sophie stepped forward and shook his hand. "I can see how happy Marci is. I'm glad you found each other."

"Marci has added a new dimension to my life. One I never thought I would ever have. She is my life," Roman said.

Sophie smiled, "I've heard Italians are great romantics."

Houston and Fons shook his hand.

Marci turned to Sophie, "when this is over, will you and Houston come for dinner."

"Of course, we'd love to."

DC,-TUESDAY
The next evening Director Cosby met with the president in his residence. A secret service man announced him.

"Hello, Gram, would you like some coffee or tea?" Emma asked.

"Coffee, please."

Emma put a carafe of coffee, cups, sugar, creamer, and small dishes for the oatmeal cookies, on a tray and took it into the living room. After setting it down, she poured coffee for Michael and

Gram. Emma put a spoonful of sugar in Grams, handed it to him, and directed his attention to the cookies. After taking a cup of coffee for herself and pouring hazelnut creamer and sugar into it, she sat on the couch next to her husband. Gram was on a Victorian armchair across from them.

"I understand you had the first briefing with the task force on the operation today, Gram," Michael said.

"Yes, we made modifications, but it's on track. I'm here because we do have a sticky wicket." Gram put two cookies on a plate and set it on the side table next to his chair.

"You mean a fly in the ointment, don't you?" Michael laughed. It was an ongoing argument since they were in grade school. Gram had an older teacher that always used the term sticky wicket, and Michael's mother always said fly in the ointment.

They both snickered. "Whatever," Gram relented and turned his attention to Emma. "Emma, you know Marci and Sophie lived in Austin, right?"

"Yes, I'm aware. Is that a problem?"

"Maybe not, but the fact that Lawson Cornett is the doctor *is* a problem. He was one of Sophie's best friends. He is going to recognize them immediately."

"So, what do we do?" Michael asked, knowing Gram wouldn't come without a solution. Gram had to swallow the bite of cookie he just took and sipped coffee to wash it down before answering.

"I believe if we send someone the doctor trusts to explain they are undercover, he would be on board."

"Who do you suggest," Michael asked.

"You met Emmet Scott in Trenton, didn't you, Emma?" Gram asked, turning his head toward her.

"Yes, Sophie adopted him as her grandpa when she was very young."

"That's right. And he is close to Lawson and his family too," Gram paused before saying the rest. "I know you are going to Dallas tomorrow to raise money to subsidize your projects.

"True, there are a lot of generous women there who believe in what we are doing for women and children."

"I thought if you met with Emmett and went to the doctor together, he would be more inclined to believe the necessity of his cooperation."

Michael turned his head to address his wife. "You won't be far from Austin, sweetheart if you want to do it. My only concern is you will have to keep it off the radar, and with your security, that will be difficult."

"If we drive instead of fly into Austin, we could go directly to Camp Mabry. Trish will be with me. We can leave the base incognito, without security, and go to the home of Emmett Scott."

"You can't go by yourself, darling."

"I won't be alone. Trish will be with me; she can drive."

Michael thought about it for a moment. It was risky for her to travel without security, but not unprecedented. "Alright, but I want you and Trish to wear a tracker. You'll see to that, Gram?"

"Yes, of course, sir. And Trish has all sorts of floppy hats that will help to keep you disguised."

Sophie was missing Bully; she wished now she hadn't left him in Trenton. She and Houston were on the couch watching a movie. Bully usually jumped on the couch and snuggled up to her.

That wasn't the only thing on Sophie's mind. She had missed her cycle. She bought a pregnancy test but hadn't used it yet. There was no morning sickness or any other indication she might be pregnant. She didn't want to tell Houston until, she was sure. Even then, she considered waiting until after the first trimester.

Sophie didn't want to get his hopes up just to have them shattered again. Besides, he would not want her on this mission if there was even a slight chance, she was pregnant.

Houston and Sophie were on a task force operation to take down a North Korean counterfeiter, Yon Min-ji, when she had a miscarriage. Houston still blames himself, even though the doctor told him it was not a contributing factor.

Based on the two briefings she'd gotten; the mission wasn't going to be strenuous. Her hand went to her abdomen subconsciously. Houston noticed.

"Soph, are you not feeling well?"

"No, I'm fine," she moved her hand to the popcorn bowl.

DALLAS. WEDNESDAY

The First Lady's appeal to the Women on a Mission Organization went well. She updated them on the once trafficked women. Emma asked for their continued support for those who were not self-reliant yet.

The group brought in one hundred women who paid five thousand dollars a plate to have dinner with the First Lady. Emma stayed and worked the room, knowing everyone wanted to speak and get pictures with the First Lady. Emma did three fundraisers a year to support her projects. The charity didn't just support freed trafficked women. Her other project as First Lady was a monitoring system for children in Foster Care. The non-profit hired people to monitor homes on a regular basis. State Foster Cared Systems, didn't have the workforce to continually monitor the homes the foster children are in. The State's Child Protective Services were not on board and fought the program, but she knew the right people to keep it intact.

The First Lady arranged with the Secret Service to take her to Camp Mabry at 8 am. Her security was not in agreement with her plans.

AUSTIN, TX

As soon as they pulled into Camp Mabry, Emma and Trish changed clothes, took a bathroom break, and headed to Emmett's house. The Secret Service had provided them with the address and a car. They chose a more non-descript Cadillac, a few years old, in a neutral color.

Trish was driving and had no problem following the navigation system's instructions. They pulled up to the curb in front of Emmett's house. There was a new Ford F-150 in the driveway.

"That has to be Emmett's rig," Emma said.

Trish turned off the Cadillac, and they stepped out, putting on the floppy hats Trish brought along and sunglasses. Trish looked around to see if anyone noticed them, but there weren't any houses nearby. Emma knocked on the door. They could hear someone coming.

Emmett opened the door to find two ladies in floppy hats, sunglasses, blue jeans, and V-neck T-shirts. He had no idea who they were.

"Good morning, ladies; how can I help you?"

"Emmett, can we come in?" Emma asked. He had no idea how the lady knew him, but there was no way he would keep ladies out on the porch.

"Of course," Emmett stepped back.

Emma took off her hat, so he'd recognize her. "Emmett, it's me, Emma Madden; we met in Trenton."

"Madam First Lady, what on earth are you doing here? And where is your security?"

Emma laughed, "I thought Texans were hospitable. This is my dear friend Trish Cosby. She braved our little outing today with me. I left my security behind."

"Forgive my manners. Please come sit in the kitchen. I have sweet tea or coffee."

"Coffee for me," Trish said.

"Me too. Unless you have hot tea."

"I do," Emmett said and filled his Elite Glass Water Kettle. "This will only take a few minutes. He poured coffee for Mrs. Cosby. Sugar and an assortment of teas in a ceramic holder were already on the table. Emmett opened the fridge and poured cream into the matching creamer.

The glass kettle beeped, and Emmett poured a cup of water into a China cup and set it in front of the First Lady.

"Thank you for the tea, Emmett," Emma said before she explained her visit. "I know this is unorthodox, but I needed to talk to you, and no one can know I'm in town."

"What is it I can do for you?"

"I need you to accompany me to the hospital to talk to Dr. Lawson Cornett...."

Emmett interrupted, "Are you ill?"

"No, Emmett. When I spoke to Sophie in Trenton, I asked her and Houston to accept a new assignment. Houston had refused, saying his wife needed time off. Later he called and they accepted the mission."

"I figured it was something like that," Emmett nodded.

"The mission will bring Marci and Sophie here, undercover. The person they will be imbedded with needs heart surgery, and Doctor Cornett is the surgeon.

"From what Ms. Star has said, Dr. Cornett knows her. I am here to persuade the doctor to act like he doesn't know her or Marci.

"I understand you are close with him. I know he will trust me if you are with us."

"Madam First Lady, I'm happy to help, but he is not the only one who will recognize them. Sophie was well liked in school, and she knows a lot of people."

"Ms. Star will not be leaving the hospital except to stay the nights in either a hotel or the RV they will be arriving in."

"Who's her backup?" Emmett asked.

"We are sending two men in to drive the RV, and Houston and two other men will be out of sight.

"If you are willing to stay around the hospital, you could divert anyone she knows from seeing her."

"I can do that," Emmett said.

"Do you have an appointment with Lawson? He doesn't take walk-ins."

"Yes, someone set up a second opinion appointment for Trish at 2 pm. Are you free to come?"

"Yes. Since we have some time, let me make lunch for you."

SEIZE ON THE HIGH SEAS

CHAPTER TWELVE

Emmett drove the ladies to the Heart Hospital. They kept the floppy hats on until they were called back to Lawson's office. Emmett went into the office with them.

Lawson was surprised to see him, "Emmett, what are you doing here?"

"I came with the First Lady and Mrs. Cosby."

"The First Lady?" Lawson started to say, but after the women took their hats off, he recognized her.

"Madam First Lady, are you the patient?"

"No, Doctor Cornett, this appointment was a ruse, so I could come in to see you without being recognized."

"Please sit down," Lawson pulled up another chair so Emmett could sit, then went behind his desk and sat down.

"Doctor Lawson, the man you know as Enzo Ricci, is coming here so you can do heart surgery on him."

"Yes, that's correct."

"He's only a couple of days away. There will be two women accompanying the family. Those women are working undercover, and that fact must not be revealed to the family or anyone else. You know them, Dr. Cornett."

"I can't imagine how I would know undercover agents," Lawson disagreed.

"They are part of the President's Task Force. You do know them. Marci Beauchene and Sophie Star."

"Sophie Star?" Lawson's breath caught, and his pulse went up. "No one has seen her in years," he turned to Emmett. "Have you found her, Emmett?"

"Just a week ago. That short trip I took, it was to meet up with her."

"Why haven't you told the family, Emmett. I know Lizzy doesn't know or she would have said."

"I can't, Lawson; Sophie asked me not to. She said she would consider coming home after this mission."

"Are you telling me Sophie is in law enforcement?"

"Not exactly. Sophie is a consultant," Emmett said.

"Doctor Cornett, Sophie Star is an invaluable member of the president's team. You can't infer you know her personally. Not to the Ricci family or to anyone else in the hospital. And you cannot tell anyone outside of this confidence that she is here," Emma paused. "Can you do that?"

Lawson wasn't listening; he was looking out the window. *Sophie, after all these years. Why does it scare me to see you again?*

"Doctor Cornett?" Emma said.

"Oh, yes. I can do that. But who is this man? If he is a criminal, I want to know."

"I can't tell you that. It's classified. I can only say Mr. Ricci is the person of interest in this operation. It is imperative he gets this surgery and then be back on the move," Emma said.

"Lawson, are you sure you're all right. You look a little pale," Emmett said.

"I'm fine, just surprised."

"Doctor Cornett, how long will Mr. Ricci have to stay in the hospital after the surgery?"

"If there are no complications, it would normally be three days. But since this is still an experimental device, I will need to monitor Mr. Ricci here for at least five days."

Emma lowered her head for a moment. Then whispered to Trish, "Call your husband; he needs to know." Trish excused herself and went to the furthest corner of the room.

"Alright, Doctor, we weren't expecting that long a stay. But we don't have a choice." Emma noticed Trish standing next to her with the phone.

"Gram is on the line."

"Thanks, Trish. Excuse me," Emma got up and moved away.

"Gram, we might have a complication."

"What is it?"

"This new device has a protocol that requires the doctor to monitor him for five days. That's way beyond the safe zone for him to stay here."

"Will he deviate from that?" Gram asked.

"No, it's an FDA protocol until the device is approved."

"That's no good; we wanted him gone in three days."

"I know."

"Ask him again if he will deviate from his protocol?"

"I'll let you ask him, Gram."

"Doctor, Director Cosby is on the phone. Will you speak with him?" Emma handed the phone to him.

"Yes, this is Doctor Cornett."

"Doctor Cornett, keeping Mr. Ricci in the hospital for five days will jeopardize my people. Can you deviate from the protocol?"

"No, sir, if I do that, I will be out of compliance with the FDA. I'll have to start over."

"It has to be five days?"

"Yes, sir."

"Please hand the phone back to the First Lady." Lawson gave the phone to her. She moved away again.

"What do you want to do, Gram. This device is too important to break his protocol. It wouldn't be fair to his other patients. Can you find a solution?" Emma asked.

"I don't know any other options. I'll call Houston," Gram said and hung up. Emma returned to her seat.

"Doctor Cornett. We will get back to you with our decision. I do need you to know we got word Mr. Ricci has gotten worse on the trip."

Lawson stood when the ladies stood. "Alright, Madam First Lady, Mrs. Cosby, I'll wait to hear back from you. Let me give you my personal cell number." Lawson wrote it on a card and handed it to the First Lady. "Emmett, I'll talk to you later." Emmett nodded.

Emma turned when she reached the door. "Doctor Cornett, you realize everything we told you today is confidential. You can't tell anyone."

"I understand," Lawson answered, and they left.

Emma and Trish picked up their car and returned to Camp Mabry without incident. The Secret Service immediately drove them back to Dallas and got them on the plane back to DC. Emma could tell they had been anxious waiting for their safe return. Her secret service agents were dedicated, and she knew they would take a bullet for her. She tried hard to never put herself in a position where they would need to.

"Emma, what is the problem with them staying here for five days?" Trish asked after the seatbelt light was turned off.

"These men are extremists, terrorists with a zeal for Jihad against Americans and Israelis particularly. I can't imagine they will want to pass up an opportunity. And what if their followers find out they are here. They may consider it an honor to him to kill our citizens."

"I see."

Emma's cell rang. "Emma, I heard we have a problem with the post-surgery," the President had spoken with Director Cosby.

"Yes, Makhtar needs to be monitored for five days. What did you decide?"

154

"It's too risky to have him here in the US unless he is detained. We talked about arresting him at the hospital. But having SRT secure them puts too many civilians at risk. And if his followers find out, and they would, they could take hostages to force us to release him.

"The Hijazis need to get back on that yacht. Ms. Star suggested we stick with the plan and have a Navy doctor stand by to travel with Makhtar when the Italians transport him to Italy," Michael relayed.

"If it meets the standard for the FDA, I don't think Dr. Cornett will have a problem with it, Michael. But what about the time he is on the yacht?"

"Alright, someone needs to ask him that question."

YACHT ON THE ATLANTIC. THURSDAY

Makhtar was feeling better today. The yacht had outrun the storm, sailing under clear skies and a calm ocean.

Anwar and Khaan helped their father to the lower deck, partially covered by the upper sun deck. They sat him down on the U-shaped couch and put his feet on a hassock in front of him.

Anwar called for his sister, who had been cooking for the family. The only crew was the Captain and his First Officer, who was his son. The guests had to fend for themselves. But knowing his guest were Iranian, the Captain stocked the galley with food items that were popular in that country.

Ojala, Makhtar's only daughter, made Berber pancakes and brought them up on a tray with dates and a pitcher of fermented milk called leben. She had already brought out dishes, silverware, and glasses.

There was no thank you, her father simply nodded to her, and she left. Ojala returned to the galley to start the biryani; a rice, meat, and vegetable dish her father liked.

Ojala put the meat mixture on low heat, took some Berber pancakes, slathered them with butter and honey, and a glass of juice, and headed for the sun deck to eat.

Ojala had never been on the ocean. She dropped her arm over the railing to feel the salty sea mist stirred up from the yacht moving in the water. The temperature of the Atlantic waters in the spring was in the 70s, but the chill in the air still caused it to bring goosebumps to her arm. Ojala leaned her head over the railing to feel the mist on her face. She licked her lips and tasted the salt.

I wonder why the ocean is filled with salt, not lakes or rivers. When I run away. I will go to a library and find out all the secrets of the universe. Ojala had decided she would find a way to escape her family when she heard they were traveling to America.

Ojala pulled herself back up over the railing and ate her breakfast. The conversation on the lower deck filtered up to where she was sitting. She moved a little closer so she could hear more clearly.

Ojala didn't care for her brothers. They treated her like their slave. Her father wasn't like that, probably because he loved her. And at one time, he loved her mother and treated her uncommonly well for a radical follower of Muhammad in Iran.

When they moved to Afghanistan, things changed. He became a more visible leader, and his kindness to Ojala and her mother changed. Her father began to beat her mother for the slightest infraction.

Ojala's mother died a few years earlier. Ojala blamed her father. The last time he beat her mother, she became very sick. Ojala begged her father to let her take her to a doctor, but he refused. She died from internal bleeding.

The men spoke in Arabic, so the Captain and First Officer couldn't understand.

"Walidaya, I did as you asked and withdrew five hundred thousand US dollars from our account before we left Geneva. I have contacted Salman Ebeid to let him know. I told him I would bring him funds to support his network if he swears to complete the mission you give him. Salman reports that a hundred followers crossed the southern border last month. He has set them up in cells across the state of Texas."

Makhtar patted his oldest son's face. You have done well, my son. You will take my place when I die, Anwar."

"Walidaya...you cannot leave us."

"Ah, but I wish to see Muhammad, peace be upon him, and receive my reward."

"Walidaya, you are a great leader; your reward will be great," Khaan, his younger son, added.

"You must be strong when I go. Know that I will be happy with my rewards. Make sure your sister marries a wealthy man, so she will be taken care of. Preferably a first wife, but at 16, it will be hard to negotiate. We should have found someone when she was 14, but we needed her to take care of us while in Geneva."

"Walidaya, you are speaking as if you expect to die. Have you seen your death?"

"No, but a wise man prepares his sons."

"Anwar, you believe Salman to be a true believer and follower?"

"Yes, I do. He will follow your wishes to the letter. What will you have him do?"

"To honor me after we leave. I wish for Salman to destroy the hospital where I have the surgery. Those honored to minister to me must not live to serve anyone else."

"Walidaya, it is fitting. So, you wish me to give him the entire five hundred thousand?"

"No, give him two and have him spread it to the other cells. When we return home, I will send word about what the others are to do."

157

"Walidaya, are we going home to Iran?" Khaan hadn't spoken much on this trip. He had been battling motion sickness since they boarded the yacht.

"No, my son, when I have recovered, we are going back to Afghanistan. My return will be celebrated."

Ojala heard their plans but stayed quiet, not that it would matter. They would never consider her a threat to their schemes. Her brothers considered women irrelevant. Suitable only to serve them.

The Broker ordered that she wear western clothes without a head scarf, but the minute they got on board, her brother ordered her to wear a hijab. She hated her brothers; they were mean and beat their wives. When the family left Afghanistan because the entire world was hunting her father for the bombing in Italy. Anwar and Khaan left their wives and children behind with their fathers-in-law. They feared their wives might get accustomed to a world where beatings were unacceptable.

Ojala loved her sisters-in-law. But they didn't know a life without abuse and accepted it submissively. Ojala tried to intervene when Anwar gave his wife a particularly brutal beating. He turned on her and beat her. When her father heard of it, he admonished Anwar but did nothing to punish him.

Khaan was not as vicious but was still a horrible man. All she wanted to do was get away. This could be her chance. Ojala would escape in Austin. If Anwar has five hundred thousand dollars with him, she could steal a few thousand to stay alive until she can get a job. He would never notice that small amount missing.

QUANTICO

Director Cosby called in all the teams involved for an update. They arrived at Quantico forty-five minutes later. Director Perry a few minutes after that.

"Good morning. Mr. DeCarlo, do you know when the yacht will dock in Corpus Christi?" Cosby asked.

"They are less than 48 hours out. The captain said that Makhtar's health improved after they sailed out of the storm."

"Alright, Lieutenant Denison, we need you and your team in Austin. You will leave at 0700 tomorrow. Meet up at the Bolling Air Force Base. Same with your Seal Team, Chief Abbott.

"Dr. Cornett has been contacted and knows that Ms. Beauchene and Ms. Star will be traveling with the patient. He is not aware of who his patient is.

"We have one last issue. Dr. Cornett has informed us that because the device is still in the application stage, one of the protocols is that the patient is under the doctor's supervision for five days. Under normal circumstances, he would be discharged in three if there were no complications.

"It is too risky to keep Makhtar and his family free on our soil for that long. However, we will continue as planned. Chief Abbott, your team will board the yacht as discussed."

"Yes, sir." Abbott turned to Sophie.

"Ms. Star, can you find a way to have all the non-combatants on the upper deck before we arrive; without making our targets suspicious. We don't want civilian injuries when we breach at 1 am."

"I'm sure Marci and I can come up with something," Sophie turned to Director Cosby. "Sir, have you found a Navy Doctor to complete Doctor Cornett's required protocols?"

"Yes, there will be a doctor on board the Coast Guard Cutter that will shadow the yacht and transport the Seals. He will communicate with Doctor Cornett once Dr. Lawson approves the plan, so he knows precisely what is needed."

"Thank you," Sophie responded.

"But we still need to have him watched while he is on the RV to Corpus Christi and on the yacht. Do you have any suggestions?" Cosby asked.

"Maybe Dr. Cornett would be willing to travel with us. He won't know about the seize, of course, but if he is willing, that would solve our problem," Sophie suggested.

"I'll have the first lady contact Mr. Scott. He can contact Dr. Cornett to approve the Navy doctor, but he won't understand why we need the Navy doctor if he is traveling with him. We'll have to tell him what is going to happen, and we can't do that."

"Then we'll just get approval for the Navy doctor, and we'll deal with the rest later," Sophie suggested.

"Director Perry, do you have anything to add?" Cosby asked.

"No, we have covered everything. I will be here monitoring the teams' progress and movements."

After the teams were dismissed Director Cosby spoke privately with Director Perry. "Stew, have you let Lorenzo Vittore know about the doctor needing to accompany the prisoners?"

"No, I'll call him today."

"Thank you."

ON THE YACHT SOMEWHERE IN THE ATLANTIC.

Ojala went down the stairs to the bottom deck. She picked up all the plates and put them on the tray. She kissed her father's forehead and took the tray heading for the galley.

I need to find where Anwar has the money. I won't touch it yet. He may notice. I'll wait until just before we dock. Ojala left the tray on the counter in the galley and stretched her neck to look around the door. She could see past the inside lounge area and the stairs leading up to the lower deck. It was clear.

Ojala snuck down the hall. Anwar's cabin was across from her father's. She turned the knob, not expecting it to be unlocked but found that the knob turned. She slid in and closed the door quietly.

The money has to be in his luggage. The room was identical to hers. Ojala stepped over to the small walk-in closet and opened the door. She saw the two suitcases Anwar had brought on board. A larger one and a smaller one. Only a few things were hanging on the dowel; the rest of Anwar's things were still in the suitcase. One suitcase was on a luggage rack, open. The other was against the wall. She could tell it wasn't in the open bag without feeling around.

There wasn't much room, but Ojala stepped into the closet and turned on the light. She grabbed the other suitcase and laid it down. She tried to move the zipper, but it was held with a tiny lock. *Of course, he would lock it.* Ojala grabbed one of the bobby pins that kept her hijab in place and scratched off the small rubbery end. Then she jabbed it into the lock and played with it until it opened.

Good job, Ojala. She quietly opened the luggage. Without disturbing the contents, she pressed down on each section, knowing that much money would be large and solid. She felt the right side and found nothing. A divider was connected to the left side; she detached it and started feeling around. She halted. *This has to be it.* Ojala carefully moved the shirts placed over the bundle and saw a pillowcase. Lifting it, she peeked inside. It was the money. She pulled it out of the case and saw it wrapped in that heavy see-through plastic, the same stuff the airports use to cover luggage if you are willing to pay for it.

No way I can take money out of this. I'd have to cut the plastic. He would notice. Discouraged, she put the money back in the pillowcase and covered it back up, closing the divider. Before she could close the suitcase, she heard voices in the hallway.

Oh no, oh no, Anwar can't find me in here. He will kill me. Her hands were trembling, but she closed the suitcase, locked it, and set it back in its place. She turned off the light and went to the door to listen to what they were saying.

"Walidaya, you must rest in your room."

"Yes, you are right. Now that the Great Satan has left Afghanistan, we can do our work openly. I need to be well to lead the people."

Ojala heard them open the door across from her, and then Anwar said to Khaan.

"Father needs another pillow; take one off my bed."

Ojala panicked; she ran back to the closet, got in, and quietly closed the door as the cabin door opened. Khaan grabbed a pillow off Anwar's perfectly made bed and ran back out, not closing the door.

I have to get out of here. Ojala snuck out of the closet, closed it, then peeked around the open door. She saw that both her brothers were focused on her father, their backs turned away from her. She moved around the door and ran down the hall to the galley as quietly as she could.

Ojala started doing the dishes and checked on the meat dish on the stove. A few minutes later, Khaan came in.

"Could you not see that your father was in distress. What kind of a daughter are you. He called for you; you did not answer."

"I'm cleaning the kitchen. I couldn't hear him."

Khaan moved closer to her. "Go to your father." When she stepped away from the sink, he shoved her. "Hurry."

Ojala refused to move faster but did go to see her father. She sat by his bed until he fell asleep.

CHAPTER THIRTEEN

QUANTICO

As the group moved to the smaller conference room, Denny stopped Fons to speak with him.

"Fons, I know the Director said a satellite is following the Hijazis on the ocean, but we need a dedicated satellite feed when they hit US soil and access to all Austin's DOT cameras. The sooner, the better. I have the GPS coordinates the satellite needs to be directed to. We'll monitor it once the yacht reaches the slip in Corpus Christi.

"I'll grab Director Cosby while he's still here and get it approved." Fons moved to where Houston and Sophie were sitting at the conference table looking at the blueprints of the Heart Hospital.

"I'm going to get approvals for a dedicated satellite. I'll be back."

"Thanks, Fons." Houston directed his attention to Lt. Troy Denison,

"Troy, there are a lot of exits in the hospital. Can you devise a plan to make sure they are all covered without your men coming in?"

"Yes, sir, I will work on it with my team."

Sophie and Houston left the blueprints with Lt. Denison and went to the break room where the rest of the team was.

"Would you like some coffee, Sophie?" Houston was at the coffee pot pouring himself a cup.

"Will you check the fridge and see what kind of soda they have in there if any," Sophie requested.

Houston was surprised that the fridge was stocked with drinks and food items. He opened the freezer to see ice cream, then stepped over to the cupboards to see if there was any food. The cabinets were filled with snacks.

"These cadets are spoiled; this place is fully stocked for them. Too bad we are in the field on this one. There is a Dr. Pepper in here." Houston set it in front of her with a glass filled with ice from the ice dispenser on the refrigerator door.

"Oh, good. But if there is only one, it might belong to someone."

"There is a whole case," Houston's said.

"Ok, thanks."

"We need to figure out how to get Makhtar out of the hospital on the third day without him getting suspicious."

"Well, it was your idea. You don't have the answer?" Sophie laughed.

"I look at the big picture; you look at the details," he smiled at her. "You already have an idea, don't you?"

"Yeah. I have an idea. On the evening of the third day, Roman could come into Makhtar's room and announce that the Broker had contacted him. He'll say there is chatter that someone has recognized him in the hospital, and we need to get him back on the yacht and in international waters; ASAP."

"Ok, but that still doesn't solve the problem of Dr. Cornett's FDA protocol," Houston took a drink of his coffee. "This coffee is better than the stuff we had in our operations center."

"I can ask Emmett to see if Lawson would be willing to come with us."

"That won't make sense when he is contacted by a Navy doctor," Houston responded.

"True. We'll have to tell him the Navy doctor is meeting up with us somewhere."

"That could work. But he can't tell the Hijazis that a Navy doctor will be taking over at some point."

Sophie thought it over, "We are going to have to bring him into the loop; at least partially. Otherwise, he won't go along with it. If he has some idea of what is going on he could be in the room when Roman makes the announcement, and he can volunteer to come with us."

"I'll call Emmett, he needs to talk to Lawson before the Navy doctor makes contact." Sophie pulled out her phone and called Emmett.

ON THE YACHT, SOMEWHERE IN THE ATLANTIC.

Makhtar was too weak to eat in the lounge. Ojala took his meal on a tray to his cabin. She sat with him to make sure he ate. After lunch, he fell asleep again. She took the tray and washed the dishes.

Ojala told her brothers to serve themselves. They were not happy with her attitude toward them, but she felt Anwar wouldn't act on it with her father so close.

Ojala went to the lounge and picked up their empty plates, knowing they would not clean up after themselves. When she finished the dishes, she made sure the fish for supper had thawed in the refrigerator and went to sit on the lower deck with a book.

Her brothers were talking in the lounge. It was hard for her to hear, so she moved closer to the door, hoping they wouldn't notice.

"Anwar, how will you get away from the hospital to see Salman Ebeid. I should be the one to go."

"The surgery should take at least three or four hours. I'll go while father is in recovery. It will not seem strange that I leave the floor during that time."

"Can I come?"

"No, Khaan, someone has to watch Ojala and the two women the broker is forcing on us."

"There is no place for Ojala to go. I want to be a part of this."

"Let me think about it. But there is a problem. We will need transportation."

"Anwar, would Salman leave a car for us in the hospital parking lot?"

"That is a good idea, Khaan. I will text him now, then he can let me know where it is parked when we get there."

When Anwar sees Salman Ebeid, he will have to take the money. That means he will cut the plastic. It could be my chance to get the money. I'll wait until he's gone; maybe Anwar will change his mind and let Khaan go with him. This could work. It was the first time Ojala had smiled in a long time.

"Ojala," Anwar bellowed. She hoped he didn't notice her listening. She got up and went to the lounge.

"Khaan and I would like some tea and some khajur."

"Get it yourself; you're not an invalid." Ojala's contempt for her brothers and the knowledge she would soon be leaving was making her overconfident.

Anwar was up on his feet in a flash. He crossed from the lounge to where she was sitting in a few strides. He pulled down her hijab and grabbed her hair.

"You have pushed your insolence to the limit." He dragged her into the galley by her hair. "I said, get us some tea and khajur."

Ojala never said a word; she held back her tears until he left the galley, then she broke down. Covering her mouth with her hand to muffle the sound. She slid down the wall and sat on the floor until she could pull herself together.

Ojala knew if she couldn't get away from them before they got back on the yacht, they would marry her to some old man. No young man would marry her now that she was sixteen. The thought of being forced to be intimate with someone who she didn't love was more than she could bear.

I will not get back on this yacht. I don't know how, but I won't. I will not be treated like this or worse for the rest of my life.

QUANTICO

Fons came back to the break room. "We have approval for a dedicated satellite and authorization to monitor Austin's DOT cameras."

"That's perfect. Sophie has a plan to get Makhtar out of the hospital. My question is, how does the Seal team get to the targets, without a firefight or a hostage situation on the yacht?"

"I can answer that," Terry entered the break room and grabbed some cookies and a small milk carton from the fridge.

As he sat, Houston asked, "What's your plan?"

"Same as we did when we stole the counterfeit money off the Korean ship," Seal team leader, Terry Abbott, said, shoving a cookie in his mouth.

"You're going to attach the Zodiac Milpro to the ship's hull?" Fons asked.

"Exactly. Ms. Star will have to get all the civilians corralled on the upper deck, to keep them from being hurt or used as hostages. We'll begin our seize at 1 am."

"You want everyone else asleep when you breach?" Houston said, agreeing with the plan.

"Denny will send us live feed from the time the Hijazis land at Corpus Christi," Fons said. "With the dedicated satellite, we will have full coverage."

ON A YACHT SOMEWHERE IN THE ATLANTIC

Ojala served the seasoned fish and rice she had prepared for supper. This time she served her brothers first, then took a tray to her father. She sat with him until he finished and fell asleep. Her father had been sleeping a lot; Ojala knew that was a bad sign.

It was time for 'salat'; her brothers took their rugs to the lounge, as had been their custom on this journey. Usually, their father joined them, but he was too weak.

Ojala went to her room. She would not participate in the radical beliefs that her brothers did. She wanted nothing to do with the kind of religion that produced such hateful men. She knew all Muslims were not radicals, most were good, peaceful men.

Dori, Ojala's only friend in Geneva, would sneak into her room when her brothers left and visit with her. Dori was always happy; her family treated her like a precious jewel. She often talked about the church she went to. Dori sat with her family; the men and women weren't separated. There was happy music, and the pastor spoke of a mighty God who sent his son Jesus to die for our sins.

Ojala didn't understand any of it, but if she were to pray, it would be to Dori's God. *I wish I knew if you were real. If you were, I would ask you to help me get away from my family. I love my father, but I won't be forced to marry someone, and be traded as if I am property, like a sheep or a goat.*

AUSTIN, TX

Lawson opened the gate leading to Emmett's back patio. That's where family and friends went when they visited. The back sliding glass door was partially opened, and Lawson stuck his head in and called out for Emmett.

"Lawson, come in, grab something to drink from the fridge. I'll be right there."

"Thanks, Emmett."

A few minutes later, Emmett came out of the garage with a dozen packages of butcher-wrapped meat in his arms. "Can you open the fridge for me, Lawson?"

Lawson hurried to the fridge and opened it, taking some packages out of his hands.

"I need to thaw out some more steaks for this weekend. I picked up another quarter cow from the butcher."

"Is the BBQ at your house this weekend?"

"No, I'm going to send this over to Xander's. He's back in town and wanted it at his house. I like to help supply the meat."

"I'm glad he's back from LA. I miss him when he's gone."

"He was meeting with the studio to get funding for his dad's new script."

"Why do they even have to ask anymore. Everything they touch turns to box office gold," Lawson asked, closing the fridge after Emmett put the last package in.

"It seems ridiculous, doesn't it. But those studio types like to flex their muscles." Emmett grabbed a cup of coffee and sat down for a minute. "I have chicken and baked potatoes on the grill. They should be ready soon."

"I could smell them on the way in."

"Grab your juice, and I'll baste some more BBQ sauce on them." Emmett grabbed the salad he had made and the dressing from the fridge, and they headed outside.

"Emmett, you should market your BBQ sauce. It's the best I've ever tasted." Lawson said as he watched Emmett slather the chicken with more sauce.

"I'll let Jared do it if he wants to. I don't want to deal with it."

Lawson sat quietly, watching Emmett turn the chicken and slather the other side. "You found Sophie?" He asked softly.

"Not me. Cade and Dex."

"How?"

"Sophie was at one of Cade's concerts, and he saw her."

"Why haven't you told anyone?"

"She asked us not to. If Cade hadn't noticed her, I doubt she would have contacted him."

"Why, Emmett? Why won't she come back? Does she hate us?"

Emmett turned and saw Lawson was upset. "No, Lawson. Sophie had managed to separate herself from the painful memories of her past. She told me the first few years she was gone were difficult. Sophie finally distanced herself from the heartache. She said it started to feel like the memories weren't hers but belonged to someone else. That eventually gave her peace, and the memories stayed locked away.

"Recently, she started having dreams. Sophie said she would wake up crying, recognizing the heartbreak but not the dreams. Then one day, she remembered the dream and the memories. Now she is afraid of being rejected."

"How can someone do that? Just shut down their past."

"Trauma. Losing her father and her fiancé a few weeks apart was too much. Besides the fact that Duke took the bullet meant for her... she blames herself for the pain David and Anna were going through."

"She never even said goodbye to me."

"Lawson, you told her to leave you alone," Emmett started putting the chicken on a platter.

"True. Does Sophie look the same...? Is she married?"

"Yes, she's married to a man who was once her bodyguard. And she looks great; age has added a new dimension to her."

"Her bodyguard? Why did she need a bodyguard?" Lawson asked.

"Apparently, she worked for the Morano family, who ran a drug empire. The DEA and several other agencies had been after the family for years but couldn't prove their case.

Sophie didn't just leave us when she walked away. She walked away from her faith in God too. She ended up going to work for the Moranos.

"Sophie left the organization to escape the man running the empire at the time, Nikko Morano. While hiding, she found her way back to the Lord. When she did, she decided to try to help the DEA take down Nikko Morano.

"They put together a task force, and she called the shots. She insisted on protection. Houston was on her detail."

"Sophie always managed to find trouble. I hated that she would put herself in harm's way." Lawson shook his head. After Emmett put the food on the table and they said grace. Lawson grabbed a chicken breast, a thigh, a baked potato, and salad, placing them on his plate. "This looks great, Emmett."

"I hear your patient will be in town soon," Emmett said.

"I heard that. Who is this guy I'm doing surgery on? And why is Sophie involved with any of this?" Lawson asked, finishing up the last of his chicken. "I know she belongs to some task force, but why is this guy so important?" Lawson looked past Emmett to the big tree the kids used to climb. He missed being Sophie's friend.

"I can't tell you that. I don't know the whole story; it's classified."

"I'll do the surgery, of course. And I'll do anything to keep Marci and Sophie safe. But if this is a really bad guy, I should be told."

"Why, Lawson? Do you decide now, who is worthy to live and who isn't?"

Lawson didn't like being called on the carpet. Not many people called him out these days. He was a highly regarded doctor. That's why it was important for him to be around the people who knew him most of his life, people he trusted. They had no problem with telling him when he was wrong. Besides, Emmett was right.

"No, I would still work on him. I guess I just want to know."

"Lawson, I got a call from the First Lady. She wanted me to bring you in on some of the details of the mission. Since you need five days of monitoring, the task force has asked a Navy doctor to finish up the protocol, so you won't be in default with the FDA. But there is a complication."

"You said a Navy doctor will monitor him from there. As long as he fills out the paperwork, it's not a problem." Lawson said.

Emmett hesitated, "the First Lady explained that the family will be arrested on the ocean. The Navy doctor will take over once they are arrested. But in the interim the task force wants to know if you will monitor the patient until they are arrested."

"They want me to travel with them until my patient is arrested?"

"Yes, and his two sons."

"How long?"

"I think less than 24 hours. I was not given details," Emmett said.

"I'd have to look at my schedule but if it's for a short period of time, I should be able to do that. I don't understand. Why this charade? Why not just arrest him and let me do the surgery on him. Why wait until later?"

"I have no answer to that. That would seem like the logical path, but what do I know," Emmett laughed. "Lawson, are you going to be alright seeing Sophie again? Can you work with her without your emotions getting in the way?"

"It will be hard. When I got back from Germany, I thought I was over her. But the minute I saw her, all the feelings came flooding back. It was painful."

"I saw the Good Morning Austin segment you did. Lawson, it's obvious you still love her."

Lawson looked at Emmett, "Why can't I let this go?"

"Have you prayed about it?"

"No."

"Do you think you haven't prayed about it because you know Jesus will heal you? Maybe you want to hang onto the pain of her loss because you feel it keeps a piece of her with you. The only thing of her you have left."

Lawson lowered his head. He'd learned early in his Christian life when the Holy Spirit was dealing with him. Lawson knew what Emmett said was true.

"Emmett, I loved her so much. I can't find anyone who stirs those feelings in me like she did."

"I know you loved her, still do... but Lawson, the life God had planned for her would never have melded with the life He planned for you.

"You're a doctor; you save the lives of God's tiniest children and now adults. You were made to do that. Sophie saves lives, too but in a different way. I can't tell you about some of her operations, but I can tell you what she has done is remarkable. But you two had different paths to walk.

"The man she's married to is her partner. He is the right person for her. And God has the right person for you, too. But until you let go of Sophie, you will never see it. You don't want to lose your opportunity to be happy by hanging onto something you wanted but was never meant for you."

Lawson's eyes watered. He knew it was true. He just couldn't do it.

Before Lawson could answer, Jared came around the corner, "Hi, Dad." Then he noticed Lawson and could see they were having a serious conversation. "Sorry, I didn't know you had company. Hi, Lawson. I can come back."

"No, son, come in; chicken and baked potatoes are on the grill." Emmett felt Lawson needed a break. He needed to process what he heard.

"Are you sure?" Jared stepped closer.

"Yes, son, come eat."

CORPUS CHRISTI, TX. FRIDAY.

Fons and Roman headed to the Hertz rental counter to pick up the SUV the FBI rented for them. Roman received a text from his contact that said he delivered the RV; it was parked a few miles away. Houston, Lt. Murphy, and Rocky headed to the carousel to pick up the luggage.

Fons and Roman pulled up in front of the luggage area and waited for the others to come out.

After everyone was on board, they headed to the RV.

They decided after they picked up the RV, they would find a hotel for the night. Roman spoke with the captain and was told they wouldn't be at the slip until late tomorrow afternoon.

They found a nice motel on the outskirts of town and got rooms.

Before they retired for the night, they decided to eat at a BBQ joint they passed on the way to the motel. They figured they could treat themselves to authentic Texas BBQ.

"Someone needs to call the doctor to tell him we will be at the Heart Hospital late tomorrow night."

"I'll call him," Marci said. "I'll tell him I'll call when the yacht docks. It's a four-hour drive from there.

"Emmett will be our lookout for anyone who might know Sophie or me. But he knows not to acknowledge us in any way," Marci informed them.

"He is a good man. I trust him," Houston said.

CHAPTER FOURTEEN

ON A YACHT SOMEWHERE IN THE ATLANTIC. SATURDAY

Anwar and Khaan helped their father to the lower deck to get fresh air.

"Father, would you like some tea," Khaan asked as he eased his father down to the oversized couch. Anwar lifted his father's legs to the hassock.

"Yes, that would be good…and khajur too."

Khaan stepped down into the lounge and hollered for his sister. Ojala stepped out of her room. She had been staying as far away from her brothers since Anwar's last abuse.

"Yes."

"Father needs tea and khajur. He's on the lower deck."

"Alright."

"Do it quickly," Khaan spit out.

"I heard you," Ojala spat back and got a glaring stare from her brother.

As Ojala brought tea and khajur on a tray to her father and brothers, she saw the captain speaking to them.

"We should be docking at 5 o'clock this evening. An RV will pick you up and take you to Austin from Corpus Christi." Captain Mandrapilias spoke in heavily accented English.

"Thank you, Captain. Will you be taking us back to Sanremo?" Makhtar asked pleasantly.

"Yes, Mr. Ricci, I will stay here until you come back."

"Thank you, Captain."

"Prego."

Ojala waited until the captain left before she stepped up to the lower deck from the lounge. She set the tray on the small coffee table next to her father. After pouring him tea and placing some khajur on a plate, she kissed his forehead and left when her father stopped her.

"Ojala, we will be docking soon. Pack my things for me."

"Yes, Father."

How am I supposed to get away from my brothers? I'll only have a few days to do it. Once we return to this yacht, I will never have another opportunity, especially if we return to Afghanistan. But I have no one to help me, and I will be on the streets if I cannot get a little of the money in Anwar's suitcase. Ojala took her father's suitcase from the closet and set it on the bed, then she plopped down next to it, covered her face, and sobbed quietly.

Oh, how I wish Dori's God was real. That he would love me like he does Dori. He would help me.

CORPUS CHRISTI

The team in Corpus Christi ate breakfast at the hotel they were staying in. A loud bout of laughter came from their table.

"Marci, there should be a confidentiality clause that attaches to parents and their children," Sophie complained as her childhood shenanigans were the subject of the other's laughter.

"Oh, Sophie, dear, there would be no entertainment in our lives without the stories of our children," she chuckled.

"Yes, indeed. But you have been a good sport, Sophie," Roman acknowledged before Rocky's cell rang. He looked at the caller ID.

"It's the captain," Rocky said.

"Yes, Captain. Do you have news for me?" They were speaking in Italian.

"Yes, we should be docking in Corpus Christi at 5 o'clock, their time."

"Thank you, and you will stay in the house I've arranged for you near the slip until they return?"

"Yes."

"Thank you, Captain. And the bonus I mentioned will be put into your account when you've completed your end."

"Thank you. I am at your disposal anytime."

"I'll keep that in mind. Arrivederci."

"Arrivederci," the captain ended the call.

"They will be here at 5 pm, Roman."

"Alright, we will have to clear our hotel rooms and separate. You have our route to Austin, as we discussed, Houston?"

"Yes. I wish you would let us put a tracker on your RV."

"No, the Hijazis are very cunning men. They might check the RV for listening devices and trackers before they get on."

"I'm sure you are right. We will stay far enough ahead of you that your passengers can't make us."

Roman insisted on paying the bill for the group, and after collecting their things, they checked out.

Roman and Rocky went down to the slip when the yacht came into view. Sophie and Marci stayed by the RV. Sophie's eyes landed on the passengers; there was no way to tell by looking that the Hijazis were terrorists and killed more than eight hundred people with one bomb. Sophie looked up to the sky; gray clouds were closing in, and she could feel a chill in the air.

The older man and one of the sons were built the same, broad shoulders and chests. But the son was muscular, unlike his father, who looked weak. The younger brother was smaller and looked more like a professor than a terrorist. Sophie saw the girl take her hijab off her head and drop it on the deck. Her hair was long and black, and she was maybe 5'2", slim, like the younger brother.

When the yacht docked, the captain's son jumped off and landed on the pier to secure the ship. The Hijazis waited on deck.

Captain Mandrapilias laid a ramp to cover the short gap between the yacht and the pier. After the family disembarked, the captain handed the luggage to his son, who remained on the dock.

Roman directed them toward the RV. He did not introduce himself or his brother or help them with their luggage. They supposedly were hired to drive, and they were acting the part.

When they reached the RV, Rocky placed their suitcases in the outside luggage compartment and latched the cover. As the girl came closer, Sophie noticed she wore heavy eye makeup.

"Mr. Ricci," Marci addressed Makhtar. "My name is Marci Smith," she turned to Sophie, "and this is Sophie Jones. We have been hired to escort you to the hospital and back here to ensure you have no complications during your stay."

Makhtar nodded. "Yes, I was told you would be here."

"We need to get my father inside and lay him down, Ms. Smith. Please excuse us."

"Of course," Marci moved aside.

Sophie watched as Khaan walked around the RV with a small black box in his hand. *Roman was right; he is checking for trackers.*

While Anwar was settling Makhtar, Marci sent Emmett a text with their estimated arrival time to pass on to Lawson. Then she and Sophie boarded, and Marci closed the curtain that separated the driver from the rest of the RV. Khaan was the last to step in; Rocky closed the door to the back and got into the front passenger seat.

Ojala sat next to Sophie. She looked to see if her brothers were watching her. Then spoke, "my name is Giada, Mr. Ricci is my father, and those are my brothers."

"Yes, it is a pleasure to meet you, Giada."

"Are you American citizens?" Ojala asked.

"Yes."

"If I tell...." Ojala was interrupted by Anwar hollering for her. She went to the bedroom in the back.

"I don't want you talking to those infidels; they will put nonsense into your head," Anwar ordered.

"I can't ignore them; we are supposed to act like westerners," Ojala blurted back.

Anwar got in her face, his jaw set, "do what I say. Sit in here with your father."

Anwar and Khaan nodded to Marci and Sophie, who sat in the seats closest to the driver. The brothers sat on the bench seats at the table. They whispered softly in Arabic so no one could understand their conversation.

Marci hit record on her cell. She planned to send it to Denny at the command center for interpretation when they finished speaking.

Sophie could hear the rain hitting on the metal roof of the RV. There was something sinister going on with those men. Sophie prayed and asked the Lord to reveal their plans so they could stop it. She leaned over and whispered to Marci.

"I'm not sure having them here, in the US, is a good idea."

"Why not?"

"I don't know, but they are planning something. I can feel it."

Marci nodded to her cell, and Sophie realized she was recording the brother's conversation. The brothers spoke for several hours. Anwar went in to check on his father off and on.

Sophie was startled by Ojala yelling something in Arabic from the bedroom. She was crying, telling her father to wake up.

Everyone hurried to the back bedroom to see Ojala shaking her father.

Ojala looked up as her brothers came in.

"He won't wake up!"

"What did you do? Move out of the way," Anwar shoved her aside to get to him. Ojala moved to the doorway where Sophie and Marci were looking on.

Anwar checked to see if he was breathing.

"He's unconscious but breathing," Anwar put his fingers on Makhtar's wrist to check his pulse. "His pulse is weak," Anwar looked at Marci.

"I'll call ahead to the hospital and let them know we will be at their emergency room in…." Marci looked at her watch, "forty minutes."

Anwar moved to the hall where Marci stood with her phone to her ear. "If he dies, you will die too."

Sophie pushed him back, "Back up, or I'll have the driver stop this thing, and you will walk from here."

He swatted her words away like they were flies.

Marci was talking to the emergency room, "we have an elderly patient of Dr. Cornett's. He is unconscious; we are about thirty-five minutes from your hospital."

"You are certain he is breathing?" the person on the other end asked.

"Yes, and we found a weak pulse."

"Alright, I will contact Dr. Cornett, and we will expect you at the ambulance bay."

"Thank you."

When Marci hung up, she turned to Anwar. "You must stay with your father and let me know if he quits breathing. We'll need to start CPR if he does. The hospital is expecting us at the ambulance bay. I'll tell the driver to speed. If the police stop us, they will escort us the rest of the way."

Marci pulled back the curtain that separated the driver from them. "Mr. Ricci is unconscious; we must get to the hospital fast."

Roman nodded and pushed his speed to eighty-five, fast for an RV of this size. Rocky texted Houston to let him know what was going on.

It didn't take long to pass Houston's SUV.

THE HEART HOSPITAL. AUSTIN

Roman pulled into the ambulance bay, and Rocky jumped out, running inside to get help. He returned and opened the door for the doctor and nurse who followed him.

It was close quarters, so the doctor asked everyone to leave the RV so he and his nurse could attend to the patient.

Two men with a hardboard stretcher came in a few seconds behind them, and a gurney was left just outside the RV door.

Makhtar was placed on the stretcher, carried out to the gurney, and then rolled into the emergency room. Anwar and Khaan followed them.

Ojala was trembling, standing outside the door watching her father being rolled away.

"Giada, don't you want to follow them?" Sophie asked, gently putting her arm around her. Ojala shook her head.

"Sophie, I need to register him," Marci said. Roman went with her. Rocky asked Sophie if they were going inside. Sophie shook her head, and she and Ojala stepped back up into the RV. Rocky closed the door and got into the driver's seat, heading to a parking spot in the closest hospital parking area. The RV was too large to take into the three-layer parking garage attached to the hospital.

"I know how scary it is to see your father sick like this." Sophie tried to calm the girl down.

"Ms. Jones, I love my father, but he is not a good man. If I tell you something that would save lives, would your government allow me to stay in the US?"

Sophie was surprised by her statement. "It depends on if, by telling us, your life would be in danger if you go back to your home country. And we would have to be able to verify it."

"Yes, if I tell you this, my family will kill me. But whether you help me stay or not. I cannot go back with them."

"What is going on, Giada?"

Ojala turned to face Sophie more directly. "You are not aware, but my family are jihadists. You call them terrorists. I heard my father and brothers talking. My brother told my father that many of his followers had crossed the southern border in the last few months. Anw...Paolo will meet with one while he is here to give him money to support the cause."

"Where is this money coming from?"

"It's in his suitcase. I saw it myself."

"Ok, but that is not against the law."

"No, but what they plan on doing with it is," Ojala lowered her voice and her head.

"Do you know what they plan to do with it?"

"Yes," she looked back at Sophie. "They plan on blowing up this hospital as soon as my father leaves."

Sophie sucked in a breath. "You are certain of this?"

"Yes, I was on the upper deck; I could hear them. My father told my brothers what he wanted them to have done," Ojala paused. "Can you help me?"

"Do you have family here?"

"No. I don't know anyone. But I won't go back, even if I have to live on the street. My father will force me to marry some old man who will make me his slave and beat me." Ojala covered her face and wept.

Sophie hugged her. "I'll help you, Giada. Just give me time to figure it out." She waited for Ojala to stop crying and said, "we better get you inside before your brothers come to find you."

"You promise you will help?"

"Yes."

It was raining hard outside. Ojala grabbed a jacket with a hood, and Sophie put on her jacket, lifting the hood too.

Rocky followed Sophie and Ojala in. Roman was at the entrance to the hospital, closest to the emergency room. Rocky pulled him aside. He spoke to him in Italian.

"The girl," he pointed to Ojala. "Told Sophie her brothers are having the hospital blown up once they are gone."

Even though Roman knew of their treachery, he was shocked. "We need to talk to Houston." He pulled out his phone and sent a text: **We need to meet. NOW.**

The response came: **There is a Catholic Church across the street. Meet us in the foyer.**

Roman didn't reply. He and Rocky started heading toward the church.

Lawson had gotten the call from the hospital that his patient was unconscious. He went to his office and waited to hear when the patient arrived.

When he got the call, he headed down to emergency and found Mr. Ricci being worked on by the emergency room doctor.

"What are his vitals?" Lawson asked.

"HR is 50 bpm, BP is 50/45, RR is dropping, O2 is up now that he is hooked up, and his temperature is 96.8°."

"Thank you, doctor; we need to get him prepped for surgery," Lawson turned to the nurse. "Can you get an orderly here and transport him to the surgical floor. My team is on standby."

"Yes, Doctor."

Lawson headed to the second floor. His team was already there prepping the room. Lawson's scrub nurse helped him get ready for the surgery.

Anwar and Khaan wanted to follow their father's gurney. The ER nurse told them to go out through the ER waiting room and take the elevator to the second floor.

As they headed to the elevator, they saw Marci speaking with the registration desk. Anwar stopped.

"Is everything taken care of, as promised?" Anwar asked, agitated.

Marci excused herself from the lady taking the information. "Yes, I'm registering him now."

"Alright, we are going to the second floor to wait. They are prepping my father for surgery," Anwar looked around. "Where is Giada?"

"She was in the RV when the driver went to park it. She will be here in a moment." Marci looked up as the entrance door slid open, and Sophie and Ojala walked in.

Anwar turned. He stepped over to her and grabbed her arm. "You stay with us. Do you hear me?"

"Yes, let go of me. You can't abuse me here."

"Don't push me, Oj...Giada."

Ojala got on the elevator with her brothers. Sophie waited until Marci finished registering Makhtar before speaking to her.

"Did you say Emmett is here?" Sophie looked around for him.

"He said he would be here," Marci moved closer to her.

"I need to talk to him," Sophie pulled out her cell and moved to a corner away from everyone."

"Hello?"

"Hi, Grandpa."

"Sophie, I didn't recognize your number."

"It's a task force secure cell," Sophie paused. "Grandpa, are you at the hospital?"

"Yes."

"Marci and I need to leave for a moment. Can you watch Mr. Ricci's sons? They are in the waiting room on the second floor."

"Sure."

"Grandpa, the older one...I'll send you a picture. Can you watch him and call immediately if he leaves the second floor? It's imperative we do not lose track of him," Sophie said. Marci pulled up Anwar's picture on her cell and sent it to Emmett, while Sophie was still talking to him.

"Yes, I can do that. I'm on the second floor now."

"Be careful, Grandpa," Sophie said and hung up, then turned to Marci.

"What's going on?" Marci asked.

"We need to talk to DC. Ojala told me her father ordered this hospital bombed when he leaves."

"What?" Marci lowered her voice. "How does she know this?"

"Ojala heard them make plans on the yacht. She wants asylum in the US."

"Alright, let's bring Houston and Roman up to date."

Marci pulled out her cell to text Roman: **Where are you?**

The reply came instantly: **The Catholic church across the street.**

The rain had slowed down, but Marci hadn't taken her jacket with her when she left the RV because it was under the ambulance bay cover.

"Take my coat, Marci. I have a thicker shirt on than you."

"No, I won't let you get wet."

"I insist."

A lady passing by heard them arguing and handed Sophie a small plastic item. It was folded like an accordion, she realized it was a pocket-size rain bonnet.

"Thank you, but I can't take this; you will get wet when you leave," Sophie said to the stranger.

"I insist," she said. "My husband will pick me up under this portico when I'm ready to leave."

"Are you sure?"

"Yes, dear, I'm sure."

"Thank you."

Sophie took her hooded jacket off and gave it to Marci, then snapped the plastic rain bonnet on, and they hurried across the street.

As they walked, Sophie realized she hadn't asked the older woman's name.

When Marci and Sophie reached the church door, the rain had picked up again. The men were waiting in the foyer for them. Houston noticed his wife's clothes were wet. He took off his light jacket and helped her put it on.

Sophie looked around the foyer. It looked like the church she and her friends hid in from Turkish mobsters when she lived in Adana, Turkey.

There was a small gift shop with a display window showcasing rosary beads and confirmation Bibles. On the other side of the opening to the sanctuary was a baby room where mothers could take crying infants and still hear and see the Mass.

"You need to get out of those wet clothes, sweetheart," Houston said.

"I will, but first, we need to get some information to Director Cosby. We can't stay gone long. Grandpa is watching the brothers for now."

"Rocky gave us a rundown of what Ojala said," Fons spoke softly.

"Let's sit in the back of the sanctuary; we can be overheard out here," Roman directed his wife to the inside door and opened it for her, then held it for the others. They sat in the last few pews, away from the door, and angled themselves so they could speak quietly.

Sophie noticed a woman putting money in a small metal box next to the display of candles at the front of the church. She lit one, then knelt to pray. There were other people scattered around close to the confessionals. The light was on, indicating the priest was there to hear confessions.

Sophie told them what Ojala said. "Before we hang up with the director, I want to talk to Ms. Martin about getting Ojala asylum papers. I promised her we would help."

"Flynn brought his secure computer with him," he looked over to Flynn. "He'll get us a secure conference video set up with Denny, so we can talk to Director Cosby."

"Already on it, sir."

"I believe her; Makhtar has already proven he would do something like this," Rocky said.

"I do too. We are going to need more help. We can do what we did when we tracked the counterfeit money the cell leaders picked up from the storage shed," Fons agreed.

"That worked well. But I don't know if it will work here. We will have a live bomb in play. If we lost Anwar's contact even for a moment ...," Sophie said.

"I thought he said they wouldn't blow it up until after Makhtar left," Marci said.

"Yes, but he could place the bomb anytime. Then all he needs to do is detonate it." Sophie said.

"And he could do that from anywhere," Houston finished her train of thought.

"Exactly," Sophie nodded.

"Ma'am, I have a connection; Agent Smith is calling Director Cosby now," Flynn said.

"Flynn, will you call Trindi for me. See if she can get to Quantico right away. We can't discuss this over the phone.

"I'll call her," Flynn moved away.

CHAPTER FIFTEEN

Fons was manning Lt. Murphy's computer while Flynn was on the phone. He saw Denny's face come on screen and turned the volume up enough to hear him.

"Director Cosby is walking in now," Denny announced. Fons turned the computer to Sophie.

"Ms. Star, why are you contacting me? Is there an issue?"

"Yes. Makhtar's sixteen-year-old daughter, Ojala, asked if we would give her asylum if she gave us some important information."

"Alright, Ms. Star. What is it?"

"Will you guarantee her asylum and immunity?" Sophie asked.

"Ms. Star, we have been this route before. We cannot give out asylum like its candy on Halloween. Even if the information is important, would it be verifiable? And why would she need immunity?"

"The information is a matter of urgency, sir. And she needs immunity because she is part of the family and could be accused of being a participant."

"You are certain she isn't?"

"Yes, sir."

"And I take it she has already told you the information?"

"Yes."

"Then I insist that you tell me, Ms. Star."

"Yes, sir, but I want to make sure the promise I made to her will be kept."

"You know that is up to the DOJ, but haven't we always?" Director Cosby was getting annoyed.

"Yes, sir. Ojala told me she overheard her father tell Anwar to give money to one of their trusted followers. This man is the head of over one hundred of Makhtar's followers who came over the southern border in the last few months. They have scattered the new men across Texas and created six-man cells.

"Apparently, this man is the head of this network and the go-between for Makhtar and these followers. He wants this man to blow up the hospital once he has left."

"What?!" Cosby couldn't mask his shock.

Roman scooted over, so Cosby could see him on the screen. "Director, I believe her. He blew up the hospital in Milan. It's in his wheelhouse."

"Yes, I'm aware, but we can't just take her word for it."

Houston motioned to Fons to move the screen in his direction. "Is SRT here, sir?"

"Yes, they are being housed at Camp Mabry," Cosby replied.

"Sir, if he leaves the property like she said, then we must also believe the rest is true. Our team has been discussing the pros and cons of repeating the action we took with the terrorist cells when they split up the counterfeit North Korean money. We captured the leaders and most cell members in that network." Houston paused. Flynn caught Sophie's eye and nodded, indicating Trindi would get there ASAP.

"What are the cons, Agent Townsend."

"Sir, if we lose the network leader, even for a second, he could plant the bomb. And if we arrest him, the others will go underground, and we won't be able to arrest them."

"I thought you said he wasn't to blow it up until the Hijazis left."

"He's not, but that doesn't mean he can't plant it and detonate later when he gets word they are far enough away."

"We are getting ahead of ourselves. How do we find out who this cell leader is? Did the girl give you his name or where he lives?"

Fons turned the computer back to Sophie. "No, sir. But she heard Anwar say he would take money to the man to split it with the other cell leaders to support their network."

"So, that is why you thought we could do what we did before. Do you know how much money they are talking about?"

"Yes, two hundred thousand dollars. Ojala saw way more than that in his suitcase."

"Cash?"

"Yes. Anwar plans on meeting with the man while his father is in recovery. Lt. Denison's men can follow Anwar and find where this man lives."

"How is he going to leave the hospital? Steal a car? He can't drive that RV around. It's too conspicuous."

"Ojala said the cell leader was leaving a car for him in the hospital parking lot."

"Did she hear what kind? We could put a tracker on it."

"No, sir. But Khaan has a small tracking detector with him. I saw him go around the RV with it."

"Alright, Houston, Fons, one or both of you will have to surveil him if he leaves the hospital before SRT gets there. Don't get spotted."

"Yes, sir."

"That leads us back to the rest of this network. This might be our only chance to catch them. Do you have a plan, Ms. Star?" Director Cosby asked.

"Yes. We can loan Lt. Murphy and his drone to Lt. Denison. As long as they don't lose our main guy, we could give the SRT a few days to locate and surveil the other cell leaders. They just can't take anyone into custody until after the bomb maker is captured. I'm sure SRT brought their surveillance equipment."

"Yes, and what they don't have, we can borrow from Camp Mabry."

"Sir, Ms. Martin said she was heading to Quantico so I could talk to her about the asylum issue. Houston and Fons will work out all the logistics with Lt. Denison. They can coordinate with the operations center," a shiver ran through her. The wet clothes had lowered her body temperature. "I need to change out of these wet clothes." Sophie turned the computer over to Houston. Then whispered to Marci, and they moved out of the pew.

"Marci, you better get back to the waiting room. I'll change my clothes and meet you there. I'm sure that surgery will take hours, but we need to ensure Anwar doesn't leave. I need to wait for Ms. Martin."

"Alright."

Roman overheard. "I'll walk you as far as the RV and bring back Sophie's bag so she can change."

"Thank you, Roman," Sophie said.

Houston stepped over to his wife. "Fons and I will coordinate things from our SUV. We'll be ready to follow Anwar if he leaves before SRT arrives."

Sophie was changed when Flynn called her over. Ms. Martin was at the operations center.

Denny came on the screen; Flynn raised the volume enough so they could hear. Ms. Martin came into view. Sophie sat down in front of Flynn, who was smiling seeing his girlfriend on the screen. He turned the screen toward Sophie and balanced it on the back of the pew he was sitting in. Sophie was on the bench behind him.

"Ms. Star, what is so important I had to leave DC for it?" Trindi always took that cold, austere tone with her. Flynn once told Sophie that Trindi needed it to get respect from the male prosecutors at DOJ. But she was nothing like that outside the office.

"Thank you for accommodating me, Ms. Martin."

"It seems I spend a lot of time doing that," this time, she gave herself away when her lips almost pulled up into a smile.

Sophie explained the portion of what was going on that would be pertinent to the asylum request.

"Ojala asked for asylum and immunity for the information. I told her if the information was verifiable, she would be eligible."

"You often promise things that are not in your purview. But why immunity if the girl is not involved?" Ms. Martin asked.

"You know why. And I realize I ask a lot of you, but the information I shared with you certainly qualifies."

"Yes, it does. I'll get the paperwork started."

"Thank you, Trindi," Sophie smiled. Ms. Martin was surprised at the informal response from her but smiled.

"I'll send you a copy when they are signed. But the other issue is her age. The girl can't just be put out on the street if she is sixteen. We need to have a guardian for her," Ms. Martin said.

Roman was sitting close and heard the statement. He moved closer so he could be seen on the screen. "Ms. Martin, Marci, and I will take responsibility for her."

"Who are you?"

"I'm Marci's husband, Roman DeCarlo. Director Perry will vouch for me."

Trindi knew Director Perry was the head of the CIA clandestine unit.

"In that unit, you will be out of the country more often than not. This girl needs guardians who are around."

"Marci and I are retired."

"It seems not. You're on a mission as we speak."

"At the request of your government."

"Point taken. I'll check it out."

"Thank you," Sophie moved back into view and signed off. Flynn turned the computer back to him and officially signed off.

"Roman, are you sure Marci will be all right with this. It's a huge commitment," Sophie whispered. Rocky was sitting next to Roman.

"If Marci isn't alright with it, my wife and I will take her," Rocky volunteered.

Roman smiled, "Marci will agree."

Houston spoke up. "We need to get into the SUV in case we're needed. Flynn will get us online with Lt. Denison."

"Ok, Houston, I'm going back to the hospital," Sophie said.

"Rocky and I will stick around the cafeteria and the front entrance to keep an eye out. Will you let Marci know? The brothers won't think it strange seeing us around since we are their ride back."

"I'll tell her. Thanks, Roman." Sophie headed to the door. Houston carried her suitcase as he walked with her as far as the RV and placed it inside. Then he gave her a quick kiss and they parted ways.

"Be careful, sweetheart."

"I will; you too."

Sophie got off the elevator on the second floor. She saw Emmett sitting in the area by a small chapel. They did not acknowledge each other in any way.

Sophie walked toward the surgical waiting area and saw Anwar and Khaan sitting together, whispering. Ojala was seated next to Marci. Sophie stepped up to the brothers.

"Did anyone say how long the surgery will take?"

Anwar looked up at her, "No. No one has told us anything."

Sophie nodded. "If you need me to get you some food at the cafeteria, let me know." Anwar nodded, and Sophie went to sit with Ojala and Marci.

"Were you able to get me asylum?" Ojala whispered.

"Yes, and immunity," Sophie said.

"Why would I need immunity? I'm not part of what they do," Ojala said, her eyes big, frightened.

"We don't want to take the chance that some prosecutor will decide you are."

"Oh, ok. Thank you. Can I leave now?"

"Giada, you are sixteen. We can't leave you alone in a country where you know no one. We will set up guardians for you."

"Do I get a say in who I stay with?"

"I think so. But Giada, you must stay with us until we get your family safely off US soil. We will take you with us when we get off the yacht."

"No, I can't stay with them. They won't let me leave. I need to go now."

"Giada, it's part of the agreement. You must stick with us until we are in international waters."

Ojala started to cry. Khaan turned and looked at her. He assumed she was crying about her father and turned around.

"Please, don't make me stay. I can't take any more abuse," Ojala cried.

"Shh…. Do you trust us?"

"I don't know you?"

Marci put her hand on Ojala's chin and turned her head, so she was looking at her. "Giada, trust us. We will not let them take you." Giada nodded and took the Kleenex Marci handed her.

While they waited for news about the surgery, other patients' families came and went. Sophie wondered if they were SRT plants. She didn't think there were so many surgeries on Saturday. The brothers were sitting in the row closest to the surgery unit's door. She, Marci, and Ojala were seated in the furthest row against the wall.

When Sophie changed, she put a cardigan over her outfit, so the brothers wouldn't notice. Her cell vibrated in the pocket.

Sophie pulled out her phone and read the text: **Recorded conversation translated. Know where the car is and the name, Salman Ebeid.**

Sophie didn't reply. After showing Marci, she deleted it even though the phone would do it in ten minutes. The FBI created an App after an undercover was killed when his target got ahold of his phone. Their phones were programmed to delete phone numbers after one use, and texts were deleted after ten minutes.

Houston arranged with Lt. Denison to meet behind the Central Park Shopping Center, one block from the hospital. The loading dock was on one side of the alley, and a ten-foot unmaintained strip of property was on the other. They parked there.

Houston saw four non-descript vehicles and one black SUV with tinted windows. The caravan pulled up behind Houston, who was standing outside of his SUV with Fons.

Lt. Denison stepped out of his black SUV and walked over to Houston. "Hello, Agent Townsend, Agent Rodriguez," they shook hands.

"Good to see you, Lieutenant," Houston said. By then, the other drivers had formed a small circle around them.

"Have you been briefed?" They all nodded. "Lt. Murphy found the car left for Anwar. He said he could get into the car's computer system from under the dash; he's doing it now. Once we have the address, how do you want to handle this, Troy?

"Once he gives us the address, Costa and Dunlap will head there. We're hoping to find a way to get eyes and ears inside," Denison said.

"The man is likely home if he's left his car here for Anwar," Fons mentioned. His cell dinged. Fons took it out of his pocket and read it aloud.

"Salman Ebeid's address is 2508 Janice in the Tarrytown area."

"Alright, head out," Denison directed Costa and Dunlap. "I'll send some back up soon." The men took off in one of the nondescript vehicles. Lt. Murphy jogged up behind them.

"Good job, Flynn," Houston said, turning back to Denison. "What's your plan, Lieutenant?"

"The op center sent us everything they had on Salman when they translated the conversation Marci had recorded. That's not his real name, which is why we had trouble locating him. His real name is Russ Keeton. He was a civilian worker in Afghanistan and ended up indoctrinated and became a follower of Makhtar. That's when he changed his name to Salman Ebeid. The op center had no address for him or utilities in his name," Lieutenant Denison said.

"Flynn, get into your secure network and find out who owns that property," Houston said. "We need to know if other people are in that house."

"Yes, sir."

"In the meantime, we need to keep an eye on the brothers."

"We'll cover all exits to ensure neither brother leaves the hospital without a tail. Who do you have in there now?"

"Sophie and Marci are in the waiting room with them. We have a civilian on the floor as a backup. And we have the DeCarlo brothers available in the hospital for whatever we need," Houston said.

"A civilian?" Troy questioned.

"Someone known to Sophie," Houston responded. "We'll be here three days, then we will find a way to get him back on the yacht."

"The property is under the name of Rachel Wendell, sir," Murphy spoke.

"A girlfriend?" Fons moved over to look at Murphy's screen.

"No way to know, sir. She may have sublet to him."

"Alright, Lieutenant, you need to give your people a heads up. We don't want an innocent to be caught up in this. In the meantime, have the command center get what information they can on Rachel Wendell."

"Yes, sir." Denison moved away to make the call.

Anwar said something to his brother and stood. Sophie looked over to Emmett to see if he was watching. He was. She watched Anwar as he headed to the elevator: Emmett went down the stairs.

Sophie texted Houston: **Anwar is on the move. Emmett is following.**

Houston responded: **Copy that.**

"Ok, Anwar is leaving the hospital. Do you want to follow him, or do you want us to do it?" Houston asked.

"Lt. Murphy, will you join Magnus and head over to the hospital and follow Anwar when he pulls out," Lt. Denison asked.

"Yes, sir." The two men hopped into an older Taurus and drove off.

"Fons and I will trade off on surveillance, so we can get some sleep. Rocky and Roman DeCarlo can do the same. We'll share our vehicle with them. Sophie and Marci will likely stay in the RV.

"Alright, Agent Townsend, I'll work out a routine for my team. We'll keep you up to date on everything that comes in."

"Thank you."

Costa and Dunlap parked off the side of the alley behind Salman's house two doors down. There were no cars in the back or in the front. The two men carefully walked into the backyard of Salman's home. Costa peeked into the detached garage and saw that it was empty. Dunlap quietly stepped to the back door and looked through the small window. No lights were on, but the sunlight shone through all the windows; lights weren't needed.

Costa came up beside him. They gave hand signals indicating they would each go around opposite sides of the home. There were no neighbors outside to worry about seeing them, so they continued.

Costa made it to the first window with no window covering. It was the kitchen. Nicely decorated and clean. *Too nice to be a bachelor pad.* The next window was a bedroom. The blinds were open, so he could see inside. One queen size bed. The bed was made, but there were clothes on the floor. *Ok, maybe he does live here alone.*

Dunlap looked through a window, it looked like a laundry room. The next window had curtains but there was enough of a gap that he could see it was a bedroom with a single bed and a throw rug. He moved on to the next window, obviously a bathroom; the window was small with textured glass. The next was a large picture window that opened into a large dining room. No one was there, but an open laptop sat on the table.

Costa had moved past the kitchen to the next window. Closed blinds next to a small, frosted window, made him think it was likely the master bedroom and bath. The next window was big, a picture window. He carefully peeked around the side of it. It was the entry and living room. The front door opened into it.

The front of the house had two more large picture windows. One into the dining and TV room and one in to the living room. Salman Ebeid was sitting on a couch writing what looked like a shopping list. He couldn't read what was written; his back was to Costa.

Dunlap came up behind him. They moved away from the windows. "What do you see?"

"Ebeid is sitting on the couch making a list," Costa answered.

"A list of what he needs to make a bomb?"

"That's my guess. That's the living room; the front door enters it. Would there be any reason for Salman to move Anwar into another room?

"No."

"Can we use this window to get eyes and ears?"

"Yes, I need to run to the car and get my case," Costa took off running to the car."

A text came in, and Dunlap opened it: **Anwar is on the way. You have approximately ten minutes.**

Costa came back with a hard plastic case. Dunlap showed him the text.

"No problem," Costa whispered. Already getting the listening device out. He attached it to the outside window; the couch back hid it from sight. The camera was another story. Costa pulled a tiny wireless camera from the case; a suction cup was attached; it was purposed for glass. "Where do you suggest we put it. If it's seen, this whole mission is down the tubes."

"Do you have a camera with a clip?" Dunlap asked.

"Yes," Costa pulled it out of the case. He looked around, there was a tree a few feet away. One of the limbs hung down below the top of the window. It had flower buds on it, and he could hide it among those. But getting it in place without being seen was another matter.

Dunlap was watching Salman. Salman got up and headed to another room. "Do it now," Dunlap cupped his hands to lift Costa, so he could reach the branch.

Costa attached the wireless camera and then hopped down. He got in the case and turned on the screen for the camera to make sure it didn't need adjusting. The view wasn't perfect, but the whole room was covered.

"We need to get this synched with the op center." Dunlap and Costa hurried back to the vehicle.

"As soon as Anwar gets in the house, I'll place a tracker on the car," Dunlap suggested. Costa pulled out a tracker and gave it to Dunlap.

CHAPTER SIXTEEN

Ebeid came from another room to answer the knock on the door wiping his hands on a towel,

"As-salāmu ʿalaykum," Salman said after opening the door and directing Anwar to the couch.

"Wa ʿalaykumu s-salām, it is a pleasure to finally meet you.

"The honor is mine. Please be seated." Salman waited for him to get comfortable, then excused himself. Salman went to the kitchen and brought out the tea he had made. He set a cup in front of Anwar and then sat across from him in an overstuffed chair that matched the couch.

"I have the cash. You will do what you promised my father?"

"Yes, I give my word. I will fulfill our leader's wishes. I will plant it the day you leave the hospital and detonate it when you text and tell me you are off US soil."

"Yes, we must be safely in international waters. Once we are in Afghanistan, we will announce our involvement.

"Now tell me about your new network and where they are located."

Salman told Anwar about the new cell members as Anwar sipped his tea.

"They are zealots, willing to give their lives to fulfill the vision of Makhtar Hijazi. These men traveled over treacherous cartel territory in Mexico to get to the southern border.

"I can promise you every dime you supply will go to the fulfillment of your father's vision."

"I am impressed, Salman. I will let my father know he has a true follower in you. Where have you sent the men?"

"My cell is here in Austin. I sent two cells, six men each, to Dallas and Houston. The others are spread out across the state."

"Excellent. Now I must get back to the hospital."

"Is your father still in surgery?"

"Yes, I decided, because of the importance of your mission, I would come to see you now. I must return. I want to be there when he comes out of surgery."

"Surely, inshallah, such a great man would not be taken until his work is completed."

"That is true. I will pass on the blessing you spoke over him." Anwar pulled out the money he had taken from his suitcase and handed the clasped envelope to Salman.

"I will distribute it to those I know will use it in a way your father would approve."

Anwar stood, "I would expect no less. I will keep in touch. Now that the American infidels are gone from Afghanistan, we can do our work in the open as Muhammad, peace be with him, wills it."

"I wish I could be there with you," Salman said.

"No, your work is here. You will be with us in here," Anwar touched his heart. "Now, I need a ride back to the hospital."

"Yes, of course, right away," Salman grabbed the keys from Anwar's hand.

Magnus called Dunlap, "we'll be following Anwar back to the hospital."

"Good. The lieutenant wants us to look inside and plant surveillance."

"It will take at least forty minutes round trip. We'll follow Ebeid back and give you a heads up when he is close, then leave him to you," Magnus said.

"Thanks, that will give us some time to look around."

Costa started his search in the kitchen. He went through everything including the freezer and the boxes of cereal. The trick was to do it without Salman knowing anything was out of place.

Dunlap went to the bedroom where Salman slept and noticed a corner of the carpet was lifted slightly. He moved the small table away from it and pulled back the carpet. There was a trap door. Dunlap pulled it up and saw a stash of C-4.

"Costa, take a look at this."

Costa had moved to the bathroom. He came out to see what Dunlap was looking at. "He must have brought that over with him. That much C-4 purchased or stolen in the US would have been noticed."

"Yeah." Dunlap took pictures and put everything back where it was.

They called Lt. Denison to let him know what they found.

Anwar made it back to the hospital only a few minutes before Dr. Cornett came out of the surgical doors and spoke to them.

"Giada," Marci shook her; she had fallen asleep. She nodded to the doctor. Ojala got up and went to hear what the doctor had to say.

"Mr. Ricci, your father came through the surgery well. He will be taken to the ICU, and I will give permission for you to stay with him if you wish. He should come around in another thirty minutes or so."

"Where is the ICU?" Khaan asked.

"It's in the next wing," Lawson pointed. "Take the right at the end of the corridor, and there will be a sign and another waiting room."

"Thank you, Doctor," Anwar said. Lawson headed back inside the surgical unit to change.

"Father, will be well?" Ojala wanted confirmation.

"Yes. Khaan and I will stay with him in his room to guarantee he is properly taken care of. You will stay in the waiting area."

"No, I'm going to the RV to sleep," Ojala said.

"No. I say you stay in the hospital where we can check on you."

"Where can I go? I know no one here. I'm going to the RV...." Ojala demanded. Marci stepped up.

"I'll go with her; she will be safe. Sophie will stay in the waiting room in case something comes up." Marci and Sophie had discussed this while Lawson was speaking with the family. The room was full enough that Lawson hadn't noticed Sophie.

"All right," Anwar said, then turned to his sister. "But I want you here early in the morning; your father will want to see you."

Ojala nodded, then went back to where she was sitting. "Marci is going to take me to the RV, Sophie. Why can't you take me away now? Now that I know father is well, I don't need to stay," Ojala pleaded.

"Giada. If you disappear now, your brothers will not leave the country. They will stay and look for you. We need them to get back on that yacht. I promise you; Marci and I will take you with us when it is time."

Marci returned from speaking with the brothers, "come on, Giada, let's get something to eat at the cafeteria before it closes, and I'll take you to the RV." Ojala moved toward the elevator. "Sophie, why don't you eat with us. I see Emmett is still here; I'll ask him to stay until you get back."

Marci texted Emmett: **Emmett, the brothers are going to the ICU waiting room. Can you stay long enough for Sophie to get something to eat?**

The response came back: **Yes.**

"I'll meet you down there," Sophie said. She saw Emmett heading toward the ICU waiting room as she entered the chapel.

Sophie pulled out her cell and called Houston. "How are things going? I saw Anwar leave the hospital," Sophie asked.

"Everything went as planned. Anwar gave Salman the money, and we found out his plans. He is going to plant the bomb the day Makhtar is released.

"It's a bad idea to wait on picking him up. If we pick him up now, we will get the money too. That will hinder the network's ability to function. We'll find another way to get the others," Houston said.

"I agree. I don't think we can let him plant that bomb. Even if we see where he plants it. It would put the hospital and the bomb squad in jeopardy. We can't know it won't go off.

"Lt. Denison needs to stop him when he leaves his house with the bomb and arrest him on his front step. Since Salman is not planting the bomb now, that gives us time to find his cell. Besides, if Anwar tries to contact him without an answer, he will know something is wrong. We'll keep to the original plan of following the cell members and surveilling them until we take Salman down," Sophie said.

"I see your point, but SRT will need more help to follow the other cell leaders. I'll call Denison and suggest he ask for more men. Austin has an FBI headquarters; maybe he could get help from them. And someone needs to contact the local chief of police to let him know we are running a mission in his city. It could cause some real problems if they don't know what's going on."

"Where are you, Houston?"

"I'm downstairs. Fons is getting some sleep in the SUV. Are you all right?"

"I'm going to meet Marci and Ojala at the cafeteria and get something to eat. But I was thinking... maybe after the Hijazis are taken into custody... we can come back here and see my family."

"Sweetheart, I think that is a great idea. I'll ensure Director Cosby honors the rest of our 90-day leave."

"Thank you, Houston. I love you."

"I love you too. Now get something to eat. I'll watch over you."

Sophie laughed, "My own guardian angel."

"Always," Houston chuckled.

Lawson changed and spoke with his surgical team before he headed to his office. Under the circumstances, he figured he would stay the night there. He had a private bathroom and a comfortable couch. He passed through the surgical unit doors and headed to the end of the corridor. His office was down the hallway toward the ICU.

As he looked up, he saw a woman walk out of the chapel. "Sophie," he breathed to himself. His heart literally skipped a beat. *Oh, Sophie, how can seeing you after all these years still do this to me. Will I never get over you?* What Emmett said to him rang in his ears. *'Do you think you haven't prayed about it because you know Jesus will heal you, and you want to hang on to the pain of her loss because you feel it keeps a piece of her with you? The only piece of her you have left.'*

Lawson wanted to speak with her, but she had stepped into the elevator. She was more beautiful than she was the last time he saw her.

Lawson headed to his office to pray. He knew it was time for him to let go and pray through his hurt over losing her.

Magnus and Murphy had followed Salman from the hospital to Home Depot. Magnus went inside and videoed what he was purchasing. Then followed Salman to his house and contacted Costa.

"We are handing him back to you and heading back to the hospital."

"Copy that."

Dunlap and Costa had set up three cameras in Salman's house. One in the living room, one in the TV/dining room, and one in the bedroom where the C-4 was.

Salman unloaded his vehicle and placed the bags on the table in the TV room when he entered the house. They saw him assemble three detonators and connect them to three new burner phones, using the items he purchased but didn't attach any explosives. When Salman finished, he turned out the lights and went to bed.

"Salman only has six bricks of C-4. I wonder if that is enough to take down a building the size of the Heart Hospital?" Costa wondered out loud.

"You know as well as I do. It's not about how much but about where the bombs are placed. And even if it didn't take down the entire hospital, the damage and loss of life would be extensive. You've studied the Oklahoma bombing, like the rest of us."

"We saw Salman studying the blueprints of the hospital. I wonder how he gained access to the cities building and planning department. I'm sure he was looking for the load-bearing walls."

THE HEART HOSPITAL. SUNDAY

Marci and Ojala got up early, took showers, dressed, and headed to the cafeteria before going to ICU.

"Giada, what do you want to do once you live here in the US?" Marci asked as they ate.

"I want to go to secondary school, then college. When the Americans were in Afghanistan, girls were allowed to go to school. But that didn't last long."

"How do you speak English so well?"

"My mother taught me; my father objected at first, then he thought it might be beneficial for his cause if I learned."

"Did your mother teach you anything else?"

"Yes, but we had to hide it from father."

"What do you want to study in college?" Marci asked.

Ojala considered the question for a while. "I love languages. I want to learn as many as I can and become an interpreter."

"I think that is an excellent idea."

"You do?"

"Yes, Giada. It would open doors for you."

Ojala finished her eggs and took a bite of her toast; she kept her eyes on Marci as she finished her coffee. "Marci, where will they take me when I get off the yacht?"

"Most likely, they will take you to DC."

"Why?"

"You lived in Afghanistan, right?

"Yes."

"They are always looking for information; since you lived there, you might be able to give them something helpful." Marci couldn't reveal that they knew who her family was.

Marci was torn about telling Ojala what was really going to happen. *I believe Ojala wants away from her family, but she still loves them. I don't know if I can trust her with the truth. She might tell her family to save them if it came down to it. And I won't put our team in jeopardy by taking the chance.*

"I see. Will you come with me?"

"Yes, if you want."

"Then, will they put me in a girl's school?"

"Giada, my husband and I would like you to live with us. Would you like that?" Roman had texted Marci, telling her he had offered to take Ojala in.

"Oh, yes. I would like that." Giada's countenance brightened.

"Alright, we better get upstairs so you can see your father." Marci and Giada took their empty plate and trays to the dirty dish area and threw away their garbage.

As they got off the elevator and headed to the ICU waiting area, Marci was surprised to see Emmett still there. He was sitting in his spot by the chapel. *I thought Emmett had gone home. I bet he stayed to watch over Sophie,* she thought.

Marci did not acknowledge him in any way but went straight to Sophie, sitting in the back row of chairs. The room had filled up since they left last night.

"Good morning, Sophie. How was your night?"

"Quiet."

"Hi, Sophie."

"Good morning, Giada. You look nice today," Sophie smiled at Giada's reaction. Compliments were new to her.

"Why don't you get some food and some sleep. I'm going to talk to the nurse and see if Giada can see her father."

"I'll wait until you come back," Sophie and Giada sat down.

Lawson had prayed for an hour when he made it to his office after the surgery last night. He finally laid out all the pain and hurt over losing Sophie at the foot of the Cross and asked Jesus to heal his broken heart. Then he cried. He cried until his lungs ached, but when he cried his last tear, he felt a breeze wash over him. It was like a window was open on a warm summer day, and a morning breeze blew in. It carried a fragrant scent with it. He lifted his head to see if it was coming from a vent, but it wasn't. It was the Holy Spirit breathing new life into him.

Lawson was still unsure how he would react to seeing Sophie again, but he knew it wouldn't hurt the way it used to. *Emmett was right. I had been keeping the pain to keep a piece of her with me. It was all I had left. I'm sorry, Lord, I should have turned this over to you years ago.*

Lawson had slept on his couch. When his alarm went off, he took a shower and changed. His office had a full bathroom and a small closet for a change of clothes. It was something he negotiated in his contract. He knew he would have to spend nights at the hospital on occasion after a delicate surgery.

Lawson was heading to the elevator to the cafeteria when he saw Sophie heading in that direction. He almost decided to avoid her and take the stairs, then stopped himself. He needed to keep the ground he'd gained last night.

Lawson almost caught up to her when he heard his name called. He turned to see Francesco Ricci.

"Doctor Cornett," Khaan walked up to him.

"Mr. Ricci," Lawson turned away from the elevator to direct his attention to Francesco.

"Doctor, when will you come in to check on my father?"

"Is there an issue?"

"No, I just wanted to make sure you would be checking on him today."

"Yes, I should be there in an hour. I spoke with the head ICU nurse this morning; she said your father was recovering well."

"Good, I was just going to get something to eat and bring something back for my brother. You said we would be here five days?"

"Yes, the protocol on this new device requires me to observe him for that length of time. But I can move him from ICU on the third day and put him in a room on the third floor."

"Yes, good. We don't want any complications."

Lawson headed to the elevator, Khaan walking with him. Sophie was nowhere to be seen.

Sophie headed to the cafeteria after exiting the elevator. Houston stepped out from around the corner; she was glad to see him. Other than texting, she had not seen him since the church yesterday.

The food line was relatively short. Sophie got in line, picking up a tray. When she saw waffles on the menu, she knew exactly what she was having. Sophie put in her order and continued through the line taking orange juice from the glass front refrigerator and a cup of coffee from the carafe. As she headed to the cashier, she saw Lawson and Khaan heading to the food line. She saw Lawson's eyes shift her direction, it looked like he was going to say something, but she shook her head as subtly as possible. He caught it and walked on.

Sophie saw Roman at a table eating; he must have just relieved Rocky. She did acknowledge him since the Hijazis knew they were our drivers, but she didn't sit with him.

Sophie put her tray down and heard her name called. She went to pick up her waffle and marionberry and maple syrups. She watched as Lawson and Khaan found a table.

When she finished her waffle, she headed to the RV to sleep.

Fons was sitting with Lt. Denison in his SUV, doubling as their command center. He was on the phone with Costa.

"While you were inside, did you see any blueprints of the hospital," Denison asked.

"No, sir, but when Salman got home, he brought them up on his computer."

"Well, he isn't going to get that far anyway. Keep me informed. I'm sending you relief so you can sleep," Denison said.

"Houston asked Director Cosby to contact the local police chief. We didn't want any police rushing into the middle of our action and not knowing what was happening," Fons said.

"Yes. That would be a bad situation. Cosby must have called the local FBI too because I got a call from the SAC, and he said his men are on standby for whenever we need them. We don't want these terrorists to remain loose in our country. We'll pick them up after Salman is in custody." Denison replied.

Ojala returned to the waiting room after visiting with her father for several hours. Marci watched as she walked over; the girl was sad, no doubt thinking this was one of the last times she'd see her father.

"Hi, Giada, are you alright? Is your father recovering well?"

"Yes, he is doing very well. He fell asleep, so I left."

"What's bothering you?"

"I can't go back with them, but I love my father, and the idea of never seeing him again makes me very sad."

"Giada, you can stay with your family if you want. No one is making you leave."

"I know, but the things they believe… it is all so cruel, and I will never be able to go to school. They will force me to marry an old man, and he will be just as cruel. But here in America, I will be all by myself," Ojala put her hands over her face, bent over, and quietly cried.

Marci rubbed her back while she cried, then said, "You will have me. I know it's not the same, but you won't be alone."

Ojala sat up and hugged her, "Thank you. I wish my family believed in Dori's God. He would help me."

"Dori?"

"My only friend in Geneva. She used to sneak into my room when my family was gone. Her family went to church together, and she told me wonderful things about her God."

"Giada, there is only one true God, and he is my God, and can be yours too."

"He can?"

"Yes. God created all things and created man in his own image. The Bible says, 'There is neither Jew nor Greek, neither slave nor free, nor is their male and female, for you are all one in Christ Jesus.' Gal. 3:28. He loves us all the same, and when sin came into the world by disobedience, he sent His Son to earth to give up his own life to save ours. Jesus paid for our sins, so we could reconnect with our Father in heaven, through the blood of the Cross, and spend eternity with him."

"You mean the prophet, Jesus?"

"He was a prophet but also the Son of God."

"Jesus is the son of God?"

"Yes, and the scriptures say, 'For I know the thoughts that I think toward you, says the Lord, thoughts of peace and not of evil, to give you a future and a hope.' Jeremiah 29:11."

"But I'm a woman; God doesn't care about me."

"That's not true. Remember I told you God does not distinguish between male or female, and He is no respecter of persons. The Bible says, 'Of a truth, I perceive that God is no respecter of persons.' Acts 10:34.

"A woman can have a relationship with your God?"

"Giada, it is your choice to believe in Him or not. Or to have a relationship with Him or not.

"First, you must believe that Jesus is the Son of God who created the heavens and the earth. That He came to give his life so that you can have a personal relationship with Him. 'For all have sinned and come short of the glory of God.' Romans 3:23.

"The Bible shows us who God is and how to live a life acceptable to Him. I know I fall short every day, but Jesus is faithful to forgive me because I repent.

"I have a Bible in the RV. You can read for yourself what it says. Then you can decide if you believe."

Ojala looked to the ICU doors, knowing they would beat and maybe even kill her if she got caught reading the Bible.

"Yes, I would like to read it."

"Good. Are you sure you want to leave your family, Giada? Once you leave, you can never go back. You know what would happen to you."

"I do."

"Alright, then it is settled," Marci said. Giada nodded.

SEIZE ON THE HIGH SEAS

CHAPTER SEVENTEEN

Ojala went to see her father again later in the afternoon, she planned to stay for several hours. The brothers took that time to go to the cafeteria, get something to eat, and go to the RV to change clothes. The door was locked, so they knocked on it. Sophie answered.

"Good afternoon. I was just getting ready to change places with Marci. I'll leave you to rest in the RV."

"No, we aren't resting. We've been sleeping in the room with my father. The nurses brought in a second reclining chair. We just need to change."

"Well, I'll leave you to it."

"Ms. Jones, is the yacht still in Corpus Christi waiting for us when my father is released?" Anwar asked.

"Yes, of course. My boss is paying them to wait. The captain would not leave."

"Excellent, we wanted to be certain," Anwar nodded. Sophie stepped out of the RV, watched them enter, and then closed the door behind them. Lt. Murphy had given her a listening device to place in the RV; she put it in place before she went to sleep.

When Sophie left the RV, she headed to the covered three-tier parking structure. She knew Houston had parked on the ground level in a parking space against the concrete wall that faced the RV. Houston's eyes were closed, the seat in the reclining position. Sophie rapped lightly on the window. Houston jerked awake.

"Sophie?"

"Hi, darling; sorry I woke you," she pointed to the lock on the door. He unlocked it. He wrapped her up in his arms when she got in the passenger seat.

"I miss you, Sophie."

"I miss you too; that's why I woke you up. I know you need to sleep."

"I'd rather be with you."

"I just wanted to be near you. Go back to sleep; I'll watch over you," Sophie smiled.

"That's my line," he chuckled. "Anyway, I'd rather smooch with you."

Sophie laughed; it was a standing joke with them.

"Really, Houston, shut your eyes. I'll lay my head on your shoulder and rest awhile."

Houston put his arm around his wife and moved as close as they could with the console between them. She laid her head on his shoulder, and Houston closed his eyes.

Sophie hadn't realized she had fallen asleep until her phone vibrated in her pocket and woke her up. Houston was still asleep. She gently removed herself from under his arm and quietly opened and closed the door. She moved to the hospital entry door.

"Hello, Agent Timms."

"Hello, Ms. Star; I translated what the brothers said in the RV after you left."

"Good, what were they talking about?" Sophie headed for the cafeteria to get a drink to take with her to the second floor.

"Anwar told his brother everything was set for the bomb to be detonated as soon as they were in international waters."

"Anything else?"

"Anwar wants to kill you and Marci when they reach their destination."

"Sanremo?"

"No, they plan to bribe the captain to change his course. They mentioned killing him and his son too. They want to deboard in Iran and travel to Afghanistan from there."

"Why wait to kill us?"

"In case they need you as hostages."

"What did Khaan say?"

"Khaan was trying to talk him out of it. He said they might need the Broker again, and if they go scorched earth, the Broker is well known as a lethal and unforgiving man."

"Did he convince Anwar?"

"Anwar said his father would make the final decision."

"Thank you, Agent Timms. Let me know if you hear anything else."

"Yes, ma'am."

Houston woke up to find his wife was gone; he felt the loss. After this mission, he contemplated retiring from the President's Task Force and the US Marshals. The work put Sophie, and him, at times, in some perilous situations. It was time to do something else. He'd talk to her about it after this mission.

Houston called Lt. Denison to tell him he would be back on duty after he got something to eat and asked for an update. Denison told him about the brother's conversation and what Costa saw on the camera at Salman's.

Lt. Denison sent back up to Salman's house in case any cell leaders showed up to get their money. After rehashing their earlier discussion with Sophie, the team agreed not to pick any of them up until after Salman was in custody. They would follow the cell members and put trackers on their vehicles.

Houston thanked him for the update and headed inside to use the bathroom to clean up.

Lawson looked in on his patient three times already. The first few days were the most critical. If Makhtar got an infection or his body attacked the device, he would have to remove it.

"Mr. Ricci, you have recovered from the surgery very well. I am pleased with your vitals and how quickly you regained your strength."

"I can feel the difference already."

"I would like to have someone from therapy come up and help you get your balance. I want you walking so you don't develop blood clots."

"My sons can help me," Makhtar said. Anwar agreed.

"I appreciate that, but I need someone who is trained to see any stress or imbalance."

"Of course, Doctor, whatever you feel is best."

"Alright, I'll talk to the nurse to get someone up here. Have you been eating today? The nurse said you didn't eat your food last night after surgery."

"My stomach was upset, but I ate a little breakfast. By lunch, I was hungry and ate everything on my plate, and dinner should be here soon. I will eat it too."

"Good." He turned to Anwar, "See that your father does what he says," Lawson smiled.

"We will see that he eats."

"Alright, I will come back in the morning. Call the nurse if there is any setback, and I will return."

"Thank you," Makhtar said.

Lawson left the room and spoke with the nurse. He headed to the double doors and saw Marci and Giada in the waiting area. He nodded but did not speak to them. On the way to his office, he saw Sophie leaving the elevator and heading to the chapel.

Emmett was sitting in his usual place. It was a perfect spot to observe who came and left the floor. The stairs were on one end of the corridor, and the elevator was halfway between.

Lawson headed to the chapel to speak with Sophie. He wanted to say hello. He hurt her before she left all those years ago; he regretted it.

Emmett stood up when he saw Lawson heading toward the chapel.

"Lawson, you can't speak with her."

"What? Why? I just want to say hello."

"Lawson, she is undercover. If the Ricci brothers see you talking to her in a familiar way, they will get paranoid. You could put the mission and her life in danger."

"Emmett, how dangerous are these people?"

"I don't know, but Marci would have never asked me to stand guard if they weren't. Sophie doesn't even acknowledge me when she passes me by. She would never do that unless doing so would endanger the mission."

"Will she ever come home, Emmett?" Lawson's face showed his discouragement.

"After this mission is over. I believe she will."

"Goodnight, Emmett."

"Goodnight, Lawson."

Lawson got on the elevator and headed home. His heart was heavy, worried about his friend. He had no one he could share his burden with except the Lord. None of his friends knew Sophie was here."

Sophie heard Lawson speaking with Emmett as the chapel door closed behind her. Her heart went out to him. She missed his friendship but talking to him would be selfish. She wasn't going to put her team and the mission in jeopardy.

AUSTIN. MONDAY

By morning, Lt. Denison's SRT team, with the help of the local FBI, managed to track three of the other cell leaders. They kept the men under surveillance.

Marci had given Ojala her Bible to read when they went to the RV after Sophie relieved them. Ojala stayed up until early in the morning, reading it. She woke Marci up more than once to ask her questions. Marci let her sleep in. She took the Bible from Ojala's chest and put it away, so the brothers didn't see her with it.

Ojala stirred. "Marci?"

"Yes. We have some time. You can sleep some more if you like."

"No, I need to get back to the waiting room."

"Alright, take your shower and change, we'll get some breakfast, and you can stay with your father."

Ojala headed for the bathroom but stopped mid-stride. "Marci, thank you for telling me about Dori's God."

"He can be your God too, Giada."

"I think I'd like that," Ojala said.

Marci walked her through the sinner's prayer.

After breakfast, Marci and Ojala went back to ICU. Tomorrow would be the third day, and they would need to get the Hijazis out of the hospital. As soon as Marci relieved her,

Sophie called Lt. Denison, Fons, and Houston to meet up with her at the church.

"Lt. Denison, you have a secure computer; can you bring it? We'll need to contact the op center."

"Yes, ma'am, will do."

They met fifteen minutes later. The church was empty, and they took the last two pews furthest from the door.

"Lt. Denison, have you been in contact with the Seal team leader Chief Abbott?"

"Yes, ma'am."

"Have the Marina Militare arrived?"

"Yes, they will be on the Coast Guard Cutter shadowing the yacht."

"Good, we need to work the plan and get these men off US soil."

"Ma'am, I heard the translation of Anwar and Khaan's last conversation. Do we want to change our plans now that we know they want to kill you?" Denison asked.

"No, they didn't plan on doing anything until they reached land. And we don't know if Makhtar approved Anwar's plan."

"I don't like this, Sophie. That's a lot of speculation. How do you know they don't just plan on throwing you overboard on the way?" Fons asked.

"I agree," Houston said.

"They might need us as hostages, but let's see what Makhtar says first. Then we can adjust if needed," Sophie paused. "Let's talk about tomorrow. If we leave the hospital at 5 pm. It will be late by the time we reach Corpus Christi. Chief Abbott's men plan to implement the seize at 1 am. Then the Coast Guard and the Italians can take Makhtar and his sons into custody."

"Yes, ma'am. We will finish our job here. We will ask the local police to help us with our plan to evacuate Salman's neighbors. We are going to claim there is a gas leak. But we will have them evacuate from the rear of their homes. We don't want anyone too close when we take Salman into custody on his front porch." Denison said.

"What do you think, Houston? Should they include the local police?" Sophie asked.

"You'll have to close off the streets that allow ingress to Salman's home. Someone is going to have to man that. Are you going to use the local Gas Utility trucks as your cover?"

"Yes, we are going to borrow them to block off the streets and make our story believable," Lieutenant Denison said.

"It's a sound plan, Sophie." Houston said.

"Do you need Murphy and his drone to stay with you, Troy?" Fons asked.

"Yes. We can use the help."

"Alright, Troy, we will see you and your men back in DC," Fons said. Denison left the church.

"Alright then, now we just have to talk to Lawson about giving Makhtar the news he has to leave. He will need to be there to volunteer to come with us," Sophie said.

"Fons and I will follow the RV. We'll imbed with the Seals when they head out in the Zodiacs," Houston said.

"Someone needs to stay with the Italians so there are no mistakes. I'll stay with them, Sophie. Houston can imbed with the Seals. I'll need pictures of everyone, so I can make sure they know who's who," Fons said.

"I'm sure Matt or Sissy can get those for you," Houston suggested.

"Are we all agreed on this plan of action?" When everyone nodded, Sophie said, "Alright, let's contact Director Cosby and fill him in."

Fons contacted the op center, and Agent Smith connected. "Good morning, Agent Smith. Who's in the op center this morning?"

"Everyone, sir, we knew you would be calling with an update today."

"Good. Alright, put us on screen, and we'll turn it over to Houston and Ms. Star."

"Yes, sir."

When the screen showed the team at the command center, Houston went through the plan. Houston answered Director Cosby's questions, and then Sophie addressed them.

"Director Cosby, the yacht is very close quarters; I'm concerned for Chief Abbott's men. There is no cover in the hallway."

"They are training right now on a similar yacht while they are waiting for you. Don't worry about the Seals; this is what they do. Just make sure you have all the civilians on the upper deck like Chief Abbott asked, " Director Cosby said.

"Copy that. We are on track to put this in motion at 5 pm tomorrow. We should be at the yacht around 8 or 9 pm."

"Is Lt. Denison still set to arrest Salman Ebeid and the cell members as soon as Salman steps out of his house with the bomb."

"Yes, sir. We just spoke with him. He is using a gas leak story to evacuate the neighbors." Houston said.

"Sir, one more thing, is the doctor in place to monitor Makhtar?"

"Yes, he has already contacted Dr. Cornett to get all the instructions and the correct forms."

"Thank you, Director."

Director Cosby told them to be careful, and the connection was shut down.

"Houston, I need someone to contact Lawson to let him know he needs to be in the room a few minutes after 5 pm when we initiate this plan."

"I'll do it. Text Lawson and ask him when he'll be at the hospital."

Sophie sent a text off. **Lawson, Agent Townsend needs to speak with you. When will you be at your office?**

A text came back that quick. **I'm here now.**

Sophie responded. **He'll be right there.**

Houston turned to Sophie and kissed her, "You get some sleep."

"I will but let me know if anything happens."

"You know I will."

Houston went to the second-floor office of Doctor Cornett and knocked.

"Come in."

"Good morning, Doctor; I'm Agent Townsend; I work with Ms. Star."

"Yes, she said you would be coming. Please have a seat."

"Thank you," Houston sat across from the doctor. "I understand you have been briefed by the First Lady and Emmett Scott on the nature of our operation."

"I won't say briefed. But the First Lady did tell me what she needed."

"Did she mention we need to have the Ricci's back on the yacht tomorrow?"

"Yes."

"We understand that you must observe him for five days to meet your requirements for the FDA. But we can't wait that long."

228

"I had volunteered to travel with him for the two days, but now I'm told things have changed. A Navy doctor contacted me to get the protocol requirements. He emailed me his credentials; he is qualified to complete the monitoring. However, I don't understand why you still need me on board now."

"We want you to go along to keep the Ricci's from being suspicious."

"Is that their real names?" Lawson asked.

"No."

"How dangerous are these men?" Lawson asked.

"Very."

"Why would Sophie be involved with such a dangerous mission? Shouldn't the FBI or CIA be handling this?"

"Yes, but she is an integral part of this operation. I can't reveal anything more than that."

Lawson sat there for a moment. "You work with Sophie Star?"

"Yes."

"I understand she is married."

"Yes, she is."

"Is he a good man?"

Houston smiled, "I think so."

Lawson lowered his eyes to his desk for a moment. "I was one of her best friends for years. I miss her."

"I understand she may be coming back here when this operation is over," Houston said.

"You think so?" Lawson looked up at him.

"I don't know for certain, but she has mentioned it."

"So, what you need me to do, is play along?"

"Yes."

"What time."

"We want Makhtar to get the news from Roman at 5 pm. Watch for him to go in first. Then come in a few minutes behind him, like you normally would, to check Makhtar."

Lawson stood, "I will be there, Agent Townsend."
Houston thanked him and left the room.

Sophie woke up at 2 pm. She was surprised she could sleep that long. She took a shower and changed. Sophie was fixing her hair when she heard a knock. She opened the door to see Anwar and Khaan.

"Please come in; I'm just leaving."

"Thank you, Ms. Jones."

"How is your father?"

"He is doing very well. I had no idea he could recuperate so quickly."

"I'm glad to hear it," Sophie stepped out of the RV so they could come in.

"I'll be up in the waiting room after I get something to eat if you need anything."

"Thank you, Ms. Jones."

Sophie headed to the cafeteria. Roman was there having lunch. Sophie sat with him.

"Shouldn't you be sleeping?" Sophie asked.

"I'll get some sleep after I eat. What's the plan, Sophie?"

"Tomorrow at 5 pm, you and I will go to his room with the news that the boss called and said he heard some chatter that the Hijazis are in Austin, Texas, at a hospital. Then you'll say the 'Broker' insists we leave immediately. Dr. Cornett will agree to monitor Makhtar on the yacht."

"Let's hope it works."

"It will; they are afraid of being caught on US soil," Sophie was convinced of that.

Roman picked up his tray, dumped his garbage, and then returned to say goodbye. "I'm going to get a few hours' sleep," Roman said.

Sophie headed to the food line and saw Houston. She came up behind him and whispered, "Aren't you going to get some sleep?"

Without turning, he said, "Yeah, I just needed to get something to eat."

"I'll see you later. I love you."

"I'll be watching over you," Houston heard her chuckle behind him.

Sophie spotted Marci as she walked back into the ICU waiting area, but Ojala was not with her.

"Is Ojala sitting with her father?"

"Yes. Ojala turned her life over to Christ this morning," Marci had a big smile on her face. Sophie's reaction was what she expected. Excited.

"Marci, that is wonderful. I'm so happy for her."

Sophie brought Marci up to date on the sequence of things that was going to happen tomorrow. "You might want to have Ojala in the RV before we get this underway. Do you think you should tell her that her father and brothers will be taken into custody?"

"No. Ojala loves her father. Out of loyalty, she may tell him. And if she doesn't, the fact that she knew it and didn't tell him will haunt her the rest of her life."

"I agree."

They continued to discuss the plan. Ojala came out of the ICU doors around 4 pm. Marci took her to the RV.

The night was quiet, Sophie only saw the brothers once after Marci and Ojala went to the RV. They went to the cafeteria together to eat. It was the first time one of the family wasn't with Makhtar. She supposed Makhtar was asleep.

CHAPTER EIGHTEEN

TUESDAY

Marci relieved Sophie around 9 am, like she had the past few days and Ojala went to see her father. Sophie got something to eat and headed to the RV.

Sophie didn't see Houston but knew he was around. He would not sleep today; the entire team was on high alert. She had received a text saying the SRT team had located five more members of the cell teams.

Sophie slept for a few hours then made contact with the team. Everything was in place for the final leg of the mission. Sophie relieved Marci at three o'clock and after Marci and Ojala ate, she had Ojala on the RV by 4 pm.

At a few minutes to five, Lawson left his office to wait at the nurse's station for his cue. He looked Sophie's direction but didn't acknowledge her, walking through the ICU doors.

Roman stepped off the elevator and signaled to Sophie to go with him. They walked through the double doors and knocked on the door frame of Makhtar's room. Makhtar and his sons turned to them.

"I am sorry to bother you. But I need to speak with you privately."

"Can it wait? My father's doctor is coming to check on him in a few minutes," Anwar spoke up.

"No."

Roman closed the door.

"What is the meaning of this," Khaan said, angry at the interruption.

"I just got a call from the 'Broker'. He said there is chatter that Makhtar Hijazi is being treated at a hospital in Austin, Texas," Roman said.

"He is sure?" Makhtar questioned.

"Yes. We need to get you back on the yacht and in international waters. Are you well enough to travel?" Roman looked at the machine attached to Makhtar, showing his vitals.

"I believe I am. We can't take the chance of getting caught. How will we explain this to the doctor?" Anwar asked.

"I'll take care of that," Sophie said. "Just back up what I tell him," Sophie opened the door. That was the cue for Lawson to come in.

"Doctor Cornett, Mr. Ricci has just received some very distressing news. It is imperative he gets back home," Sophie said.

"Now?"

"Yes."

"No, I need to observe him for five days. It's only been three."

"I'm sorry, doctor, he doesn't have a choice."

"Is Mr. Ricci's health in jeopardy if he isn't monitored?" Roman asked, stepping nearer to the doctor.

"Yes. I must make sure my patient's body doesn't reject the device. If not me, another cardiologist needs to."

"Doctor, can you travel with us for the next two days?" Sophie asked.

"Give me a minute to talk with my scheduler. If I have no surgeries, I may be able to go with you," Lawson said. Sophie wasn't surprised Lawson was such a good actor. She knew the things he pulled when they were in school.

"Can my father's body tolerate the traveling, Doctor?" Anwar asked.

"Yes, the therapist said his balance is good. He should be fine if he doesn't have a long way to walk and has a place to rest when needed. I can keep a close eye on him if I'm with you."

Lawson left the room supposedly to make calls but had already made the arrangements.

"Do you need us to get clothes from the RV for him?" Roman asked.

"No, we brought clothes up for him already," Khaan said.

"Please get him ready as soon as possible. I will have a nurse bring in a wheelchair. I'll bring the RV to the emergency room entrance," Roman said, and he and Sophie left.

Sophie texted Houston and Rocky to tell them they were on the way to the RV. Makhtar would be out soon.

Houston and Fons were in their SUV talking with Lt. Denison's. "Ok, we are a go. Let your men know this is happening now." Houston said to the Lieutenant.

"They're ready. Our plan is in place."

"Copy that, Lieutenant."

Rocky got the message and drove the RV to the ER portico.

Anwar, Khaan, and Lawson were coming out of the double doors to the portico behind a nurse who wheeled out Makhtar to the waiting RV. Sophie and Roman were a few steps behind them. Lawson had grabbed his medical bag and a duffel from his office that he had prepared the night before.

Ojala didn't understand what was happening, when Rocky came and drove the RV to the ER and the others got on.

Anwar helped his father onto the RV and to the back bedroom, where Lawson checked his vitals.

"Anw...Paolo, what is going on. Why are we leaving? Is father alright?"

"Sit down and be quiet. I'll explain later," Khaan admonished her. Anwar simply ignored her.

When Roman got into the passenger seat, and Sophie said Makhtar was settled, they headed out. Khaan did not have time to check for trackers or listening devices. While Lawson was tending to Makhtar, Anwar sat at the kitchen booth and sent a text.

Sophie could see the phone and saw the message was in Arabic. No doubt letting Salman know they were leaving the hospital.

Sophie secretly sent a text to Houston saying she believed a text was just sent to Salman.

Salman was in a position that one of the cameras picked up the text message from Anwar.

Agent Timms had it translated and sent the translations to Houston, Lt. Denison, Sophie, and Roman:

We have left the hospital. We will be on the yacht in three hours. Keep your promise to my father.

I will not fail you. Came the response.

Sophie deleted the text and looked over at Marci.

Khaan came to Ojala and spoke to her in Arabic. "Your father is fine. Someone has found out we are here. We needed to go before we were detained."

Ojala nodded.

Lt. Denison contacted his men on Salman. "Anwar just told Salman they were out of the hospital. He was told to detonate in three hours. I don't know if he will plant the bomb now or wait a few hours. Take him down as soon as he leaves his house with the bomb."

The ruse of a gas leak was ready to roll and in place once the order was given.

Underwood and Jandrell left their vehicle. They had already scouted the area and decided on the empty house across the street to set up his 'roost' and walked into the back yard. Underwood carried his sniper rifle in a longish soft side case over his shoulder. Jandrell cupped his hand to boost Underwood enough to get ahold of the roof and hoist himself up.

Jandrell looked around for something to stand on. There was an old five-gallon paint bucket over by the fence. He stood on that and reached up to Underwood's outstretched hand. With his help, he got a foot up on the roof and hoisted himself from there.

Jandrell picked the spot for Underwood to set up his sniper rifle and rest, then used his binoculars to watch the front door.

Underwood and Jandrell were the last resort. If Salman moved to detonate the bomb when he was detained, Underwood would take him out. There was no way he was leaving or detonating that bomb.

Lieutenant Denison knew if the six sticks of C4 went off in that neighborhood, it would destroy it. He had already made plans with the local FBI and police to help pull this off. He called the Sergeant in charge of the police unit and told him to initiate the plan. Since sundown wouldn't be until 7:30 pm, it gave them two hours of sunlight and took some danger out of the takedown.

The local FBI had contacted the Texas Utility Gas provider and asked to borrow their trucks and uniforms to block the three access roads leading to Salman's house. The police would stop all traffic by saying there was a gas leak. One of Denison's team was in place with each utility truck.

The local police officers were in gas company uniforms and went from house to house, explaining there was a gas leak and they needed to evacuate. To keep Salman from noticing, they had the families leave by the back doors and ride in unmarked cars to wait at a nearby church until they were given the *all clear*. They didn't want the street to look deserted. Costa and Dunlap closely watched Salman to ensure he hadn't seen the evacuation.

Salman kept watching his clock. Now that the C4 was hooked to the detonator in his backpack, he turned off his cell phone.

The mission was hot, and the team was connected through earpieces. Costa spoke to Lt. Denison. "He's waiting on someone. He keeps looking at the clock and out the window. Do you think he was expecting another member of his network?"

"It's possible. Or Salman could have noticed the evacuation. We may need to take him down in his home."

"He's making a call on his landline. I'll patch you in."

"Gayth, where are you? I need to get to the hospital."

"I'm only a block away, but a Texas utility truck is blocking the entrance to your street. I'm behind a line of cars."

"What is going on?" Salman asked.

"I don't know. But a man is going from car to car talking to people."

Denison immediately contacted his men at the roadblocks. "Look for someone on the phone. We need to get a tracker on the car if it's one of Salman's people."

Agent Magnus grabbed a tracker from his vehicle and started down the row of cars, smiling and nodding as he went by. It was warm out, so most people in line chose to turn off their engines and open the windows. He saw a man alone in a vehicle, talking on the phone. Magnus moved closer to the car to see if he could hear what was being said. He stopped and looked back as if he was waiting for someone, trying to listen to a morsel of the conversation.

"Salman, there is a guy walking by. I'll ask him what's going on."

That was all Magnus needed. He started to walk by, but Gayth stopped him.

"Mister," Gayth hollered.

"Yes, sir."

"What's going on? I need to get to my friend's house."

"I was told it is a gas leak. They are being extra cautious because they haven't found the gas leak yet. They asked me to let people know. It shouldn't take more than an hour. If you like, I can spot you so you can turn around and come back later."

"Yeah, maybe I should come back."

"Let me see how far you can back up. I don't want you to hit the guy behind you."

"Thanks."

The agent walked in front of his vehicle to the other side and placed a tracker in his wheel well, as he passed. He reached the back of the car and directed him to go back two feet. Gayth was able to do that and make a four-point turn. The agent nodded at him as he drove off.

Agent Magnus passed on the info that there was a tracker in play. He described the car and gave the license plate number, so someone could catch up to him. "Sir, I saw him get back on his phone. He must be calling Salman back."

"Dunlap, did you pick up the tracker Magnus placed?"

"Yes, sir."

Lt. Denison told Dunlap to contact one of the local agents to direct him to the moving vehicle. "They need to have him followed and watched for the time being," he ordered.

While the brothers were distracted, Sophie took a moment to text Emmett. **We are gone now. Thanks for your help, Grandpa. I love you.**

The response came immediately. **Yes, I saw and followed you out. Come home. I'm always here for you. I love you too.**

The response brought tears to Sophie's eyes. Marci noticed. "Are you alright, Sophie?"

"Yes, I'm fine," Sophie nodded, her eyes still on the message. She deleted it and looked out the window.

Lawson came out of the bedroom and found a place to sit across from Sophie.

Anwar told Ojala that her father wanted her to sit with him.

Ojala sat by her father and took his hand. *Maybe I should stay with my family. I would miss you, father. I love you. If only you loved me like Jesus loves his children,* Ojala thought. She was beginning to feel the weight of her decision to stay in the US.

Makhtar looked over at her. "My daughter, I will miss you when we get back home. I had wished for you to be a first wife to a young man who would love you, but you are too old now. No young man will have you.

"But I promise we will find you a good husband."

"Father, why can't I stay with you. I love you. I'll take care of you."

Makhtar took his hand out of hers and cupped her face. "You have been a good daughter, but it is time you have children and serve a husband. It is your destiny."

"Father, I don't want to be married to some old man."

"You will be fine, Ojala. It is our custom. Your brothers will make the arrangements when we get to Afghanistan."

"Father, in Afghanistan, I won't be able to go to school."

"Once you are married, you won't be going anyway."

240

I will not live a life against my will. I will stay in the US with Marci. Her mind was settled now. *I love you father, but when I am married, I will not see you often anyway. If I am going to start a new life, it might as well be one I want.*

Anwar and Khaan had been whispering in Arabic, sitting at the RV's kitchen table. Khaan finally said. "Let father decide. The brothers got up and headed to the bedroom where Makhtar was resting. They stepped in a closed the door behind them.

"Father, when we dock in Iran. We need to kill all the infidels on the ship," Anwar spoke in Arabic. Ojala was horrified at his words. She began to say so when Khaan spoke.

"Father, if we do that, we will never be able to use the 'Broker' again, and we may need him in the future. What if you get sick again? And from what I hear of him, he will seek retribution, and he has the resources and connections to do it."

No one spoke while Makhtar considered both options. "No, we need the man to get us to Iran and then to Afghanistan," he touched Anwar's arm. "Anwar, for all we know, the two women may have weapons.

"Khaan, have you contacted the 'Broker' yet to tell him we want to change our destination?"

"No, Father. You need to call him now and tell him we have a change of plans. It will cost us, but it is the only way. The captain will not deviate from the Broker's original orders. He knows what would happen to him if he did. The only way the captain takes us to the Arabian Sea is if the Broker tells him to. Tell the Broker we need travel arrangements from Iran to Afghanistan too."

"What about the crew? They might figure out who we are. We need to kill them once we dock in Iran," Anwar insisted.

"No, they will only know we are in Iran, and murder will bring too much attention to who was last on the yacht. We leave them alone," Makhtar looked at Khaan. "Go do as I say."

"Yes, Father."

Khaan went into the bathroom and shut the door to keep his call private. The call was routed from Roman's contact, who screened all the incoming requests and forwarded them to Rocky.

Rocky felt his cell vibrate. He saw it was from their man. "Yes," he whispered.

"Khaan is on the line and wants to make new arrangements; what should I tell him?"

"Tell him I will call him back in ten minutes," Rocky whispered.

"Roman, Khaan is trying to get ahold of us. We need to pull over so I can call him back."

Roman pushed the corner of the curtain aside while keeping his other hand on the wheel. "Marci."

Marci stepped up next to him. "Yes."

"Tell the brothers we need to pull over; an engine light came on. We need oil. Khaan wants to talk to the 'Broker'."

"Alright."

Marci closed the curtain and told Sophie what was going on.

"Why would the brothers need to talk to him?"

"I think they want to change their plans." Marci went to the back and told the Hijazis the driver was pulling into a gas station.

They acknowledged her, and Ojala asked if she could get off and get some snacks. Her father nodded. She went to the front and said she needed to talk to Marci. They stepped off the RV and went into the convenience store.

"They want the yacht to take us to Iran so they can return to Afghanistan." Ojala was hyperventilating; she was so upset.

"Calm down, Ojala, we have it under control. Don't worry; nothing will change."

"Anwar wanted to kill you when we got to Iran, but my father said no," Ojala started crying.

"It's ok, Giada," we will all be fine.

Costa saw Salman pick up the phone and listen. Salman responded, "Maybe we are compromised, Gayth. But if I call Anwar and tell him that. He will think us incompetent and no longer fund us." Salman listened again.

"Ok, if you believe the gas leak is real. I won't call them." Gayth responded but Costa couldn't hear it.

"Alright, I'll head out now. Come by tomorrow." Salman hung up and looked out the window.

Once Salman questioned if he had been compromised, the SRT team was notified to apprehend Salman as soon as he left the house.

Underwood was put on standby. He put his rifle sight on the front door and waited. Jandrell was using the binoculars to keep watch.

Denison was watching the cameras set up in Salman's home. Salman moved to the door to pick up his backpack.

"The target is heading to the door. When Salman steps out and locks his door, take him into custody. If he tries to get into his backpack, shoot. We can't have him detonate those bombs."

Clicks came from his team, letting him know they understood.

As soon as the lock on the door clicked, Denison's men came from around the sides of the house, screaming orders to him.

"PUT DOWN THE BACKPACK AND STEP AWAY!"

"PUT YOUR HANDS IN THE AIR! DO IT NOW! DO IT NOW!"

The orders were repeated fast and loudly.

Salman was startled. Then a calm came over him. He moved the backpack in front of him, partially covering his face, knowing no one dared shoot and risk hitting the bomb. He heard the stories of how the suicide bombers were idolized by their peers; he liked the idea of becoming a martyr for the cause. The leaders constantly told them of the great rewards they would receive. He slowly moved his hand to the zipper. A shot rang out, and Salman was dead before he hit the ground. Blood oozed from a hole right between his eyes.

"Roman, what do we want to do?" Rocky asked as the two men moved to the front of the RV and raised the hood.

"Respond like it's just another deal. It won't change the plans to take them down tonight. Give them what they want."

Rocky went to the convenience store bathroom and locked the door. His voice would be distorted by the bathroom echo, but that wouldn't matter.

Rocky called Khaan. "Mr. Hijazi, why are you contacting me again. My people say you are on your way back to the yacht. You are safe."

"Yes. That is true, but we want to make some adjustments."

"What adjustments. Everything is set. I do not like to shift gears in midstream. Too much could go wrong."

"I understand, but we will pay you well."

"Continue."

"We need the yacht to take us to the Arabian Sea. We want to dock in Iran and have transportation there to take us to Afghanistan."

"I see. Well, the yacht will need to refuel somewhere. I don't know if the captain will be amenable but give me a few hours to see if this can be done. The doctor will need to deboard; he did not agree to be gone for the time it will take to get to Iran.

"You must understand, last minute changes like this will cost you. Once I agree, there will need to be another five hundred thousand in my account before you reach the yacht," Rocky said.

"I understand."

Rocky made a call to Captain Mandrapilias. "Captain, I need you to set a course for Iran."

"Sir, I have worked with you for years, but I have never agreed to go to Iran," there was dread in the captain's voice.

"I will guarantee your safety, and it will be another one hundred thousand dollars for you."

"All right, but I'm dropping them off at the most remote dock and getting out of there."

"That's fine; let me know where." Rocky hung up. It was necessary to keep the captain in the dark about what would happen later tonight. He would not hold up under pressure if the brothers got suspicious and asked him questions.

Rocky came out of the bathroom and saw Roman at the cashier, paying for oil. He nodded to his brother and continued outside to the RV.

Sophie had been talking to Houston. She told him what Ojala told Marci, but that wasn't new information. A satellite would be tracking the yacht. A change of course, wouldn't matter.

When Sophie returned to the RV, Ojala handed her Twizzlers and Raisinets. Sophie smiled and took them, thanking her.

Once everyone was back on the bus, they drove on.

Lawson couldn't help but stare at Sophie. It had been so long since he had seen her. He missed her so much. He had so many regrets. He wasn't there for her when Duke died. Lawson missed their friendship, and he hated the way he hurt her. He tried to say something to her when the brothers were in the back, but she shook her head.

Lawson was beginning to understand how dangerous this operation was. He was glad now that he agreed to come along.

At least he would be here to protect Sophie and Marci if it came to that. He turned away from her and looked out the window.

Lawson smiled, remembering some of the great times they all had. His best friends were still the same ones he had in school. Naturally, there were some new friends, doctors, and nurses, but nothing could take the place of someone who has known you your whole life. He wondered how the family would react when they found out Sophie was back. The families were so hurt when Sophie left. Lizzy was heartbroken. *I wonder if they can get beyond it and be friends again. Sophie's name seldom came up anymore, but the few times it had, Drew made it clear he'll never forgive her. She hurt China by leaving, and to Drew, that was unforgivable.*

CHAPTER NINETEEN

Houston and Fons were following the RV. When the RV made an unscheduled stop and pulled into a gas station, they were concerned something had gone wrong. Fons got off on the next exit and waited on the shoulder of the on-ramp for the RV to get ahead of them again, when Houston gat a call from Sophie, explaining the situation.

They were watching the action at Salman's house on the feed sent out by the command center. Local FBI under SAC Woolf and his team were backing up Lt. Denison's SRT.

"Salman is not going to give up that backpack," Fons said, backseat quarterbacking the action.

"Underwood is going to have to take the shot...." Before Houston could finish the sentence, a shot rang out. Houston's eyes were glued to the iPad.

They heard Lt. Denison call for the bomb squad to come in.

"They will be there for hours collecting evidence," Fons said.

"Yeah, and they better round up the rest of the network before Salman's death makes the news." Houston pulled out his cell, "I'm going to let Roman know what's happened." Before he dialed, he heard Lt. Denison give Special Agent Woolf's men the order to arrest their targets.

Houston called Roman, "I know you are still at the gas station. I wanted to let you know they took down Salman."

"Dead or alive?"

"Dead."

"Ok. We will be on the road again soon."

"Copy that," Houston acknowledged.

"Houston, they have to keep a lid on this. If the news gets ahold of it before the Hijazis are on the yacht they may take hostages," Roman said.

"I heard Lt. Denison talking with the local FBI Agents. Special Agent Woolf is going to clamp a lid on it as long as he can."

"Good."

They were only twenty minutes from Corpus Christi when Rocky texted his contact and told him to call Khaan. He was to pass on the approval for the changes they asked for.

Khaan relayed the message to his father, and Anwar sent the money.

The RV pulled close to the pier where the yacht was waiting. Roman got out and opened the outside storage area to take out the suitcases. Lawson had his duffle under the seat he was sitting in.

Rocky checked to see if the transfer came through so he could acknowledge he received it. He sent a text to the contact, who then relayed it to Khaan. The funds were received.

Captain Mandrapilias met the Hijazis on the dock and told them he knew their new destination.

"The cabins have been cleaned and are waiting for you. Be careful crossing the ramp; the waters are choppy." The captain directed their attention to the fenders hitting the dock in a rhythmic pattern.

"Thank you, Captain," Makhtar said as his sons carefully helped him onto the yacht. Ojala followed behind. Anwar turned to her, "You need to get a head covering on, and you are to stop playing the part of a spoiled infidel."

Ojala hung her head, afraid the promise Marci made was only wishful thinking. She should have run when she had the chance.

Sophie and Marci were the last ones off the RV. Rocky handed them their small suitcases and they headed to the pier. Sophie noticed the sky had turned gray and drops had begun to fall on them. They hurried aboard.

When the yacht left the dock, Roman called Houston to see where they were staging the operation.

Roman and Rocky met the others at the Coast Guard facility, where the operation was spearheaded. The Seal Team and the Italians were there also. Chief Abbott made introductions.

"Good, you have the Navy doctor with you," Houston said to Chief Abbott.

"The Italians are not crazy about it, but we made it part of the package," Abbott said. "Will Lieutenant Denison be here with his men for backup?"

"I doubt it. They have a lot of work ahead of them now that they have taken down the bomber and the cell leaders. I'm sure they will be there through the night," Fons said.

"Can you show me on the map how you plan on completing this operation?" Houston asked.

"Sure, let me bring Capitano Mazzo of the Marina Militare and Coast Guard Commander Peters in on this. We can run through it together," Abbott said as he headed to where they were standing with their men.

The men moved over to the table where an enlarged nautical map of the Atlantic, an open sea map, and the blueprint of the yacht were laid out. A red line marked the new course to the Arabian Sea.

Chief Abbott took the lead. "Commander Peters will run his cutter out of view from the yacht until one hour before the action. Then he will turn off his running light and navigate by radar within one mile of the ship. At 12:45 am, my men will load up on two Zodiac Milpros. They will row the mile to the yacht and attach the CRRCs to each side.

"I have contacted Director Cosby, and he assures me Ms. Star will have all the civilians on the upper-level deck before we breach. We are waiting for a text from Ms. Star letting us know who is in what cabin.

"If all goes well, we will get to the door of their cabins without being detected and take down the Hijazis. Then the Coast Guard cutter will turn on its light, and Capitano Mazzo will board the yacht taking custody of his prisoners. Are there any questions?"

"I would like to be a part of your team, Chief Abbott," Houston requested. "And we would appreciate it if Agent Rodriguez could be on the cutter with the Italians."

Chief Abbott considered it. He knew Houston and Fons wouldn't be in the way. "Alright. You know the players, and we don't want any civilians injured."

"Copy that," Fons said.

A call came to Abbott's phone. He answered, listened, then hung up and checked his text.

"Alright, Denny just forwarded me the cabin assignments Ms. Star sent him." He pointed to the yacht blueprints, saying who would be in what cabin.

Roman was talking to the Italians, then searched the staging area for Houston or Fons. He spotted Houston, and he and his brother headed in that direction.

"My wife is on that yacht, too. Rocky and I want to be on the cutter, Houston," Roman said.

Houston nodded and went to ask the commander for his approval. The commander looked over at Roman and Rocky and nodded. "But they must stay on the cutter until the *'all clear'*."

All the different teams loaded onto the cutter. The Italians were in their uniforms, and the Coast Guards in theirs. Abbott's team and Houston were wearing black.

The cutter was about ten nautical miles behind the yacht and wouldn't breach the gap until midnight.

Ojala and Marci made a late dinner for everyone in the galley. Lawson was given the room Ojala had been using, and she moved into Marci's room.

By 10:30 pm, Makhtar went to his room, and Lawson took his vitals. Anwar and Khaan sat on the lower deck for a while, speaking in Arabic. They yacht had sailed past the bad weather and was traveling under clear skies.

"Khaan, I am concerned, I sent a text to Salman letting him know we were on the yacht. He did not respond."

"He probably turned off his cell when moving the bomb for precautionary reasons."

"Maybe, but I brought my satellite radio, and I haven't heard a thing about a hospital being bombed."

"Maybe he hasn't detonated it yet?"

"No, he was supposed to do it once we were in international waters."

"Don't get paranoid, Anwar. It will hit the news soon enough."

"You are right," Anwar acknowledged, but he could feel something was wrong.

Anwar hollered for Giada to come down from the upper deck before they headed to their rooms.

"You need to go to bed now," Anwar demanded.

"But I want to watch the stars."

Anwar put his face right up to hers. "Don't you dare defy me."

Ojala headed to Marci's room.

When the brothers left the deck. Sophie nodded to Marci to go with her to the lounge. "Marci, Chief Abbott wants us to have the civilians on the upper deck before they board. The Seals don't want collateral damage. You'll have to bring Ojala back without her brothers knowing by 12:30. I'll tell Lawson; he knows something is going down tonight."

"What about the captain. He's already retired to his room. His son is manning the helm."

"I'll wait until 12:30, then get him up by telling him there is a problem on deck. He will come," Sophie said. "I'll fill him in then."

Marci went to her cabin to grab some blankets; it was cold outside. Ojala was sitting on her bed crying.

"You aren't taking me with you. Are you?"

"Why would you say that, Giada?"

"There is no way you can fight off my brothers. They won't let you take me."

Marci sat down next to her and turned her chin to look into her eyes. "I promised you I would take you back to the US. I keep my promises."

Ojala nodded, but she didn't believe it.

Sophie went to speak to Lawson first. She chose to whisper his name at the door, rather than taking the chance the sound of a knock would vibrate. When he opened the door, she stepped in and kept her voice at a whisper. "Lawson, we don't have much time. I need you to come on deck until this operation is over."

"Sophie, I have a right to know who these men are," Lawson said.

Sophie considered his request. He was right in the middle of this. He needed to know. "The men you know as the Ricci's are the Hijazis." Lawson's expression told her he didn't recognize the name. "Do you remember, several years ago, when the president of Italy and over 800 others were killed when a bomb took down the hospital in Milan?"

"Yes, of course."

"It was Makhtar Hijazi and his two sons. It was such an atrocity that half the world hunted them. They had to leave Afghanistan and go into hiding. When Makhtar got ill, they contacted the man known as the 'Broker'. They didn't know the 'Broker' was a CIA asset. He contacted the CIA through his handler.

"A decision was made to get him treatment then hand him over to the Italians."

"They figured if they let him die, his sons would just take over," Lawson made the leap.

"Exactly."

"But why turn him over to the Italians?"

"Our president did not respond with aid or condolences when the tragedy happened. He only sent aid after the American people forced his hand. If you remember, he didn't like the Italians. Our relations with Italy have been strained ever since.

"President Madden thought the gesture of handing the Hijazis over to Italians to be tried in their courts would heal some of the rifts between our countries."

"And the world needs to see those men on trial; see justice done for their crimes," Lawson said, looking out into the darkness around the yacht as they left his cabin to head to the upper deck.

"Yes."

When they reached the upper deck Lawson asked. "So how does that happen tonight in the middle of the ocean?"

"A Seal Team will board the yacht at 1 am and take them into custody, then turn them over to the Italians."

Lawson looked around. That's only an hour from now. There is no one out there," he motioned with his hand.

"They're there."

Marci had stayed in the room with Ojala, keeping her eyes on her watch. At 12:30, she grabbed blankets and told Ojala to come with her.

"Marci, why did you bring me back out here? It's late," Ojala asked.

"I thought it would be fun to look at the stars. Maybe you can recognize some of the constellations."

"Oh, yeah, I'd like that."

EARLY WEDNESDAY MORNING ON THE YACHT

Anwar was pacing in his room. He couldn't sleep; something had gone wrong, and he was still upset that his father wouldn't allow him to kill or at least, take the infidels as hostages.

Salman had specific instructions to call him when he detonated the bomb. *If he's been compromised, then we may be compromised too.* He thought, getting more paranoid every minute. *How do I even know the captain is taking us to Iran. I need to see his navigational chart. On a yacht the size of this the maps must all be computerized.*

He didn't trust the Broker or anyone else for that matter. His paranoia was peaking.

I need to check with the captain and have him show me he's taking us to Iran. I won't let anyone get in the way of my father returning to Afghanistan.

Anwar looked at the clock on his end table. It was 12:45 am.

Anwar knocked on the captain's cabin door, but there was no answer. Sophie had already asked him to come to the helm, explaining what was going to happen. Anwar decided to find him.

Marci and Ojala sat together, looking up at the stars under a blanket. Lawson had sat down next to Sophie.

"Sophie, I've been waiting to get a chance to talk to you," Lawson said.

"I know, Lawson; I wasn't trying to be rude. I couldn't take any chances and compromise this mission."

"No, I understand. Although I would love to hear how you ended up in this position, some other time. Right now, I wanted you to know how sorry I am for the way I treated you."

"Lawson, no need to apologize. You were hurt, and it was my fault. I'm the one that's sorry."

"Sophie, you told me upfront you liked Duke. I was so in love with you, I couldn't take it when you chose him. But I recently prayed through it. I was carrying heartache around like some sort of trophy. I asked the Lord to forgive me. I will always love you, but as the friends, we always were. I have missed you so much."

"I hurt a lot of people the way I left. No one could understand my reasons for leaving, but I had to go, Lawson."

"I get it. And I think the others did too. But it was one more blow, losing you at that time," Lawson took her hand. "Please come back; your place as our friend has never been filled. It's been waiting for you all this time."

"That's kind of you to say. I don't think I could take it if the people I love so much, reject me. I couldn't live with that."

"They won't."

"You don't know that, Lawson."

"Give us a chance. Think about it, ok?"

Sophie nodded, then whispered, "I'll think about it." Lawson let go of her hand and sat back on the deck chair.

Anwar headed to the bridge to talk to the captain. As he climbed the steps to the upper deck, he saw Ojala sitting with Marci Smith.

"Ojala, what are you doing out here? You were to stay in your room," Anwar moved over to her, not even realizing he called her by her real name. Ojala looked at him with wide eyes, wondering what the others would say. No one seemed to notice.

"I wanted to look at the constellations. Father wouldn't mind."

Anwar started toward her aggressively. He reached down and grabbed her hair. "Where is your head covering? You have been under the influence of these infidels too long. Do what you are told."

Marci stood, "get your hands off her."

"You don't tell me what to do," Anwar pulled Ojala up by her hair. Ojala was hanging onto his arm, trying to get relief from his firm grip pulling on her scalp.

Lawson stood up, trying to calm the situation. "Mr. Ricci, we can't allow you to abuse your sister. Please, let go of her."

Anwar knew they needed the doctor, he let go of Ojala. Marci put her arms around Ojala and whispered for her to sit down.

"Ms. Smith, if you try to interfere with my family again, you will regret it."

"You don't scare me, Paolo."

The Coast Guard cutter had turned its lights out forty minutes ago, running on the radar navigation system. The Seal team and Houston were lowered into the CRRCs and rowed toward the yacht. It was 'go' time, and the Seal team was only half a mile from the yacht. They rowed the last few feet and attached their CRRCs to either side of the yacht. They would remain there until 1 am.

Anwar turned and headed toward the bridge. Sophie stepped in front of him.

"Where are you going?"

"I need to speak with the captain; he wasn't in his cabin."

"I'm sorry, but the Broker does not allow anyone to go into the bridge." Sophie knew the captain would not stand up under Anwar's questioning.

"I *will* speak with him, Ms. Jones. I need to see that he received the instructions to take us to Iran," Anwar was already agitated.

Ojala had seen Anwar's violent nature her whole life; she could see he was losing his temper. She'd been on the wrong end of it before.

"Mr. Ricci, I heard the captain tell you that he received instructions to take you to Iran when you boarded the yacht. You can trust the captain to do what he is told," Sophie tried to reason with him.

"I have paid your boss a lot of money; you work for me, now get out of my way. I am going to speak to the captain." Anwar shoved Sophie to the ground. Marci ran to help her up.

Lawson grabbed Anwar's arm and turned him around. "Mr. Ricci, you need to calm down. The captain is off limits."

Anwar turned around and hit Lawson in the jaw; they struggled back and forth, and Lawson got a punch or two in, but Anwar was strong. They got close to the railing. Ojala ran over to her brother and started pulling on his arm, telling him to leave them alone. She knew Lawson's size and strength could not match her brother's.

Anwar pushed Lawson away and picked up Ojala tossing her aside. Whether it was his intent to throw her over the railing or not, that's what happened, and Ojala was heading for the ocean below.

Lawson screamed, "**MAN, OVERBOARD**." The captain instantly turned on the flood lights all around the yacht and turned off the engine. Lawson jumped in after her.

When the lights came on, it was one in the morning, and the Seal team was climbing up the rope ladder they attached to the lower deck railing.

Houston saw Ojala falling into the water and Lawson jumping in after her. A few moments later, he saw two people in the flood light break through the water. He helped Ojala crawl onto the Zodiac.

The Seal team was now on the lower deck. Chief Abbot could hear the fight on the upper deck, but his assignment was to get the Hijazis in custody. The chief used hand signals to order his men to complete their mission as he headed to the upper deck.

Houston saw someone else go over the railing. "That's Sophie," he yelled as he saw his wife falling unconscious to the ocean hitting full force on her left side. He made a final tug on Lawson to get him in the boat, then jumped into the water after his wife.

Houston hit the water; the floodlights penetrated the ocean's darkness, but Sophie was out of sight.

Houston was panicking; he couldn't see her. In his panic, he couldn't think straight; he needed to calm down, fear was his enemy. *Lord, no, no, she can't die. Help me save my wife.* Houston's lungs were burning, He needed air but knew if he went up, Sophie would be too deep, he would never find her. With his lungs screaming for oxygen, he looked around. In the light, he saw a trail of blood, and he followed it deeper into the ocean. He got a glimpse of her hand and reached out to grab it. He reversed direction and pumped his legs, kicking and using his one free arm to break through the surface. When he did, he gasped for air and saw Sophie's head was still underwater. Houston lifted her head and used a lifeguard hold to swim to the CRRC. Lawson reached out as far as he could to help Houston lift Sophie onto the Zodiac. Sophie had a large cut on her forehead, that was bleeding profusely.

Chief Abbott climbed the stairs slowly; he made it to the top stair as Sophie tumbled over the railing. Marci tried to grab her as she fell, but Sophie was already out of reach. Anwar was distracted, looking over the railing too. Marci stood next to him, searching the water for Sophie and Ojala.

Abbott lifted his MK 16 and spoke loudly, "**ANWAR HIJAZI, TURN AROUND AND PUT YOUR HANDS UP.**"

Anwar spun around, startled. *Where did he come from? How could anyone find us out here? We've been betrayed.* He grabbed Marci and put his forearm around her neck, using her as a shield. He pulled a six-inch switchblade from his pocket, swiped it open, and placed it on her neck.

"**PUT THE KNIFE DOWN!**

THERE IS NOWHERE FOR YOU TO GO. IF YOU HURT HER, I WILL SHOOT YOU. IF YOU DO NOT LISTEN TO MY COMMANDS, I WILL SHOOT YOU. YOU HAVE ONLY ONE OPTION, AND THAT IS TO DROP THE KNIFE AND LET HER GO. DO YOU UNDERSTAND ME?" Abbott s

Anwar said nothing; his mind was racing, trying to find a way out of this. Gunshots were heard from below. Anwar knew the rest of his family was captured. With the floodlights still on, he could see an inflatable parked alongside the yacht. *If I could get to that boat, I could get away.*

Ojala was still coughing up water when Houston and Lawson dragged Sophie onto the Zodiac.

Lawson turned Sophie on her side and tried to expel water from her airway. Then he laid her on her back, pinched her nose, and breathed two breaths into her. Nothing. He repeated it, and her body convulsed; more water came out when he turned her to her side again. He put his face next to her to see if she was breathing. She was, but she was still unconscious. Lawson took off his wet coat and then his outer shirt, putting his jacket aside he used the shirt to put pressure on her wound.

"Agent Townsend, we need to get them on board."

"We can't until we get the '*all clear*'," Houston said, rubbing his hands up and down Ojala's back to try to warm her body while Lawson worked on Sophie. His clothes were wet, so there was nothing he could give her of his to warm her up.

CHAPTER TWENTY

Ensign McNamara came up behind Chief Abbott. He saw what was going down and lifted his MK 16, aiming it at Anwar's head.

"Anwar, there is no way out. If you jump overboard, we will get you."

"No, if you want this woman to stay alive, you will let me get into one of your inflatables and let me go."

"I can't do that, Anwar. We don't negotiate with terrorists."

The ensign whispered to the Chief, "sir, his brother is shot. He needs a doctor."

"Anwar, your brother has been shot. We can't bring the doctor on board until this standoff is over. I've been told he won't live much longer without medical help."

"You are lying," Anwar snapped, his eyes still searching for a way out. *If I jump, I can swim to that boat.*

"I'm not lying, Anwar. Khaan is bleeding out. Are you going to let him die? Your own brother."

"Where is my father."

"Makhtar is in custody. He was not injured," Abbott said. "We will call the medic up as soon as you put the knife down."

Anwar knew it was a risk, but he couldn't surrender. If he jumped, he had a chance. He saw people in the Zodiac but figured they would come on board. He could tread water until they do. Anwar needed a distraction so he could jump the railing without being shot. He focused on the MK 16 aimed at his head, stabbed Marci in the back, then grabbed the railing and jumped.

"Get the Coast Guard cutter here now. We need the doctor," the chief hollered. Then he looked over the side. He couldn't see Anwar anywhere. "MORE LIGHT." Abbott yelled to the captain behind a closed door to the bridge on the same level. The captain turned on another floodlight and moved it across the water. The ensign tossed a lifebuoy over the side.

Chief Abbott grabbed a blanket within reach and turned Marci on her stomach to apply pressure on the wound.

Anwar swam underwater until his lungs were going to burst, trying to make it past the outline of the lights. He came up for air and treaded water, waiting for the people in the Zodiac to leave.

The lights from the Coast Guard Cutter added extra coverage to the yachts flood lights. It parked on the starboard side of the yacht. The Commander asked Capitano Masso to wait to board until Anwar was in custody.

Now that Anwar had jumped ship and was no longer a threat, they called the doctor to come on board. Roman came up to Commander Peters.

"My wife is on that yacht. I heard one of the women was stabbed; I need to get on board, sir."

The commander sent his men over to help hunt Anwar. He told Roman to wait until his men boarded. Then the commander crossed, and Roman, Rocky, and Fons followed.

Roman and his brother saw the Navy doctor running up the stairs to the upper level and followed him. One of the Coast Guard medics was directed to the cabin where Khaan had been shot.

Houston hollered for help. He and Lawson saw Anwar go over the side but had not seen him resurface. Fons followed the voice and saw Doctor Cornett, Ojala, Houston, and Sophie in the Zodiac. Sophie appeared unconscious.

"We need help getting Sophie and Ojala on board," Houston hollered.

"I can climb the ladder," Ojala said. Houston helped her get on, and she made her way up. Fons reached out his hand to help her over the railing.

"Hold on, I'll get a stretcher from the Coast Guard." Fons ran to the Coast Guard Sergeant and told him what he needed. The sergeant returned to the cutter and brought a hardboard stretcher with straps. They lowered it over the side with a rope.

Ojala was surprised to see men in uniforms fill the yacht.

They hauled Sophie up, and two Coast Guard men lifted her over the railing. Houston and Lawson climbed the rope ladder. When Lawson crawled over the railing, he went for his medical bag in his room.

Ojala stopped a man wearing black, "what's going on? Where is my father?" She turned to see men walking her father out onto the deck from below in handcuffs. She ran to him, and one of the Seals put his arm out to stop her.

"He is under arrest, ma'am."

"Father, what is going on? Why are they arresting you?"

The Seals who captured Makhtar handed him over to two Coast Guardsmen who set him down on the couch. They allowed Ojala to sit next to him.

"Father, tell me what's going on."

"Ojala, you need to go back to Afghanistan. Your sisters-in-law will take care of you."

"Tell me, why did they arrest you."

"You know, Ojala. You have always known," he said.

Ojala sat there looking around. She did know; she heard her father and her brothers making plans to bomb synagogues and iconic buildings. Ojala wanted to believe it was just talk.

Otherwise, she was the daughter of a monster. What did that make her?

Ojala saw two men bringing someone from the upper deck on a hardboard. Roman was with them. When they got closer, she saw it was Marci, and ran to her.

"Marci, what happened?"

Marci reached her hand out to Ojala. "Ojala…."

"You know my real name."

"Yes. Ojala, stay with Rocky. He will take care of you."

"Are you leaving me?"

"No, they are taking me to the hospital. Rocky will bring you when the yacht docks back in Corpus Christi."

"You promise?" Ojala started crying. Marci nodded and wiped away a tear.

Rocky stepped over to her. "Ojala, you need to change; you are shivering." Ojala nodded.

As Ojala headed to her cabin to get changed she saw several men carrying out a black body bag; she moved out of the way.

"Who is that?" she asked Lawson, who was coming out of his cabin.

"Ojala, your brother Khaan shot at the Seal team. He died in the exchange." Lawson was surprised Ojala did not react to her brother's death. Behind her, she heard her father cry out when he saw the body bag.

"Where is Anwar?" Ojala asked.

"After he stabbed Marci, he jumped ship. They are looking for him now."

Ojala nodded. She was sorry her brother was dead, but no tears came, and she didn't feel guilty about it. He was awful to her and to his wife. She would not miss him.

Ojala headed to her cabin. She took off her wet clothes, dried herself off, and put on a dry pair of blue jeans, a heavy sweater, and a jacket. Ojala sat on the bed; she didn't want her father to go to jail. She loved her father, but what could she do. She knew he was an evil man. Maybe she could visit him in prison.

Marci saw Houston kneeling next to Sophie. "Sophie!" She reached out to her.

"Darling, she is unconscious. Doctor Cornett is taking care of her."

"Oh, Roman, how could this have gone so wrong."

Roman took her hand and kissed it. He was scared for his wife; she had lost a lot of blood. "You both will be fine, love." But he wasn't sure he was telling her the truth. He couldn't face life without her.

The Navy doctor there to monitor Makhtar, took over tending Marci from the Coast Guard medic, so the medic could help Sophie. He spotted the Commander and headed to speak with him. "Sir, we need a Coast Guard rescue helicopter. These patients need to get to the hospital right away.

The Commander stepped away and used his radio to speak with his officer on the cutter.

"Yes, sir."

"Call in a rescue chopper and get an ETA."

"Copy that. Sir, the Italians want to board and take their prisoners."

"We still don't have Anwar in custody. He jumped ship."

"I'll pass it on, sir."

Lawson was back on the lower deck when he saw Agent Townsend on his knees next to Sophie, holding her hand and stroking her hair. He was speaking to her softly. The Coast Guard medic was on her other side, tending to her cut.

"I'm sorry, Soph, I shouldn't have allowed the First Lady to talk you into this. I love you. It's time to wake up now, sweetheart. You need to wake up for me. I love you."

Agent Rodrigues was standing behind him, guarding his friends, his hand on Houston's shoulder.

Lawson watched the Agent and realized he was Sophie's husband. Seeing Houston gently stroke her hair and whisper to her convinced him that Houston was the perfect partner for Sophie. Their lives aligned, and it was apparent he loved her.

Instead of being jealous or hurt, he was happy for her. Sophie had a good man.

Lawson spoke to the medic, "I'll help you suture her laceration."

The medic asked someone to bring them blankets.

"I'll do it," Fons said and ran off.

After Lawson stitched her laceration, he tried to rouse her again. He rubbed his knuckles over her chest bone, but there was no response. He covered her with the blankets Fons handed him. Speaking to the medic, Lawson said, "We'll need an MRI. No doubt she has a concussion.

"Agent Townsend, I see you are Sophie's husband. She needs to get out of these wet clothes. Do you want to do that for her?"

"Yes, I think she brought a few things with her."

"Good, take her on the stretcher into a cabin." When Houston stood, Lawson said, "And change out of those wet clothes, so you don't get hypothermia. I have another set of clothes in my duffle. My cabin is the first on the left."

Houston thanked him, and he and Fons picked the stretcher up and took her to the cabin that was marked hers on the information she had sent to the Seal team.

Fons waited outside the door while Houston changed her into dry clothes. When he removed her soaked top, he noticed deep bruising on Sophie's left arm that extended to her back. He knew what caused it; he saw her fall from the second level of the yacht. Unconscious, she couldn't right herself on the long fall into the water. Sophie hit full force on her left side. Fortunately for Ojala, she could right herself to keep from obtaining the same sort of injuries.

Houston sat beside her praying, tears running down his cheeks, when a knock came on the door. Fons had gotten the change of clothes the doctor offered. Houston took them and nodded his head. He changed and sat with his wife in the cabin until he heard the chopper.

Anwar had been treading water for thirty minutes outside the range of the flood lights. He was cold, and muscle fatigue was setting in. If he couldn't get to the CRRC unseen, then he had nowhere to go, and this was a foolish move. He was able to swim underwater to the CRRC. He planned to detach it from the yacht, pull it out of the reach of the lights, then get on board. But the connection was too high for him to reach from the water.

Anwar decided to swim to the other side of the yacht, hoping there was another way to get back onboard without being seen and hide. There was a large Coast Guard Cutter in his way. Swimming between the yacht and the Coast Guard Cutter was risky. The cutter's fenders were systematically hitting the yacht as the water moved. He decided to swim on the other side of the cutter, even though it would take twice as long, and he was already exhausted.

Anwar saw another Zodiac attached to the yacht and looked for a way to untether it without being seen. He held onto the side of the boat, trying to regain strength. His body was beginning to shake; he needed to get out of the water. He reached for the tether, but like the other side, the connection was too high to reach from the water. The floodlights were on all around the boat. But he figured most the men were watching the other side, where he jumped.

Anwar went to the darkest side of the inflatable and managed to crawl onboard without being seen. He reached for the tether and detached it from the yacht.

Coast Guardsmen were searching for Anwar in the water on the starboard side. The Cutter pilot used his flood lights to scan the water on both sides of the yacht. Chief Abbott and Ensign McNamara were on the lower deck port side.

"Chief, do you think he drowned?" McNamara asked.

"No. Keep looking," Abbott said. "THERE!" Abbott heard one of the men yell out from the other side. "He's on the Zodiac."

Abbot ordered the men to go down the ladder and keep him from taking off. But Anwar managed to start the small engine and move out of reach.

Chief Abbott and Ensign McNamara ran to the other side and down the ladder to the other Zodiac. The ensign started the motor, and they headed after Anwar.

Anwar had a good head start but heard the other Zodiac behind him. He looked around the boat for a weapon.

"Run the engine full out, Ensign," Chief Abbot ordered, grabbing the bullhorn stored under the seat. As soon as they were close enough that Anwar would hear him over the engines, he turned it on.

"ANWAR HIJAZI, TURN OFF THE ENGINE AND BE READY TO BE BOARDED."

There was no response. The ensign turned on the Goodsmann 4500 handheld waterproof floodlight and focused it on Anwar.

"ANWAR HIJAZI, THERE IS NOWHERE FOR YOU TO GO. TURN OFF YOUR ENGINE AND WAIT TO BE BOARDED."

The ensign bridged the gap between them by running the engine hot and coming at him at an angle. They were within a half mile of him when Chief Abbott took out his gun giving a warning shot over his head.

"STOP YOUR ENGINE, OR THE NEXT SHOT WILL BE IN YOUR HEAD."

Anwar was desperate; the other Zodiac was coming up fast. He had no weapon. *What do I do? There is no way I can outrun them. Should I go out in a blaze of glory?* Anwar was mulling things over. But when it came down to it, he was a coward. Anwar didn't want to die. He always believed he had what it took to be a martyr, a suicide bomber. But when it came right down to it, he wanted to live.

Anwar turned off the engine and waited for his pursuers to catch up.

Ojala was on the lower deck sitting with her father while men moved around the ship. Ojala heard someone speak over the radio.

"We have Anwar Hijazi in custody."

How did this happen to my family? I planned to leave them, but I never wanted my father in prison.

Chief Abbot drove one of the Zodiacs while keeping his gun on Anwar, who was cuffed. Two Coast Guardsmen went down the ladder to take him off the boat.

With Makhtar and Anwar in restraints and Khaan dead, Commander Peters officially turned them over to Capitano Masso. The Capitano handed papers to the Commander addressed to Roman DeCarlo and asked him to deliver them. The Commander sent one of his officers to where Roman was waiting for the helicopter to deliver the papers.

Ojala didn't recognize the uniforms of the two men who came to take her father, they looked foreign. They were moving Makhtar and Anwar to the ramp that crossed over to the Coast Guard Cutter, when Ojala ran after them.

"No, no. Please do not take my father," Ojala pleaded. One of the Militare stopped her. Capitano Masso saw her distress and halted the move.

In Italian, he told his men to allow her to say goodbye.

Ojala hugged her father; she spoke to him in Arabic, "I love you, father. I do not want you to go to prison. What will they do to you?"

"I expect they will try me and put me in prison. I want you to go home, Ojala. They will find a husband for you, and you will be taken care of. The Italians do not have the death penalty. I will find a way to do my work from prison. Prison walls cannot stop me from my mission. My followers will find a way to communicate with me."

"Will they let me visit you?" Ojala asked.

"I don't know," Makhtar kissed her forehead but never told her he loved her. She ignored Anwar, and he did not speak to her.

The Italians took her father away. Ojala watched him disappear onto the big Coast Guard Cutter.

Ojala knew now that her father would never stop killing unless he was in prison; he had no conscience. He belonged behind bars.

She was crying when Rocky came and put his arm around her.

"What will happen to me now?" Ojala looked at him. "Marci was going to take care of me, but she is going to the hospital. I don't know what to do."

"Roman and Marci still plan to take you in. We will travel with the yacht back to Corpus Christi, where the Coast Guard will provide us transportation to the hospital in Austin."

"We're going back to Austin?"

"Yes."

"My father is going to prison," she cried.

"Ojala, your father and brothers are terrorists; they bombed a hospital in Italy and killed many people. They need to pay for that crime," Rocky said.

"Khaan, what will happen to his body?" Ojala asked.

"His body will be returned to his wife in Afghanistan."

Ojala broke down. Even though they were often mean to her, she was a part of a family. Now she was all alone, and the feeling overwhelmed her.

Rocky could see what she was going through. "Ojala, you are not alone. Jesus knew you from before you were born. He is with you now. He will never leave you." Rocky held her for a moment.

It had taken forty minutes from the time they called the helicopter for it to reach the yacht. Doctor Cornett, Sophie, Marci, Houston, and Roman were lifted off the deck, and the chopper headed toward Austin.

The medic on board inserted a warm IV to help with Sophie's mild hypothermia. He did the same for Marci to keep fluids in her because of the loss of blood.

The cutter was long gone, and the captain had turned the yacht around to take it back to Corpus Christi. The Coast Guard called in the local police to meet the yacht with their bomb squad when it returned to Corpus Christi. They wanted to be certain there were no explosives hidden on board.

Chief Abbott had contacted the op center in Quantico and gave a full report. Including the injuries.

Ojala was sitting on the lower deck, staring over the side into the darkness around her. She cried until there were no tears left. *I almost forgot about the money! Father has no use for it now; it should go to me. That way, if Marci changes her mind about taking me in, I will not have to live on the street,* she reasoned. Ojala went to Anwar's room and found the money. The plastic wrap was slit open, but there was still more than half in the plastic. She took it, went to her cabin, and placed it in the bottom of her suitcase, covering it with her clothes.

Doctor Cornett called ahead to the Heart Hospital to have gurneys ready on the roof when the helicopter landed. Marci became unconscious due to the loss of blood, halfway there.

It took one hour and thirty minutes to reach the hospital rooftop from the yacht. As requested, orderlies and an ER Doctor

Svensson, were waiting for them. While unloading the patients, Doctor Cornett ordered an O- blood transfusion for Marci. Roman had no idea what blood type his wife was.

Lawson hollered over the helicopter's rotors to the ER doctor, "Order blood test on Mrs. DeCarlo so we know her type for the next bag."

When Houston reached the ICU, Sophie was in a room with several nurses, Lawson, and Doctor Long. Lawson was giving him all the relevant information about Sophie's injuries.

Roman followed behind Marci's gurney and watched as the doctor did what he could to contain the bleeding. He was hesitant to suture her wound until he knew if there was any debris lodged in it. Doctor Svensson packed the wound until an X-ray technician could get there. He ordered a blood test to find her blood type and to see her critical blood count, serum creatinine level, and platelet count.

While Marci was being treated, the head nurse asked Roman to register his wife. Reluctantly he left her ER room.

When he got to registration, he saw Houston doing the same thing.

"Houston, how is Sophie doing?" Roman asked.

Houston lifted his head from the papers he was filling out. "Roman. I see they sent you down here too. Sophie is still unconscious. How is Marci."

"I don't know, Houston. I'm worried."

Houston stood and put his hand on Roman's shoulder. "Roman, one thing I've learned living my life for Christ is that no matter how bad things look. God can turn it around in a blink of an eye. There is always hope in Him." Roman nodded.

"You're right, Houston. Will you pray with me?"

No one else was in the office except the woman who oversaw the new patient registration. Neither man cared who was around. This was who they were. Houston and Roman prayed quietly together. First, they thanked the Lord for all He has done for them, then asked Jesus to give the doctors wisdom and spoke healing into their wives, in the name of Jesus.

Houston turned his phone back on when they were done with the paperwork. He saw that he had ten missed calls. He ignored them for the time being, and he and Roman headed back to be with their wives.

Dr. Svensson received the results back on Marci's blood test: B+. He ordered a bag of her blood type then sent a copy of the test to Dr. Cornett and gave him a call.

"Doctor Cornett," Lawson answered the phone.

"Doctor Cornett, did you get the blood test results I sent you?"

"Yes, Doctor Svensson, I'm here with Doctor Long. I'm putting you on speaker. Please go ahead, Doctor."

"The X-ray showed there is no debris in the wound, but the blood tests show the serum creatinine levels are…."

"Low, yes, Doctor, we see that. And I know what you are thinking and agree we need an MRI and an ultrasound to know for sure. But it is likely the knife nicked her kidney. If we can get in there and stop the bleeding, we may be able to save it," Dr. Long said.

"Exactly," Svensson agreed.

"Doctor Svensson, will you send her for an MRI and then have her taken up here to the surgical unit?"

"Right away."

"Thank you."

"You're welcome. I hope she makes it, Lawson. I know she is a friend of yours."

"She is, thank you for your help," Lawson hung up.

CHAPTER TWENTY-ONE

I'll do the surgery, Sebastian."

"No, Lawson. You are too close to the case, and you are exhausted. You've had no sleep. I'll do the surgery."

Lawson lowered his head for a moment, looking at the results on his computer. "You're right. Marci needs fresh eyes on this."

Lawson's computer showed that more results were coming in. "These are Sophie's test results," he paused and looked at them, then turned the computer screen to Dr. Long.

"Sophie's MRI shows brain swelling but no bleeding. That could be why she hasn't woken up."

"I agree; the blood tests show she is pregnant too. Do you think she knows?" Dr. Long asked.

"Sophie is the smartest woman I've ever met. She knows. Do you think the baby can make it after so much trauma?" Lawson looked up at his friend sitting across from him.

"Lawson, you know as well as I do. We'll have to wait and see. But an ultrasound could let us know if the baby's alive."

"I'm concerned she may still have water in her lungs; she wasn't awake to help expel it."

"It happened in the ocean, right?"

"Yes, I know what you're thinking. We could be dealing with blood thickening and an enlarged heart."

"Yes, you need to get an X-ray," Sebastian suggested.

"Sebastian, when I call the family, there will be more than fifty people in the waiting room. That includes former Governor Pierce and the extended family from London. They won't leave until they know she and Marci are out of serious condition. Marci is Sophie's stepmother."

"Our waiting room can't handle that," Sebastian said.

"It will have to. I'm not sending anyone home. They are my family too. They have waited nine years to see Sophie again."

"Lawson, the administration won't allow it."

"The notoriety from my devices brings more money, grants, patients, and attention to this hospital than anything else. I have the political capital to insist. They will have to figure a way to make it work."

Sebastian nodded his head, "all right, Lawson. If you want to use your capital, that's up to you. Cher Chandler saw right through you."

"Who? What are you talking about?" Lawson looked confused.

"The host of Austin Today. I watched your interview. It was evident you still love Ms. Star."

Lawson moved his eyes away from his colleague and looked at the outside lights reflecting in the rain. "I will always love her, in one way or another, for the rest of my life. But this week, I was able to pray through the heartache of losing her. Now all I see is my best friend again."

"I'm glad for you, Lawson. You can't carry around pain like that. It hinders you emotionally," Sebastian said.

"I'll tell the husbands what's going to happen next. How long before you are ready to operate on Marci DeCarlo?"

Sebastian looked at his watch, "It's 5:52 right now. It will probably take an hour for my team to get here and get the surgical room ready. So, let's make it 7 am," Sebastian stood. "I'm sorry your friends are hurt, Lawson."

"Thanks, Sebastian," Lawson watched as he walked out and closed the door behind him. He sat for a moment, staring at the computer, wondering if he should wake the family and tell them what was happening.

Lawson turned his eyes back to the window, the black of night was being penetrated by a sun working its way above the horizon. Soon the darkness would lose to the light. *I'll call the church prayer line and the family later; maybe I'll have better news for them. Oh Lord, we wanted Sophie to come home. But not like this.*

After Lawson made the call, he headed to the ICU.

After the MRI, Marci was prepped for surgery. Lawson went to speak to Roman, who was told to go to the second floor waiting area. Lawson needed him to sign the consent forms for surgery.

Roman stood to meet the doctor. "Dr. Cornett, what's happening with my wife. Is she still unconscious?"

Lawson directed him to sit. "Mr. DeCarlo, the blood test and the MRI suggest the knife nicked your wife's kidney." Roman rubbed his hands over his face and hair. Lawson continued. "Dr. Long believes he may be able to save the kidney if he does surgery right away.

"Is he a specialist in this field? I can afford whoever she needs," Roman asked.

"He is not a urologist, but Doctor Long is an excellent surgeon qualified to do the surgery. I trust him. You have the right to call in a urologist of your choice, but that will take time, and time is of the essence here."

"I don't know what to do. I don't want to make the wrong decision. How much time do I have before he wants to do the surgery? I want to talk to my brother and Houston."

"Mr. DeCarlo, take as much time as you need; just know time is not our friend."

"Thank you, Doctor," Roman watched the doctor move to the surgical unit doors. He called out, "What about Sophie?"

"She has a concussion from hitting her head on the yacht's railing. The MRI shows her brain is swollen. She has not woken up yet."

When Lawson left the room, Roman called his brother. "Rocky, where are you?"

"The yacht just docked in Corpus Christi. A helicopter is going to take us to Austin. How are Marci and Sophie?"

"I don't know what to do. The doctors think the knife nicked Marci's kidney. They want to do surgery on her. But I don't know anything about this surgeon."

"Do you have time to get another opinion?"

"They want surgery done right away to save the kidney."

"We know the hospital is famous for its heart surgeons. Don't you think it would follow that the other surgeons at the hospital were just as qualified?" Rocky asked, realizing if the surgery was urgent; Roman didn't really have a choice.

"I guess. So, you think I should let Doctor Long do the surgery?"

"Roman, if they are trying to save her kidney, what choice do you have?" Roman didn't answer. "Brother, the chopper is here. I'll be with you soon."

"Alright, Rocky. Pray."

Lawson saw Houston holding Sophie's hand. His eyes were closed, and he could hear the man praying softly.

"Agent Townsend."

Houston looked up, "Doctor, did you get the results back?"

"Yes, let's sit over here, and I'll explain them to you."

Houston moved to the chairs by the wall and looked at Dr. Cornett with red bloodshot eyes.

"Agent Townsend...."

"Please call me Houston."

"Ok, Houston. The MRI shows that when your wife hit her head, it caused a concussion; her brain is swollen. There is no bleeding, which is a positive sign. The swelling is likely why your wife hasn't woken up yet. I believe, from her shallow breathing, that Sophie might still have water in her lungs. I'm bringing in an X-ray machine to look. I'm hoping we can prevent her from getting pneumonia."

"But you forced the water out on the Zodiac."

"Yes, but usually the patient comes to and helps the process by coughing, forcing the rest out. Sophie was unconscious. But I can try to extract the rest."

"How?"

"I would insert a suction catheter down her windpipe and try to suction it out. Hopefully, I'll be able to get all of it."

"I know Sophie would trust you, Dr. Cornett. You do what you have to. I can't lose her. What about the bruising on her arm and back?"

"I called in an orthopedic specialist. She hit the water hard. I want to be sure there is no severe muscle damage. Oh, and as far as we can tell, the baby is fine. An ultrasound will give us a better look. But only time will tell."

"The baby?" The look on Houston's face told Lawson he had no idea. "How far along?"

"I can tell you after the ultrasound."

"Thank you, Doctor."

"Please call me Lawson." Houston nodded.

Roman came into the room to talk to Houston as Lawson was leaving.

"What news did the doctor have?"

"He just told me she's pregnant," Houston looked at him, stunned.

"You didn't know?"

"No."

"Is the baby alright?"

"He ordered an ultrasound to know for sure; he thinks so. But he said only time will tell."

"Do you think Sophie knew?"

"I don't know, but if she did and didn't tell me, it will be hard for me to forgive her. I would have never let her go on this mission."

Roman sat down in the chair the doctor had just vacated. "Houston, *let her*? Your Sophie and my Marci are not women who let anyone tell them what to do."

"True, but we had an agreement. We agreed to discuss anything she or I did that would put us in danger. And that should have included my child."

"Houston. Let it go for now. You can always discuss it when she is well. All your energy needs to go to make sure she gets better. And if you are not careful, you can allow something like this to fester. It can take you over.

"I know from experience. I once loved a woman. A woman I loved so much that when she refused my proposal, I began to hate her. It only hurt me. And I almost let Marci slip by me because I let that rejection fester.

"Now I know, Marci is truly the love of my life. I could have lost that."

"You're right. I'll ask the Lord to help me not obsess over it."

"How's Marci?"

"That's why I came in. I need your opinion. The knife nicked her kidney. The doctors think if they do surgery right away, they may be able to save it. But I don't know anything about this place. If I wait for a second opinion and it causes the loss of her kidney, I'd never forgive myself."

"I know exactly what you mean. I would normally want a second opinion on something like that too. But do you really have that option?"

"No."

"What do you think Marci would want you to do?"

Roman thought about it, "she would want to keep her kidney if there was a chance."

Houston nodded. Roman got up and headed to the nurse's station. Lawson was still there speaking with the head nurse.

"Doctor Cornett, please tell Dr. Long I want my wife to have the surgery."

"Alright, Mr. DeCarlo, the nurse will give you the paperwork to sign."

Lawson came into Sophie's room twenty minutes after the X-ray technician left. A nurse brought in a tray with a suction tube to remove the water in her lungs.

When he finished removing the water, he checked her breathing and felt it had improved. Houston watched the procedure from the corner of the room.

"Doctor, do you think you got it all?"

"We'll know soon enough," Lawson saw how exhausted Houston was. "Houston, you need to get some sleep."

"I'm not leaving her room."

"Then use that recliner," Lawson pointed to it, "and get some rest. There is nothing you can do. If you collapse, you won't be any good to her."

Houston nodded.

The Seal team was getting ready to head back to DC. Their job was done. The bomb squad cleared the yacht; there were no explosives hidden onboard. The captain and his son were interviewed and then given permission to return to Italy.

The Coast Guard took custody of Makhtar, Anwar, and Khaan's possessions. After searching them, they would send them to the command center in Quantico. Khaan's body would be sent to the FBI for an autopsy, then the body would be returned to his wife in Afghanistan.

The Italians left on the same private jet they came on, with the Navy doctor provided by the US government, and headed back to Italy. They would break the news of the Hijazi's capture when they arrived home. It had been agreed that the Italians would take credit for the arrest.

President Luigi Giordano called President Madden to express his sincere appreciation for turning them over. He promised that the two countries' long friendship would be renewed.

Mission accomplished.

News had spread that the mission went south, and Marci and Sophie were seriously injured. Director Cosby needed to brief the president before the news reached him. He left Quantico and drove to the White House. He was ushered directly into the Oval Office.

"Sir, the Italians have Makhtar and Anwar Hijazi in their custody."

"I'm aware. President Giordano already called to thank me and promised to reengage our normal friendly relations."

"Excellent, sir. That means the mission was successful."

"Yes. I understand the other son of Makhtar died. I believe his name is Khaan."

"Khaan's body will be sent to his wife in Afghanistan when the FBI is done with it."

"And his daughter? I understand she wants asylum."

"That is correct, sir. She is the one that gave us the intel that they planned to bomb the hospital."

"She is only sixteen. Will she go into the foster system?"

"No, Roman DeCarlo and Marci Beauchene want to become her guardians."

"That's agreeable. The task force did an excellent job. Good work, Gram."

"I'll pass on your congratulations, sir. But we did have some serious injuries." Cosby said.

"Serious injuries? I only heard about Khaan."

"Yes. Sophie struggled with Anwar, and he pushed her; she hit her head on the yacht railing and went overboard. Anwar took Marci hostage and stabbed her to give him time to jump ship. He took off in one of the Seal's inflatables to escape. But Chief Abbott and one of the Coast Guardsmen pursued and captured him. The sister went overboard too but was not injured."

"What condition are Marci and Ms. Star in, and where are they? You buried the lead, Gram." The president was annoyed with him.

"Sorry, sir. They are at the Heart Hospital in Austin. They were both unconscious, last I checked sir. Marci is going into surgery. They think her kidney was nicked by the knife, and the doctor is trying to save it.

"Ms. Star has a concussion; her brain is swollen. The doctor is concerned about pneumonia."

"All right, you know Marci is Emma's very good friend. She will want to be with her and Ms. Star too. I want you and Trish to go with her. I have to be in Italy to meet with President Giordano. He wants to thank me in person. It's what this mission was all about. I can't put him off."

"Of course not, sir."

"And I want the Secret Service at the hospital until they are out of there."

"Sir, Ms. Star is comfortable with the US Marshals that have protected her in the past. I think she would prefer to have them. You know how she feels about security."

"Alright, that's fine, but Gram, don't bury the lead on me again."

"I won't, sir."

Director Cosby knew he had made a mistake. Typically, he gave task force operations first then discussed casualties. But Michael and Emma Madden were close friends with Marci Beauchene and were very fond of Ms. Star.

When Director Cosby returned to his office, he asked Ms. Deasun to get SAC Stanley Fremont, of the US Marshals, on the line.

Ms. Deasun buzzed him, "SAC Fremont is on the line, sir."

"Thank you, Patsy."

"Hello, Director; what can I do for you?"

"What makes you think I want something? I might want to set up another date to play golf."

"You had Patsy call. For golf, you would have called me yourself."

"True. Stan, we completed a mission that had serious injuries."

"I know, Ms. Beauchene and Ms. Star. Gram, you know how all the teams that work with the President's Task Force keep close tabs on what happens there."

"I'm aware. The president wants security at the Heart Hospital in Austin, Texas, where they are patients. And you know Ms. Star, she wants people she knows. Did you know Ms. Star is Marci's stepdaughter?"

"I had no idea; it's a small world."

"That's not very original, Stan," Gram laughed.

"You know me, not a creative bone in my body; my wife tells me that all the time. Agent Townsend generally asks for Marshals Samuels and Cooley, but they will need to be relieved, so I'll send Vang and Holder. She will recognize them too."

"Alright, how soon can you get them down there?"

"I can have them on a plane in three hours."

"I suggest you contact the hospital and let them know you're coming," Cosby said.

"Copy that. I'll text you when they are in the air," Stan said. "Thank you.

"And I'll call to set up another date for golf," Gram heard Stan laugh as he hung up.

After Dr. Long took Marci into surgery, Lawson went into his office to get a few hours' sleep. He decided to call the family when he woke up. He set his alarm for 9 am.

Fons, Rocky, and Ojala, stepped out of the elevator, Rocky noticed Roman immediately in the waiting room and headed directly to him; Ojala followed. Rocky was carrying Roman's and Marci's luggage. Ojala was pulling her suitcase behind her.

Fons was carrying his and Houston's duffle and Sophie's small suitcase. He saw the sign for the ICU and followed it. He nodded to Roman when he looked over.

Ojala was scared; she had never been anywhere without a family member. Although Marci told her she would take her in, she was totally alone. If Marci died, Roman wouldn't want to take care of her. She would end up in some stranger's home. Ojala felt selfish thinking about herself at a time like this, with Marci and Sophie in serious condition. But if she didn't take care of herself, who would. One brother was dead, and her other brother and father were going to prison for the rest of their lives.

The television was on in the surgical waiting area. The local news discussed aerial views of the FBI's takedown of terrorist cells in Austin, Dallas, Houston, and El Paso. In the end, ten-cell leaders and six other members of Salman's terrorist network were in custody. Salman was dead, and the bomb squad had located C-4 in several different homes of his network. Lieutenant Denison's team was tracking down where the C-4 came from.

They heard a commentator say, "This morning, the Italians announced they had captured one of the most wanted terrorists in the world, Makhtar Hijazi."

Rocky and Ojala set their luggage in a corner. Ojala laid her wet jacket over them to dry out.

"Fratello, how is Marci?"

"Marci's in surgery," Roman hung his head and covered his face with his hands. Rocky sat next to him, put his hand on his shoulder, and prayed for him.

When Roman looked up, he saw Ojala watching them, sitting in a chair against the wall under the windows. She looked scared and alone.

"Ojala," Roman moved to sit next to her. "I'm sorry about what has happened to your family."

Ojala nodded her head.

"You don't have to worry, Ojala; Marci and I want to take care of you. We want you to be part of our family."

Ojala broke down when he said they wanted her to be part of their family. Roman put his arm around her.

Fons stepped through double doors without asking anyone's permission. Houston was in Sophie's doorway. Fons had texted him to look for him when they landed on the roof.

"Fons," Houston got his attention. Fons grabbed him and gave him a hug, after dropping the luggage. Houston was shaking.

"Fons, what if she doesn't make it. What do I do then?"

"First of all, Houston. We don't talk like that. We are believers; we need to believe."

Houston let go of him. "I know you are right, but I'm so scared." He walked back to his wife's side, and Fons followed.

"What are they doing for her?" Fons asked.

"A Doctor Ma is supposed to be coming to look at Sophie's bruised body. She hit the water without being able to right herself."

"When is he supposed to come?"

"A couple of hours."

"I talked to Director Cosby. He is coming down with the First Lady, and they are sending US Marshals for security."

"Samuels?"

"He's one of them."

"Good, you know how Sophie feels about security," Houston smiled. "She hates people following her around. She thinks the men are being given the job no one wants, but someone draws the short straw."

Fons smiled, "She never understood that she is considered a valuable asset by the government, and it is an honor to be charged with her security."

"Fons, even now laying here, pale and unconscious, she is still the most beautiful woman I've ever known. How was I able to convince her to marry me?"

"I have no idea," they both laughed. Fons moved the luggage from where he dropped it and put it in a corner of the room.

CHAPTER TWENTY-TWO

David had an early court appearance today, so David, Manny, and Jonathan came into the office at 8 am to discuss purchasing the building from Emmett. Emmett walked in behind them. They grabbed coffee from the Keurig in the break room and sat in the small conference room.

"Dad, are you sure you want to sell? We want the building, but it's a good source of income for you."

"Yes, I'm sure. I've decided to downsize. I don't need the pressure of all these property holdings anymore. I'm also considering selling my portion of the downtown commercial building to my partners."

"Dad, you are making a huge income from that."

"I know, but I want to retire at some point and spend time with my friends and family."

"We want the building, Emmett, but we want to make sure to give you a fair price."

"I'll get an appraisal done; if you feel it's fair, I'll accept that price."

Emmett's cell vibrated. He looked at the number and almost rejected it but changed his mind. He excused himself and stepped into the hallway.

"Hello?"

"Emmett Scott, I don't know if you remember me, Glenda Carran. But I'm the head nurse in the ICU at the Heart Hospital. "

"Of course, Glenda, you went to school with my wife Carol. "Yes."

"What can I do for you, Glenda?"

"Well... I'm not sure I should be telling you this, but two women, I think you know, came into the hospital early this morning. I just came on duty and recognized their names. Marci Beauchene and Sophie Star."

"What do you mean? Are you saying they are patients?"

"Yes," Glenda whispered.

"Do you know what happened or what condition they are in?"

"I don't know what happened, but I can't tell you, their condition. I just thought you would want to know."

"Yes, thank you, Glenda; I don't want you to get in trouble."

"I think Dr. Lawson is overseeing their care. Marci is in surgery. They are both in serious condition. Oh! I shouldn't have told you that."

"I appreciate the information. Goodbye."

Emmett hung up and started to head out the door when his son stepped into the hallway.

"Dad, what's going on?"

Emmett made an executive decision as Sophie's grandfather. The family needed to know. He stepped back into the conference room and told them that Sophie was in town on an undercover mission. Something went wrong, and she and Marci Beauchene were in the hospital in serious condition.

"Sophie? You knew Sophie was in town? Why haven't you told anyone?" David asked.

"I'll get into all that later. Right now, I'm heading to the hospital. Lawson is taking care of them. Someone needs to tell the rest of the family."

"David, you go with your dad; I'll make the calls," Jonathan said.

"I have a client coming in. After that, I'll cancel the rest of my day and meet you at the hospital," Manny told them.

Lawson's phone rang, waking him up from a fitful sleep. Marci was out of surgery. He freshened up, changed his shirt, and headed to the surgical recovery room to speak with Dr. Long.

Lawson saw David and Emmett in the waiting room with Roman and Rocky. They hurried over to speak with him.

"Lawson, what's going on with Marci and Sophie?" David asked.

"How did you find out they were here?" Lawson asked, surprised to see them.

"You know this town, Lawson. Now tell us what you can," Emmett said.

"I'm just heading in to talk to Doctor Long. Marci is in recovery now. They will take her to ICU when she comes around. Why don't you go to the ICU waiting area? I'll ask Doctor Long to come out and explain how the surgery went."

"What about Sophie?" Emmett asked.

"She is already in an ICU room. Her husband is with her."

Fifteen minutes later, Lawson came out with Doctor Long and explained what he had done during surgery to save Marci's kidney.

"Was the surgery successful?" Roman asked.

"Yes. I will need to closely monitor her for the next 72 hours. We will be transferring her to the ICU, in twenty minutes. You can see her once she is in a room."

Roman shook Doctor Long's hand, "Thank you, Doctor."

"Roman, the ICU waiting area is just down the next corridor," Lawson pointed.

Doctor Long went back through the surgical unit doors and Roman and Rocky headed to the ICU waiting area. Emmett stayed and asked Lawson to explain what happened after they left the hospital with the Ricci's. By then, Manny and Jonathan were there, and Anna, Zoey, and Ruby were just getting off the elevator and headed to the surgical waiting area where Lawson was speaking to the others. Lizzy, Jett, Drew, and CJ were behind them. Lawson waited until they were all there before he continued.

"Marci and Sophie came to Austin on an undercover mission. The plan was to get surgery for Mr. Ricci, then hand him over to the authorities when in international waters."

'What on earth are you saying, Lawson. Sophie is some sort of agent for the government?" Manny asked.

"No, her husband is, but Sophie is a consultant for the task force he is assigned to."

"Sophie's married?" Lizzy asked.

"Yes, to Agent Houston Townsend. He is a good man and truly loves her," he paused. "Anyway, things were going as planned when one of the targets got paranoid and aggressive. During a struggle with Sophie, the target pushed her. She hit her head on the yacht railing and fell overboard. Marci was taken hostage by the same man. The man stabbed her as a distraction so he could jump ship and try to escape."

"A yacht? Jump ship? Who were these people?" CJ didn't understand.

"CJ, I can't tell you more than that," Lawson said.

"Emmett said they were both unconscious," Anna said.

"Yes. Marci lost a lot of blood, and the knife nicked her kidney. She just got out of surgery."

"What about Sophie?" Jonathan asked,

"The MRI shows her brain is swollen, but there is no cranial bleeding. Look, I shouldn't be telling you any of this without their husbands' approval. Don't pass any of it on until they say so."

"Alright, Lawson. Please get permission so you can keep us updated," Emmett pleaded.

"I'll ask. I'm heading to the ICU now. You all can wait there with Rocky and Roman. Marci should be taken there shortly.

Earlier, Lawson had maintenance bring an extra recliner for Fons. Houston didn't realize he had fallen asleep until he woke up when he heard a hospital bed being rolled down the hall. He sat up and rubbed his face a few times.

Fons was in the recliner next to him. "Fons."

Fons startled awake, "yeah, I'm awake. What's happened?"

"I need to find out if Marci is out of surgery. But I want to clean up first. You brought my duffle, right?"

"Yes, it's in the corner with Sophie's suitcase," He had nodded to where he set the bags in the corner. I'm going to the cafeteria to get us some coffee.

Sienna walked into the bakery's back door after taking Teresa and Kato to Parkcrest Academy.

"Did you get them to school on time?" Jean-Paul asked with a smile. Jean-Paul was Sienna's business partner, now fiancé.

"Yes, they got into the buildings before the bell rang. Thank you very much," Sienna snarked. He always chided her about waiting until the last minute to drive them to school.

"Get a ticket?"

"No," she said. "It's hard to believe they have been with me for three years. Teresa is going to graduate high school next month.

Jean-Paul stopped decorating the wedding cake he'd been working on since three this morning. It had to be delivered today to the Catholic Church reception hall by five.

"Amour, you know getting Teresa into college will be a problem. She has never given her and Kato's last name and either doesn't have or won't show you, her identification. That worked at Parkcrest because they have the policy to allow undocumented children access to their school if they can afford it or if their quota for scholarships isn't filled."

"I know, I've talked to Teresa about it, but she still won't tell me what happened to her family. I'm certain they are not undocumented aliens."

"What are you going to do?"

"I don't know yet. No one has really questioned where they came from or how they came to live with me. With the border wide open, everyone assumes they are undocumented. I can't bring dad or Uncle David's law firm into it because if someone asks questions, I don't want them involved."

"You registered them with your last name. I'm sure most people think you are related somehow. Chérie, I want to help, whatever you decide."

"Thanks, sweetheart. There is a company that worked with Uncle Manny doing things he couldn't. I might go see them. "

Sienna's phone rang. She laid down the piping bag used to make her famous strawberry macaroons and wiped her hands on a kitchen towel. She looked at the caller ID before she answered.

"Hi, Dad."

"Sienna, I just got a call from Jonathan. Sophie is here in Austin in the Heart Hospital. She and Marci were injured somehow. Your mother and I are heading to the ICU waiting area."

"Sophie? Are you sure?"

"Yes."

"Ok, Dad. I'll meet you there."

"Sienna, what has happened? You are as pale as a ghost." Jean-Paul went to her. She was leaning on the long stainless-steel worktable to keep steady.

"Sophie... she is in Austin, at the hospital."

"What? How?"

"I don't know," she started untying her apron. "I need to get there. Will you pick up the kids?"

"Of course. We'll meet you there after school."

Sienna had to stretch to reach his 6' 1" frame so she could kiss him. She grabbed her purse as she ran out the back door.

Fons went through the ICU doors and noticed people sitting in the waiting room. He recognized one of them. He knew Emmett had helped watch the Hijazi brothers at the hospital.

Fons was headed toward the elevator when Emmett approached him.

"Agent Rodriguez?"

"Yes."

"My name is Emmett Scott; I'm Sophie's grandfather."

"Yes, I remember. I saw you here helping us watch the brothers."

"We haven't seen Houston; we'd like to know what's happening."

"We?"

"This is my son David," Emmett introduced David standing next to him. "The others are Sophie's family, too." Emmett turned and nodded to the small group sitting in the waiting room looking at them. "More family and friends will be here soon," Emmett replied.

"Did Lawson call you?"

"No, but news travels. Agent Rodriguez, please ask Houston to come talk to us."

"I will."

"Thank you," Emmett said and stepped out of his way.

Fons walked back through the double ICU doors. "Houston. Emmett, his son David, and a bunch of others are in the waiting room. They asked if you would go out and speak with them. He said more people were coming."

"Who are they?"

Fons shrugged, "Emmett said, family."

"I will when I know something." Houston headed into the bathroom to get cleaned up. Fons decided to wait on coffee.

Lawson stepped into Marci's room to speak with Dr. Long. He heard him explaining how the surgery went to Marci now that she was awake. The fluids and blood had stabilized Marci enough to wake up after the anesthesia wore off. Ojala was sitting on the recliner with her feet under her, listening.

"So, you were able to repair my kidney?" Marci asked.

"Yes. The operation was successful. We will keep an eye on you today. If your vitals and blood work continue to look good, we will send you to a room on the third floor."

"That's great news; thank you, Doctor," Roman shook his hand. "I'd like a private room for her."

"You'll have to speak to administration about that," Dr. Long said.

"Yes, of course."

Lawson moved closer to Dr. Long. "Thank you for doing the surgery."

"I didn't think we had a choice, but it was a small nick and didn't take long to repair. I made sure the wound was clean, then sutured it."

"Marci seems to be stabilizing well." Lawson responded.

"I'm heading home, but I told the nurse to send her vitals every two hours. I'll be back if there are any problems.

"Doctor Titus Nelson is on duty now. I will fill him in before I leave."

"Thank you, Sebastian."

After the doctor left, Lawson spoke with Marci, Roman and Rocky.

"I expect you will make a full recovery, Marci. Your body has had a traumatic experience; it is adjusting. You still need time to heal."

"Thank you, Doctor Cornett, for everything," Rocky stepped closer, to hold Marci's hand.

"No need to thank me."

Houston and Fons waited for Lawson to finish speaking with Roman before they stepped in. Lawson stopped to talk to Houston.

"Dr. Ma, the orthopedic and vascular specialist I told you about, should be coming to see Sophie in a half hour."

"Thanks, Lawson. Will you be there?"

"Yes. I'm not leaving the hospital. I'm going to see a few other patients, then go to my office. I'll be there if you need me," Lawson started to leave, but Houston put his hand on his shoulder, stopping him.

"Lawson, you have gone above and beyond, caring for Sophie and Marci. I won't forget it."

"Houston, they are both important to me. I'm doing this for myself and the family," Lawson replied. Houston nodded and took his hand off his shoulder.

As Lawson left the ICU, he called maintenance to bring up two more recliners for the DeCarlo room.

Houston walked over to Marci's bedside next to Roman. "I hear your surgery went well. It's good to see you awake, Marci."

"I'm just happy to see her beautiful eyes," Roman directed his comment to Houston, while patting Marci's hand and smiling at her, a tear threatening to fall.

"You are such a charmer, love. I'm sorry I scared you, Roman," she turned her eyes to Houston again. "How's Sophie?"

"She is still unconscious; did you know she is pregnant?" Houston asked.

"No, Houston, is the baby alright?"

"Doctor Cornett thinks so. They are doing an ultrasound soon. It should give us more information."

"Please let me know as soon as you hear."

"I will."

"I guess there is family waiting to hear how you and Sophie are doing," Houston told Marci.

"I'd like to see them, but I'm really tired right now. Maybe later," Marci said. "Roman, why don't you go speak to them. Tell them I want to see them when I wake up."

"I'll go with you. I just need to wait for Doctor Ma," Houston said.

"Come and get me when you're ready," Roman said.

"I will."

Fons and Houston went back to Sophie's room.

"I feel bad for that young girl. She is all alone and frightened," Fons said.

"Why don't you take her to breakfast and try to reassure her she has a place with all of us. Ojala is probably worried about what her future looks like in a country she knows nothing about."

"Yeah," Fons went back into Roman's room.

Rocky decided to go with them to get something to eat and bring back some food for Roman and Marci. As the three of them stepped through the doors, they saw a crowd in the waiting room.

"Are all these people Sophie's family?" Rocky whispered to Fons, surprised to see such a large group of people.

"In one way or another. I've never heard Sophie speak of her family."

The crowd turned to look at them when they stepped out the door. David moved toward them.

"Agent Rodriguez, are Houston and Roman coming out to speak with us?"

"They know you are here. This is Rocky DeCarlo, Roman's brother," Fons turned to him. "Do you want to let them know what's going on with Marci?"

"I think it would be better if Roman fills you in. But she woke up after the anesthesia wore off. Roman said he and Houston will come out soon to speak with you." He scanned the faces of those looking at him.

"Do you think we could see her," Anna said. "We were good friends when she lived here."

"She is taking a nap right now, but she said she wanted to see you when she woke up."

"What about Sophie? How is she," CJ asked, Lizzy, clutching his arm, frightened for her best friend.

"She is still unconscious. They are doing more tests."

"Could my wife sit with her? Lizzy was Sophie's best friend," CJ asked.

"I'll ask Houston," Fons told Rocky he would catch up to him and went back to Sophie's room to speak with Houston.

"Thank you," CJ said.

"Houston, you need to go speak with the family. There is a crowd out there. I'll stay with Sophie," Fons insisted.

Houston turned his head when he heard Fons. "A crowd?"

"Yeah, a young woman says she is Sophie's best friend. She wants to sit with her."

"I'll get Roman; we'll go speak to them."

Houston and Roman came out of the ICU doors, surprised at the number of people waiting for them. They moved towards them, so they could hear.

"Houston, Roman, please tell us what you know," Emmett said.

"Marci is out of surgery. She was stabbed in the back by a man trying to escape authorities. Dr. Long noticed her kidney was nicked in the tests he ran.

"Marci was unconscious when she arrived. She woke up after the surgery, and the anesthesia wore off. She lost a lot of blood, but Doctor Long feels she will recover fully." Roman turned to Houston.

"During a struggle, Sophie hit her head on the railing of the yacht she was on, giving her a concussion. She went over the railing into the ocean unconscious. She hit the water in a bad position causing severe bruising on her body. An orthopedic surgeon will be coming in to see her soon.

That's really all I know. Dr. Cornett is her primary physician," he paused. "I don't know anyone here but Emmett, but I know she planned on coming to see you all after…."

Lizzy stepped to the front. "Mr. Townsend, my name is Lizzy Young. I'm Sophie's best friend; I'd like to sit with her now if you let me."

"Lizzy, I'm sure she would like that. I'll get you after Dr. Ma has completed his exam."

"Thank you," Lizzy had Jett in her arms.

"Is this your boy?" Houston asked, smiling at him. "And this must be your husband, CJ."

"Yes." CJ extended his hand. Houston shook it."

"I need to go back to her. It could be a long time before she wakes up," Houston spoke to the crowd. "If you want to go home, I'll call as soon as she wakes up."

"Houston, most of us won't leave here until we know she is out of serious condition. Please keep us informed," Emmett requested.

"Alright," Houston turned, and he and Roman went back through the ICU doors.

It was 10 am when Dr. Ma examined Sophie and ordered a CT scan. He told Houston he was worried about vein damage. Severe bruising like this could cause blood clots that could travel to her lungs. With her lungs already weak from the drowning, he was concerned.

When the orderly came in to take her to get the scan, Houston and Fons went to the waiting room to update the family.

When they stepped out, the crowd had grown. "Uh, Emmett," Houston lifted his voice to get his attention, and the others crowded around to hear.

"Dr. Ma, the orthopedic and vascular specialist, is sending Sophie for a CT scan. He is concerned the bruising from the fall into the ocean may have created vein issues. Specifically, he is concerned blood clots could travel to her lungs," Houston heard someone gasp. "I'll let you know more when he gets the results."

Lizzy took his hand as he turned. "Mr. Townsend, please don't forget to get me when she returns. I don't care if she's unconscious. I want to be with her."

Houston could see how upset Lizzy was. Fons spoke softly to him. "You know Sophie would want her there."

"I'll get you as soon as she is back," Houston told her then spoke to Fons as they headed back to Sophie's room. "When she gets back from the CT scan, I'm going to change Sophie. She might have one of her pajama sets in her suitcase. She wouldn't want people to see her in the hospital gown."

"I'm going to get something to eat. Rocky and Ojala are in the cafeteria already. I'll bring you something." Fons stopped when he saw the Marshals coming down the corridor.

"Houston."

Houston stopped at the doors and turned to see four US Marshals heading toward them."

Houston and Fons greeted Samuels and Cooley with a hug. "Fons said you would be here."

"I'm sorry Sophie got injured, Houston. How's she doing?" Marshal Samuels asked.

"Sophie's condition hasn't changed. Now they're worried about blood clots."

"We were told to do a full-scale security sweep. We'll vet the nurses and doctors who treat Ms. Beauchene and Ms. Star. Vang and Holder are going to sweep this floor now," he turned to them. "Start with the ICU, Holder. SAC Fremont already informed the hospital we would be here and doing a security sweep."

"Yes, sir," Deputy Holder responded.

"Cooley and I will stand guard at the doors."

Emmett interrupted the conversation. "Houston, what's going on. Is there a threat?" Emmett stood with the other men in Sophie's family. Houston turned to them.

"Emmett, this is US Marshals Samuels and Cooley. The ones that just left are Holder and Vang. The president ordered them here."

"Why," former Governor Mitch Pierce asked.

"Sir, the president requested Ms. Star and Ms. Beauchene be protected until they leave the hospital," Deputy Samuels answered,

"It's just a courtesy, Emmett. We don't expect trouble," Houston tried to assure him.

"If that changes, will you let us know?" Emmett asked.

"Yes, of course, Emmett," Houston turned back to Daren Samuels when Emmett gave them room.

"You know Sophie will want to see you when she's awake, Darren."

"That's why Cooley and I are taking the day shift. Right now, we have to help sweep the hospital," Samuels and Cooley nodded to the men that had gathered and headed out.

"Emmett, I'll come back when I know something," Houston told him.

"Alright, Houston," Emmett said, walking back to the family.

The orderly was bringing Sophie's bed down the hall when Houston went through the ICU doors. He waited for him to secure it in place. A nurse came in behind him and plugged her back into the equipment.

When the nurse left, Houston went through Sophie's suitcase and found her pajamas. He pulled the curtain for privacy so he could change her and clean her up. Houston couldn't get her right arm in the top because of the IV. He pressed the button for the nurse, who unhooked her and helped put her arm through.

CHAPTER TWENTY-THREE

Houston finished brushing Sophie's hair and pushed back the curtain. Fons entered the room with a Styrofoam container and placed it on the table for Houston. He put a cup of coffee in his hand.

"Fons, I can't get over my resentment that she didn't tell me she was pregnant before we agreed to go on this mission."

Fons put his hand on his shoulder. "Houston, don't you think she was waiting to see if this baby was viable before she told you. You both were so broken when she miscarried before."

"Maybe, but I also think she knew I wouldn't want her going on this mission if there was even a chance, she was pregnant."

"Houston, you need to pray through this before you confront her. Whatever happens in this pregnancy, she'll need your love and support."

"Roman told me something similar. I'm so scared, Fons,"

Houston asked Fons to see if Lizzy still wanted to come in.

"What about the other family? I don't think they will leave until they see her."

"If they ask to see her. I don't think it would hurt."

Doctor Cornett was filling out paperwork when a knock came on his office door. He stood and opened the door.

"Dr. Ma?" Lawson moved out of the way, so the doctor could step in and directed him to the small conference table by the window. The rain had started up again, and the wind was causing it to hit his window.

"Dr. Cornet, I wanted to consult with you. What I saw on the CT scan worries me. The bruising is very deep, and I have no doubt the veins have been compromised."

"You're worried about blood clots?"

"Yes. I know you have compression sleeves on her legs but the injury to her arm might be where a clot would come from. I would recommend blood thinner, even though I understand she is pregnant. The chart indicates the patient drowned in the ocean. Why haven't you put her on blood thinners already?"

"I know there is the possibility of her blood thickening up from the ocean water in her lungs, but as you said, Mrs. Townsend is pregnant."

"What about the LMW heparin blood thinners?" Dr. Ma suggested.

"There is still a small chance it could affect the baby. I'm not sure her husband will be willing to take the chance if it lessens the baby's chances of survival." Lawson looked out the window considering the question. "Dr. Ma, what are the chances she will get blood clots?"

"I'd say her chance of getting them in the weak condition she is in is probably 50/50."

Lawson leaned forward on the small table between them. "I would be inclined not to use them yet. But it has to be Houston's decision."

"I'm on my way to give him the CT scan results. Do you want to come with me?" Dr. Ma asked as he stood.

"Yes."

Fons was out speaking to Marshal Samuels when he saw Dr. Cornett and Dr. Ma heading to the ICU. Fons followed them into Sophie's room.

Houston was sitting next to his wife, holding her hand, and praying. Lizzy was sitting on the other side. Dr. Ma knocked softly.

"Houston, will you sit over here with us?"

There were only two chairs and the doctor's metal stool in the room beside the recliners. Houston moved the doctor's stool over and sat across from them. Fons leaned against the windowsill. He could hear the rain hitting the window and felt a chill come through the glass.

"Do you have the results?" Houston asked.

"Yes. Houston, the bruising goes deep. I am concerned there might be vein damage. If there is, clots could form and move into her lungs."

"That's bad, isn't it?" Houston's face turned sickly.

"It's only a possibility. We can't use regular blood thinners because she is pregnant, and it would harm the baby."

"You said regular. Does that mean you have irregular blood thinners?"

"They are not irregular, just made differently. They are called LMW heparins."

Houston looked at Lawson, confused, "So what's the problem, Dr. Cornett?"

"Houston, there is still a small chance it could affect the baby. I'm concerned because of the condition she is in. But the chance of her getting clots is 50/50."

"Dr. Ma, if we wait and she does get a blood clot in her lungs, will the blood thinner still work then?" Houston questioned.

"Yes, but I would rather prevent it than try to cure it."

"Dr. Cornett, what do you think?"

"He is right. Preventing is better. But there is still a chance, even if she is on blood thinners, that she could get a clot," Lawson explained.

"So, Dr. Ma, you are recommending we put her on an LMW heparin even though there is still a chance of her getting a blood clot."

"Yes. That is my recommendation."

"Thank you, doctors. Can I have some time to think about it?"

"Yes, of course."

When the doctors left, Houston put his elbows on his knees and covered his face. Fons sat down in one of the chairs vacated by the doctors.

"Fons, how do I make a decision like this," his voice was muffled by his hands.

"We don't; we let God make the decision. You need to go to the chapel and pray about it. I'll join you after I talk to Sophie's family."

"I don't want to leave her alone," Houston said.

"I'll stay with her," Lizzy said softly.

"Thank you."

Fons and Houston stepped into Marci's room. Roman helped her change into her own night clothes and sat beside her; she was asleep.

Houston explained what the doctors said about the risk of blood clots.

"What are you going to do, Houston," Roman asked.

"I don't know; I'm going to the chapel to pray."

"Rocky and I will come with you; we can pray for Marci, too," Roman hesitated and turned to his wife. "I don't like leaving her alone."

"I'll stay with her," Ojala said, standing and moving to the recliner next to Marci's bed, but she didn't sit.

"Ojala, you were so quiet; I thought you went to the waiting room."

"No, I didn't want to be a bother."

Roman took her shoulders, "Ojala, listen to me. You are not a bother. We want you to be a part of our family. Family is never a bother."

Ojala nodded.

"If there is any change, come get us. The chapel is on the main corridor by the elevators."

The small group of men stepped out of the ICU doors. It was noon, and the family was still waiting. Houston, Roman, and Rocky headed to the chapel. Fons stayed to explain what was happening.

"Marci is sleeping. But if any of you would like to see her when she wakes up, she would like that."

"What about Sophie?" Anna asked. Fons explained the decision that needed to be made about the blood thinner.

"She's pregnant, and it brings some risk with it," Fons said.

"She's pregnant?" Ruby asked.

"Yes. We are heading to the chapel. Houston needs the Lord's help in deciding what to do."

"Do you think Houston would mind if some of us joined him?" Governor Pierce asked.

"No, I'm sure he would appreciate it."

The women decided to stay and see Marci.

"Can we see Sophie too?" Carmen asked.

"If you like, but she's not awake."

"We know, but we want to pray for her." Aileen, the governor's wife, said.

When the men stepped into the chapel, they saw Houston kneeling in the front, his shoulder slouched, crying out to Jesus for direction. Roman was kneeling next to him.

The men formed a circle around him, knelt, and began to pray. Henry Whiteing didn't know how long they had prayed before he felt a presence around him. He opened his eyes, thinking someone had joined them, but no one new was there.

Henry had been a believer for many years. He didn't have a miraculous experience with the Lord as some do. He just decided the Bible was the Word of God and believed by faith. He was encouraged by Hebrews chapter 11. It spoke of the patriarchs of old who walked in faith and pleased God. But right now, at this moment, he felt something. He couldn't explain it, but the power of the unified prayers seeking a common answer, changed the atmosphere around them.

A scripture came to his mind, Matt. 18:20. 'Again, I say to you that if two of you on earth agree about anything they ask for, it will be done for them by My Father in heaven. For where two or three gather together in My name, I am there in the midst of them.'

That's what he was feeling. The presence of the Lord in a way he never had before. He opened his eyes and could see the other men's bodies react as the presence of the Lord passed by them. Henry kept praying but couldn't bring himself to close his eyes, afraid he would miss what the Lord was doing.

Houston felt the presence of the Lord and raised his hands. He began to praise and thank the Lord for all He had done for him. And for the hope of a baby.

The others in the group started doing the same, and soon the tears turned into laughter and singing. The Spirit of the Lord finally lifted, and peace came over Houston. He would never be able to explain it to anyone, but he knew what he needed to do. He got off his knees, turned, and sat quietly in the same spot. The other men sat quietly with him.

It had been forty minutes since they began praying, but it didn't feel that long.

"Thank you for praying with me. I know what to do, but I would like your opinions." Houston looked around at these mighty prayer warriors, he now felt a bond with.

Jared spoke, "Houston, none of us will give you our opinion, but if you tell us what you have decided, we will tell you if we felt the same answer." The others nodded in agreement.

"I do have peace about my decision. I'm going to request Sophie be given the LMW heparin. How I understand it, the risk is minimal, and the chances of her getting clots are much larger." Houston looked around and saw the men nodding in agreement. He looked at Emmett, who sat across from him. "Emmett, what do you think?"

"Houston, I don't see that you have many choices. And if you are at peace with it, then you know whatever happens, it's the Lord's responsibility to take care of it. It's out of your hands."

Houston nodded and stood. "I can't tell you how much your prayers mean to me."

"Yes. Thank you," Roman added.

As the men returned to the waiting area, Anna and Zoey came out of the ICU doors. Anna went up to Houston.

"We've been laying hands and praying for Sophie," Anna started crying. "We have missed her so much. She has to get better."

David held his wife. "She will, darling."

Houston addressed the group. "It's getting late, and you all have been here all day. When everyone has had a chance to visit with Marci and see Sophie, why don't you go home? If anything changes, we will call you."

"What about that young girl? I think her name is Ojala," Sienna asked. "Do you think she would come to stay with me tonight?"

Roman wasn't sure. "Come with me. You can ask her. Her world has just been knocked off its axis, and she could use a friend."

"Before I go, I'll bring you some food from the cafeteria," Carmen said.

"Xander and I will help you, sweetheart," Henry added.

"Thank you," Houston reached into his pocket to give them some money.

"Don't even think about it," Henry said with a scowl.

Roman and Sienna entered Marci's room and addressed Ojala. "Ojala, Sienna wanted to know if you would like to spend the night with her tonight. She will be coming back tomorrow."

Ojala's eyes got big. She didn't want to be rude, but she didn't want to leave the only people she knew in the US. Marci woke when they entered and could see the conflict in her eyes.

"Sienna, do you mind if she stays with me tonight. I would like her to stay close," Marci said.

"No, of course not, Aunt Marci," she turned to Ojala. "But you are welcome to stay with us anytime if you like."

Ojala nodded and thanked her.

Houston stepped to Dr. Cornett's door and knocked.

Lawson hollered, "Come in," thinking it was Dr. Ma. Lawson was researching the LMW heparins, the results looked promising. Lawson was surprised to see Houston walk in.

"Houston, please, have a seat."

"I've been praying about it, and I've made a decision, Dr. Cornett."

"Good. What did you decide?"

"I want to get her started on the LMW heparins. Based on our choices, I feel it's the best thing to do."

"I agree."

"You do? I thought you were concerned about it?" Houston asked, confused.

"Yes, I've been researching the LMW heparins since I talked to you. I looked over the test groups, and the results are excellent."

Houston felt relieved, "Thank you for telling me that. Do I need to tell Dr. Ma?"

"No, I'll order it. You need to rest."

"I won't leave her room, Lawson. And Fons won't leave Sophie or me. I imagine that goes for Roman and Rocky too. Thank you, Lawson… for everything."

"Like I said, there is no need to thank me, Sophie was a great friend until I messed it up. I hope we can be friends again when this is all over."

Houston nodded and left. He headed to the chapel for privacy to call his folks.

Houston sat down in the last pew and took a few deep breaths. He felt he had followed the Lord's leading in his decision. He knew that did not guarantee the outcome. But he trusted God. Like Fons said, 'we are believers; we need to believe'. He thanked the Lord for his friend and dialed his folk's landline in Trenton.

"Hello?"

"Mom. It's me."

"Hello, son. Let me get your dad on the line. "Jack, it's Houston; get on the line." A moment later, his dad picked up.

"Hello, son."

"Hi, Dad," Houston choked up. It was so hard saying it out loud.

"Houston, tell us what's happened," Jack insisted.

Houston told them that Marci and Sophie were injured during a mission. He couldn't tell them much about the incident, but he told them about Sophie's condition and the treatment she was getting.

"Son, we will hire a private plane and be there as soon as possible," Jack said. He could hear his mother crying.

"Dad, bring Bully; he'll need his service vest. It's there somewhere."

His mom must have hung up and stood by his father. He knew his father well enough to know he was holding her close. Houston heard her say she knew where the vest was.

After Houston hung up, he set the phone down and ran his hands over his face and hair. Then he leaned his head against the wall and closed his eyes. He felt someone sit next to him. He lifted his head and opened his eyes; he saw Lizzy's husband sitting there.

"Oh, CJ, were you looking for me? Has something happened to Sophie?"

"No, I saw you come in here and wanted to make sure you were alright."

"Where is your little guy?" Houston attempted a smile.

"Mr. Hudzik and his wife, Ivy, took him home for us. I'll pick him up when I go home. I'm still waiting to see Sophie and Marci."

"You were Duke's best friend, right?"

"Right, we met Sophie and Lizzy when they were in second grade. We were two years ahead of them, but we took the same bus from the Incirlik Base housing to school."

"Sophie almost married Duke?"

"Yes. I knew I loved Lizzy the moment I saw her when she was in second grade. It took longer for Duke to realize he had loved Sophie the whole time. He spent most of his time getting her out of trouble," CJ couldn't help but laugh.

"Tell me, I'd like to know what she was like as a kid."

"The first time we talked to her was on the bus when Sophie stood up to a bigger kid who bullied a young boy into giving him his lunch. The bully was in our class, and he'd been doing it for days. The driver was off the bus talking to someone. Sophie stood up and told the bully to give back his lunch. The big kid pushed her down. Duke got up and told him to leave her alone and give the kid back his lunch."

"That sounds like my Sophie," Houston smiled.

"Duke turned to help her up, but she told him she could take care of herself. When she dusted herself off and sat down, Lizzy told Sophie she was rude to Duke, who was only trying to help.

"She stood up and came to where we were sitting and apologized. From that day on, Duke spent most of his time getting her out of one jam or another," CJ said. Houston couldn't help but laugh.

"She is exactly the same now," Houston paused. "I'm sorry your friend died."

CJ nodded, "Me too. But I know I'll see him again someday. It broke my wife's heart when Sophie left us."

"That's why Sophie was so afraid to come back. She was afraid she wouldn't be forgiven."

"As you can see," CJ motioned toward the waiting room. "That's not the case."

Houston nodded. "I need to get back. Thank you for telling me that story."

Carmen, Henry, and Xander came back with trays of food. Carmen went into Sophie's room to bring food for Lizzy, Fons, and Houston.

Fons' eyes got big when Carmen came into the room. "Your Carmen Whiteing, the famous movie star."

Houston stood to save his starstruck friend, even though he was just as starstruck. "I apologize for my heathen friend, Mrs. Whiteing. Thank you for bringing us food. You know my wife, right?"

Fons took the food tray and set it on the small table, still staring at the beautiful actress.

"Sophie and her friends saved my son from a very lonely life. Xander had a serious heart condition when he was a child. I'm embarrassed to say I kept him in a bubble until he was in sixth grade. He was pale, skinny, and had little muscle mass."

"You can't be talking about Xander Whiteing; he looks like a movie action hero," Fons blurted out.

"He didn't then. He told me later that no one would speak to him in his classes. It was like he didn't exist. When he went to the lunchroom that first day, he froze at the door. Half the school ate lunch together at a time. He was afraid someone would embarrass him and tell him to scram if he sat at the wrong table.

"Then he saw this young girl walking his way. He was praying she could see him. That maybe she would even talk to him. It was Sophie. She invited him to her table and treated him like nothing was wrong with him. Eventually, he believed that too. They have been friends ever since."

"That was a nice thing to do," Houston smiled at his wife.

"Oh, their whole lunch table was made up of misfits; anyone who looked like they didn't have a friend was invited. Eventually, the school called it Sophie's table.

"Those misfits make up some of Austin's most prominent citizens now. It's amazing what a little kindness can do." Carmen went over to Lizzy and kissed her cheek. "Do you plan on going home tonight, dear?"

"No, I'm not leaving her."

"Alright, we plan to stay until visiting hours are over. I love you, Lizzy."

"Love you too, Aunt Carmen."

Houston moved over to his wife's bedside. "Lizzy, you need to eat."

"No, I won't leave her," Lizzy blurted out. "Oh, Mr. Townsend, I'm sorry. You probably want some private time with your wife."

"It's all right, Lizzy. I'll bring your food over to you."

"Thank you," Lizzy said.

When Houston sat at the table to eat, Fons said, "That was Carmen Whiteing. I can't believe I met her."

"She really is something. I appreciated her telling me how she knew Sophie."

CHAPTER TWENTY-FOUR

Glenda, the head nurse came in and switched the IV bag to one with the LMW heparin. Houston sat next to his wife and held her hand.

"Ma'am can you have another recliner brought in? Sophie's best friend wants to stay with her tonight."

"Of course, Agent Townsend. I'll have an orderly bring it in."

"Thank you."

Lizzy had been talking to Sophie most of the afternoon; she only stopped when others visited her and prayed.

"Lizzy, I've heard some of the stories you were reminiscing with Sophie about. It sounds like you two did everything together," Houston said, trying to understand the woman Sophie was most afraid would reject her.

"There was never a Sophie or Lizzy; it was always Sophie and Lizzy, even though our personalities are so different. We balanced each other.

"Sophie always went headlong into everything. She never considered her own well-being when she saw something wasn't right.

"I'm not sure how old we were; maybe nine. We lived in Turkey then. Sophie saw something hidden in the bushes by the fence surrounding the Base. She wanted to check it out. Come to find out, it was drugs. Some enlisted men were smuggling drugs onto the Base through crates that came through the Military Household Goods and Transport Division. They had a dead drop where they would leave the drugs in exchange for cash through the fence.

We told my dad about it; he was the day sergeant for the Military Police. He set up a sting. The Turkish mob lost the drugs and the money. And their sources providing the drugs on the base were arrested. As you can imagine, they were upset.

"The head of the Turkish mob wanted me kidnapped so he could leverage my dad into giving him back his money and drugs.

"CJ, Duke, Sophie, and I were at the bus stop. We begged our parents to let us take the bus back from the mall. The bus stop was right across the parking lot. As we waited, two men in a van pulled up and tried to take me. The others fought back hard. CJ got hit in the head with the butt of a gun. They told me to run, and I started to, but I saw they were still struggling, and I ran back.

"The men saw onlookers coming to help and decided to cut their losses and took Sophie. I don't think they really knew who was who, anyway. Duke wouldn't let go of her, so they shoved them both in the van and took off.

"Before they shut the van door, Sophie hollered to me to take care of CJ. He was still unconscious on the ground. So, I did. I wouldn't let anyone force me to let go of his hand. Not the EMTs and not the nurses at the hospital. I stayed in the hospital room with him in a recliner, not much different than this one. I had to keep my promise to her."

"Wow, you obviously got them back."

"Yes, a huge task force was formed, Turkish police and US military. But it was Uncle Luke and Uncle David who found them and brought them home."

"And here you are again, the faithful friend, staying by her side," Houston said.

Lizzy started crying, "It broke my heart when she left us." Lizzy looked up at Houston, "I understood why she had to, but she was a big part of who I was."

"Sophie was most worried about how you would respond to her if she came back. She said she couldn't take it if you rejected her," Houston whispered.

"I could never reject her," Lizzy said.

"I can see that."

"I know you don't live here, but do you think you will come and visit us."

"I'm sure we will."

"How did you two meet?" Lizzy asked, but they were interrupted by more visitors.

Henry, Emmett, Mitch, and Jared were the last to enter Sophie and Marci's rooms. They laid hands on Sophie and prayed for her. Emmett leaned down when they were done, kissed Sophie's forehead, and stroked her hair.

Emmett whispered, "Come home to us, Sophie, we love you."

When the men moved into Marci's room, Roman and Rocky greeted them. Marci was awake, they visited, and they all prayed together.

While the family was in with his wife, Houston would sit in the waiting room trying to get to know Sophie's family and friends.

Houston noticed a couple of younger boys sitting together. The boys looked to be about 10 years old. He saw David sitting with Jonathan. Houston heard a piece of the conversation as he walked over to them.

"… court in the morning, so I'll take Drew and Anna home in an hour. Jonathan, do you have…."

"I don't mean to interrupt."

"No, Houston, please join us. Any progress with Sophie yet?" Jonathan asked.

"No change. Those young boys over there. I can't place him with anyone."

"Drew is my son," David pointed to him and smiled. "Kato and Teresa, the teenage girl sitting with them, live with Sienna, the governor's daughter.

"Was Sophie here when your son was born?" Houston asked.

"Yes, Sophie was here when we got Drew."

"Got?"

"Yes, he was only a few months old when we became his parents. His mother was a client of mine and was in an abusive marriage. She wanted me to handle her divorce and change her Will to ensure Drew would be taken care of. She appointed me as his guardian if anything happened to her. When his mother died, we adopted him."

"I assume her husband murdered her."

"Actually, it was her husband's mistress. She killed Drew's father, went to his mother's home, and shot her."

"Whoa, that's quite the story. I remember Emmett saying he had to get back home to be here when you told Drew he was adopted or how his parents died?"

"Yes. We just told him a few weeks ago. We were afraid some hotshot newsperson would start looking for him for some 'Where is he now' piece."

"How did he take it?"

"A lot of our extended family is adopted. Drew understands how much they are loved and sees no distinction between being adopted and being born into a family.

"At least, that is what I hope is happening. Drew didn't say much. We showed him pictures of him with his mother. She had put together a baby album."

"You're talking about Dex and Cade, right?"

"Yes, and Emma, Blaze, and China," David said.

"Did Sophie tell you about them?" Jonathan asked.

"No. I've only met Cade and Dex and their wives. Cade was performing in New York. We were given tickets for the concert. Cade saw Sophie in the audience and asked her to come on stage and play with him."

"That seems like such a random coincidence," Jonathan said.

"More like a 'divine appointment'," Houston said.

Everyone had a chance to visit with Marci and see Sophie several times before the announcement came over the intercom that visiting hours were over.

CJ went to see if Lizzy would come home and rest, but she wanted to stay with Sophie.

As David, Anna, and Drew were heading home, Drew scooted up, poking his head between the front seats.

"Drew, do you have your seat belt on?"

"Yeah, sorta. Dad, Sophie made everyone cry when she left, but now they all treat her like nothing happened. Like she just got back from a vacation. You talk about consequences all the time. Shouldn't she have to pay for hurting everyone like that?"

David considered the question; he understood where Drew was coming from. He loved China and Lizzy, and their hearts were broken when Sophie left.

"Let me ask you something, Drew. What if one day you are mad at me and say something horrible. Then you think about it and realize how awful you were, and you're afraid I may never forgive you or love you the same way I do now.

"Would you want me to show you love and forgiveness? Accept your apology and love you the same. Or would you want me to hold it against you forever?"

"I'd never be mean to you, Dad."

"I know that son. Ok, let me explain it this way. You know the Bible story of the prodigal son, right?"

"Sorta, yeah."

"This man had two sons. He gave them their inheritance money, and one stayed with his father and worked in his father's fields. The other young man spent all his money on a sinful life and disgraced his family name. After he spent all his inheritance, he ended up feeding the pigs on someone's farm and watched them eat while he starved.

"One day, he woke up and decided to go home and ask his father to let him work as one of the servants. After all he had done, he knew he didn't deserve to be considered a son.

"The son didn't know that the father would go out every day and stand on the highest place on his property and look for his return. Every day he went out and came home sorrowful.

"But one day, the father looked out and saw a figure walking a long way off. He knew it was his son, and even though he couldn't see his face, he ran and threw his arms around him. The young man told his father he was not worthy of being his son, but could he come home and be his servant.

"The father called for one of his servants to bring his finest robe, placed it on his son, and put a ring on his finger. The father had a feast prepared, and they celebrated."

"I bet that made the brother mad?" Drew scoffed.

"It did. When the other brother came in from working the fields, he heard the party and asked why there was a celebration. The servant told him his brother had returned.

"The brother was so angry he would not go to the celebration. When the father came looking for him, he found his son was angry.

"'I have stayed with you and worked the fields, and you have never thrown me a party. But my brother comes from squandering his inheritance, and you kill the fatted calf? It isn't fair.'"

"Yeah, Dad, see, it wasn't fair," Drew said, empathizing with the brother.

"Do you want to know what the father said?" David asked patiently.

"Yeah."

"The father said, 'you are always with me, and everything I have is yours. But we had to celebrate and be glad because your brother was dead and is alive again; he was lost and is found.'

"You see, Drew, it's the same way with our Father in heaven. We, as His children, sometimes leave Him by sinning. But when we come back and ask forgiveness, He welcomes us like we had never left and forgives our sins, never to remember them again.

"Isn't that how you would want to be treated?"

"Yeah, if you put it that way, I guess," Drew said. "But I'm not sure China will see it that way."

Rocky and Ojala fell asleep in their recliners, but Roman sat by Marci's bedside. She had fallen asleep. Marci opened her eyes, and he whispered, "Hi, love. How are you feeling?"

"I'm hurting a little."

"Do you want me to get a nurse?"

"Not yet; I want to be with you a moment," she lifted her hand to his face and cupped his cheek. "I love you, Roman." He put his hand over hers and leaned into her touch. He turned his head and kissed her palm, then took her hand and held it to his chest.

"Marci, you scared me. I thought I was going to lose you. You can't do that to me. I waited so long for what I have with you," Roman whispered. She smiled.

"Are the Hijazis in Italian custody?"

"Yes, Makhtar and Anwar. Khaan shot at the Seal team, and he was killed in the action, Roman said.

"Do you think we can help Ojala?" Marci asked.

Roman looked over at Ojala; she was asleep in a recliner in the corner.

"Darling, I don't know. Do you think Ojala will be able to acclimate to this country? She lost her family and everything she knew."

"I hope so. She is such a sweet girl. How's Sophie?" Marci asked.

"She was unconscious when she went over the railing and hit the water hard. The doctor is concerned that the bruising caused vein damage and may cause blood clots to form and travel to her lungs."

"Oh, Roman, how could I have let this happen?"

"You?"

"I convinced you to take this to Director Perry; you would have been content to tell Makhtar you were retired."

"No, darling, it was the right thing to do. I'm not happy about the fact that you and Sophie were injured. But the plan was a good one. We couldn't foresee Anwar getting paranoid and wanting to speak with the captain in the middle of the night."

"Do you think Sophie will be alright?"

"We went to the chapel and prayed. I trust the Lord will keep her," Roman said. "Now close your eyes and get some sleep. I want you to get well fast," Roman kissed her lips.

"You'll stay with me?"

"I'm not going anywhere."

HEART HOSPITAL. THURSDAY

It was 4 am; the room was quiet. Houston woke up, picked up the metal doctor's stool, and moved it to the side of Sophie's bed. Lizzy was asleep on her left, and he didn't want to wake her. Lizzy's commitment and loyalty to her best friend was genuine, and he could relate it to his own friendship with his partner, Fons.

Houston took Sophie's hand, being careful of the IV in her forearm. He gently rubbed it on the scruff of his face. He smiled, thinking how she would wake up in the morning and do that. She liked how it felt.

He placed her hand carefully on her stomach. Then folded his arms and laid them on the side of her bed, putting his head down.

Houston didn't remember falling asleep, but he was woken by the beeping of the machine next to him. He had no idea what was wrong, but a nurse and a nurse practitioner came in and hurried to her. Houston moved out of the way. The practitioner took a stethoscope and listened to her chest. He whispered to the nurse to call Dr. Cornett.

"What's going on? Is something wrong?" Houston asked, panicked.

"Mr. Townsend, Sophie is having trouble breathing; her oxygen level has gone below what we like to see. Dr. Cornett will be in. He told us he would be staying the night. The nurse went to call him."

The commotion startled Lizzy. She sat the recliner up.

"Houston, what's going on."

"I'm not sure, Lizzy."

Dr. Cornett came in disheveled. He listened to her chest and ordered her to be taken for a CT pulmonary angiogram. The nurse left to call an orderly.

"Lawson, what's happened?" Houston wanted a straight answer.

"It sounds like she might have blood clots in her lungs."

Houston plopped down on the little stool. "I thought the blood thinner would prevent that."

"Dr. Ma and I were hoping it would, but it's good that she was on them," Lawson was interrupted by an orderly. The nurse returned and unhooked Sophie's leads to the machine, and the IV. The orderly unlocked her bed wheels and pushed her bed down the hall.

"When will you know for sure?" Houston asked, his voice trembling.

"A CT pulmonary angiogram doesn't take long, but a radiologist will have to read it and put the results in the hospital computer. I'll go to my office to wait for the results on my computer."

"Can I wait with you, Lawson?"

"Sure."

Fons had woken up when Lawson came in. He stayed in the room when Houston left with the doctor.

"Lizzy, what happened?" Fons asked; she had tears running down her cheeks.

"I don't know, but Lawson said he thinks she has blood clots in her lungs. Lawson ordered a CT pulmonary angiogram."

They both just stood there looking at the empty space where her bed had been. Fons stepped over to Lizzy.

"Lizzy, she will be all right. I have to believe that. I can't bear to think what would happen to my best friend if..."

Lizzy sat down; Fons moved the metal stool closer to sit by her.

"How did they meet?" Lizzy asked to take her mind off her fear.

"Houston and I worked for the DEA at the time when a woman came in to speak with the SAC James Hampton. She told him she could hand over Nikko Morano on a silver platter. The Morano's had the most prominent criminal empire on the East coast.

"Hampton was skeptical, as you would imagine until she told him her name. Sophie had worked for the Morano's, and she knew everything. She had been in hiding for more than a year. Nikko was obsessed with her. When she refused his proposal of marriage, he beat her, severely. I saw the pictures; it was brutal. The detective who worked the case said it was worse than the pictures portrayed.

"I can't go into the undercover op, but Sophie successfully led the takedown, and Nikko and most of his crew went to jail.

"Houston and I were part of her protection detail. He fell for her hard the moment he saw her."

"It sounds like there is much more to that story," Lizzy said.

"There is, but maybe another time."

Lizzy stood and walked to the door looking for Sophie. "Should I call the family?"

"Lizzy, I wouldn't; we don't know what's going on yet. There is nothing they can do, and they will be back in a few hours," Fons looked at his watch; it was 5:30 am.

"Ok, I'll call the church prayer line. Someone answers, 24/7."

"That's an excellent idea."

Lawson sat behind his desk and opened the in-house hospital site for physicians. He entered Sophie's name and his name as the primary so he could see the results as soon as the radiologist uploaded them.

Houston was standing at the window looking out into the dark. Houston and Sophie used to sit out on the balcony of their Manhattan penthouse. The lights mesmerized her. Sophie would make up stories of the people who lived in the houses or offices with lights on. He loved listening to her voice. Houston turned away and sat opposite Lawson at his desk.

"What's going to happen, Lawson?" Houston's voice was pensive; he was almost afraid to ask.

"Houston, I don't think it's a good idea to worry about worst-case scenarios." Lawson turned his eyes away from the computer to Houston.

"I need to know, Lawson."

"The results should be coming shortly. We'll discuss it, then call Dr. Ma to get his opinion."

Houston nodded, then went back to the window. It looked like the rain had slowed down; a few drops were still sliding down the window. But the wind had picked up, he couldn't hear it but could see the wind move the tree limbs in unnatural positions below them. He stared at the lights from the moving cars on the street, it was hypnotic. He could feel the cold outside when he touched the window.

"I didn't think it rained this much in Texas," Houston whispered to himself.

"We get our fair share. But it usually doesn't last long. Raining all day like this is unusual," Lawson answered. Houston looked at him for a moment, he hadn't really expected an answer.

Lawson watched Houston. The only thing he knew about this man was that he was hard-core law enforcement. It flew in the face of his own bias about FBI agents to see his tender love and commitment to his wife. It reaffirmed his original judgment that Houston was a good man.

Watching Sophie in this condition was hard for Lawson. The heartbreak and the pain of her rejection were gone, but he still loved her. He would never leave her bedside if her husband weren't here, but it would be inappropriate under the circumstances. So, he'd been staying in his office. Xander had been bringing him clean clothes from his condo.

A ping sound came out of the computer, and Lawson sat up and hit a few keys. He was reading the diagnosis when Houston sat down.

"Lawson, what does it say?"

"The radiologist said there are several small and large clots in Sophie's left lung and a few small ones in her right lung. He also said it appeared her heart was slightly enlarged."

"That's not good, is it?" Houston asked.

"It's not what we were hoping for."

"So, what do we do now?"

"We continue the blood thinners."

"But...?" Houston knew one was coming.

"We'll need to watch for side effects. The thin blood could lower Sophie's platelets and cause bruising. The clots can cause difficulties in her breathing."

"What happens then?"

"The smaller blood clots will dissolve in time. But if the side effects get too serious, we may try to remove them to protect the baby."

"How?"

"Normally, we would go through the groin with a catheter and suck them out. I'll consult an obstetrician to see what's best for the baby. If we go that route, Dr. Ma will do the procedure."

Lawson didn't want to scare Houston, but he needed to prepare him. "Houston, you need to consider your answer if it's between the baby's best interest and your wife's."

"How does anyone make a choice like that, Lawson."

"I don't know, Houston. Just pray it doesn't come to that."

Lawson called the nurse's station and ordered oxygen for Sophie. Houston thanked Lawson and left his office. It would be a while before Lawson consulted with the other doctors.

The waiting room was empty except for the two US Marshals sitting close to the large double doors to the ICU. They no longer wore their US Marshals jacket, trying to be less conspicuous. He went to the large window and saw a glimmer of pink coming over the horizon.

Houston sat in one of the empty chairs and put his head in his hands. *Oh, Lord, you are my only hope. Only you can save my wife and my child. 'I know in whom I have believed and am persuaded that He is able to keep that which I have committed unto him against that day.'* The scripture from Timothy 2:12 ran through his mind.

Lord, I do believe, and I trust You. I commit my life, my wife, and my child to You. There is nothing I can do but believe and trust you.

Houston sat alone for a few more minutes, then returned to Sophie's room.

CHAPTER TWENTY-FIVE

The First Lady, Trish, and Director Cosby landed and were escorted to the hospital. It was 10:30 am by the time they pulled under the hospital portico.

Two secret service men went in with them. The other two stayed outside. Director Cosby went to the reception desk and inquired about the room numbers.

"We don't have a Marci Beauchene, or a Sophie Star registered here, sir."

"Marci DeCarlo and Sophie Townsend, then."

"Yes, they are in ICU, sir." Then the young woman whispered, "Is that the First Lady, Emma Madden?"

The director didn't answer but asked what floor the ICU was on.

The small group got on the elevator and headed to the second floor. When they got off the elevator, one Secret Service man went ahead, and one stayed behind.

Marshals Samuels and Cooley had relieved the men on night duty. They stood to their feet when they saw the Secret Service coming. Deputy Samuels went to speak with the lead Agent.

"Whose here?"

"The First Lady. Where are Ms. Beauchene and Ms. Star? And who are all these people?"

"This is their family," Samuels nodded to the crowd. "Mrs. Star Townsend is in the first room to the right, and Mrs. Beauchene DeCarlo is in the room right next to her."

"Good, thank you, Marshal."

The other Agent kept the First Lady from going into the waiting room until he got the all-clear from his partner. They were standing a few feet away from Dr. Cornett's door. When Lawson stepped out, he was surprised to see people in the hallway.

"Can I help you," Lawson said before he recognized the First Lady and an Agent stepped between them.

"Madam First Lady."

"I've come to check on Ms. Star and Ms. Beauchene."

"I'm their primary physician."

"How are they," the Agent stepped out of the way so they could speak when he saw Lawson was no threat.

"I'm sorry, ma'am, I can't give you that information, but I can let Mr. DeCarlo and Mr. Townsend know you are here, and they can speak with you."

"Yes, I would appreciate that."

Lawson headed to the ICU, and Director Cosby and the others went to the waiting room.

The room was full, but when the newcomers walked in, the men sitting in chairs got up to offer them to the new visitors. It took a minute for them to recognize who they were.

Emma recognized Emmett from when she visited Sophie in Trenton. She went up to him. "Emmett?"

"Madam First Lady. Are you here to see Sophie and Marci?"

"Yes, how are they?"

"Marci is doing well. Sophie has not woken up yet. Something happened last night, but we had gone home, so we don't know what yet."

"And this is Sophie's family? Marci said Sophie left behind a lot of people who loved her."

"Yes. May I introduce them?" Emmet asked.

"I would like that..." they were interrupted when Houston and Roman came out of the ICU.

"Roman, how is Marci?" Emma asked about her friend first.

"Good morning, Madam First Lady," he smiled at her. He always teased her about her lack of manners. "The stab wound nicked her kidney. Doctor Long did surgery and managed to take care of the bleeding. She is awake now, and they may take her out of ICU to another ward later this afternoon. Would you like to see her?"

"Yes, of course, Roman. But I want to hear about Sophie first." Emma turned to Houston.

"Madam First Lady, thank you for coming. Sophie hasn't been conscious since the incident. Last night she developed blood clots in her lungs. Doctor Cornett is waiting for the orthopedic specialist and an obstetrician to consult with."

"An obstetrician? Is Sophie pregnant?" Trish asked.

"Yes, about six weeks," Houston said.

"After you visit Marci, you are welcome to see her."

"Thank you, Houston."

The First Lady turned to the family. "Emmett, can I take a rain check on the introductions?"

"Of course."

Emma, Trish, and Director Cosby went through the doors to the ICU, the Secret Service swept the ward. One Agent stood at the entrance of the room the First Lady was in, and the other stood by the Marshals.

Houston stayed in the waiting room to explain things to the family. They didn't know that Sophie developed clots in her lungs.

"When did all this happen, Houston?" Anna asked. "And how do Marci and Sophie know the First Lady?"

"I can't tell you that, Anna, but the blood clots happened early this morning. Her oxygen level went down, and Dr. Cornett ordered a CT pulmonary angiogram. They found blood clots and that her heart was enlarged."

"What are they going to do?" Ricky asked.

"That's what the consultation is going to decide," Houston bowed his head. "You have to pray that I don't have to choose between my wife and my child." He looked up again, "Please."

"We will, Houston. Why didn't you call us earlier?" Zoey asked.

"There was no reason to wake you. I knew you would be here in a few hours anyway. And Lizzy called the church prayer line."

Fons stuck his head out the ICU door. "Houston, the doctors are here."

Houston nodded to him, and he excused himself from the family.

Emma, Trish, and Gram stepped into Marci's room. Marci turned her attention to them. She raised her bed so she could sit up and smiled.

"Emma, Trish, Gram. I'm so glad you're here."

"Are you sure you feel up to it?" Emma asked.

"Yes, I hear they are sending me to another floor this afternoon."

Emma stood beside Marci, kissed her cheek, and took her hand. "I was so worried when I heard what happened. How did this spiral so badly?"

"The Seal Team wanted all civilians out of the way when they got on board, so we stayed on the upper deck.

"I don't know why but Anwar started getting paranoid. He decided to speak to the captain in the middle of the night to ensure he was taking them to Iran. His aggressiveness started as anger toward his sister when he saw her out of her room. He had ordered her to go to bed. Anwar got abusive with her, so Sophie and I told him to leave her alone. He became increasingly aggravated and started questioning why we were all out here at this hour. He noticed Dr. Cornett was with us; that was when he realized something wasn't right.

"There was a struggle between Anwar and Doctor Cornett after he pushed Sophie to the ground. Ojala tried to stop her brother from hurting the doctor."

"Ojala is the sister, right? You asked to have guardianship of her."

"Yes, she has no one. She went down to get breakfast with Rocky. I'll introduce you when she gets back."

Emma looked over at Roman, "If you have trouble getting guardianship, let me know."

"I will, Emma," Roman said.

"Anwar is a big man with a broad chest and a muscular upper body. He picked his sister up and tossed her aside. They were standing close to the railing, I'm not sure he intended to, but he threw her right over the railing. Doctor Cornett dived in after her to save her.

"Anwar started shaking Sophie, ordering her to tell him what was happening and who she worked for. They scuffled, and she hit her head on the railing and went over the side.

"By then, the Seal Team had come on board. Chief Abbot heard the commotion and appeared on deck, surprising Anwar. He grabbed me when Chief Abbot pointed his MK 16 at his head.

"The chief tried to talk him down, but Anwar felt he could get away if he could get to one of the Seals inflatables. I believed he stabbed me as a distraction so he could jump before he got shot."

"I'm so sorry you're hurt, Marci."

"I'll be fine, but Sophie is still in serious condition. Roman saw some doctors go into her room," Marci looked up at Emma. "Could you go see what's going on?"

"Of course, Marci."

"Trish and I will wait here," Gram said.

The First Lady walked into Sophie's room. There were three doctors around her bed. Houston was standing with them, listening. Emma moved over to where Fons and Lizzy were looking on.

"What's going on, Agent Rodriguez?"

"Hello, ma'am. The obstetrician just called for a technician to come with a portable ultrasound machine. Doctor Neel Banerjee is the one standing next to Houston. Doctor Ma, the orthopedic surgeon, is standing next to him, and Dr. Cornett, her primary, is on the other side of the bed.

"Dr. Banerjee is concerned the baby won't survive the time it will take to dissolve the clots," Fons explained.

"They stood there while a young man came in with the ultrasound machine and pulled the curtain.

Houston watched as the tech pushed up Sophie's pajama top enough to expose her abdomen and squirted gel on it. The screen came to life as the tech ran the transducer probe back and forth. Dr. Banerjee moved closer to the screen and explained what they were seeing to Houston.

"Mr. Townsend, see here? This is the fetus, who appears to be developing properly. He turned a button on the machine, and they could hear the heartbeat. A look came over the doctor's face. He turned to Dr. Cornett, who understood."

"What's wrong," Houston asked, realizing there was a problem.

"Mr. Townsend, the fetus... "

Houston interrupted, "Baby."

"All right. The baby's heartbeat is weak, he is in distress." He turned to the doctors, "Doctor Ma, her heart is working too hard to get blood and oxygen to the baby. If we want to save the baby, we need to remove the blood clots so that Mrs. Townsend can keep her oxygen level up and remove some of the stress on her heart." The doctor lifted Sophie's right arm. "She is already showing signs of side effects from the blood thinner. Look at the bruising."

Dr. Ma turned to Lawson, "Doctor Cornett, you are her primary; what do you want to do?"

Lawson addressed Houston. "If we remove the blood clots, we cannot stop the blood thinner. She could develop more."

"What is the right decision to keep my wife and my baby alive, Doctor Cornett."

"Houston, I agree with Doctor Banerjee that we need to remove the blood clots, which Doctor Ma can do. I don't see where we have a choice."

The ultrasound technician wiped off Sophie's abdomen and pulled her pajama top back down. Then took his equipment and left.

Houston looked at the doctors, who were waiting for his answer. Houston pushed back the curtain to speak to Fons. He was surprised to see the First Lady standing there.

"Houston, I hope you don't mind that I listened."

"No, I was just going to ask Fons what he thought. I'd like your and Lizzy's thoughts too." The others waited for the First Lady to speak first.

"I have had experience with another friend that had blood clots. I do think Sophie needs the blood thinner. But, Houston, every person's body reacts differently.

Houston turned to Fons, "Houston, what do *you* feel is the right thing to do?"

"I'm leaning toward letting them take out the blood clots," Fons answered.

"Lizzy?"

"Sophie will want whatever is going to give her child the best chance."

Houston turned back to the doctors. "Doctor Ma, will you remove the blood clots?"

"Yes. We need to wait twenty-four hours after the blood thinner stops," he turned to Dr. Banerjee. "Do you think we should go through the neck?" Dr. Ma asked.

"No, if you are careful the groin will give us the best results."

"What about continuing the blood thinner after the surgery?" Lawson asked.

"Yes, I agree we need to continue it. If the side effects worsen, we will deal with it then," Houston said.

"Alright, Houston. We'll stop the blood thinner until after the procedure, then restart it." Dr. Ma turned to Dr. Banerjee, "will you be in the surgical room when he does the procedure?"

"Yes. I will stand by."

"All right, thank you. Someone will contact you tomorrow when the surgical staff and room are ready," Dr. Ma said.

The other doctors spoke with the first lady and left the room. Lawson stayed.

"Dr. Cornett, this is First Lady Emma Madden," Houston said.

"Yes. We've met before. It's a pleasure to see you again, ma'am."

Emma turned to Lizzy. "I apologize for not introducing myself to you when I stepped in."

"Madam First Lady, you need no introduction. My name is Lizzy Young. I'm Sophie's best friend."

"It's a pleasure to meet you, Lizzy."

The first lady excused herself to fill Marci in, and Houston asked Lizzy and Fons to inform the family.

Lawson started to leave, but Houston stopped him.

"Dr. Cornett, Sophie hasn't eaten in two days. Won't that hurt the baby?"

"We have supplements in the IV for her and the baby. We will insert a feeding tube if she doesn't wake up soon."

"Why hasn't she woken up?" Houston asked, letting his eyes drift over to her.

"She'll wake up when her body is ready, Houston. Don't worry."

Lawson left, and Houston went to his wife. He bent down over her and kissed her, stroking her hair. He put his mouth next to her ear and whispered to her.

"Sweetheart, I know you can hear me. You have to wake up. Our baby and I need you. Fight to come back to us," he sat down on the stool next to the bed, tears making a trail down his cheeks.

When Emma stepped out of Sophie's room, six nurses were waiting for her in the hallway.

"Madam First Lady, we don't mean to detain you, but we wanted to say how much we admire you for what you have done for the women freed from sex trafficking." Glenda, the head nurse, spoke for the small group.

"Please introduce yourselves," Emma requested. The nurses went around giving their names.

"It's a pleasure to meet you all, but I could not do what I do without your support. When I called for help for those women, from doctors, nurses, teachers, and social workers, you came from around the country. So much so, we had to ask people to stop coming; we had enough help. You are the ones to be admired."

"Thank you for that. We won't keep you; we just wanted to let you know we admire you," the head nurse said.

As the nurses moved out of her way, Emma spoke again. "The woman in that room," she nodded to Sophie's room, "She is the one who found a way to save all those women. Sophie is the one to be admired; she is a real hero. I only helped after the fact." Emma excused herself and went into Marci's room.

Lizzy and Fons went into the waiting room to find Wes and his family had arrived. Dex had been watching the door waiting for someone to come out. They had arrived on a private plane an hour earlier. An SUV was waiting for them, and they came straight to the hospital.

Dex rushed up to Lizzy, giving her a hug. Emmi, Bridgett, China, Cade, his wife Chantel, Wes, and Lady Be surrounded her. They hugged her as the rest of the family came to gather close. Lizzy introduced Fons to Wes' family and then went on to tell everything she heard the doctors say.

Drew had Jett, and when he moved up to Lizzy, Jett saw his mother and started to cry, reaching out for her. Lizzy took him, held him close, choking up as she continued to tell what she knew.

CJ saw how exhausted she was. He stepped up behind her and wrapped his arms around her so she could lean back into him for support.

Emma told Marci about the final decision. "I need to call Michael; he wanted to be kept in the loop about your and Sophie's condition." Emma stepped over to the corner and sat. Trish and Director Cosby went to see Sophie.

While Emma was on the phone, Marci spoke to her husband. "Roman, when Ojala returns, I want you to take her out to be introduced to the family. She is already feeling homesick and lonely. It doesn't matter that her family abused her. It was all she knew.

"I know this family. They will instantly welcome her. That's what she needs right now."

"Alright, darling, but I think Rocky was going to do that when they returned from breakfast."

"I'm wondering if we should move down here, Roman. There would be plenty for her to do. I know Parkcrest Academy is a good school, and she would have an instant family."

"We can discuss it, Marci. Let's get you well first, and we need to get the legal paperwork out of the way."

"They want to move me in an hour, but I don't want to leave the floor until I know Sophie's alright."

"Marci, I'm sure they need the room. After you're settled, I'll bring you down in a wheelchair to see her," Roman said. Marci nodded.

An orderly took Marci up to the third floor. Emma, Trish, and Gram Cosby went to tell the family.

Emma spoke to the family, noticing new faces in the crowd. "Marci wanted me to let you know that she will be on the third floor and would love to see anyone who wants to visit. Roman is going to send us the room number. I'm afraid we have to go to

Dallas now, but I will be back to check on Sophie tomorrow," she paused. "Before we go, we would like to be introduced."

Emmett came forward and started introducing the family. The First Lady already knew Dex, Cade, and Cade's wife. She asked where Dex's wife was. Dex explained she was with her father, the senator, and would come in later today.

Before they left, Ojala and Rocky came up from the cafeteria, and he introduced Ojala to the first lady and her friends.

"Ojala, I'm so happy I met you before we left. I'm sorry for what you are going through. Marci is my dear friend, and I know she and Roman will do what they can to make you feel comfortable in the US," Emma said, taking Ojala's hand. Ojala whispered a thank you with her head down.

The First Lady put her finger under Ojala's chin and lifted her face. "Ojala, you saved many lives by telling Marci what your brothers and father had planned.

"It will take a while to adjust, but you can be happy here in the US. You know you can never go back to Afghanistan," Emma hugged her when she saw the tears in Ojala's eyes. She could see that the young girl felt scared and alone.

When the first lady left. Emmett introduced Ojala and Fons to the rest of the family.

"Agent Rodriguez, we want to see Sophie. Do you think her husband will let us?" Wes asked.

"Yes, come with me," Fons led Wes' family and Drew into Sophie's room. Houston was sitting by her side, praying.

Fons stepped up to Houston, "Houston," he waited for him to turn around. Houston stood and noticed the people Fons brought with him.

"Houston, this is Sophie's stepfather, Wes Cornish."

"Stepfather?" Houston asked. Wes extended his hand, and Houston shook it.

"I married Clair, Sophie's mother. And this is my wife, Countess Phoebe," Wes said. Lady Be stepped forward to give him a brief hug.

Wes took over the rest of the introductions," these are Sophie's brothers and sisters, Dex, Cade, and Cade's wife, Chantel." Wes placed his hand on Emmi's shoulder, "This is Emmi, China, Drew, and Bridgett."

"Blaze will be here soon, I couldn't reach him. He was on the way to Portland, Oregon meeting with a big athletic shoe company when the news reached Lennox Estate. They want to name a shoe after him." Wes explained. "We want to pray with Sophie if it is all right with you."

"Yes. I'll give you some privacy," Houston watched as Wes went to Sophie, kissed her forehead, and stroked her hair. He saw the tender way he related to her. They must have been close at one time. Then he walked out with Fons to the waiting room.

Houston wanted to talk to Director Cosby before he left. But he didn't see him, so he dialed his number.

"Agent Townsend, is everything all right? We just left the ICU."

"Nothing has changed. I need to talk to you before you leave."

"We are down in the lobby getting ready to go. I could wait if it's important."

"It is."

"Alright, I'll have the ladies get in the SUV. I'll wait for you."

"Thank you."

Manny had stepped up to him but waited until he got off the phone. Houston acknowledged him.

"Manny, I must speak with Director Cosby before he leaves. I'll be right back."

"Of course, go," Manny said.

Houston took the stairs, knowing it would be faster. He opened the door to the first level and saw the director standing by the seating area. When Cosby saw Houston, he moved toward him.

"What is it, Agent Townsend."

"Sir, I just wanted to give you notice. I am resigning from the President's Task Force. And Sophie will no longer be available to consult."

"Houston, this is no time to make that kind of decision. You haven't even been able to discuss it with her."

"If God has mercy on us and our baby lives. I will not expose him or her and their mother to any danger. You know yourself; every mission we go on brings its own level of danger. We have had injuries and even deaths on our watch. I can't do it anymore."

"What will you do?"

"I don't know. Neither one of us needs to work, you know that."

"Will Agent Rodriguez be resigning too?"

"I just made up my mind. I haven't told him, but I doubt it."

"Alright, Agent Townsend, but I will need it in writing to go along with your verbal resignation, and I will hold it until you have a chance to speak with your wife."

"That is your prerogative, sir. But I won't be changing my mind."

Director Cosby nodded, patting Houston on the shoulder. "I understand," he turned to the SUV waiting. "I have to go."

"Of course, sir. Thank you for waiting."

SEIZE ON THE HIGH SEAS

CHAPTER TWENTY-SIX

Wes' family formed a horseshoe around Sophie's bed and prayed for her. Then they took turns sitting by her side and talking to her.

There weren't enough chairs in the room, so Drew and China sat on the wide ledge of the windowsill. Drew looked over at China; she was crying.

"Why are you crying. Aren't you still mad at Sophie?" Drew asked, putting his arm around his sister. She shrugged.

"I guess, but Dex told me I was being selfish. Sophie had lost her dad and Duke. He said she had reason to leave us when she did. Dex said they were on their way to the church to get married when he was killed," China paused to look at her papa. "I don't know how I would react if my papa died. I love him so much."

"Yeah, and the Bible says God won't forgive us if we don't forgive others," Drew said, dropping his arm.

"Look at you, little brother, remembering scripture," China smiled at him.

"Well, Dad has drummed that one into me. But I usually remember the Sunday School stories," Drew said. "China, did you know I was adopted?"

"Not until you told me. You were a little baby the first time I saw you. It never dawned on me that you appeared out of nowhere," she looked at him. "Why does it matter? You know all of us are adopted," China motioned to her family.

"I'm not sure. The pictures Mom and Dad showed me of...her, looked like she was rich. I sometimes wonder what it would be like to be rich like that."

SEIZE ON THE HIGH SEAS

"First of all, your folks are well off like mine. Don't make up some fantasy of what life would have been like—if. You know nothing about her except she handpicked Aunt Anna and Uncle David to be your parents. If she was rich, she probably knew lots and lots of people. She obviously did not want you raised by any of them.

"Being rich isn't a bad thing. But it can never replace love. Your folks never made any distinction between you and Duke. Not every child is loved as much as you are."

"I know, and I love Mom and Dad. It's just strange to think I had another mother."

"Do you think I'm not your real sister because I adopted you?"

"No, of course not, sis."

"Sometimes, I wonder what would have happened to us if Sophie and Lizzy hadn't found us in that barn. I don't remember much of it, but I remember being hungry. She saved our lives, and I can't imagine not having Mama and Papa. I love them so much."

"I know, sis," Drew whispered.

"And don't ever do what Blaze did. When he was fourteen, he started sneaking out of the house to meet up with his friends from the cottages. They would sneak behind one of the cottages and smoke.

"Pa was looking out his bedroom window late one night and saw Blaze heading toward the cottages. He got dressed and followed him. He saw the boys sitting on the ground smoking. He stepped up to them and told them to put out the cigarettes. Blaze was so embarrassed he blurted out, 'You're not my dad; I don't have to listen to you.'

"Pa told him that Blaze may not think of him as his dad, but he would always think of Blaze as his son. He told him he was wrong about one thing; they were related by blood. They had the same Father, and that Father sent His son, Jesus, to shed his blood for us. That made them related by blood.

"Blaze saw the hurt and pain on Pa's face. He didn't know why he had said such a hurtful thing. He regretted it immediately. He didn't mean it. Blaze had told Pa the same thing when he first came to the manor. But they had no bond or history then, and he was only eight and hurting from the loss of our mum.

"Pa walked the other boys to their cottages and told them to tell their folks or he would. Blaze stopped Pa on the way back to the manor and told him he was sorry; he didn't mean it. Pa said he knew that, but Blaze couldn't get the look of hurt on Pa's face out of his mind.

"Blaze was grounded for a week. The following day, he went to Pa again and hugged him, repeating that he didn't mean it. Pa told him he forgave him and would never think of it again.

"Pa has never treated Blaze any different, but Blaze says he can't get over the hurt he saw in Pa's face. He doesn't think he'll ever get over it."

"Wow. How come I never heard about it? Blaze and Uncle Wes are so close, I can't imagine him saying anything like that to him."

"Well, you will be surprised what you'll do when you are embarrassed or mad. But Blaze and Pa never spoke about it to anyone. They kept it between themselves.

"Then how did you know?

"Blaze told me when I turned thirteen, he was afraid I would get in trouble and say something stupid like he did. He didn't want me to have the same regrets he does."

"Yeah, I guess."

"Listen, Drew, don't make up some imaginary fantasy about life with a woman you never met. You have a wonderful life right here with the family you have."

Wes' family left Sophie's room when Anna, Carmen, Aileen, Ruby, and Zoey stepped in to be with her. Houston and Fons were sitting with the family, listening to stories about Sophie.

CJ had taken Lizzy home to take a nap. She objected, but he told her he would bring her back this evening. David, Jonathan, and Jared got off work early and were sitting with Houston and Fons. Lawson, Xander, and Sienna were sitting close by them. Kato was with Drew and China, and Teresa was with Emmi and Bridgett. Kato and Teresa spent two weeks at Lennox Estate the last two summers. They had grown close to the family.

"I love hearing all your stories of Sophie when she was young. I can see who she is now in every story you tell." Houston said after hearing the story about how Sophie convinced Lizzy to sneak out of the house to go to the teen club.

Houston spotted his family coming off the elevator and stood to close the gap between them. His dad was holding Bully's leash. Bully was whining and pulling on the leash, trying to get to Houston. Jack finally let go of him.

Houston got down on one knee to brace for impact. Bully ran full force and knocked Houston down; licking his face, Houston couldn't help but laugh.

"Alright, Bully, let me up," Houston stood and hugged his family. Mr. Katsumi, Izumi, and Lee came with them. Fons went to his wife Carol, who also traveled with them.

Carol whispered to him, "how is she?"

"Sophie's having a procedure done in the morning. It's been tough, babe. I've missed you," Fons said, then hugged Houston's family.

Sophie's family stood, waiting to greet them. Houston walked them to the waiting area and introduced his family.

"This is my mother, Lily; my father, Jack; my sister, Spring; and my brothers, Sam and Ted." Then he moved to Mr. Katsumi,

"And this is also my family, Mr. Katsumi, his son Izumi, and his wife, Lee." Katsumi and Izumi bowed low to Sophie's family, humbling themselves.

"Emmett, please introduce your family. I don't want to mess up anyone's name."

Emmett introduced everyone, and the two groups merged, giving hugs and handshakes. Houston was surprised to see Ojala sitting with Teresa, Bridgett, and Emmi. Houston wanted to hear more about their story when this was over.

China, Drew, Ojala, and Kato descended on Bully, mesmerized at how pretty and big he was. Bully allowed them to pet him but never left Houston's side.

"Houston," China got his attention. "What kind of dog is he?"

"He is a Belgian Malinois."

"He is a big dog; how come he can come inside the hospital?" Drew asked.

"He is a service dog," Houston knelt beside them and told them how he saved Sophie's life and protected her. They were spellbound.

Lawson called maintenance to bring more chairs to the ICU waiting area. The men stood to allow the new visitors to sit until more chairs arrived.

Jack went to Houston, "Son, let's go get you something to eat, and you can tell me what's happened."

Houston stood and headed to the cafeteria with his father. "All right, Dad," Bully started to get up, but Houston told him to stay.

Houston and Jack got in line at the cafeteria and found an empty table. Fons and Carol came in a few minutes later and did the same.

Houston hadn't eaten all day. After taking a few bites and drinking some coffee, he looked at his dad, letting him know he was ready to talk.

"Son, tell me what you can about how this happened."

Houston told him the story leaving out names, and explained the procedure Doctor Long was doing in the morning. Houston took a few more bites, then put his fork down.

"Dad, I told Director Cosby I'm resigning from the President's Task Force. I can't abide Sophie being in harm's way all the time. And if God gives us this baby, there is no way I will allow any harm to come to him."

"If that's your decision, I agree, but have you asked Sophie?"

"She has never wanted to do this. She has a gift, but we will find another way to use it. I can't lose her, Dad." Houston lowered his eyed to his plate. Jack put his hand on his son's shoulder.

"Sophie and your baby will be fine. I trust the Lord."

When Houston, Jack, Fons, and Carol were back upstairs, they didn't hear the usual sound of chatter. When they turned the corner, they saw everyone was spellbound by Izumi, who was telling how he became a believer.

"Once I read the Bible and believed, I knew I could no longer live the life of a 'saiko komon' for the Akuza. I didn't leave immediately, feeling I needed time to bring my father to the Lord. But I did not have time. One day an Akuza kobun came before the Kumicho to get permission to kill his servant. His servant had consistently run away, and this last time he was caught with the kobun's wife's jewelry on him.

"My father, as Kumicho of the Akuza, had no choice but to give the man the remedy he was entitled to, by Akuza law. The servant was to be beheaded. Though I had been present at executions before, I could not stand by and allow it; I had to intervene. The Akuza law allows a member found guilty of a crime to bring a replacement to take his punishment. Usually, the replacement was a servant or a member of the family, a daughter, who was considered of little value in most Akuza families.

"Although this had always applied only to Akuza, the law did not specifically say so. It had simply never been done. So, I told my father I would take the man's place. There were objections from all sides, but I stood firm.

"Then my sister stepped in and spoke up. Sophie demanded the Kumicho honor his promise to her. She had done a favor for my father that no one else could do, and he promised to give her anything she asked in return. Sophie had never taken him up on it.

"More objections erupted; my father was looking for a way out and agreed to keep his promise to her. He asked what she wanted, and my sister asked for my life.

"After that, my father had to save face and appease the kobun and his men. He expelled us from his presence from that day forward. Being expelled from the presence of the Kumicho was considered a horrible fate."

"Mr. Katsumi, please tell us how you became a believer after that," Governor Pierce insisted.

Katsumi told the story of his life and of his miraculous salvation experience. The room was spellbound.

"Mr. Katsumi," Mitch motioned to the other men. "We belong to the Austin Christians Businessmen's Association. Would you consider telling your testimony to them sometime?"

"I am unworthy to speak to your group. However, Jesus is worthy; if it brings Him glory, it will be my honor."

When Anna and the ladies came out of the ICU doors, Houston headed back to her room. Bully followed and began to whine next to Sophie's bed; he put his front paws on the mattress but couldn't reach her.

Lawson followed Houston in to check her vitals.

When Lawson was done, Houston's family came in to see Sophie. Lily stopped in her tracks when she saw her lying there not moving.

"Oh, Houston," Lily put her hands to her mouth.

Houston took his mother in his arms, "I know it's startling to see her like this, Mom."

The family moved around Sophie's bed and laid hands on her, praying for healing. Lily kissed her forehead and smoothed back her hair.

"Houston, do you have clean pajamas for her?"

"Sophie only had one set in her suitcase."

"Anna told me she brought a new set of pajamas for her when they came this morning."

"I didn't know that; let me look in the closet." Houston found them and gave them to his mom.

"Press the button for the nurse when you need her to unhook Sophie's IV and equipment."

"We will. Spring and I will change her," Lily pulled the curtain around.

Houston, his brothers, and his father were sitting, visiting, when Lizzy stepped in. She had come back after taking a short nap at home.

"Houston, is it alright if I stay the night with Sophie again?

"If you'd like to, Lizzy."

"Thank you. I'll wait until everyone says good night to her," Lizzy saw the curtain was drawn, then went back to the waiting room.

Everyone had a chance to say goodnight before visiting hours were over. Houston's family was planning on getting hotel rooms, but Emmett and Jared insisted they stay with them.

Izumi and Lee stayed in Emmett's cottage. Mr. Katsumi, Jack, and Lily stayed with Emmett, and Spring, Ted, and Sam stayed with Jared.

Jack, Katsumi, and Emmett stayed up late into the night, talking about the Lord, and listening to Katsumi's life in the Akuza.

Wes' family stayed at Blaze's home in the same gated community Xander lived in, by Emmett's house. China and Drew insisted that Ojala stay with them until Marci left the hospital. Marci and Roman felt it would be good for her.

Before they left, Drew, China, Kato, and Ojala took Bully for a walk. Liam and Ricky escorted them.

Fons insisted on staying with Houston at the hospital, and Zoey invited Carol to stay with her.

A nurse brought a bowl of water for Bully, and Fons went to a store nearby to get him dogfood and a doggy dish to eat out of.

Bully lay next to Sophie's bed and whined. Lizzy moved her recliner as close as she could without displacing Bully and fell asleep with a blanket laid over her. Fons was in a recliner on the other side of the room. Houston moved his recliner as close to her as the medical equipment would allow.

Houston would wake up every few hours when the nurses came in to check on her and draw her blood. They did their best to maneuver around him. This time he heard the nurse speaking softly to someone.

"I don't think you are supposed to be up here," she chuckled.

Houston opened his eyes to see that Bully had squeezed himself beside Sophie. Two legs were under his body, the other two dangling off the bed. Bully's sad eyes moved to the nurse, who didn't have the heart to shoo him off.

Houston closed his eyes again, leaving Bully where he was.

HEART HOSPITAL, AUSTIN. FRIDAY

At 7:30, Houston was awakened by a nurse trying to change Sophie from her pajamas into a hospital gown without waking him. She needed to prep her for the procedure Dr. Ma was doing to remove the blood clots.

Lizzy woke, too, and they moved out of the way. The nurse closed the curtain and finished preparing Sophie. An hour later, the orderly came and rolled her away.

When Jack, Lily, and his siblings returned to the hospital with Emmett and Jared, Sophie was still in surgery.

Houston and Lizzy were sitting alone in the waiting room. Fons went to get them food from the cafeteria.

Others started coming around 10 am.

It was 10:45 when Dr. Ma and Lawson stepped into the waiting area. Everyone stood.

"Mr. Townsend, all the clots are removed, and Dr. Banerjee said the baby was not disturbed."

Houston took the doctor's hand, "Thank you, Doctor." Dr. Ma smiled and left after speaking with Dr. Cornett for a few minutes.

Houston rushed to the room to wait for Sophie to return. Bully padded behind him. The orderly rolled Sophie into her room, and a nurse hooked her up to the machine and started an IV with the LMW heparin.

Lawson came in, took his stethoscope out of his white coat pocket, and listened to her lungs. "They sound good," he smiled at Houston.

"Lawson, how will we know when the anesthesia has worn off if she is still unconscious."

"Anesthesia puts you in a state deeper than a state of unconsciousness. We will be able to tell by her brain activity."

"Are you going to hook her up to a machine to check her brain waves?" Houston asked.

"Yes, if she doesn't wake up soon, I'll connect her to an EEG. I'll wait until morning to put a feeding tube in."

"Alright, Lawson. Will you let everyone know? And if anyone wants to see her..."

"I'll let them know," Lawson said as he left.

SEIZE ON THE HIGH SEAS

364

CHAPTER TWENTY-SEVEN

HEART HOSPITAL. SATURDAY

Lizzy came into Sophie's room last night when visiting hours were over. Bully lay next to the bed. Lizzy and Fons had fallen asleep hours ago. Houston couldn't sleep; he was mesmerized by the lines on the monitor showing her brain waves. Finally, he pushed the recliner back and fell asleep.

At 3:30 am, Houston was startled when he heard a raspy voice, almost unrecognizable. He sat up and saw Sophie petting Bully, licking her face. He had managed to get up on her bed again when he fell asleep.

"Bully," she whispered. "What are you doing on the bed? If Houston sees you, you will be in trouble," she smiled.

Houston scooted up close to her and whispered. "Sophie, sweetheart. I thought I might have lost you forever."

"Have I been asleep long?" She looked at her surroundings. "Where are we?"

"What's the last thing you remember?"

Sophie considered the question for a while and tried to remember. "Oh, we were on the yacht, and Anwar started getting angry. He was fighting with Lawson. Ojala tried to stop him. Anwar tossed her off the ship," Sophie's eyes got big. "Oh, Houston, is Ojala all right?"

"Yes, Lawson went after her; she's fine."

"Good."

"Did they arrest Makhtar, Anwar, and Khaan and turn them over to the Italians?"

"Khaan died in a gunfight. But yes, Makhtar and Anwar are in Italy now."

"Everyone else alright? Marci?"

"Anwar stabbed Marci in an escape attempt. She is recovering after surgery in a room on the third floor."

"A room? We're in a hospital?"

"Yes, Sophie, you have been unconscious."

"What day is this?"

"It's Saturday morning," Houston said.

"I've been out for three days?" Her brows furrowed, "I don't remember being injured."

"Sweetheart, when Anwar tossed Ojala overboard, he went after you. He knew they had been sold out. He started shaking you, and there was a struggle. In the process, you hit your head on the railing and went overboard. You were unconscious and couldn't right yourself. You didn't come to when you hit the water. I was in the Zodiac with the Seal Team. We were boarding when we saw Lawson go after Ojala, and then you hit the water. I went after you.

"Sophie, I couldn't find you. The waters were so dark, even with the floodlights. It was the scariest 90 seconds of my life. I followed the trail of blood and was able to reach you."

"Why has it taken me so long to wake up?"

"When you hit your head, your brain swelled. Lawson's been taking care of you. You bruised yourself when you hit the water flat on your side. The impact of the bruising caused veins to be compromised, and blood clots passed to your lungs. Dr. Ma took you to surgery and did a procedure to suck out the clots. You are on blood thinners to prevent more."

Sophie remembered she thought she might be pregnant. "Houston, am I pregnant?"

"Yes."

"Is the baby alright?"

"It was touch and go, but Dr. Banerjee believes the baby will be fine," Houston said. Sophie laid her head back and let out a breath.

"Sophie, why didn't you tell me you were pregnant?" Houston couldn't help the little bit of anger in his tone.

Sophie tried to lift her hand to his face, but her arm hurt too much. She saw the bruising for the first time. "Oh, love, I was afraid to take a pregnancy test. I didn't want either of us to be disappointed again. And I knew we were going on this mission. I figured I'd take the test when we got home."

"You know I would have never let you go on this mission if I thought you were pregnant."

"I know. I would have refused if it weren't Makhtar, but he killed so many people, he needed to be stopped. And Italy needs to be the one to bring him and his sons to justice.

"None of us thought Marci and I would be in danger," Sophie said.

"Sophie, I thought we had this conversation. You can't make those kinds of decisions without me."

Sophie turned her eyes to Bully, who had snuggled his head next to her. She stroked him with her good hand. She turned her eyes back to Houston.

"You know I can't just sit by when there is a chance, we can save someone."

"Yes, but you weren't making the decision for yourself. You were making it for my baby."

"Your baby?'

"Well, isn't that what you said to yourself, that it was your baby. That I had no say in it. You want to separate the fact that the baby is mine too. You left me out of the equation."

Sophie realized he was right. She did not consider him when she made the decision.

"I'm sorry, Houston. And when this baby comes, I don't want to be working for the task force."

"I've already given Director Cosby our resignation."

"Houston, you love your job."

"I love you more," he kissed her hand.

"What will you do?"

"I don't know. We can figure that out together when you are well. I better let the nurse know you are awake." Houston pushed the call button.

Lizzy had woken up when she heard voices, but she felt Houston needed this time with his wife. She tried not to eavesdrop, but she heard that Sophie and Houston had been part of a task force that captured Makhtar Hijazi. Lizzy knew the name from the hospital bombing in Italy. It was on the news for weeks, and now his capture was the lead on most channels.

Anna flew to Italy when it happened to help with the sick and wounded; she stayed a week. Jared and Emmett flew her over and waited, helping to clear the debris. They all said it was a horrific site.

When the nurse came in, Lizzy felt she could get up and not intrude. Fons was up, too, standing by Houston.

Houston had waved Bully off the bed; he wasn't happy but obeyed. Bully went to get something to drink out of his bowl.

Fons was talking to Sophie, laughing at something. Sophie hadn't noticed Lizzy yet.

"Sophie."

Sophie turned to see Lizzy. "Lizzy," Sophie started crying. Lizzy did too. "I'm sorry I left you."

"I know, Sophie. I'm so glad you're home."

Houston interrupted, "Lizzy wouldn't leave your side."

"Of course not; she is my best friend," Sophie reached up her one good arm to hug Lizzy. Lizzy leaned over and wrapped her arms around her.

The nurse checked Sophie's vitals, then called Dr. Cornett.

Lawson came in, checked the report on her last blood test, listened to her lungs, and checked her pupils. He asked her questions to find out if her memory was intact.

Lawson addressed Houston and Sophie, "Sophie, your lungs sound clear. Your pupils look normal, and your mind is not fuzzy. The fact you woke up tells me the swelling on your brain went down."

"And our baby is alright?" Sophie asked, her hand touching her abdomen instinctively."

"Dr. Banerjee was in with Dr. Ma when he extracted the clots from your lungs. He felt the baby came through in good condition."

Lizzy rubbed her shoulder. "Sophie, that is wonderful news. Do you want me to call the family and tell them you are awake?"

"No, let them sleep. It will be a nice surprise if they come to see me later."

"Sophie, the family has been here from the time you arrived. Houston had to insist they go home to sleep. There is no doubt they will be here," Lawson said.

"Lawson, I understand you have been my doctor. Thank you, I don't know anyone I would trust more to advise Houston on the difficult decisions he had to make."

Lawson smiled and touched her cheek. He knew it was inappropriate, but he didn't care. "Sophie, you are one of my best friends. I couldn't let anyone else be your primary."

"We are friends again?" Sophie was hopeful.

"Yes, I'm sorry I hurt you. I treated you so badly, even though from the start you told me…. Well, I'm sorry, Sophie."

Fons looked at Houston to see if the exchange bothered him, but if it did, he didn't show it.

"Should I call the church prayer line and tell them their prayers were answered?" Lizzy asked, pulling out her cell phone.

"Yes, and tell them how much we appreciated their prayers," Houston replied.

"Lawson, how much longer do I have to stay in the hospital?"

"You are still in jeopardy of having more blood clots. We have you on a blood thinner, so we are confident that will do its job, but you should stay in the ICU for two more days. Then I'll have you move to the third floor for another day or so."

Sophie nodded, "If you think that's best."

Bully wanted her attention, so he put his paws back on the mattress. Sophie ruffled the fur around his ears. "My sweet Bully. I've missed you."

Lawson went back to his office.

Houston knew it was time to take Bully out for a walk. He and Fons left, allowing Lizzy and Sophie time alone.

When they came back Houston and Fons fell asleep while Sophie and Lizzy continued chatting away speaking softly and laughing. Houston had no idea when the ladies finally went to sleep, but they were asleep when he and Fons woke up.

When Lizzy woke, she sent a text to the family to be at the hospital at 10 am. There was news.

The nurse brought in a wheelchair and unhooked Sophie from the IV at Lizzy's request. Lizzy took her into the shower. While Sophie sat on the shower seat and used her good hand to wash. Lizzy dug through the clothes she had brought for Sophie the day before. She took out her hair dryer, dried Sophie's hair, and put it in a French Braid. Lizzy asked Houston if Sophie had a makeup bag in her suitcase. Houston dug through her things and found it.

Lizzy rolled Sophie out of the bathroom.

Houston kissed his wife, "You look beautiful, sweetheart."

"The family is going to be here in an hour," Lizzy told Sophie. "Can they all fit in here, so we can surprise them all at once?"

Houston lifted her into the bed. "Darling, there will be over fifty people. Why don't we roll you out to the waiting area."

"Fifty people?" Sophie looked over to Lizzy.

"Your family and friends, Wes and his family, and Houston's family. The First Lady even came to see you."

"Emma came here?"

Houston answered, "yes, with Director Cosby and his wife, Trish."

Sophie covered her face with her hands. "Oh, Houston, after the heartache I put my family through, I don't deserve them."

"Sophie, you must have done something to warrant their loyalty." Houston took her hands away from her face.

"A nurse came in to hook Sophie back up to the IV but did not hook her back up to the machines.

Houston addressed the nurse, "Nurse Glenda, can Sophie go out to the waiting area to see her family later."

"I can't see a problem with that. I'll bring a wheelchair with an IV pole," the nurse looked straight at Houston. "Don't let her overdo it. She is still fragile."

"I'll watch her, thank you."

Lizzy decided to go out with the family to wait for her to come out. She wasn't sure her face wouldn't give away the surprise.

Lizzy gave Sophie a last hug and headed out. When she pushed through the ICU doors, she saw the room filled with family, their faces concerned. She went over to her husband, holding Jett, and kissed his cheek. CJ put his arm around her, and Jett leaned over to have her take him.

Fons told Deputy Samuels and Cooley that Sophie would be coming out. He didn't want them to be caught off guard.

BLAZE

Wes was convinced that Blaze had come out of the womb playing football... soccer, in the US. From the time he came to them, he dragged his siblings out to play football with him every spare moment they had. When no one else wanted to play, he would spend time kicking the ball and learning to do tricks with it.

Wes knew Blaze needed to be on an organized team. The family liked being tutored, so Blaze didn't have a school team to join. Wes went to the school in Chertsey and asked if Blaze could play on their school team. The principal looked through his regulations and determined there was no regulation against it.

Wes or Duke drove Blaze to practice every day and waited two hours while the team practiced. They went to every game, and by the time Blaze was in grade twelve, university and professional teams were vying to sign him.

Wes was concerned about Blaze joining a professional team at his age. But Blaze would be 18 a month after he received his grade twelve certificate. Blaze wouldn't need their input.

Wes didn't like the idea, but he realized not everyone wanted to go to college. Blaze was an excellent student and could pick any university, but that wasn't who he was. All he cared about was kicking a ball.

They had a family meeting. Lady Be and Dex objected to him joining a professional team until after he went to university. Blaze tried to make his case, but they didn't budge.

Blaze turned to his pa. "What do you say, Pa?"

"Are you willing to abide by my decision, Blaze?'

Blaze thought about it. He loved Pa and didn't want to do anything to disappoint him. "Yes."

"Blaze, you have a gift. You are too young to go to a professional team, but I also want to avoid forcing you to attend university. If you attend one year at the university, I would be more comfortable about you going to a professional league. You would be nineteen then, it's still young, but you know who you are, and I expect you to live what you believe."

'I will, Pa. I promise,' Blaze said.

Lady Be disapproved. She said she would go along with it if Blaze took classes or trade school on his off time.

Blaze agreed.

The first year, Blaze took his London based soccer team to the playoffs for the World Cup, but they didn't make the cut. The UK had not won a World Cup Tournament since 1966. Wes had negotiated a yearly contract for Blaze. He wanted him to have the option to move to other teams if he chose. The second year they made it into the World Cup but lost. This year they won the World Cup.

Advertisers wanted Blaze endorsements on everything from cereal to clothing. Wes advised him against it. He told Blaze that when he lent his name to a company, he endorsed their office culture, politics, and any unethical decision they made. Blaze saw the wisdom in that. He was one of the highest-paid team members in the EU, making millions a year. Money wasn't what drove him.

After his team won the World Cup, a well-known athletic shoe company contacted him. They said they wanted to name a shoe after him and wanted him to endorse it and give input on the design.

Blaze's ego was having a hard time turning down the opportunity. Wednesday, he got on a flight and went to Portland, Oregon, to speak with the CEO. He was on the plane when the news about Sophie came. No one could get ahold of him. Once he hit the ground, the company picked him up and kept him busy showing him their headquarters. The next day he sat with a designer. The evenings were spent at dinners in his honor. He forgot to take his phone off airplane mode.

When he finally got a minute alone on Friday night, he checked his phone and saw he missed twenty texts and calls. He called his brother immediately and took the first flight out to Austin.

Dex picked Blaze up from the airport. He had been communicating with him every hour since he heard about Sophie.

"Did you see her right after they took her to the hospital?"

"Yeah, late Wednesday. Sophie was in bad shape, Blaze. But now that the blood clots are gone, they are hopeful she will improve."

"You said her husband and the family prayed in the chapel and you called the prayer line."

"Yes."

"And she's pregnant, huh," Blaze smiled. "I can't wait to see a little Sophie. I have no doubt she will be a whirlwind."

"What makes you think it will be a girl," Dex took his eyes off the road for a second to look at him.

"I just do."

"We don't know if the baby will survive yet."

"She will; I have faith."

Dex parked, and he and Blaze headed inside.

Houston lifted his wife from her bed and placed her in the wheelchair. Sophie laughed.

"Houston, I can get out of bed on my own."

"I know, but this is the only way I can hold you," he kissed her cheek. After he set her in the wheelchair, he spoke to Fons.

"Fons, will you leash Bully and handle him. I'm afraid when so many people surround Sophie, he might get nervous and think she is in danger."

"Yes, I'll handle him."

Blaze was becoming more anxious as they entered the hospital. When they got off the elevator, he rushed to the ICU doors intending to walk right through to Sophie's room. Dex told him which room she was in.

As he drew closer, Deputies Samuels and Cooley stepped in front of the doors.

"Sir, who are you here to see?"

"My sister, Sophie. I need to see her," Blaze was getting more anxious, wondering why there were Marshals there.

Dex caught up with Blaze. "Marshal Samuels, Blaze is my brother. Sophie will want to see him."

"One moment please," Samuels pulled out his cell and sent a text to Fons, asking if Blaze Cornish was cleared.

Fons replied that he was.

The Marshals moved out of the way, and Blaze rushed into Sophie's room. Bully could feel Blaze's anxiety and interpreted it as danger. Fons had just put on his leash as Bully tried to intercept Blaze and started growling. Fons pulled him back and told him to lie down. Bully obeyed but would not put his head down. His ears were forward, and his hackles were still up. Fons kept patting him on his side and speaking softly to him that there was no danger. Finally, Bully relaxed.

Sophie turned her head to see why Bully was upset and saw Blaze. She was in a wheelchair, but when she saw Blaze, she tried to stand. She was too weak; Houston helped her.

Blaze enveloped her in a hug and cried. "We thought you weren't going to make it, sis."

"It was touch and go for a while, but I'm much better, as you can see. I'm sorry I scared you. And I'm sorry I left you, Blaze," she leaned back to see his face. Tears ran down both their cheeks. Sophie wiped his away. "You look so handsome, Blaze," she said as she sat back down.

Blaze smiled at his sister's compliment. Houston stretched out his hand. "Blaze, my name is Houston, I'm Sophie's husband, and this is Agent Rodriguez, my partner."

Fons stepped over to him with an outstretched hand, "please call me Fons." Blaze smiled and took his hand.

"We were just getting ready to let the family see that Sophie woke up," Houston said.

"May I take her?" Blaze asked.

"It's up to her," Houston said. Sophie nodded.

"Ok, then, we'll follow you."

As they went through the ICU doors, Sophie saw the Marshals. She lifted her hand for Blaze to stop.

"Deputy Samuels and Deputy Cooley, you drew the short straw again. But I'm happy to see you."

Samuels squatted down next to her wheelchair and took her hand. "No, ma'am, it is always an honor to watch your six." Sophie patted his hand and smiled. She nodded to Cooley, who was on the other side.

The family saw her come through the doors and started clapping. Roman had brought Marci down from the third floor to see her stepdaughter and family.

Blaze pushed Sophie into the midst of the crowd so everyone could get a good look at her. They visited for a while before Houston saw the First Lady's protection detail coming. The two Marshals met them and gave them an update, letting them know the scene was secure.

The First Lady, Trish, and Director Cosby followed behind the Agents. The family noticed and made room for them to get to Sophie and Marci.

The First Lady spoke to Marci and gave her a kiss on the cheek.

"I'm so glad to see you up and about, Marci," she reached over to Sophie, who was in a wheelchair right next to Marci's. "And you, Mrs. Townsend, you had us all worried. Look at you now; you look wonderful."

"Thank you, Madam First Lady. I heard you came to see us when we first got here. Thank you for caring."

"Don't be silly, Sophie. The president and I think of you as friends."

Emma noticed Blaze had joined the family. She heard Michael, Gram, and their son talking about Blaze while watching soccer games. "Houston, I see you have more family here. Would you introduce us?"

CHAPTER TWENTY-EIGHT

The first lady stayed and visited with them for over an hour, then tapped Houston on the shoulder and asked if she could speak to him privately. They moved to the corridor.

"Houston, Gram told Michael you put in your papers. Michael wanted me to talk you out of it. But I won't do that."

"Thank you, Madam First Lady."

"I understand your reasons for leaving. I can't say that your and Sophie's loss to the team won't be significant. But you have trained the team to see beyond procedure and use their instinct. Understanding the target well enough to know what they will do in a given situation is not something taught at Quantico."

"That was all, Sophie, ma'am."

"It was both of you. And I want to thank you for your service."

Houston hung his head for a moment. "Thank you for understanding. It was a hard decision."

Houston and the first lady returned to the group. Her secret service agent whispered in her ear; Emma looked at her watch.

"Thank you. I need a minute."

She said her goodbyes and kissed Marci and Sophie on the cheeks. Emma asked former Governor Pierce if he would speak with her as they were leaving. The Governor followed her to the elevators, where the secret service, Gram, and Trish waited for the elevator. The Governor and First Lady stepped away.

"Mitch, you've heard the vice president has cancer and will not be able to finish his term.

"Michael would like to talk to you about stepping in."

"I would be glad to discuss it with him, Emma. Just let me know when."

"Good. We have known you for a long time. Michael trusts you."

"We do see things the same way. Most of the time," Mitch smiled. Mitch waited for them to get back on the elevator before returning to his friends.

The family continued to visit. Sophie loved Jett; she held him on her lap. Bully was lying next to her wheelchair. Kato and Drew were petting him. Jett would lean down as far as he could to try to reach Bully. Bully would raise his head and put his nose to Jett's cheek and nudge him. Jett would giggle, the two continued the little game repeatedly until Jett was giggling hysterically. He squirmed his way off Sophie's lap and laid his whole body on Bully, wrapping his arms around his neck. Bully was content to let him do so.

"Lizzy, he is so handsome. I can see both of you in him."

"CJ and I are so blessed."

Anna noticed that Sophie's eyelids were getting heavy. She knew Sophie would never say she was tired, so she stood.

"I'm afraid we have worn Sophie out. She is still weak and needs her rest."

Lawson stood and backed her up, "We don't want to overtax her."

"But my family…," Sophie objected.

Emmett spoke, "Sophie, now that we know you are on the mend, we will come and visit you in shifts. That way, you won't get too exhausted. But right now, you need to rest."

"Lawson, can I get her something to eat from the cafeteria?" Ruby asked.

"Yes, but for the next day or so, it should be soft food, nothing greasy, no bread, no meat."

"I'll go get her something," Ricky said. "Any soup but pea soup, right, Sophie?" Everyone laughed.

Houston looked confused. "I'll tell you about it later," CJ said.

Sophie said goodbye, and Houston wheeled her toward the ICU doors. Bully lifted his head but didn't want to tumble Jett by standing up. Drew grabbed Jett and Bully stood. He turned to follow Sophie but touched his nose to Jett's cheek and nudged him one more time. Jett giggled and reached out to hug him, but Drew held on so Bully could leave.

"Fons, why don't you spend time with your wife and the family. Sophie's awake now; no need for you to stay."

"Alright, but I'll take Bully for a walk first."

China heard and asked if she and Ojala could walk him.

"I'll go with them," Fons said.

Before Fons left, Houston turned, "Fons, thank you for being here for us. Just knowing you were here…," Houston choked up.

"Hey, Houston, there is no need to thank me. That's what brothers do for each other." Houston nodded and wheeled Sophie back to her room. Houston worked hard to keep her awake until Ricky brought tomato soup, yogurt, and grape juice.

After eating half her soup, Sophie fell asleep.

Henry and Carmen asked Jack, his family, and Mr. Katsumi and his family to join them for lunch.

Wes and his family headed to Blaze's house. Drew, Kato, Teresa, and Ojala went with them.

Sophie slept for three hours. Houston was sitting by her bed; Bully was lying down. When she woke, Houston called the cafeteria for yogurt and chicken and rice soup.

"I'm sorry, Houston."

"What for, darling?" Houston cupped his hand on her cheek. She leaned into it.

"For putting you through this. I know I would have been scared if our places were reversed."

Houston took her hand and kissed it. "I can't lose you, sweetheart."

"I'm glad you put in our papers. I don't want either of us to go through this again. But you never said what you want to do," Sophie questioned. Houston looked at her quizzically.

"Do?"

"For a job. We can't sit around and look at each other all day," Sophie chuckled.

"Why not, I could look at you all day." Houston leaned forward and kissed her lips. Sophie giggled. Houston loved that sound.

"I'm not sure." Houston went quiet and looked out the window.

"Houston, what's on your mind."

"We can move here if you want. You seem whole here, happy."

Sophie moved her hand to stroke his cheek. "Houston, I'm happiest whenever we are together."

"It seemed that a piece of you was missing before. Here with your family, you are whole," Houston took her hand from his cheek and held it to his chest.

"In a way, a piece of me *was* missing. But my life is with you; wherever you are, I will be whole. I would never ask you to leave your family."

No one spoke for a few minutes as the cart came in and the server put a covered tray on the rolling table and placed it in front of her.

Sophie took the cover off and placed it aside. She took the plastic spoon and ate a little of the soup. Then Houston spoke.

"I thought we could open a detective agency. That way, we can pick the cases we want."

"Houston, I don't see you doing anything without Fons. He is your partner."

"You are my partner. But if he retires from law enforcement, I would love to work with him."

"We could back the costs ourselves and pay him what he makes on the task force until the business could pay for itself," Sophie said.

"You'd be ok with that? But where would you want to live?"

"Houston, we don't have to leave New York for me. But I will want to spend a lot of time coming back here to see my family. I won't desert them again."

"We'll figure it out. I'm so grateful you're alive; nothing else matters."

FROM THE AUTHOR

I enjoyed reuniting Sophie with her family. There are a lot of things still left up in the air. Where will they live? Will the baby survive to term? Will they open a detective agency with Fons?

For now, you will have to use your imagination. In the meantime, I hope you see how their faith carries them through all life's tragedies. One of my favorite scenes is the men all praying together in the hospital chapel. Unity in prayer is a powerful way to get prayers answered.

Like the scripture says, 'Again, I say to you that if two of you on earth agree about anything they ask for, it will be done for them by My Father in heaven. For where two or three gather together in My name, I am there in the midst of them.' Matt. 18:20.

If you enjoy reading the Sophie Star Series and the Sophie's Story series, please take the time to review the books.

With appreciation to my readers,
L. J. Webb

If you enjoyed this book, please write a review on Amazon.

ljwebbauthor@gmail.com